D0201037

Hillsboro Public Library
Hillsboro, OR
A member of Washington County
COOPERATIVE LIBRARY SERVICES

WITHDRAWN

THE WHISPERING WARS

JACLYN ✦ MORIARTY

Arthur A. Levine Books
An Imprint of Scholastic Inc.

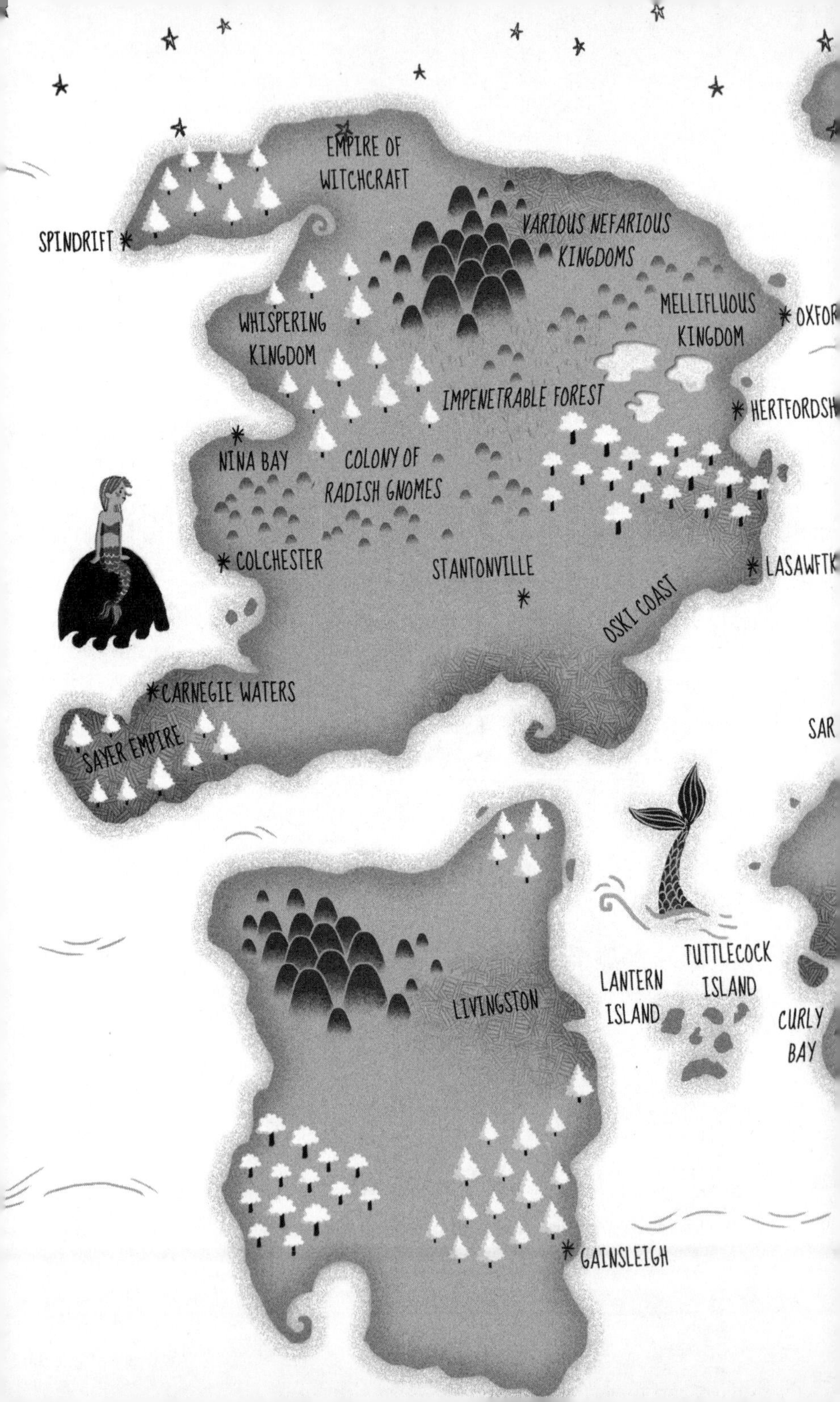
EMPIRE OF WITCHCRAFT
SPINDRIFT
VARIOUS NEFARIOUS KINGDOMS
WHISPERING KINGDOM
MELLIFLUOUS KINGDOM
OXFOR
IMPENETRABLE FOREST
HERTFORDSH
NINA BAY
COLONY OF RADISH GNOMES
COLCHESTER
STANTONVILLE
LASAWFTK
OSKI COAST
CARNEGIE WATERS
SAYER EMPIRE
SAR
TUTTLECOCK ISLAND
LANTERN ISLAND
LIVINGSTON
CURLY BAY
GAINSLEIGH

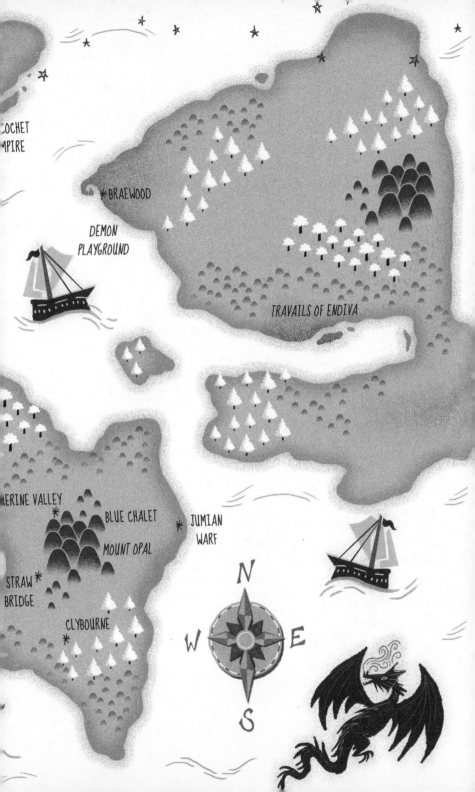

Text copyright © 2019 by Jaclyn Moriarty

Illustrations copyright © 2019 by Davide Ortu

All rights reserved. Published by Arthur A. Levine Books, an imprint of Scholastic Inc., *Publishers since 1920*. SCHOLASTIC and the LANTERN LOGO are trademarks and/or registered trademarks of Scholastic Inc.

The publisher does not have any control over and does not assume any responsibility for author or third-party websites or their content.

No part of this publication may be reproduced, stored in a retrieval system, or transmitted in any form or by any means, electronic, mechanical, photocopying, recording, or otherwise, without written permission of the publisher. For information regarding permission, write to Scholastic Inc., Attention: Permissions Department, 557 Broadway, New York, NY 10012.

This book is a work of fiction. Names, characters, places, and incidents are either the product of the author's imagination or are used fictitiously, and any resemblance to actual persons, living or dead, business establishments, events, or locales is entirely coincidental.

Library of Congress Cataloging-in-Publication Data available

ISBN 978-1-338-25587-4

10 9 8 7 6 5 4 3 2 1   19 20 21 22 23

Printed in the U.S.A.   23   33614081672890

First edition, October 2019

Book design by Baily Crawford

To my brave and beautiful niece, Maddie, the first child to visit the Kingdoms and Empires.
To my other lovely nieces, also adventurers: Anna, Emily and Piper. And to my Charlie, who can run as fast as Finlay.

Opening Words

I was taken by Whisperers at 2:00 p.m., so I never pulled the lever for the laundry chute.

That's what bothered me most.

I live in the Orphanage, see, and the laundry cart comes once a week to collect our dirty laundry. If it's your birthday that week, you get to pull the lever.

Some of the children stand back and watch the clothes slide down the chute. Little smiles on their faces. When it's done, they walk away, still smiling.

They have hearts that are dead easy to please, those kids.

Some children pretend they are the clothes themselves. They pull the lever, then squawk and screech: *Where am I going? Oh, I'm just a simple nightdress belonging to Avril, and I never thought to have such an adventure!*

SPLAT.

Waaah!

WHERE AM I?

Is this a LAUNDRY CART? It is!! But I don't WANT to be clean!

And so on. They're pretty funny.

But *one* child?

Here is what he does when it's his birthday.

He jumps into the chute. Rockets down along with the skirts, dresses, petticoats, and drawers, and hits the cart with a *THUD*. (It's a soft thud, since the clothes are like a pillow, so don't worry.) The cart horse, Clodswald, twitches his nose and says *pfft*, but the Orphanage director, Lili-Daisy, who stands on the pavement supervising, well, she screams. She screams like the sirens. Or like the dentist has his pliers clamped around her favorite tooth.

The whole thing is crackerjack. The ride down the chute, the thump into the cart, Lili-Daisy's screams. Doors fly open up and down the street and everyone runs out in a fright. "What is it? What's happened? Oh *Lili-Daisy*, for goodness' sake, he does this every year. Would you hush?"

Better laugh than the cinema.

Anyhow, it's me. Finlay. I'm the child who rides the laundry chute each year.

But not this year. Not my eleventh birthday. The Whisperers got us at 2:00, and the laundry cart doesn't come till 3:00.

This is way ahead in the story, though. A lot happened before that. I'm only saying it up front because it bothered me so much, the missing out.

PART 1

CHAPTER 1
FINLAY

Finlay here.

I'm starting the story, but a girl named Honey Bee takes over in the next chapter. You'll miss me then. You'll say, "Oh, I wish that Finlay was back, I liked him."

You won't like Honey Bee. Trust me on that. This is her fault. With some people, you don't like them and it's not their fault? They're accidentally annoying? But with Honey Bee, it's her fault.

Don't worry, though. I'll be back. Honey Bee and I are taking turns.

The story begins on the day of the Spindrift Tournament.

That's an annual competition that takes place on the Spindrift Town Green. (*Annual* means once a year. *Spindrift* is my town.) At the tournament, the local schools compete in athletics. (*Athletics* are running, high jump, and so on. *Compete* means—)

Listen, from now on, you can look things up in the dictionary if you don't know what they mean. Otherwise, this will take forever.

That morning, I woke up and dropped straight out of bed onto the floorboards to do my push-ups. I do twenty first thing every morning. Only did seventeen that day, though, not wanting to wear myself out before the tournament.

Glim's bed is by the window and she was kneeling on her pillow, drawing pictures in the mist on the glass. She's not much of an artist, if I'm honest. But she tells us all crackerjack stories each night, pressing her nose against the glass as she speaks. (She likes to watch the goings-on in the town square.)

The twins, Eli and Taya, were reading newspapers under the covers. They always do that. They're big for ten, Eli and Taya, so every morning it's like a pair of boulders have got ahold of a paper each and climbed under the blankets to read.

I won't describe what the other kids were doing, as that would take too long. Also, I don't remember. Three beds were empty: I know that. Amie, Connor, and Bing had all been taken.

Back then, we didn't know who or what had taken them.

Jaskafar would have been on top of the wardrobe because that's where he always ends up. He climbs there in his sleep. It took Lili-Daisy about six months to stop screaming about this.

"A rat! A rat on the wardrobe!" she shrieked, the first time she saw him there.

"I am not a rat," Jaskafar replied, waking up. "I am a five-year-old boy —" And he bumped his head on the ceiling and realized where he was. "A five-year-old boy on a wardrobe!" He was that surprised.

Everybody had scolded Lili-Daisy for calling Jaskafar a rat.

"Jaskafar looks *nothing* like a rat!" we shouted.

"Still. Have a gander at his teeth," Daffo observed. "They stick out a bit." Then everybody shouted at Daffo to shut his trap. But he did have a point.

"They stick out in a cute-little-boy way," Glim said. "Not a rat way. Also, he has no tail — we'd have noticed if he did."

Glim also had a point.

Lili-Daisy had pulled Jaskafar down from the wardrobe and apologized for calling him a rat. It was just she could only see his hair at first, she explained; that's where the mistake had come in. Then she sat on a bed, Jaskafar on her lap, and made up a song:

> *"Not a rat! Not a rat!*
> *But a dear little boy, oh drat!*
> *Oh drat that I called you a rat!*
> *Oh, how foolish I can be*
> *When I've not had my morning tea —"*

"And when you've *had* your morning tea," I interrupted—and now *I* had a point. Lili-Daisy can be foolish any time of the day. She raised an eyebrow at me and carried on singing:

> *"Oh drat!*
> *You're not a rat!*
> *If you were, I'd get a cat!*
> *To eat you!"*

Jaskafar had been very cheerful and said, "It's okay! You can call me a rat if you like." But we all bellowed, "No!" except Daffo, who said, "Thanks, I'll do that."

Lili-Daisy had sung more loudly, and then it was time for breakfast.

But the next day, Jaskafar was on the wardrobe again and Lili-Daisy came into the dormitory and screamed, "A rat!"

Anyway, she got used to Jaskafar being on the wardrobe in the end.

On the morning of the Spindrift Tournament, everyone was trying to brush Jaskafar's hair at the breakfast table. Lili-Daisy was dabbing at his face with a washer. Avril was brushing dried mud from his shoes. Jaskafar himself wore a thoughtful expression on his face.

"What if I accidentally eat the flowers?" he asked.

He had a special job that day, you see. The queen and the prince were coming along to the Spindrift Tournament as part of their tour of the kingdom, and Jaskafar was the child chosen to give the queen a bunch of flowers.

Queens always need bunches of flowers. I don't know why. I think they have a special interest in them.

"What if I accidentally eat the flowers," Jaskafar repeated, "before I give them to her?"

We asked him if he was in the habit of eating flowers and he said no, he'd never done it before. Well then, we said, it probably wouldn't happen today. Glim suggested he have extra toast for breakfast so as not to have an appetite for flowers.

I was having trouble eating breakfast myself. It's not that I get *nervous* on the day of the tournament, it's just that it seems like grasshoppers are kicking each other around in my belly.

Here is what always happens at the tournament: I win most of the boys' events. My best friend, Glim, wins most of the girls' events. My other best friends, the twins, being a boy (Eli) and a girl (Taya), and both big and strong for their age, win the rest of the events between them.

Between us, we four make the Orphanage School the champions of the Spindrift Tournament. Every single year.

Which is a big responsibility. I think that's why the grasshoppers.

This year, Sir Edgar Brathelthwaite Boarding School was competing in the tournament for the first time. That school is just outside town, and they're usually too rich and important to join in. But Millicent Cadger, local councilwoman and director of the Spindrift Tournament, had begged them to come today, on account of the queen and prince attending. Royals need the *better* sort of children, see? The sort who polish their faces and shoes, and tilt their chins at the sky.

We were not worried about the boarding school kids winning anything. They just lazed about on cushions eating cake all day, as I understood it. They'd be clueless about sport. Even if they tried it, they'd run into a wall or a tree, on account of their chins pointing up.

We knew we would win.

We washed up, tied our shoelaces, and set off for the tournament.

And that is the beginning of the story.

(Honey Bee will probably say, "No, no, I cannot *abide* that beginning." And she'll try to tell you a different one. Ignore her.)

Okay, here she is. It's Honey Bee. Good luck.

CHAPTER 2
HONEY BEE

Ahoy there!

I am Honey Bee, and I *completely* agree with Finlay about the beginning of the story. It did start on the day of the Spindrift Tournament.

I do not know what *crackerjack* means, but I *did* like Finlay's chapter.

He is funny! The joke about me being annoying, especially. That had me rolling on the floor. But he's right that you'll be missing him. I'll try to be quick.

I live at Sir Edgar Brathelthwaite Boarding School.

The morning of the Spindrift Tournament we marched around the courtyard, chanting the school motto, as per usual.

> *"Brathelthwaite students are*
> *Better than the best!*
> *Brathelthwaite students,*
> *Put us to the test!*
> *We will conquer all*
> *We are ever so tall*
> *We will never ever fall*
> *We will never drop the ball*
> *We would never have the gall*
> *To come second!*
> *What?*
> *Second?! [then you must pretend to spit, as if you've tasted some-*
> *thing nasty]*
> *No way!*
> *We will come first!*
>
> *Ohhhhhhhh*
> *Brathelthwaite students,*
> *We are fine and well-pressed,*
> *We are faster and stronger and much better-dressed,*
> *We are — we are — we are the BEST!!"*

Uncle Dominic, who is deputy headmaster, swished his horsewhip about our ankles as we marched. He only does that for show, of course, and has never once horsewhipped a student.

Oh, other than Carlos. Uncle Dominic did horsewhip Carlos the day he kicked the windowpane out of the school's second-best carriage. It had filled with smoke, you see. Madame Dandelion had tossed her cigar inside and the seat caught alight. Carlos ought *never* to have damaged school property, Uncle Dominic said—he ought to have squeezed himself and the other children into a corner, away from the flames, and *waved* the smoke away. Never mind that little Reenie has the asthma and was turning blue, Uncle Dominic said.

Uncle Dominic also horsewhipped Sarah-May, I just remembered, when she accidentally dropped a tray of fine china. She was carrying it down the stairs for deportment class. Wood lice had gotten into the floorboards and her foot cracked right through a step, causing her to drop the tray. But never mind that, Uncle Dominic said, she ought to have guessed about the wood lice.

Oh yes, and Jeremy, when he was thrown from a dragon during prelim officer training and broke his ankle—he was horsewhipped too. (The dragon had been spooked by a snake.) Jeremy ought to have held on, Uncle Dominic said. Brathelthwaite students never *ever* fall. It's in the chant.

I just thought of four or five more children who have been horsewhipped, but I must get on. Suffice to say, Uncle Dominic has (practically) never once horsewhipped a child.

After we finished marching and chanting, we filed onto the sports field for our daily sprints and drills. Next, on to the dining hall for breakfast, where Sir Brathelthwaite, our headmaster, gave a rousing speech about the tournament. He is a fine-looking man, Sir Brathelthwaite, little and dapper, with a mustache and a perfectly bald head. This glows fiercely under the school's chandeliers, and you often see him patting it affectionately. Another thing he often does is brush down his immaculate suit jacket.

He wears bright white shirts that flare out from his jacket sleeves dramatically.

My Uncle Dominic, as deputy, tries to dress the same way but he is a much larger man, and his buttons tend to pop. Also, he's always getting those flaring shirtsleeves in his soup.

"Today," Sir Brathelthwaite said, "my fine students, the queen and prince are going to be *dazzled* by your athletic prowess! The people of Spindrift will be stunned!"

We all nodded as we buttered croissants and sipped tea.

"Now, the little local schools," Sir Brathelthwaite continued, and he counted them on his fingers, "Spindrift Public, Harrison Boys, Thea Ashley Girls, and the Orphanage School—will *not* be accustomed to seeing such skill. I ask myself: Ought we to *let* them win an event or two, so as not to crush their spirits?"

We waited, curious to know how he might answer himself.

"No! We ought not!"

Ah.

"It would be wrong to hold back!" Sir Brathelthwaite continued, and he gave his own head an encouraging little pat. "The local children *deserve* to see the splendor of *true* athletics. Certainly, they will be horribly depressed by their defeat, but I think, in the end, they will be grateful. Watching *you* will be rather like a pageant to them!"

Here, Victor Ainsley wiped his mouth with a napkin and raised his hand. "Respectfully, sir," he said. "May I interject?"

"Certainly, Your Grace!" Sir Brathelthwaite replied. "Do you think me wrong?"

The teachers all call Victor *Your Grace*, as that is his proper title. Even though he is only twelve, he is already a duke. But most of the children just call him Victor. Because he might be a duke, but he is also a horrid little toad.

Victor chuckled. "No, no, Sir Brathelthwaite," he said. "You? Wrong? Impossible to imagine!"

Sir Brathelthwaite beamed. "Oh, you make me blush, Your Grace. What a delightful boy you are. Go on, then. What is it?"

"Sir, is it quite the thing for us to associate with local riffraff? Could not a wicked outsider conceal him- or herself amidst the ... *unwashed* crowds? Personally, I am not at *all* concerned about the danger, but some of our younger children might be nervous?"

"Indeed," Sir Brathelthwaite replied solemnly. "You make a fine point. Dear students, please try to be as considerate as our young duke. For His Grace is correct. Seventeen children *have* been taken from Spindrift in the last few months. *Hundreds* have been stolen across the Kingdoms and Empires. But I ask you, my dear students, has a *single* student of Brathelthwaite Boarding School been taken? Have they?!"

We all cried, "No!" and cheered, which was what he meant us to do.

"So, be calm, dear students. It's true that the townsfolk will be at the tournament, but they will be seated in the stands. Children will be seated *across the field* with their school groups, well-guarded by the local constabulary. The ten most highly trained constables will focus on protecting *our* school. I have demanded this."

Sir Brathelthwaite cleared his throat. "In addition," he said, "your teachers will be vigilant for your safety." He waved his hand at the teachers seated around him at the high table, and they all nodded seriously, trying to look vigilant. Uncle Dominic tried so hard to look vigilant that pastry crumbs spilled down his chin.

"Then the only danger," Victor said, spooning a sugar cube into his tea, "will be the local children themselves? We could catch diseases from them, say, or slovenly habits?"

"Oh, I *say*," Hamish Winterson piped up. "Last time I caught slovenly habits, I was laid up in bed a *week*. I can't be catching *that* again!"

Everyone spluttered, and Carlos, who was sitting next to me, laughed so hard he almost knocked over the cream jug. I reached over and caught it just in time. Carlos breathed a sigh of thanks. You could get horsewhipped by Uncle Dominic for knocking over the cream jug.

"Slovenly habits are *indeed* to be feared, Hamish," Sir Brathelthwaite chuckled, "but not in the way you are thinking. His Grace makes another excellent point. We *must* keep our distance from the local children today."

Once again, the other teachers nodded and sent stern looks around the room.

"When you win your event," Sir Brathelthwaite continued, "*never* shake your competitors' hands. Nasty germs on local children's hands. Merely remark that they have put in a 'good effort,' perhaps offer a word of advice, and briskly walk away. You will certainly see slovenly habits today, but I *know* you would never copy them! Students, let's tell Hamish what sort of slovenly habits we are likely to see, especially from the Orphanage School?"

"Bad grammar!" somebody called.

"Dirty fingernails!"

"A limited vocabulary?"

"Ragged clothes!"

"Crumpled stockings!"

"Worn-out shoes!"

"Smallpox scars!"

"Skinniness!"

"Oh yes, their bones do stick out awfully," Rosalind Whitehall put in. "Those Orphanage children! Horrible to see! So thoughtless. They ought to eat more."

"Excellent, excellent." Sir Brathelthwaite nodded, reaching for his teacup and slurping on his tea. "Got the hang of it now, Hamish?"

"I believe so, sir," Hamish said, shuddering. "I say though, sounds *awful*. Must we go to the tournament and see all this?" Hamish is tall for ten, and lanky. His father is terrifically rich and owns most of the kingdom's diamond region, so Hamish is allowed to be as daft as he likes. He is also allowed to skip haircuts, which means his white-blond hair is always in his eyes. He flips it aside but it falls back into place at once, so he only gets to see for half a second.

Sir Brathelthwaite nodded at Hamish. "Yes, Hamish, we must go today. Imagine if the royals came to Spindrift and *only* saw local children and their slovenly habits!" Children shook their heads, aghast. "Now and then," Sir Brathelthwaite continued, "we must do our duty for our kingdom. No matter how horrific we might find it."

So we finished our breakfast, dressed in our sports kit, and set out to the Spindrift Tournament.

CHAPTER 3
FINLAY

"Finlay," hissed a voice just at my shoulder.

"Lili-Daisy?" I replied.

We were following the cart through the streets of Spindrift on the way to the tournament. A proper crowd of us, small children in the middle, big ones encircling them.

The blue sky was up there, you know, in the sky. The day was as crisp as spring.

This is because it was spring.

"Finlay, I need—" Lili-Daisy began.

"Morning, Lili-Daisy!" That was a voice from across the street.

"Good morning, Baker Joe!" Lili-Daisy called back.

"Fine day for it!" Baker Joe shouted.

"It is indeed!"

"Morning, Lili-Daisy!" Now it was the fishmonger. Lili-Daisy also had to wish the bookseller, news vendor, a fortune-teller, a couple of local pirates, and three witches a good morning—and to agree with each that it was indeed a *very* fine day—before she could carry on. The roads and pavements were crowded with happy people, some clutching streamers, others bottles of beer, one a pet chicken (bundled, squawking under his arm). The whole town was heading to the Green for the tournament.

"Finlay," Lili-Daisy said at last. "You and your lot *will* keep an eye on the little ones today, won't you?"

By *you and your lot* she meant me and my best friends, Glim and the twins.

They were walking alongside me and listening to Lili-Daisy too. The twins were reading newspapers as they walked, but they can read and listen both at once. (From the moment they wake up until they fall asleep each night, the twins read newspapers. Never stop except to break something, punch someone, or take a temperature—they've got an interest in health, the worse the health the better.)

"Of course we will," Glim declared.

"We've promised you often enough," I reminded Lili-Daisy.

The twins coughed in a determined way, meaning that yes, we were *always* promising Lili-Daisy to keep an eye on the little ones and that, to be honest, they were sick of it.

"Only, I have a bad feeling about today," Lili-Daisy admitted.

The twins cursed. They curse beautifully. Lili-Daisy pretended not to hear them.

"We know," I sighed. She'd been on about her bad feeling all morning.

"They've got extra constables coming, remember?" Glim said soothingly. "So it'll be fine."

"That's exactly what bothers me," Lili-Daisy pronounced. "It's when you get *extra* of anything that things go wrong."

All four of us gave her sidelong glances.

"Don't look at me like that," she complained. "Remember when we persuaded the grocer to give us an extra sack of rice as it was such an icy winter and you were all so hungry and cold? Well, didn't the rice spill while we were carrying it into the kitchen? And Avril slipped on the grains and twisted her ankle! Remember that?"

"Of course we remember!" It had happened just the month before. Avril was still limping. In fact, right at that moment, she was riding up in the cart with the picnic blankets.

"Well!" Lili-Daisy said. "So you see? That's what happens with extras."

Before we got a chance to tell Lili-Daisy that she was talking a great big crate-load of crabapple, we were swinging through the gateway to the Green.

The first thing we saw was a row of constables looking fierce.

A lot of children had been disappearing lately, see, all across the Kingdoms and Empires. At first, we thought they were running away, but they didn't pack bags and they never came back. Ordinarily, when a child runs away, it's about a squabble or some small complaint like finding mathematics homework unnecessary. A night out in a cold field begins to make the squabble or complaint seem pretty daft. So the child comes back and copies someone else's homework. That's my experience of running away anyway, and I've done it four or five times.

When Connor disappeared from the Orphanage on apple crumble day, we knew he must have been kidnapped. He loves apple crumble the way you might love your grandma. (If she's a kindhearted grandma who always gives you extra pocket money. Never having had a grandmother myself, I'm very interested by them.)

Anyhow, the disappearing children explain all the constables.

By the way, it's me, Finlay, talking again. You probably guessed that. I hope you are all right after your time with Honey Bee, and don't have too serious a headache.

Before I continue, I need to tell you about Spindrift. If I'm honest, I thought Honey Bee would do that. I got the story started, and then Honey Bee should have spoken about geography.

But she didn't. So it's up to me.

Spindrift is a small town on the coast of the Kingdom of Storms. (Its proper name is the Kingdom of Gusts, Gales, Squalls, and Violent Storms, but that's too long to be convenient.) Spindrift has a harbor and a beach with yellow sand — known as the Beach with the Yellow Sand — which means that people in bathing suits like to visit. They get cranky on rainy days, windy days, hailstorm days, and typhoon days, these visitors. This is because they are daft gits who ought to have noticed that this is the Kingdom of *Storms* when they booked their vacation.

As for the Kingdom of Storms, you don't need to worry about that. It's just your regular kingdom. There's a bunch of diamond mines up north and the capital city, Cloudburst, is right in the middle. Never stops raining there, laundry's always strung out to dry on covered balconies. Even on the fancy balconies of the Royal Palace where the queen and prince live. This is what I hear anyway, from kids who've visited on school trips.

Now you might be wondering about surrounding Kingdoms and Empires, and you are right to wonder. To the west, of course, is the sea. South is the Whispering Kingdom, a quiet little place that never caused anyone a bit of bother. But north and east? Crowds of Kingdoms and Empires and almost every one is wicked and nefarious. (Nefarious is just another way of saying *wicked*, to underline how bad these places are.) It's crackerjack, all the wickedness. There's an Empire of Witchcraft, a Colony of Radish Gnomes, the Cailleach Kingdom (filled with sirens, fire sirens, and sterling silver foxes), and many more. Imagine Shadow Mages everywhere you turn and you have it right.

Now and then, folks from these places come all the way here to Spindrift, buy a cottage, and move in. Look just like regular folk, by the way — well, witches wear socks and sandals; and radish gnomes are very short with long, sharp nails (claws, really); sirens have largish mouths; and sterling silver foxes wear a lot of jewelry and have pointy ears, but those are little things. Generally, they're just like regular folk and you hardly notice a difference.

They have to sign a form promising to stop using Shadow Magic, and then they can settle right in.

Ah, now I wish Glim was writing this. I need her to explain about what Shadow Magic is, in case you're a daft git and don't know. And she likes magic, Glim. Hang on and I'll fetch her.

GLIM

Hello, this is Glim. Setting aside the mending for a moment since Finlay just called you a "daft git" if you don't know about Shadow Magic. But you could be from far away where they don't have *any* kind of magic. So you're not a daft git, you're just a sad git. Ha-ha. No. Not a git at all.

He's my best friend, Finlay, but he can be a bit harsh.

About me: I'm shy.

It's tricky being shy. You miss out on things and you blame yourself for it, and other people blame you too.

"Speak up for yourself!" they say, getting cranky.

Finlay and I found a toy in the junkyard once, a sort of wooden maze in a glass box. You put a marble through the hole at the top and the marble runs down wooden paths: slide, then *pop* down to the next level, slide, then *pop* down, slide and pop. Clatter, roll, clatter, roll, all the way to the bottom.

That's what happens to my voice when I'm shy. It's a marble rolling down,

down, down, deep inside me. No chance I can get it back. The more you say, "Come on, child, speak!" the more my voice drops away. Especially if you're an angry or important grown-up.

I would *never* be able to speak to the queen!

One final thing about me: I love magic, but I'm not a mage.

Now I will tell you about mages. Skip this bit if you already know it.

A mage is someone who can do magic. There are three types: Shadow Mage (or Dark Mage), True Mage, and Spellbinder.

Shadow Mages are witches, radish gnomes, sterling silver foxes, ghouls, sirens, and so on, and they generally cast wicked spells.

True Mages are elves, water sprites, Faeries, and so on, and they mostly cast sweet spells like for healing and love and so on. They often instill objects such as saltshakers or pencils with their magic.

Spellbinders have a very useful talent: they can bind the wicked magic of a Shadow Mage. They are born with this talent but have to train for years to use it, the way even a musically gifted person has to learn and practice the trombone before playing it. We have a few trained Spellbinders on our police force, in case any of our local Shadow Mages forget their promise to be good. Nobody knows which those constables are, of course: Spellbinders keep their identity a secret.

All mages do their magic by pretending to weave, stitch, knit, or crochet the spell or binding. They just move their hands around in the air, imagining the thread. Legends say that long ago they used *actual* thread for this.

Sometimes I walk along and secretly run my hands through the air, imagining the magic curving and winding around my fingers. *Everywhere I go*, I think, *I am walking through magic.* When I remember this, I feel a bit less shy.

Here's Finlay back.

CHAPTER
3
(continued)
FINLAY

Thanks, Glim. Perfect. (I'm never harsh, by the way, only honest.)

Anyhow, there's plenty more I can say about Spindrift, but that'll do for now. Like I said, it's what Honey Bee should have told you.

Speaking of Honey Bee, I'm about to share the first time I ever heard her voice.

Through the gateway and onto the Green, and there was the row of constables. Beyond them were crowds of townsfolk swarming in one direction, crowds of children swarming in another, popcorn and apple cider vendors hollering, *"Come and get it!"* and the blare of the town band tuning up.

"Come on, then," Constable Dabnovic called to our group, waving us through. "Good luck today, kids!"

"Hold up!" boomed a voice. "*Hold* up!"

A little bald guy was blocking our path, a hand in the air. He had the daftest flappy sleeves.

"The children of the *Orphanage* will wait, *if you please*, for the students of Brathelthwaite Boarding School!"

"Oh," said Lili-Daisy. "I didn't know you were first. Beg your pardon, go on, then."

So there we were, squashed against the gate, while kids with backs as straight as masts and hair as shiny as oil slicks went marching by, chins propped up as if a puppeteer was overdoing their chin-strings.

White sports kit, they wore, and giant, round red hats. Like walking toffee apples.

Just as she passed me, one of these toffee apples — long legs, long braid — glanced towards the town band. "Oh," she said. "I cannot *abide* the sound of violins!"

She could not *abide* them. That's what she said.

It's because she's rich, see. Regular people would say, "I don't like violins," meaning they'd prefer to stay away from violins, thanks.

But rich people cannot *abide* things, and what they mean is, violins should not even exist.

And that was Honey Bee.

CHAPTER 4
HONEY BEE

And here she is again! Honey Bee!

That is to say: me.

I cannot abide the sound of violins. This is true.

But on to the events of the day!

There was a great deal of chatter as we settled ourselves under our marquee. The maids had lined up folding chairs alongside a trestle table. Platters of fruit, cakes, and savory pastries were placed atop a linen cloth. We also had a drinking fountain, a stack of fresh towels, and a makeshift changing room.

Sir Brathelthwaite was making a fuss because he had been promised the ten most highly trained constables to guard us, and there were only nine. It was *not* relevant, he said, that the tenth constable was at home with a nasty toothache. Nor that another was rushing back early from her vacation and would soon arrive. It was simply not good enough!

Uncle Dominic, meanwhile, was growling at Orphanage children. A handful of these were straying too close to our marquee. He was very much like a guard dog, Uncle Dominic, but this only made the Orphanage children creep closer, giggling.

Everyone was chattering, as I mentioned. "Where's the queen? Where's the prince?" But that was a little daft. The royals were not due to arrive until the afternoon. The queen was going to present the trophy to the winning school. Sir Brathelthwaite had combed his mustache in preparation.

The mayor opened the tournament by taking the carrot from her mouth.

Everyone complains that Mayor Franny is too young to be a mayor and that she chews carrots too much, but I like her. Now she shouted into her megaphone: "And we are away, folks! It's open! The tournament is *open*!"

Standing alongside the mayor was Millicent Cadger, Spindrift Tournament director. She raised her arms and shouted, "Woot! Woot! Hooray!"

"Tch, tch," muttered Sir Brathelthwaite.

Off I went, to warm up for my race.

CHAPTER 5
FINLAY

My first race was boys' long distance. Three times around the track, it is.

Glim and I train for this by getting up at 5:00 a.m. a couple of days a week and running by the shipyards, along the Beach with the Yellow Sand, around the tallow factory, and up and down the steps of the lighthouse. The lighthouse keeper, Randalf, is usually having his kippers and tea when we arrive. We shout up to ask if we can borrow his stairs.

"Be my guests," he calls down. But, after a while, he sighs each time we pass him, and he imitates the sound of our puffing breath and banging footsteps. "Get away with you," he says eventually.

Now I looked around at my competitors. There was that solid little kid from Spindrift Public, who gives me a scare each year by zooming out front for the first two laps. But he always runs out of puff by the third, and has to sit down on the track.

There was Ro Lee Hat from Harrison Boys, who's pretty good at this event, and generally comes second to me. You never know when he might close the gap, so I'm always uneasy about him. What if he'd been training this year? He was squinting down the track, psyching himself up.

"Good luck," I said, to mess with his focus.

And to wish him good luck.

Ro Lee Hat bowed. "And to you, Finlay."

Everyone else, I knew I could take. Five boys from Brathelthwaite Boarding School were huddled together a little distance away, doing the daftest warm-up stretches I'd ever seen. Honestly. The rest of us were trying not to guffaw. *Guffaw* means to laugh so loudly you could use up all your energy for the race.

"Are you boys planning to *be* in this race?" the official called to them. We were ready to start, but the Brathelthwaites were still curled up like caterpillars.

One of boys spun around. Tall kid with white-blond hair that fell to his nose. Realizing he couldn't see through his hair, he flopped his head sideways to get a clearer line of vision. He seemed surprised to see us there. I honestly think he'd forgotten where he was.

"Right you are!" he said. "Come on, chaps!"

The five boys jogged over and joined us at the line.

"On your marks," said the official.

I took a deep breath. Stared down the track.

"I say," said the blond boy, pointing at my feet. "Old chap, you've forgotten your shoes!"

Crack! went the starting gun.

The first lap, I seriously considered quitting the race to take him out. One solid *thwack* to the nose with a closed fist.

I'd give him a moment to brush his hair aside first: wouldn't be right to hit a boy who couldn't see. But absolutely right to hit that boy. Distracting another racer at the start of the race! It's as close to cheating as you can get without actually tripping me up. Plus, I hadn't *forgotten* my shoes. I'd just been growing lately. Lili-Daisy had wanted to get me new runners in time for the tournament, but she also wanted to get medicine for the kids with whooping cough. So, no shoes.

By the second lap, I decided I'd finish the race and *then* smack him.

By the third and final lap, I remembered I was *in* a race.

I started paying attention.

The solid kid from Spindrift Public was just ahead, as usual, but I could see his legs wobbling and I could hear him gasping for air. "Three, two, one," I said to myself, and he sat down on the track.

He scooted himself off to the side to be out of my way, and gave me a sad wave as I passed. I could still hear him panting as I rounded the next bend.

Someone's got to tell the kid to pace himself.

A clear run to the finish line stretched before me. I was almost at the crowd in the stands, and there was a lot of cheering, clapping, and "Go, Finlay!"

Who cares about a daft boarding school kid? I decided. It was good to be running. My rhythm was just right, my stride felt good. I decided to give the kid a break and not hit him. Just a proper talking-to.

I ran by the stands, and the crowd was really roaring. Screaming even. I glanced over, thinking they were getting a little carried away, and caught glimpses of Baker Joe and the witch from the red-roof cottage. Both were waving madly at me, sweeping their hands through the air towards the finish line, as if they thought I'd forgotten where to go.

"Take it easy," I muttered. "I know the way."

And that's when I sensed it.

Right behind me.

Another runner.

Ro Lee Hat. So he *had* been training. I quickened my pace. Behind me, Ro Lee Hat did the same.

I could hear his breathing. His thudding feet.

The finish line was just ahead.

I quickened my pace again—but so did he. Still directly behind me. I'd used up all my speed: this was as fast as I could go—and Ro Lee Hat was making a move. He was shifting to my right.

I kept my eyes ahead. The shadow to my right went *thud, thud, thud.* It was *tall*, that shadow—too tall. I glanced over.

It was *not* Ro Lee Hat.

It was the boy with the white-blond hair in his eyes, arms swinging, legs pounding, inching slowly by me.

He was ahead of me.

He was almost at the finish line.

I ran like I never had before. Like the grass was on fire, like a tidal wave was after me.

He was just ahead, just ahead, and then I passed him, stuck my head forward, and crossed the finish line.

Beat him by a nose.

CHAPTER
6
HONEY BEE

I almost missed the starting gun for my race, the girls' long distance, because the uproar was so loud.

Also, I was distracted by my fellow students, over in our marquee.

Their faces looked exactly as if they'd just watched their homes picked up by a tornado, carried off, and dropped into the sea. Uncle Dominic was weaving his horsewhip through his fingers in agitation. Sir Brathelthwaite was as white as a whitecap and then, as I watched, the white darkened into thunderclouds.

A boy from the Orphanage School had won the first race of the day.

We simply could not believe it.

That boy was Finlay, of course, and that race was the first time *I* had ever seen *him*. He is a wonderful runner. You don't believe it at first because he's such a little, skinny, scrappy boy, arms and legs like twigs, and he was running barefoot. He did *none* of the things that *we* learn in our drills. His arms were held much too far from his body and his posture was ungainly. It would have been funny if it wasn't superb—somehow his rhythm and stride were perfection.

The ending was *so* close. Finlay's final sprint to defeat Hamish Winterson was a magnificent *surge*. I could hardly breathe. The crowd, as I said, roared.

And the Brathelthwaite marquee fell deathly silent.

You see, Hamish Winterson is our school's best runner. He has been boys' champion at the Cutler Sarkys (the private and exclusive schools' athletics competition) for the last five years in a row.

But he had just been defeated! By an *orphan*!

Hamish himself was so astonished that he forgot the rules about local children and gave Finlay a hearty slap on the back. "Oh, I say!" I heard him bellow as he shook Finlay's hand. "Well *done*! Jolly fine show!"

Finlay seemed very cross about something, but I didn't see what happened next, as I had to run.

I won my race, but only just.

A girl from the Orphanage was beside me the entire time. It was thrilling to have competition — not to boast, but I am usually girls' champion at the Cutler Sarkys, and I never have to work for it; I just have long legs. But the final lap of *this* race nearly did me in! I was terribly puffed out.

Like Hamish, I also forgot the rules and shook the girl's hand. I couldn't help it: I wanted to thank her for the marvel of her pace.

She was very polite, and seemed shy. She had short dark hair, dark skin, and bright eyes. "You're good," she informed me, getting her breath back. For some reason, hearing these words from *her* pleased me more than hearing them from my coach at school.

"Might I know your name?" I inquired.

"You might," she said, serious but with dimples. "It's Glim."

"I'm Honey Bee," I offered.

"I'll see *you* at the next race, Honey Bee," she said, dimples again. I think she meant she was *not* going to let me win twice. *What a lark!* I thought.

After that, the day became intense.

Mayor Franny kept announcing the point scores, and I rather wished she wouldn't. It was too much for Sir Brathelthwaite to bear. His face kept changing color and he was breathing as if he *himself* had been running races. Uncle Dominic, meanwhile, was clutching his horsewhip to his chest like a comfort blanket.

It was *so* close, you see, and the lead kept changing. One moment Brathelthwaite would be winning the day, the next the Orphanage School, then back to Brathelthwaite again. Back and forth, all the time.

Here is a sample.

Finlay won the boys' *middle* distance too. A gloom fell upon our marquee, and people tore the crusts of their sandwiches to pieces. I thought Uncle Dominic might damage his nose, his nostrils were flaring so violently.

But then Hamish won the boys' sprint! A cheer swept through our marquee and everyone began passing around slices of cake and shouting our school chant.

However, next thing, *Glim* beat me in the girls' middle distance, and our school went back to tearing crusts and weeping.

And so it went on.

Glim also beat me in the sprint, but then I (just) beat her in the long jump. Hamish beat Finlay in the hurdles, but Finlay beat *him* (just) in the long jump. A pair of twins—a boy and girl—from the Orphanage both won the shot put, discus, and javelin, but then—

And so, as I said, it went.

By 3:00 p.m., we were dead even.

Only one event remained: the mixed sprint relay.

If we won this event, we would win the day.

If the Orphanage School won, *they* would be victor.

This was unthinkable.

Our marquee was silent. We were seated in our folding chairs, our backs very straight. Sir Brathelthwaite cleared his throat.

"The following students will come forward please," he said, and, very solemnly, he read the names of our relay team. "Hamish Winterson. His Grace, the Duke of Ainsley. Sarah-May Cohen. Honey Bee Rowe."

We each stepped up.

"You are the mixed relay team, am I correct?"

We nodded. "Yes, sir. You are correct, sir."

Millicent Cadger was terrifically strict about her tournament rules, and we had registered our names for the events a month earlier. We'd been training as a relay team daily. Our baton handover was perfect.

"There is only one thing I want to say," Sir Brathelthwaite began, but Victor cleared his throat, interrupting.

"Might I have a quiet word with you, Sir Brathelthwaite? Before you go on?"

"Certainly, Your Grace."

We other members of the team waited while Victor and Sir Brathelthwaite stepped aside and spoke in low voices. We could not hear their conversation but, after a moment, Sir Brathelthwaite said, "Oh-ho! Ha!" and he and Victor stepped back to us.

"I have only one thing to say to you," Sir Brathelthwaite repeated, his smile vanishing. He paused and looked hard at each of us in turn. He stared at me for so long I could have drawn a picture of the blood vessels in his eyes. At last, he spoke, lowering his voice. "It is *vital*," he hissed, "that you win this."

Beside him, Uncle Dominic swished the horsewhip.

CHAPTER 7
FINLAY

Whoosh! Was that a freight train going by?

Honey Bee just told the *whole day* in a few paragraphs! Reminds me of the solid kid from Spindrift Public who can't pace himself. I mean, you could get whiplash trying to keep up with the girl's storytelling.

If you'd been with *me* for that chapter, I'd have taken you through each race and event, one at a time. You'd have enjoyed it.

Too late now.

I will say this though: after the long distance race, I had a go at Hamish.

"Golly!" he replied. "Thought you'd misplaced your shoes, old chap! Sort of thing *I* might do, forgetting my shoes, see? Awfully sorry, but I truly—" He'd have kept right on talking, but I was tired of his voice and walked off.

In the other races, he started without interrupting me, and in the sprint, he was just ahead of me the whole way. *Legs!* I thought. *Go faster!* My legs just bellowed back: *Going as fast as we can! YOU go faster.*

And Hamish beat me.

Sprinting is my thing. It's *who I am*—the fastest boy in Spindrift.

Or that's who I was. Then Hamish beat me.

Meanwhile, Lili-Daisy was running around hugging everybody, thinking this would make it all right about Brathelthwaite winning half the events.

When she wasn't hugging us, she was staring at the Brathelthwaites. We all were. We were sprawled on old blankets, nothing but our hats to shade us, and they had chairs under a silk marquee. Giant pots of flowers in each corner.

Glim and I were stretching, getting ready for the mixed relay. The twins were sitting on our feet to help with the stretches, their heads inside their newspapers.

"This one's ours," Glim said.

"You bet," I agreed.

But we didn't really believe it. Our relay team was not the best. Daffo was on the team, and he's pretty quick, but the other fast girl at the Orphanage is Avril, and her twisted ankle was propped up on a basket.

Leesa was taking her place. She's speedy but she's only eight years old, so not yet as speedy as she will be. At this point, her eyes were darting around like a scared little frog, and she was chewing her knuckles. I worried she would drop the baton.

"Just do your best," Lili-Daisy advised, squeezing our shoulders. "Be proud of yourselves, *whatever* happens."

"I'll only be proud," I said, "if we win."

Across at the Brathelthwaite marquee, the children were eating cream puffs and watching their head teacher speak. A huge man, shoulders like a tanker, stood alongside the head. He kept swinging a whip as if the flies were bothering him. "That's their deputy," Lili-Daisy whispered. "Dominic Rowe." She shuddered.

Then she told us to relax and think happy thoughts, and she went off to notify Millicent Cadger about the change to our team. We'd registered Avril back before she twisted her ankle, and had kept her name down in case of a sudden recovery.

But no recovery.

"All done," Lili-Daisy said when she returned. "Relay is about to be called! Would you like a cold boiled potato for energy?"

"Lili-Daisy," I said, "eating a potato right before a race would be ridiculous."

"Oh," she said. "Finlay, I'm ashamed."

"No need," I told her. "We all make mistakes."

And the relay race was called.

CHAPTER 8
FINLAY

Still me, Finlay. Seemed like time for a new chapter. Honey Bee agrees, and suggests I carry on.

I'll just repeat that last sentence.

And the relay race was called.

Everything went whisper quiet, right across the field. The kids from the different schools, adults in the stadium, teachers, officials. Everyone knew what this race meant. Nobody would blink for fear of missing a moment.

Four lanes. Spindrift Public in Lane 1. Thea Girls and Harrison Boys Combined Team in Lane 2. Brathelthwaite Boarding School in Lane 3. Orphanage School in Lane 4.

The starting gun cracked.

Little Leesa ran first for us. She flew like a puff of dandelion caught in a slipstream. Handed over the baton smooth as butter, putting our team in second place behind Brathelthwaite.

Daffo narrowed the gap a little. He's fast.

He handed over to Glim.

The other schools had fallen behind. It was Brathelthwaite versus the Orphanage. Glim is lightning-fast, but she was up against Honey Bee.

Here I will say that Honey Bee may be an annoying girl who *cannot abide violins*, but she runs like she's supposed to be running. Her face, which is generally smiley but with worried lines around the edges, becomes smooth and clear. She reminds me of a sailboat skimming the ocean.

Anyhow, I couldn't watch Glim and Honey Bee racing, because I had to face forward, ready for my turn.

Slap went the baton onto my palm and, *at the exact same moment*, I heard Honey Bee slam hers into Hamish's hand.

Glim had closed the gap. We were even.

I took off with my heart singing happy thoughts about Glim. She must have given everything she had.

Now it was up to me.

Hamish was right alongside me.

Every time I surged, he surged as well.

His breath was in my ear. His pounding legs. Sunlight shining on his flopping hair.

You have to run faster, I said to my legs, and they started up their complaining about how they were running as fast as they *could* and how—

But I said: *Yes.*

Yes, I said, calmer than I've ever been. *You must.*

And I was flying. He was flying too, but I was flying faster.

Crossed the finish line first.

The Orphanage had won the day.

CHAPTER
9
HONEY BEE

There was no time to congratulate the Orphanage team. Nor was there time to rush back to school, pack my bag, steal a horse, and ride away into the sunset, far from the wrath of Sir Brathelthwaite and Uncle Dominic—

As a matter of fact, there was no time even to *look* at Sir Brathelthwaite and Uncle Dominic, to check their facial expressions. (Or whether they still *had* faces: I feared they might have fallen right off.)

For along came the constables, scooting children back to the sidelines, waving adults back into the stadium, and there was Mayor Franny with her megaphone, shouting: "Positions, everybody! It's the queen!"

A different sort of hush fell, a giggling, excited, craning-to-see hush. The gates swung open.

"Two, three, four," hissed the band conductor, and the trumpets blazed their fanfare.

The royal carriage rolled onto the Green, drawn by six fine horses. The drummers started up. I *do* like the sound of drums. I feel the rhythm deep inside my tummy.

Nothing whatsoever happened, and then a hand reached out of the carriage window, held itself still in the air—and waved. Cheering erupted.

The carriage halted in the center of the Green. The drummers stopped drumming.

It seemed that the royal carriage had arrived a *little* earlier than expected, and there was a deal of hissing and clicking fingers as officials hurried about. Everyone else waited with interest. The children who'd just run the mixed relay had gathered together in a sort of huddle near the finish line. Some of us were still panting. The four children of the Orphanage team were grinning hugely.

"I say," hissed Hamish. "Jolly good show out there! When I saw your tiny runner? The little girl who ran first? Well, I thought, *golly*, this'll be a shoe-in for us! No offense intended there, little girl—oh dear, that *shoe-in* sounded like I was insulting your bare feet, Finlay—put my foot in it, didn't I? Oh, I've done it again! Foot! No, honestly, all an error. Anyhow, then she took off like a—" but the rest of us said, "Shhh," and Hamish stopped.

A red carpet was spread along the grass perpendicular to the royal carriage. Next, a small platform was carried out and placed at the other end of this carpet. Various chairs were hustled onto it, along with a table, the immense Spindrift Tournament trophy, and an enormous megaphone.

Once again, the queen's hand emerged from the carriage window and waved, and once again the crowd went mad to see it.

Quite soon, I thought, *the town is going to tire of the queen's hand. They're going to want to see a little more of her. A glimpse of her ear, say? Or elbow?* I smiled at my own small joke.

A small boy was hustled out of the Orphanage section, across to the platform, and handed a bouquet so large it hid his face. Mayor Franny leapt up beside him and made a show of trying to find the boy behind the flowers. He tipped the bouquet sideways to reveal his beaming little face, and Mayor Franny pantomimed amazement. The crowd laughed in a loving sort of way.

"Are we right, now?" the mayor called to an official.

Millicent Cadger shout-whispered, "Wait! Wait!" rushed up, and polished the trophy with the hem of her dress. Again, the crowd giggled. But Millicent did not seem to mind. She adjusted the trophy's position on the table, checked her reflection in its surface, and nodded.

The constables stood at attention.

An official pointed at the band conductor, who faced his band, arms raised high.

The carriage door was opened.

Out stepped the queen.

* CHAPTER *
10
FINLAY

She looked like the queen.

I have a strong feeling that Honey Bee wants me to say that the queen glowed like starshine and smelled like seashells, or something.

But she did not. Well, to be honest, I couldn't smell her from where I was standing.

She wore queenly clothes and her hair was puffy like a queen's hair. That's about all I can remember.

The crowd cheered like they couldn't believe it really was the queen and not just her hand.

Everyone waited for the prince to hop out too—he's about eighteen years old and what people call "dashing" or "dishy" or "darling," usually starts with a *d*—but nothing happened. Seemed the prince was staying put. We stared at his silhouette behind the carriage window. The silhouette leaned forward but then settled itself back.

So we turned back to the queen.

The queen did a little pivot. Crowd cheered even louder.

Next she marched along the red carpet. She seemed fit enough for a grown-up. Had no trouble with the steps up onto the platform.

Now came Jaskafar's starring role.

He tugged on the queen's sleeve. I'm pretty sure he wasn't supposed to do that part. But the queen was only startled for a second. She recovered and crouched down. Jaskafar bowed his head, the way we'd taught him. Then he stuck the flowers in the queen's face. We hadn't taught him that part either. Once again, the queen was pretty smooth, ducking just in time so she wouldn't get stabbed in the nose by a rose. She did a good job acting amazed by the flowers, as if she'd never been given them in all her queenly days.

Jaskafar stood back, grinning his head off. The queen patted his head. He looked less happy after that: tidy hair is important to him.

The queen appeared to have a friendly chat with Mayor Franny and Millicent Cadger, who hefted up the megaphone and offered it to her.

"My people," said the queen, taking it like a pro and speaking directly into it. Clapping and excitement again. Honestly, this would never get done.

"My good people of Spindrift," the queen said next. "What a joy it is to attend your Spindrift Tournament!"

Well, she hadn't attended it.

It was over.

But we let that go.

"I understand that the healthful benefits of fresh air and outdoor activities are enormous!" the queen carried on.

More cheering, but I was a bit bored by the queen and her excitement about fresh air, to be honest, and I'd started looking around.

What I saw was the head teacher of Brathelthwaite—I'll call him Sir Brath; his name's too long otherwise. He'd somehow hopped up onto the platform too, and was whispering into Millicent Cadger's ear. Millicent shook her head.

Mayor Franny had the megaphone now. "Your Majesty!" she boomed into it. "We are over the moon to have you and the prince here in Spindrift! If you can hear me in there, Prince Jakob, welcome!" She waved towards the carriage.

After a long moment, a hand reached out of the carriage window and gave a sort of salute. Everyone laughed.

The queen leaned into the megaphone. "The prince apologizes," she said. "But he was stung on the cheek by a zapper eel while swimming in Careening Bay yesterday and the royal doctor has instructed him to keep out of the sunlight!"

The prince's hand rose up in a sort of apologetic shrug. Again, the crowd laughed. Dead easy to please we are sometimes, here in Spindrift.

"Victor!" Sir Brath shouted suddenly. "Take the prince a cream puff! To cheer him up!"

The kid standing beside me—Victor, I guess—zipped over to the Brathelthwaite marquee, then zoomed to the carriage, carrying a single cream puff on a silver tray. He held this up to the window. The prince's hand reached out, gave a thumbs-up signal, and took the tray.

Oh, everyone loved that.

Ha-ha-ha, they all laughed.

People are peculiar, aren't they?

Victor pelted back to us relay runners, looking dead pleased with himself.

Honestly, we'd all grow old and cobwebby before we got our trophy.

Mayor Franny must've read my mind. "Now, we invite Her Majesty to present the trophy to the winning school!" she cried.

Finally.

At this point, Jaskafar was sort of in the way. Nobody had told him what to do once he'd handed over the flowers, so he'd hopped up on the table and sat there, swinging his legs. He was blocking the trophy.

There was a bit of a kerfuffle, but he scooted along and the mayor grabbed the trophy.

Back to the megaphone she came. "It's been a ripper day, Your Majesty," she said. "Most nail-biting tournament we've ever held. It was neck and neck right up until the final race! But the winner of the day is clear. The winner is — wait, could we get a drumroll please?"

The band obliged.

"The winner is . . . the *Orphanage School*!!!"

Another storm of cheering.

"Come on, Lili-Daisy! Hop over here and accept the trophy on behalf of the Orphanage School!"

Over in our section, the kids were all leaping around Lili-Daisy. She peeled herself away from them and walked towards the platform. She was trying to be quick so she wouldn't keep the queen waiting, but also trying to be slow so she would look proper and regal. It's impossible to be quick and slow at the same time. Lili-Daisy looked like a stork that is wading through a pond and making sudden darts at fish.

I was watching her and maybe there was a little tear of happiness in my eye, even while I was trying not to bust my gut laughing at her walk. But then voices distracted me. Sir Brath was on at Millicent Cadger again, and Millicent Cadger was pointing to something on a clipboard. Sir Brath peered over her shoulder. He reached out a finger and stabbed at the clipboard himself.

When I turned back, Lili-Daisy had reached the platform. Her foot landed on the first step.

"One moment!" sang a voice. It was Sir Brath. His voice was cheery. He was rocking on his heels.

Lili-Daisy stopped on the bottom step, confused. Beside Sir Brath, Millicent Cadger was still studying the clipboard while rubbing her fist against her forehead.

"Just a little hiccup!" Sir Brath called. "My sincerest apologies, Your Majesty!" The queen nodded once in a queenly way, and smiled. You could tell she was fond of Sir Brath, on account of him having sent a cream puff to her son. Beside the queen, Mayor Franny frowned.

Millicent Cadger gave a helpless sort of look and took the megaphone.

"There's been a mistake," she said. "A technical violation. The Orphanage School has been disqualified from the mixed relay. Which means that the winner of today is *actually*—uh, drumroll please?"

There was no drumroll. The drummer was busy staring with an open mouth.

"The winner of today is actually the Brathelthwaite Boarding School," Millicent continued. "Er, Sir Brathelthwaite? Would you accept your trophy?"

Sir Brath beamed and stepped forward.

CHAPTER 11
HONEY BEE

The children under the Brathelthwaite marquee applauded loudly and broke into the school chant:

> "Brathelthwaite students are
> Better than the best!
> Brathelthwaite students,
> Put us to the test!
> We will conquer all
> We are ever so tall
> We will never ever fall
> We will never drop the ball
> We would never have the gall
> To come second!

What?
Second?! [and they all noisily spat on the grass]
No way!
We will come first!"

This did not seem very sporting.

You will recall that I, Honey Bee, was standing in a gathering of relay teams. The four children from the Orphanage School team were blinking in shock.

"Golly," piped up Hamish. "Did we truly win? How'd we pull that off? I could have *sworn* the orphans beat us in the relay just now. And didn't that mean they'd won the day? Or was the *arithmetic* wrong somewhere? Or am I *dreaming* all this? I *do* dream, you know. I often—"

"Do be quiet, Hamish," Victor sighed, stretching his arms above his head in a very lordly way. "They *did* win the relay but they've been disqualified. Technical violation, she said. I expect there was a problem with one of their baton handovers."

Finlay and Glim swung around to look at each other. Meanwhile, the little girl who had started the relay for the orphans bit her lip. Her eyes filled with tears.

"Did I do something wrong?" she asked. "Did I ruin it?"

The boy who had followed her—his name was Daffo, and he was terribly rough-looking with scabby arms and unkempt hair—tapped the little girl's shoulder. "You did nothing wrong, kid," he told her. "If there was a problem, it must have been me." This was sporting of him.

But the other school relay teams were shaking their heads. "There was nothing wrong with your handovers," they told the orphans. "The officials gave the thumbs-up for each. They'd have called it when it happened."

"In that case"—Victor yawned—"it must have been one of my suggestions."

Up on the platform, the queen was handing the trophy over to Sir Brathelthwaite. The director of the Orphanage, Lili-Daisy Casimati, was lingering on the bottom step, staring up at him.

"One of your suggestions, Victor?" I asked. I remembered Victor taking Sir Brathelthwaite aside before the relay. But whatever could he have said?

"The rules of this tournament are terribly detailed," Victor explained. "I told Sir B that if we *didn't* win the relay, there was sure to be a loophole. This one's not wearing any shoes, for instance. I bet it's a violation."

He waved his hand at Finlay's bare feet.

"Oh cripes," Hamish said, aghast. "I did try to warn you about the old shoes, old chap."

But the other children protested that it was *not* against the rules. Children from the Orphanage often ran barefoot, they said.

Meanwhile, Sir B was making a speech about how proud he was of his students, and how they had conquered adversity. They had sat outside on the Green all day, poor things, competing with a different *sort* of student to the usual sort. But it was all worth it, he said, because they had triumphed!

"Hmm," Victor said, still gazing at Finlay's feet. "Perhaps the orphans changed their relay team, then? Not allowed. I pointed that rule out to Sir B."

"We did change our relay team!"

"But we *notified* Millicent!"

"It *is* allowed!" the orphans all bellowed.

They were so loud that people stopped listening to Sir B and looked over at us. Even the queen peered in our direction. Noticing this, Sir B sniffed.

"Oh my," he said. "It seems the orphans are making a fuss. Not quite the thing, is it? Not quite sporting. Lili-Daisy, perhaps you could control them?"

He tapped his fingertips together in the direction of Lili-Daisy.

"But, Sir Brathelthwaite," Lili-Daisy called up. "I don't understand how your school came to win!"

"Simple!" Sir B grabbed the megaphone again. "You notified Millicent about the change to your relay team, yes? But the change is only *valid* if Millicent signs off in the *right-hand* column on her clipboard. Which she did not!"

Millicent curled her hands into fists, distraught. "He's right," she called down to Lili-Daisy. "I'm so very sorry. I accidentally signed in the *left* column."

"And that means they were disqualified?" Lili-Daisy said, amazed.

"Yes."

"There's *nothing* you can do?"

"Nothing."

Mayor Franny put her hands on her hips. "Are we kidding here?" she demanded.

The queen looked around for a lady-in-waiting to rescue her from this nonsense. (At least, I think that's what she was seeking.)

But Sir B was still smiling and clutching his trophy. "In effect," he boomed, "the Orphanage School *cheated* by changing their relay team improperly. But we won't make too much of that. That is for the orphans to think deeply about. Life must be done *properly*! Meanwhile, we at Brathelthwaite are proud of our victory today—and proud that we achieved it in the right way, *without* cheating."

"There," said Victor languidly. "Told you so."

At this point, Finlay punched him in the nose.

CHAPTER 12
FINLAY

It was the right thing to do. The only thing to do.

To be honest, it was a beautiful thing to do. My fist in that Victor boy's face.

He staggers back, his face turns purple, and he's roaring straight for me. Pummelling my belly. So I laid into him.

Around this point, things fell to pieces.

A bunch of Brathelthwaite kids tore across the grass to help out Victor. A bunch of orphans streamed over to help me.

Some adult was shouting into the megaphone. The crowd was whooping and screaming. (The people of Spindrift love a good fight.) "Fight! Fight! Fight!" a few witches and pirates chanted, and they rallied the crowd to join them. "Fight! Fight!" everyone roared.

And we did.

The little kids scooted out of the way. The rest of us got stuck in. Kicking and punching, scratching and tearing. Hair-pulling and screeching. Three big boarding school guys got ahold of me, and I spun around like I've seen in the cinema, kicking them one at a time. One tipped sideways into the second, he knocked into the third, and they all crashed down.

Victor came after me again and got his hands around my throat. Glim hooked an arm through his and spun him in a beautiful circle in the air. He hit the ground with a thud.

Daffo was a whirlwind, taking on about five boarding school kids at once. The twins, Eli and Taya, stomped and stampeded.

I guess it only lasted half a minute.

Before we knew it, the constables were dragging us apart; teachers were shouting; and somebody had gotten ahold of a bucket of water and flung it over us.

I stood there, glaring at Victor, blood and water dripping everywhere.

"Stop that at once!" a woman's voice was bleating. I wasn't sure who it was. "As your queen, I *command* you children to stop fighting!"

So then I knew it was the queen.

The crowd quieted down. They'd been jumping up and down, but now they sank back into their seats, a bit shamefaced. (The people of Spindrift also love their queen.)

"Fight! Fight!" a couple of witches called, trying to rev the crowd up again, but the queen snapped, "Do you witches *want* to spend the night in the dungeon?"

So the witches sat down too.

Lili-Daisy had scurried over to try to stop the fight, and she was standing alongside me now, her hand quite firm on my shoulder. When I say quite firm, I mean her nails were digging into my skin like talons.

"Lili-Daisy?" I said.

"Finlay," she replied, in a voice that suggested she knew exactly what her nails were doing and wasn't planning to stop.

"Now then," the queen began, in her most queenly voice—but at this point Lili-Daisy did lift her hand from my shoulder.

She swung around, this way and that. She muttered to herself.

She took a step towards the platform. Still peering in every direction. Next thing she was running.

"Where is he?" she said. "Where's he got to?"

"Who?" demanded the queen, exasperated.

"Jaskafar!" Lili-Daisy cried. "I can't see him! Where's he gone?"

And she stopped still by the platform and screamed: "JASKAFAR?!"

CHAPTER
13
HONEY BEE

He was gone.

The little boy from the Orphanage who had given the queen flowers.

Everybody searched the Green, but he had vanished.

He'd been right there on the platform, sitting on the table, swinging his legs. So many adults! The queen, Mayor Franny, Sir Brathelthwaite, Millicent Cadger—they'd *all* been up there with him. The queen's guards had been lined up on the red carpet! Constables all over the place!

But once again, a child had been stolen and nobody had seen a thing.

CHAPTER
14
FINLAY

Day and night, we swept through the streets of Spindrift searching for him.

Everyone from the Orphanage, crowds of people from right across the town—all of us looked. Plenty knew Jaskafar and loved him, and we marched the streets shouting his name and banging on saucepan lids.

We turned the place upside down.

Other children had been taken, and we'd always searched for them, of course, but not like this. This was *Jaskafar.* Taken *right before our eyes!* While our *queen* was in town!

We'd had enough.

We climbed roofs and trees, upturned baskets of fish and trash cans, shone lamps into basements. We crept into the radish gnome caves along the coastline, and hunted through the ships docked at the wharf.

The constables ran around the Green with magnifying glasses and box cameras, and interviewed everyone who'd been at the tournament. The queen decided to stay in town another fortnight in the royal suite of the Ocean View Hotel, the best hotel on the Beach with the Yellow Sand, and she sent for five of her best palace spies to help out. These palace spies galloped into town and ran around the Green with their own much fancier magnifying glasses and cameras. They interviewed everyone who'd been at the tournament again, asking exactly the same questions, only using bigger words and longer, more menacing pauses between questions.

Randalf the lighthouse keeper aimed his spotlight at every corner of the town to help. This caused a few near-shipwrecks, so he had to go back to aiming it at the sea. Local witches and sterling silver foxes suggested they dust off their Shadow Magic to help in the hunt. "We'd *never* use it ordinarily," they all promised. "We've practically forgotten how!"

"Hmm," said the constables suspiciously.

Friendly pirates dragged out treasure chests from the backs of their closets and posted notices:

REWARD
Used Treasure Chest in Fair Condition
(few scratches but hinges polished)
for Any Information Leading to
the Return of Little Jaskafar.

The siren sisters who live on Danbury Street very kindly shrieked, "Jaskafar! Jaskafar! Come back at once!" in voices so horrible that, if the boy had been *hiding*, he'd have come running right away to make it stop. Eventually, everybody else asked the siren sisters to please stop.

But there was no trace of him, not a single clue. Jaskafar's bed was empty each night, and every morning, the top of the wardrobe was bare. "A rat?" murmured Lili-Daisy hopefully, looking up there each day.

Now and then, Glim and I took a short break from searching to go see our friend Snatty-Ra-Ra, a fortune-teller in the town square. There are six or seven fortune-tellers who sit at card tables or inside tents around the square, and all of them will tell you the future for a couple of silver. Far and away, our friend Snatty is the best.

The others all claim to be the best, of course. Some will tell you they trained in Baebelot with the crystal-gazers. Some claim to be part Sibyl. Two of them, a pair of brothers who dress in matching smart suits, swear they are actually visitors from the future who came here to Spindrift through a gap in a hedge. "The Time Travel Brothers," they call themselves.

"So *we* can certainly tell you what happens in the future," they crow. "We're *from* there."

Now, there is an old story about a hedge in the Oakum Woods where people used to squeeze through a gap and time travel. But most folk are pretty sure that the story is a great big crate-load of crabapple, invented by a local gardener after seven or eight pints too many. My friends and I had scratched ourselves to pieces one summer, squeezing between every gap, half gap, and plenty of actual non-gaps in every hedge we could find in the Oakum Woods, and we'd reached a solid conclusion: hedges don't help you time travel. All they do is stand there looking hedgy.

Still, some do believe the Time Travel Brothers, most probably because their suits are so snazzy. It stands to reason, people think, that suits in the future will be snazzy. So customers hand over their silver.

Not Glim and me. We don't give our silver to the two in the suits, nor to any of the other fortune-tellers.

Well, we don't actually have any silver.

But let's say we did? We'd only ever give it to Snatty.

Snatty has long gray hair, all the way to his ankles, which he wears in a ponytail. He also has the best nose you ever saw. Like a sail it is, long and thin, flappy and sharp. When Glim and I were tiny, we used to sneak out of the Orphanage and visit Snatty because he let us pull on his nose. Each time we pulled, he'd make a sound in the back of his throat. Like this: *Gong!* We thought it was his nose making the noise. We'd crawl around his lap pulling on his nose, laughing our heads off at this guy's crazy, *gong*-making nose. He was very patient. *Gong*, he'd go.

Gong.
gong.
Gong.

Anyhow, Snatty is from the Whispering Kingdom, where the people can Whisper thoughts into your head. Some of the Whisperers, Snatty amongst them, can also hear Whispers from the future. That's how *he* does his fortune-telling.

He never makes much money, though, because he's honest. If he can't hear a Whisper about a particular customer, he'll give the silver straight back. "Nope," he says. "Sorry. Got zippo here. It's like you don't even *have* a future."

Customers don't tend to like that.

As I mentioned, Glim and I dropped in on Snatty each day while we were searching. We wanted to know if he'd heard any Whispers about Jaskafar. Each day, Snatty would shake his nose. I mean, he shook his head, but his nose is so long it always seems as if that's what he's shaking.

Snatty loved Jaskafar too, so he was listening to the future as hard as he could, but day after day went by without a word.

Finally, a week after the tournament, Snatty told us that he'd heard a *very* faint Whisper from tomorrow.

"I heard that Jaskafar is a good distance away," he said.

"No point looking for him in Spindrift anymore, then?" Glim asked.

Snatty shook his nose.

"You hear anything else? Like an *address* maybe? If he's okay?"

The nose shook again.

We sighed for a bit.

"Cheer up," Snatty said, but he said this in a Whisper. It feels like a tickle in your brain when Whisperers Whisper at you. Feels like you're thinking to yourself: *I'm going to cheer up now*, in a scratchy little voice. I gave a little shake and the Whisper fell away.

"Snatty," I said sternly.

"Sorry," he replied.

He knows it's not polite to Whisper.

"I don't *want* to cheer up," I added.

"Me neither," Glim agreed. "I want to be sad."

Snatty wound his long ponytail around his wrist and offered for us to pull on his nose. But we said no, thanks all the same. We've pretty well grown out of that.

Sorrowful, we walked back across the town square towards the Orphanage.

"I want to be sad," I said, expanding on the thought, "because I feel so bad."

Glim nodded. "We promised Lili-Daisy we'd keep an eye on Jaskafar."

"But we were fighting with the Brathelthwaite kids," I continued grimly. "It's *my* fault. I'm the one who punched that boy."

"Don't blame yourself," Glim argued. "The boy deserved it. Right prat, that one. I'd punch him myself this moment if I could."

"Same," I agreed. "Nothing would make me happier—"

"—than to lay into those boarding school kids again."

"The way they acted at the tournament!"

"Cream-puff-eating, silk-tent-lazing toffee apples!"

"Snooty bunch of toffee-nosed jackasses!"

"And that *crabapple* way they stole the victory from us! The trophy!"

"*Of course* we had to fight them!"

"It's *their* fault Jaskafar's gone!"

"Of *course* it's their fault!"

"And have you noticed that every person in town has been searching for Jaskafar, *except*—"

"—for the Brathelthwaite kids!"

Suddenly, we were not at all sad.

We were extremely mad.

"Let's find the twins," I said.

"And attack Brathelthwaite," Glim agreed.

CHAPTER 15
HONEY BEE

For a week after the tournament, between 6:00 p.m. and midnight, the whole school had to march around the courtyard chanting our school motto. This was to remind us of how wicked we had been in almost coming second.

"My dear students," Sir Brathelthwaite said on the night of the tournament. "My dear, dear students. There may come a day, later in your lives, when you experience a crushing disappointment. It will hit you like a steam train in your belly. It will make you want to don boxing gloves and beat your own face."

"Oh my," Hamish muttered, clasping his hands to his face. "I just . . . I find that rather foolish an idea. I mean to say—"

"When that happens to you, dear students"—Sir Brathelthwaite's voice rose over Hamish's—"you will get *some* idea of how I feel right now."

We all stared. We were in the dining hall but there was no dinner on the table, only empty plates.

"These empty plates will help you understand," Sir B continued, "the *emptiness* I feel in *my soul*. Oh dear students—" He had to stop there, as his voice was cracking, and he picked up a cloth napkin and buried his face in it, blowing his nose. Uncle Dominic, who was standing alongside and flicking his horsewhip about, reached out and placed a gentle hand on Sir B's shoulder. When Sir B looked up, he gave Uncle Dominic an emotional nod. "Dear students, you *almost* lost today! Had it not been for the young duke, Victor, pointing out the tournament rules—had it not been that the riffraff at the Orphanage *had* indeed broken the rules—why, we could have—we might have—"

Again, he had to stop and turn away.

We all waited. I was awfully hungry. Running all day makes my stomach ache for food.

"We could have *lost*," Sir Brathelthwaite finished hoarsely. "And Brathelthwaite students *never, ever* lose."

Then he told us, very sorrowfully, that we would have to march around the courtyard each evening for a week. It was the only thing he could think to do, he said, to help us remember how very wrong, how *shameful*, it was to lose.

He hated doing it.

Hated it.

"*All* of us?" Rosalind Whitehall asked, raising her hand.

"No, of course not all of you," Sir Brathelthwaite *tch*ed, brightening a little and nodding towards Victor. "His Grace may remain indoors with the teachers. It is thanks to *him* that you only have to do this for a week. Had we, actually … *lost* … you would have had to march at least a month. Please. A small round of applause for His Grace."

We applauded Victor, and he bowed, giving a little shrug as if to say: *It was nothing. A mere trifle.*

"But *all* of us?" Rosalind Whitehall persisted. "I mean to say, sir, I did not compete in any events. So *I* did not lose. It was really just the mixed relay team that almost lost the day for us, so should it not be athletes who failed us, who march?"

Sir Brathelthwaite sadly shook his head. "When *one* fails, you *all* fail. That is the Brathelthwaite way. The athletes will *learn* from your suffering."

Many of the students cast irritated glances at me and the other athletes for having failed them.

"Oh, I say," Hamish said. "Awfully sorry, old chaps. But it will be grand to have you out suffering with us! Thanks for that. And your suffering will help me run faster in the future!"

This did not improve their glances.

My friend Carlos raised his hand.

"Carlos?" Sir Brathelthwaite sighed.

Carlos had caught a nasty cold a few days earlier and could not speak for a moment, as he was shivering violently. Sir Brathelthwaite's mouth turned into a little pinch as he waited.

"Only," Carlos said, getting control of his shivers, "I thought we could help search for the little orphan boy? Jaskafar? The whole town is going out with lanterns tonight."

Sir Brathelthwaite gave a great shrug. "It is a tragedy," he said, "that another child has been stolen. But my dear students, it is not *our* tragedy. We must stay well away from the search. What if one of *us* were to be stolen? If we do not look out for ourselves, we *fail* the town and the kingdom. Do you see what I mean?"

"No," Carlos said.

"You are confused?" Sir Brathelthwaite inquired.

"Yes."

"In that case," said Sir Brathelthwaite—and Uncle Dominic loosened his horsewhip, but Sir B shook his head slightly. "In that case, Carlos, *you* will march the courtyard until *dawn* each night this week. Perhaps that will help clear your mind?"

Now I should perhaps let you know that my friend Carlos is a foundling. He was left on the steps of Brathelthwaite one frosty morning, a baby wrapped in a shawl inside a cardboard box. There was a note in the box, which I have seen because it is pinned to Sir Brathelthwaite's office wall:

THIS IS PRINCE CARLOS, HEIR TO THE THRONE OF THE KINGDOM OF JOYA AMARILLO (IN THE NORTHERN CLIMES). OUR KING HAS BEEN OVERTHROWN BY REBEL FORCES! PLEASE KEEP PRINCE CARLOS SAFE UNTIL OUR MONARCHY IS RESTORED! YOU WILL BE REWARDED WITH MOUNTAINS OF GOLD.

When I came to Brathelthwaite three years ago, Uncle Dominic advised me to stay away from Carlos.

"At first," Uncle Dominic confided in me, "Sir Brathelthwaite was *terribly* excited to have a little prince at his school. But years have gone by and it seems the royal family of Joya Amarillo is *never* going to win back its crown and come for the prince."

Sir Brathelthwaite had become fed up with the whole thing, Uncle Dominic explained, and couldn't *stand* Carlos anymore—he thought Carlos was actually *stealing* from the school by promising a mountain of gold and not delivering one.

"I don't understand," I said. "Carlos was only a baby when he was left here. It's not *his* fault that his family are losing their battle?"

Uncle Dominic rolled his eyes and muttered, "How can *we* be *related*?"

Then, of course, Carlos and I became friends.

I tried to explain to Uncle Dominic that this was truly an accident, but he did not understand at all. You see, Carlos is funny and kind and seems more *ordinary* than the other children. For example, each Saturday we are allowed a free day to take a stroll outside school grounds, provided we go in pairs and never stray near to a local. The other students promenade about the Spindrift Gardens, avoiding the downtown altogether. However, Carlos and I always run directly to the beach or into town, and we break the rule about straying near locals, as we find them so much more fun and lively than Brathelthwaiters.

Anyhow, by the end of that week, we were all weary, but Carlos especially. Often his colds turn to bronchitis, and it had happened again. His face was deathly white, he stumbled often as he walked, and coughed almost ceaselessly.

As a special treat, on this final night of marching, Carlos was permitted to stop at midnight with the rest of us. We all walked around to the front of the school and into the school building together. We passed the welcome sign:

BRATHELTHWAITE BOARDING SCHOOL
A RENOWNED ESTABLISHMENT
WHERE JUSTICE, ACADEMIC EXCELLENCE, KINDNESS,
AND COMPASSION
FORM THE CORNERSTONES OF OUR BELIEFS.

We crawled into our beds, greatly relieved that at last the punishment was over.

"Not punishment!" Sir Brathelthwaite scolded. "I would never *punish* my dear students. It is merely a *reminder*, to *help* you."

But just as we began to drift towards sleep, we were startled awake by this:

> *Splat!*
> *Splat!*
> *Splat!*

Along with angry shouts from our security guards.

The news flew up and down the corridors. Children from the Orphanage had climbed over the school walls! They were hurling rotten eggs at the building!

> *Splat!*
> *Splat!*
> *Splat!*

The next morning at breakfast, Sir Brathelthwaite said, very sadly, that this attack was truly our own fault. As we had *almost* lost the tournament, we had caused the orphans to forget their place. They no longer went about admiring and being awestruck by us. Instead, they threw eggs.

Now, he added, we would have to march the courtyard *another* week, to remind us of our place as number one.

"I'd like to remind those *Orphanage* kids of their place," Victor muttered, crinkling his nose at the stench of rotten egg. "Who's in?"

CHAPTER 16
FINLAY

What a night that was! Cheered us right up, attacking Brathelthwaite.

First thing that happened was, Glim and I found the twins and made the suggestion. They were in before we'd finished the sentence.

"A witch's coven has dumped a cartload of rotten eggs outside of town," Eli said.

"Read that in the paper today," Taya agreed. "They must have had one of their curse battles."

So we agreed we'd creep out at midnight, collect the eggs, and head to the boarding school with them.

Perfect.

I was already in a good mood when we set out too, as we'd listened to the Raffia–Takejby rugby game after dinner. Most of us kids support the Kingdom of Raffia even though it never wins the cup, and we'd all crowded around the wireless. Lili-Daisy is the most passionate supporter, as she grew up in Raffia—actually, she's the reason we got behind the team in the first place—and she always puts on her Raffia scarf and woolen hat to listen. So there we were in our pajamas, drinking our cocoa, waving our arms around and spilling our cocoa, because they won! Against Takejby! Five-time cup holders!

Close match too: 28–24.

Right as the game finished, the announcer said, "We interrupt this program for a Special Announcement from Waratah Teevsky."

That had us shaking our heads at the near-disaster. *Imagine if Waratah Teevsky had interrupted the game!*

"It doesn't bear thinking about," Lili-Daisy told us darkly.

Waratah Teevsky is the director of the K&E Alliance, in case you don't know that. The K&E Alliance is an organization that represents all the Kingdoms and Empires. They get together to try to stop wars and to sort out issues like how fast ships can go without smashing into each other, and things like that.

Listen, look it up in a book if you need to know more. I'm not that into politics or, you know, events.

"I am speaking to you all today," Waratah Teevsky blared on the wireless, *"about the children who have gone missing all over the Kingdoms and Empires."*

"HUSH UP, EVERYONE," Lili-Daisy cried, grabbing the wireless and turning up the volume. "WE NEED TO KNOW WHAT SHE SAYS!"

Waratah Teevsky took a deep breath. It was loud coming through the wireless, and Lili-Daisy adjusted the volume back down a bit. "The K&E Alliance *vows* to do all in its power to track down the culprits and return the children!"

"Blahdy blah," Glim put in. "All talk but nothing gets done."

Lili-Daisy nodded grimly at Glim. We all looked at the empty beds where Amie, Connor, and Bing should be, and up at the top of the wardrobe. Where was little Jaskafar?

"My proposal," Waratah Teevsky carried on, "is that we transfer a huge chunk of the diamond regions in several different Kingdoms and Empires to the Whispering Kingdom. They already have their own diamond mines, of course, but they would appreciate more. In return, they have promised to listen out for Whispers from the future that might help locate the children. The paperwork will be drawn up within the next two days. Thank you and good night."

Lili-Daisy switched off the wireless.

We were all silent for a bit, probably thinking about huge chunks of diamonds.

"Strange," I put in eventually. "Why would the Whispering Kingdom need *diamonds* to hear Whispers about the missing children? Wouldn't they want to help just for the sake of helping?"

"It's always about money," Taya said darkly.

Glim and I told everyone how Snatty-Ra-Ra had heard a Whisper from tomorrow that Jaskafar was not in Spindrift anymore.

"See?" we said. "He didn't even need a single copper coin to tell us that."

"Jaskafar is not in Spindrift anymore?" Lili-Daisy asked sadly.

"He won't be tomorrow anyhow," we said.

Lili-Daisy sighed, unwound her scarf, and pulled off her hat. "We'd better call off the search, then," she said. "You'd all better start lessons again."

That part was a shame. But we'd known lessons would have to resume at some point anyway.

At midnight, like I said, we headed to Brathelthwaite. The twins and I did our egg-tossing in a fairly random way, but Glim has beautiful aim and she hurled hers straight at the boarding school's welcome sign.

Most letters in the sign got hidden by egg splatters. The only ones left, I've underlined here:

BRATHELTHWAITE BOARDING SCHOOL
A RENOWNED ESTABLISHMENT
WHERE JUSTICE, ACADEMIC EXCELLENCE, KINDNESS,
AND COMPASSION
FORM THE CORNERSTONES OF OUR BELIEFS.

If you like, you can write down the highlighted letters and see what Brathelthwaite was now announcing about itself.

I like Glim.

The next day, we were back doing lessons, sleepy but happy.

The schoolroom in the Orphanage gets hot and stuffy, so we open all the windows. But then it gets noisy because we look straight onto the town square. So we close the windows.

Then we get too hot and open them.

And noisy, and we close them.

And so on.

Our teacher, Anita, laughs so hard she falls over sometimes. She's tiny, with dark-gold skin, ears a bit too big for her face, and long eyelashes that curl around—you notice these when she blinks like mad, which she does when she's cross about losing a game. She's eighteen years old but she still joins in games with us kids sometimes—usually wins, but is very irritated when she loses. We tease her for that.

Anita grew up in the Orphanage herself. When she was seven, her family's farmhouse burned down and her parents died in the fire. So she walked from the countryside into Spindrift carrying her baby brother. But the baby was sick. "And if I'd been a doctor," she says sometimes, blinking her angry eyelashes. "I might have been able to make him well…"

For this reason, Anita is studying to be a doctor at night. During the day, she teaches us.

Sad story, I know. But most of us orphans have sad stories. You get used to it. Don't let it get you down.

"If a cornfield has turned blue," Anita said, starting off today's lesson, "it could be common corn mold. How would you treat that?"

Anita likes to teach us about farming, as it reminds her of her childhood. The Yellow Jewel, her family's farmhouse was called, because her dad once spilled a tin of yellow paint on the roof, after which the house glowed like a jewel in the sunlight. She tells us that often, sort of dreamily.

"Common corn mold?" Eli replied, not looking up from the newspaper on his desk. "Spray it with the tears of antelopes from the Underling Cross Islands. They cry *all* the time, those antelopes. Very sensitive. I read that in an article on animal mood swings."

Anita allows the twins to read in class because they remember every word—handy—and because they can multitask. They can read a newspaper, recite multiplication tables, and throw shot-put balls, all at the same time.

She doesn't let them throw shot-put balls in class though.

"Exactly!" she said now. "The tears of the antelope! Well done, Eli. And does anybody know where the Underling Cross Islands are?"

"To the east of the Empire of Ricochet," Taya replied, turning a page of *her* newspaper and smoothing it out. "But, Anita, maybe your cornfield is blue because you've accidentally planted blue elouisas? Have you thought about that?"

"As I've never heard of blue elouisas," Anita replied, "no, I have *not* thought of that."

"It's a flower. Only grows in the Kingdom of Kate-Bazaar," Eli put in. "Read that in an article about a horticulture fair."

"Only Faery children are allowed to pick blue elouisas," Taya added. "Read that in a piece about *rules* once." She twitched her nose. The twins are not fans of rules.

Somewhere outside, a siren shrieked with laughter. "Noisy," said Anita. "Could someone close the windows please?"

I hopped up and closed them.

"And why else," Anita continued, "might a cornfield turn blue?"

"Maybe a colony of Blue-Hatted Elves has moved in?" Leesa suggested shyly.

"Excellent!" Anita gets very excited when timid kids speak up. "So, kids, if you ever have a farm and your cornfield turns blue? Do *not* rush outside to spray it with antelope tears! Or what might happen?"

"Elves could drown!" everyone shouted.

"Right! Check for elves *before* you use the tears. If no elves? The tears. Moving on. If your face turns blue, what could that mean?"

"That you're choking?" someone asked.

"Exactly! Well done! Or else?"

"That a sterling silver fox has stolen your laughter?"

"Brilliant! What a class I have! What kids you are!" Anita smiled happily for so long that we began to chat amongst ourselves. "And if your elbows turn blue?" she cried suddenly. "What could that mean? Oh brother, it's *hot* in here! We need some air!"

I hopped up again to open the windows.

Outside in the town square, locals were buying loaves of bread from Baker Joe, or choosing fruit and vegetables. Some were tossing back beers, or playing chess, or getting their boots repaired. All of this they were doing as noisily as they could. A pair of siren sisters was sitting out there having coffee and accidentally screaming—they forget themselves when they gossip.

Tourists wandered amongst the locals, getting their fortunes told, buying chocolates, staring at Shadow Mages, and blocking their ears against the sirens' screams.

Across the square, alongside the drinking fountain, I could see a girl and a boy around my own age. I didn't recognize either of them. They were standing perfectly still, looking over towards the Orphanage. Both had shiny dark hair, and both wore fancy coats and hats. The girl wore a blue coat, the boy a dark gray.

"Boarding school kids," I muttered.

For the first time, it occurred to me that the Brathelthwaite kids might try to get revenge for our rotten egg attack.

Surely not.

Surely they'd see that they *deserved* the rotten eggs?

But these were *Brathelthwaite* kids. They're so daft that every time it rains, they probably go, "I *say*, whatever is all that *stuff* falling out of the sky? Looks like water! But that usually stays in the ocean, doesn't it? Golly, has the ocean lost its mind, then?"

Slow on the uptake, is what I mean. Heads muddled by cream puffs.

Meanwhile, those two kids were out there staring.

Spies.

They were boarding school spies.

Calculating our weaknesses. Planning their counterattack.

When I turned back to the room, ready to beckon Glim and the twins over to check out the spies, Glim and the twins were on the floor. All the kids were on the floor. They were pulling off their shoes and studying their toenails. The twins' newspapers were spread around their feet so they could carry on reading as they did this.

"If your toenails turn blue," Anita was explaining, "and then turn back to normal? It means you are a Spellbinder and can train in the art of Spellbinding. Oh brother, it's so *loud* out there, I can't hear myself think! Finlay?"

I was still by the windows, so I swung around ready to shut them again.

Not possible.

The windows were streaming with rats. Big rats, gray rats, brown rats, whiskery rats, twitching rats, sharp-clawed rats, *hundreds* of rats, and all of them tumbling over each other in their rush to pour into the room.

CHAPTER 11
HONEY BEE

I heard about the rat attack while I was at the Spindrift Town Meeting that night.

How frightful it sounded!

Orphanage children innocently learning away and then KERPOW! an influx of stampeding rodents! It really would put you off your geometry.

Poor little rats were confused and terrified themselves, of course, so their claws were out, teeth primed to tear flesh. As if *rats* running all over the floor and desks, with fur brushing bare skin wasn't enough, many children were scratched or bitten.

For some reason, the children were not wearing any shoes—

Oh, but I know the reason. Now that I've read Finlay's chapter, I know. The children were checking their toenails to see if they were Spellbinders. Fair enough.

But such rotten timing! It meant rats running across bare feet!

At the time, of course, we couldn't understand their shoeless state.

"They really are too poor for words," Rosalind Whitehall muttered, screwing up her nose. "No shoes! I mean to say, be poor in the privacy of your own home if you must, but the *rest* of us do *not* need to see that poorness! *Erk!*"

"They *were* in their own home," I whispered. "They were *in* the Orphanage."

Rosalind rolled her eyes as if I'd said something terribly daft. She turned back to Victor.

"Where did you get the rats from anyway?" she asked.

"Picked them up super cheap," Hamish replied. "Fire sale at the Sterling Silver Depot. *Jolly* good deal they were, glossy coats on the lot of them. They came in boxes about yea big, although *some* of the boxes were more *yea* big—"

"SHUSH!" cried Mayor Franny, and hammered her gavel.

This conversation, as I mentioned, was taking place at the Spindrift Town Meeting. Why was I at the town meeting? you may wonder.

I shall tell you.

Students of Brathelthwaite are future leaders, Sir Brathelthwaite says, and will one day rule Kingdoms and Empires, laying claim to most of the money and all the biggest houses. Therefore we must practice bossing people about.

So five Brathelthwaite students attend the town meeting each week. We sit in the front row and we are supposed to call out, "Objection!" whenever the town council says anything "foolish or disagreeable." Then we must make a "rousing speech that will show the simple townsfolk the errors of their ways." I don't believe any student has ever done any such thing though, as Mayor Franny would tear us to shreds—much like the rats tore the orphans to shreds.

This week, it was Victor, Hamish, Rosalind, Carlos, and I. Victor had just whispered excitedly about how he and Hamish had attacked the Orphanage with rats. Rosalind was shiny-eyed to hear the story, but Carlos was frowning. Usually, my friend Carlos follows up his frowns with words—he is kindhearted and would not generally like the idea of children being attacked by rats—but he was very unwell with bronchitis by now, and wheezing too heavily to speak.

Anyhow—"SHUSH!" cried Mayor Franny. So we shushed. Up on the stage, Mayor Franny and the other town councillors were proposing a "buddy system" for children so we'd never wander the streets alone, as well as extra training for constables.

Two local constables leaned against the wall, "keeping an eye on things," and I noticed them raising their eyebrows at each other when "extra constable training" was mentioned. Behind us, about twenty townsfolk were scattered amongst the wooden benches listening. Every now and then, they contributed thoughts.

"When I trained my puppy," Baker Joe called, "I found it helpful to say *'good boy!'* to him. In a voice like this"—and he put on a passionate, loving voice— *"Good boy!! GOOD BOY!!*

"Now," he continued, "what say we use this approach in training local constables? *Good boy.* Or, for female constables, *good GIRL.*"

I glanced at the constables to see how they would respond to this, but their faces were carefully blank.

My thoughts drifted. I agreed with Carlos's frown and did not think the rat attack fair. Certainly, the Orphanage had attacked our school by hurling eggs, and that *had* led to another week of punishment. But the eggs hadn't *hurt* us, and the orphans couldn't have known that Sir Brathelthwaite would punish *us* for—

BOOM!
BOOM!
BOOM!

A sudden pounding on the town hall door!

We all swung around. The door flew open. (It's never locked, so there was no need for pounding. I think they just wanted a dramatic entrance.)

A Royal Soldier in a dashing red uniform burst forth.

"All rise," he boomed, "for Her Majesty, the Queen of the Kingdom of Gusts, Gales, Squalls, and Violent Storms!"

A gale seemed to blow across the room now, but that was just gasping and excited jiggling as everyone shoved each other aside, craning to see.

In came the queen.

There were three guards ahead of her and three behind, but she looked just like an ordinary, pleasant lady, hurrying to do her shopping.

Mayor Franny took the carrot out of her mouth and grinned. "Ahoy there!" she said. "Come on up, Majesty! Glad to have you!"

"This will be the Royal Prerogative," Victor told us in his languid way.

"Eh?" Hamish blinked.

"Royal visitors are entitled to attend any town meeting and have the final say on any issue," Victor said. "There must be something she's wanting final say on."

Up on the platform, the queen got busy discussing dull issues like bylaws with Mayor Franny and the other councillors. Clipboards and papers passed between them. The queen's guards gathered around her, their hands clasped behind their backs. I suppose that holding your hands like that gives you good posture. Try it.

"Any other attacks planned for the Orphanage?" Rosalind Whitehall asked in a low voice.

"Steady on," I whispered. "Surely the rat attack was enough?"

Carlos wheezed to show his agreement. Hamish turned to Victor, uncertain. "What do you say, chap? We've done enough now, no?"

But we were distracted then, as the voices onstage had grown louder. There were also mutters amongst the townsfolk. The voices settled down quickly, and we shrugged and turned back to each other.

"Hamish and I have formed the Anti-Orphanage League," Victor murmured.

"*Have* we?" Hamish said, pleased. "I had no idea. But delighted. Absolutely honored. By the by, what is it?"

Victor ignored the question. "First meeting tonight, green common room—"

"Your *Majesty*," several voices said at once.

Again, we looked up.

"What's going on?" Rosalind whispered.

None of us knew.

"Indeed!" The queen's voice rose above the clamor. "Indeed we shall! The town of Spindrift will be transferred to the Whispering Kingdom." She held up a paper. "It's all here in print."

"I *say*," Hamish gasped. "Is that quite the thing?"

"Has she lost her mind?" Victor asked, his eyes shining. Oddly, he seemed delighted by the idea of a queen losing her mind. He's often bored, you see, and likes a good plot twist.

Now some of the townsfolk were shouting.

"No offense, Your Majesty, but this is a cartload of crabapple!"

"You can't be giving our town away!"

"Why? I don't understand, *why?*"

"Yes!" many others yelled. *"WHY?"*

"It will benefit *everybody*," the queen declared. Her eyes looked a little wild. "The Whispering Kingdom will send in people to patrol the streets! No more children will be stolen! In return, they ask only for total control of your ship repair and fishing net industries! It's *more* than fair!"

This last bit we only just heard because the ship repair and fishing net business owners had given up all pretense at politeness and were on their feet, bellowing like sea otters. These are rather large men and women, the ship and fishing folk, and their bare arms and shaking fists showed off quite marvelous muscles and tattoos.

One or two of the guards behind the queen began marching ominously towards the boisterous audience members. Honestly, it was very exciting.

But then one of the local constables who had been leaning against the wall—Rachel Rally, I think her name is; she'd been picking her teeth for much of the meeting—anyhow, she stepped forward. Up to the stage she strode. A curious expression was on her face—rather like somebody who has discovered a pin in her soup and is alarmed, angry, *and* fascinated to find it there.

Rachel stopped behind Mayor Franny and spoke quickly into her ear. Mayor Franny blinked quickly and nodded slowly.

Like this: quick blink, slow nod.

Rachel now turned towards the royal guard immediately behind Her Majesty. This guard was a rather small woman, with a great clump of braids knotted at the base of her neck.

I do not know if anybody else noticed this, but Rachel Rally's hands began to twirl and spin.

Spellbinding, I realized suddenly.

I had always known that some of our constables were Spellbinders, but had never known which. *Rachel Rally is a Spellbinder*, I thought. A warmth fell over me and, for some reason, I felt very fond of Rachel.

I glanced sideways but I did not think the other children had noticed. Rachel's hands were low, almost out of sight, their movements subtle, and the children were distracted — their heads kept spinning from the queen to the crowd and back again.

But I stared fixedly at Rachel Rally and at the guard with the braids. These two faced each other. Rachel's hands fluttered but her face and shoulders were calm. The guard's eyes narrowed and she bit her lower lip, decidedly annoyed.

Suddenly, the guard took a step back. She looked up at the ceiling.

Rachel's hands dropped to her sides.

"Oh my," said the queen. "I have a dreadful headache. What were we talking about?"

"Well, Your Majesty," Mayor Franny began doubtfully.

But the queen was pushing her chair back. "What is this nonsense?" she said, rustling the paper in her hands. "Whyever would we want to give Spindrift to the Whispering Kingdom?"

"Indeed," murmured Mayor Franny.

"I must get back to the prince." The queen stood. "He has a nasty cold, you know. We've been advised to stay in Spindrift until he gets better. I wonder if I'm catching it? My head aches so!" And she pressed her fingertips to her forehead and swept from the room.

Her guards hurried after her.

Silence fell.

Mayor Franny cleared her throat. "Well," she said. "Moving on, then." And she began to talk about plans for a new hospital wing.

"So *odd*," Hamish whispered. "Is the queen having a sort of breakdown, do you think? Ought not we stage a *coup* and take power from her? What a hoot!" But then he squinted thoughtfully. "No, no. Treason, that would be. Never mind. What were you saying, Victor?"

"The Anti-Orphanage League," Victor replied, low-voiced. "Meeting tonight, green common room, 8:00 p.m. Are you in, Rosalind?"

"Absolutely." Rosalind's shoulders wiggled with joy.

"How about you, Honey Bee?"

"No!" I said. "I think it's silly! Why do we have to be anti the Orphanage? We *did* use a technicality to steal the tournament victory from them, which is why they fought us, which led to the little boy being taken! If you ask me, we got off easy when they threw eggs at our building. Attacking them with rats was an overreaction, and we need to let it go now."

Beside me, Carlos nodded once.

"Suit yourself." Victor shrugged.

As the meeting closed, it began to rain. We were drenched making our way from the town hall to our carriage, and Carlos shivered violently all the way back.

"Fortunately, we are back in time for showers," I told him. "A hot shower is exactly what you need."

Halfway through shower time, however, there were shrieks from every bathroom in the school. The hot water had been switched off. Ice-cold water rained down on unsuspecting heads.

It was the orphans again. They'd broken in and extinguished the pilot light on our hot water heaters. They must have had information about our bathing times. Spies, perhaps?

Afterwards, I found Carlos wandering the corridors in his pajamas. His face was purplish-blue. His eyes were heavy-lidded.

"You must go to the infirmary," I told him. "You don't look well at *all*, Carlos. An ice-cold shower was the *last* thing you needed."

"What's an infirmary?" he said. "Who are—? Who are you again? Who—where am I?"

I placed my palm against his forehead. My hand jumped back, burned.

Feverish.

I hustled him to the infirmary, where the school nurse exclaimed and hurried to telephone a doctor.

"I do not know," I heard her say, "if he will last the night."

The clock was chiming 8:00.

At the green common room door, I paused.

Victor, Hamish, and Rosalind were seated in a huddle of armchairs by the fireplace. They looked up at me.

"Let's take those orphans down," I said.

Poor little rats, she says.

Poor.

Little.

Rats.

Well, those poor little rats tore gashes in Glim's calves and almost blinded Eli. A claw swiped over his right eye. He had to have it bandaged for a week.

Everyone scrambled—onto the desks, onto the bookshelves, even out the windows. Blood and screaming everywhere.

People in the town square heard us and ran to help. A couple of old sterling silver foxes set aside their card game and summoned the rats away. The siren sisters sang out the wily ones hiding in a chalk box.

Anita then spent the afternoon washing and disinfecting bites and scratches, applying ointment and patching us all up. She herself had a scratch running all the way down her arm, but she seemed cheerful. She's training to be a doctor, as I mentioned, and likes practice. So that was all right, at least.

But little Leesa *still* wakes up screaming with nightmares about the rat attack.

And *"poor little rats,"* Honey Bee says.

Didn't I tell you that Honey Bee was annoying? I did. Back when I first said it, you probably thought, *Well now, she can't be that bad, can she?* Whereas now you're thinking: *Oh, sorry, Finlay. You were right.*

After that, it was on.

Same day as the rat attack, we switched off their hot water at shower time, as Honey Bee mentioned. (How were we to know her friend was sick? Anyhow, Lili-Daisy says a bit of ice-cold water's good for the soul.) Eli knew the Brathelthwaite schedule because he'd read it in the paper once. The *Spindrift Daily News* has a children's section that holds contests where you describe a Day in Your Life. One year, the runner-up was *A Day in the Life of a Student at Brathelthwaite.* Worst entry he'd ever read, Eli said.

Helpful though.

Brathelthwaite got us back for the hot-water thing by throwing flour bombs at us as we crossed the town square. We were on our way to the coast with Anita to study the architecture of radish gnome caves.

I remember it was taking us longer than usual to cross the square that day. Crowds of people were gathered, trying to see the noticeboard. Mayor Franny had pinned a big sign there. Here's what it said:

IMPORTANT NOTICE
From the Association of Spellbinders

Evidence is mounting that certain Whisperers are using "superpowered" Whispers to control people. Alarmingly, it appears that they are drawing on Shadow Magic to do this. As Whisperers are not Shadow Mages, they must have the help of Shadow Mages. Usually, as everyone knows, it is very easy to shake off a Whisper. But these new "superpowered" Whispers are IMPOSSIBLE TO RESIST.

We have grave concerns that some of these Whisperers have infiltrated major security organizations, town councils, Royal Advisory Boards, Royal Security, and possibly even the K&E Alliance.

We have notified the K&E Alliance of our suspicions.

If you or anybody you know appears to be making <u>strange or foolish</u> decisions—and suffering from <u>fierce headaches</u> when you try to change your mind—it could be that you have fallen under the influence of a super-strengthened Whisper. Go to the authorities <u>IMMEDIATELY</u> and request the assistance of a Spellbinder. Spellbinders are able to bind the Shadow Magic and thereby destroy the Whisper.

Thank you,

The Director,
Association of Spellbinders

A lot of people were shouting at the sign. "There's no *way* any Whisperers would do that!" they were bellowing. "Whisperers are the *nicest, quietest* folk you ever meet! They'd never team up with Shadow Mages!"

All good points.

Other people were muttering: "Oh, that's just silliness. That's the

Spellbinders trying to rustle themselves up extra work. Cash flow problems, no doubt."

And one person was blasting: "It's scare-mongering, is what it is! They ought to be ashamed!"

Meanwhile, others were doubtful. "Hmm, it's often the sweet ones who turn out to be evil, am I right? The *secretive* ones. Still waters run deep, don't I always say that?"

However, most were making jokes. "I *did* make a strange and foolish decision!" The butcher's wife prodded her husband with her elbow. "The strange and foolish decision to marry you! It all makes sense now! A Whisperer made me do it! *And* I had a *dreadful* headache the day after my wedding day! Proof!"

"That was a hangover, you daft git! And marrying me was the greatest decision of your *life*."

That kind of thing.

We were trying to jostle our way through this noisy crowd and had just made it past the noticeboard when the Brathelthwaite kids launched their flour bomb attack. We had to go to the seaside sneezing flour dust and looking like ghosts.

The townsfolk found it hilarious, which was annoying.

We got them back by pouring dried Diego peppers into their dinner. That was a risky operation. First, we climbed over the school walls at 5:35 p.m. We knew from the schedule that their cooks would be preparing dinner at that point. Next, we rang the school's alarm bells. Everyone, including the kitchen staff, ran outside. While they were outside, we climbed in through the kitchen windows and dragged a sack of dried Diego peppers out of their pantry. Usually, you'd just sprinkle a tiny pinch into a stew for flavor—it's super spicy.

What did we do? We tipped the whole sack into the tureen on the stovetop.

Then we got out of there.

The next day nothing happened, probably because their tongues were still on fire. Glim and I happened to be crossing the town square that day, carrying a couple of cabbages for Cook.

We stopped to say hello to another of our buddies, Ronnie-the-Artist, who sits on a rug in the town square painting pictures of tourists. He gets the tourists to pose with their arms sort of propped into the air, and then he paints in any sort of Shadow Mage the tourist wants. Charges extra for the scariest.

Ronnie's blanket is right alongside the Time Travel Brothers—those men in sharp suits who say they came from the future—and there were a couple of witches at their card table today. They wanted to know what was going to happen with the deadline.

"What deadline?" Glim asked.

"No silver, no mystical knowledge," a Time Travel Brother answered her smoothly, holding out his hand for payment.

"Ah, put a sock in it, Jack," Ronnie said easily. He's a big guy, Ronnie-the-Artist, with crazy hair. "That's not *mystical* knowledge; it's common knowledge. *Everyone's* talking about the deadline. Here, I'll show you, Glim."

He shifted a stack of brushes and handed Glim a paint-streaked local newspaper, folded so we could see the front page. I won't make you read the whole article, just the most important bit:

The K&E Alliance has given the Whispering Kingdom twenty-four (24) hours to explain these new supercharged Whispers, and to reveal which Shadow Mages are helping them. Whisperers

have been EXPELLED from a number of Kingdom
and Empire Security Forces, as it is now clear
that they have been influencing the decisions of several kings and queens (including our very own queen, who very nearly signed
away Spindrift but was saved by a local
constable).

   The K&E Alliance has also EXPELLED the
Whisperer members on its own executive com-
mittee, on suspicion that they have been controlling proceedings. Waratah Teevsky has
apologized to all the Kingdoms and Empires for
having fallen under the spell of these supercharged Whispers and proposing that diamond
mines be transferred to the Whispering Kingdom.
"I would never normally make such a ridiculous
suggestion," she stated. "I am furious with
myself."

"So the Spellbinders were right?" I asked. "There *are* Whisperers using super Whispers?"

"Seems like it." Ronnie nodded, and the three of us turned to see what the Time Travel Brothers would tell the witches.

"You are going to be extremely surprised by what happens next," one brother said.

"It will be in all the newspapers," the second brother agreed.

"It's madness," the first brother said.

"Would *never* happen in the *distant* future, where *we're* from."

"It's all so *reasonable* and *sensible* there."

They always say things like that, the Time Travel Brothers. No actual predictions but very smug and superior about the future.

Across the square, our buddy Snatty-Ra-Ra was looking a bit lonely and bored. He had no customers, but he'd put up a sign that said: *Not hearing a peep from the future today — will give it a go for you, but don't hold out any hope* — so, no wonder.

The day after *that*, Brathelthwaite got revenge for our pepper attack by intercepting our laundry cart and dyeing all our clothes bright pink.

I have no real problem with the color pink, and my clothes get filthy fast anyway, so you can't tell what color they are. But the twins were so annoyed they tore a few shirts to shreds with their bare hands before Lili-Daisy stopped them. And Glim surprised us by crying. She almost never cries. However, she'd sewn a new blue tunic using an old coverlet not long before this. She mends most of the children's clothes for them but never makes new things for herself. I'd caught her admiring the tunic in the mirror. Now it was ruined, streaked in muddy pink.

We got them back by stealing their carriages while they were at a picnic by Spindrift Lake.

Four carriages stood waiting for them — the carriage drivers were hovering around the children, probably for extra security — so Glim, Eli, Taya, and I just climbed aboard one each and drove away. It was a crackerjack stunt. We took the carriages back to the boarding school and tied them up just outside the front gates. Left the horses with water and hay, so nobody could accuse us of actual stealing or horse neglect.

They would have had to walk three hours to get back.

After dinner that night, we were in the dormitory listening to another rugby game. This time Raffia was playing Braewood, another strong team. Two minutes left in the game and it was dead even.

It was noisy that night, I remember, as Daffo had accidentally sent Avril's seashell collection flying—she keeps about two hundred shells lined up on a window ledge and somebody is *always* accidentally sending them flying—so a bunch of kids were crawling around under the beds trying to retrieve them. I was in a cheerful mood again. We were crackerjack at getting the boarding school! Way better than *them*. I'd spotted those Brathelthwaite spies again while I was peeling turnips during kitchen duty earlier—the girl and boy with the fancy coats, staring at us from the town square—so I knew they were plotting their next step. But I wasn't worried.

If pink dye was the best they could do, bring it on.

"Shields passes it to Jeffreys, and Jeffreys spreads it to Khatri—I think Farrugia's got this tackle—no! Khatri has avoided it! Khatri has got by Deakin! He does an amazing step off the left foot past Runcy! Oh, what a *swerve*, listeners, if you could *see* this, he's SPRINTING FOR THE TRY LINE, HE'S *PELTING* FOR IT, SVORKIN IS AFTER HIM, SVORKIN IS CLOSING IN, BUT KHATRI IS—"

"We interrupt this program," said a smooth voice, "for a Special Announcement."

"NOOOOO!" the whole dormitory screamed. Lili-Daisy bounced on the bed so angrily that a voice beneath it cried, "Ow!"

"The Whispering Kingdom has *missed* their deadline to explain their new super Whispers," the radio announcer continued. "We will now hear a special message from the Whispering King himself."

Most of us stopped screaming "NOOOOO" to look at the wireless with interest. The Whispering King was going to speak?

"PUT THE RUGBY BACK ON!" Daffo bellowed, but we shushed him.

Bit of static.

And then there was the voice of the Whispering King. "Forgive me interrupting a rugby game," he began. "I wish to address the K&E Alliance, and *all* the Kingdoms and Empires. I will let you get back to the rugby as quickly as I can." Sounded like a nice guy. Affable.

"He can't super-Whisper us over the wireless, can he?" little Leesa hissed.

Lili-Daisy shook her head. "Whisperers can only Whisper people who are nearby," she explained in a low voice. "About the length of this dormitory is as far as they can reach. Some are stronger and can cover a football field, but that would be unusual."

"Super Whispers still only have the same range," Eli added helpfully. "Or so I've read."

"We will *not* explain why we now have supercharged Whispers," the Whispering King was saying on the wireless. He sounded a bit miffed now. "Why is that anybody's business? *Nor* will we explain which of the Shadow Mages are our friends. Again, whose business is that? Do I ask you which brand of toothpaste you favor? Do I demand to know your preferred beer?"

"Hmm," said Lili-Daisy. "Not sure those are quite the same."

"It hurt our feelings deeply," the king continued, "when our members were expelled from the K&E Alliance and various security forces. But we have now decided not to mind. In fact, we are going to form our *own* club. A Shadow Club. We invite any pirate ship to join, along with any witch, radish gnome, siren, sterling silver fox, or other Dark Mage kingdom or empire."

"Crikey!" said Daffo.

But the king was not finished: *"It is time for Dark Mages to come out of the shadows,"* he said, very dramatic. *"And take their rightful place as rulers of the Kingdoms and Empires."*

"Thank you to the Whispering King for that fascinating message," the radio announcer declared. "And now back to your regular programming."

The rugby game had finished, but the announcer apologized for that and told us that Khatri *had* scored the try in the last minute, meaning that Raffia had won. Good old Khatri. You beauty, Raffia.

We switched off the wireless then, to talk about the Whispering King's promise of a new Shadow Club.

Lili-Daisy shook her head. "So strange! Whyever do they think they are the rightful rulers of all the Kingdoms and Empires?"

"This is brilliant," we all said. "Hilarious."

We thought it was like a comic strip, see? The Whisperers had always been super-nice guys and now they were playing at being villains. Nothing to worry about. The good guys—us—would take them down in a flash.

The next day was a Saturday, and another warm spring day. We all went to the Beach with the Yellow Sand for a swim. While we were in the water, the boarding school kids stole our towels and clothes. So we had to go back to the Orphanage shivering in our swimsuits. I mean, it was *warm*, but there was still a leftover winter breeze in the air. Everyone laughed at us again as we came through the town square, but their laughter was interrupted because Jean-Pierre, the newspaper vendor, suddenly bellowed: "Read all about it! Breaking news! Read all about it! Breaking news!"

"What breaking news?" everyone asked, turning to Jean-Pierre. But he wanted people to buy his papers, and wouldn't tell us. He quickly turned the papers upside down so we couldn't even read the headlines. Baker Joe and Motoko-the-Chocolatier both sighed and reached into their pockets for copper coins, handed these over, and bought a paper each. They held them up to their faces, reading fast while we waited.

"It's the *Whispering Kingdom* that has been stealing all the children!" Baker Joe shouted suddenly.

"No!" everyone shouted back.

"The children are all in the *Whispering Kingdom*!" Motoko-the-Chocolatier roared. Her necklaces clinked against each other. When she looked up, her eyes were wild: her niece had been one of the children stolen.

"Read all about it! Breaking news!" Jean-Pierre called hopefully from his newspaper stand.

"Hush," everyone scolded him.

"The Whispering King has *admitted* it!" Baker Joe cried. "He's *proud* about it!"

"They've been using their superpowered Whispers to steal the children!" Motoko-the-Chocolatier put in, frantically turning the pages so she could read on.

"The Whispering Kingdom has been sending their *own* children to other Kingdoms and Empires to *lure children away from adult supervision*! Then adult Whisperers use super Whispers to make the children accompany them back to the Whispering Kingdom!"

"The K&E Alliance has given the Whispering Kingdom twenty-four hours to release *all* the children. If not, an invading force will be sent to rescue them!" That part the baker and chocolatier read in unison, so it overlapped a bit, and we made them say it again.

"Twenty-four hours," a few people complained. "They're always giving the Whispering Kingdom twenty-four hours. Madness. Just attack *now*."

"Read all about it!" Jean-Pierre tried again.

"We just did," the chocolatier pointed out.

"*Hush*," everyone else commanded. They were busy reading the baker's and chocolatier's copies.

So the newspaper vendor sat back down behind his stand, disgruntled.

By the next day, the Whispering Kingdom had not responded to the demands, so a fleet of K&E Alliance ships sailed on the kingdom.

"Release the children at once!" the admiral demanded from the decks of the flagship, speaking through his megaphone. "Or we attack."

The Whispering Kingdom did not reply except to shoot a cannon at the ship and sink it.

Right away, a fleet of pirate ships rounded on the other K&E ships—they'd been lurking by the cliffs ready to defend the Whispering Kingdom (in exchange for diamonds, most likely)—and there was a mighty battle at sea in which hundreds of K&E sailors were killed.

The following day, a regiment of K&E soldiers attempted to invade the Whispering Kingdom by land, but this turns out to be a tricky thing. You see, the Whispering Kingdom has the sea on one side and an Impenetrable Forest surrounding all the other sides. That's a magical Impenetrable Forest, by the way: nobody can get through. Meanwhile, the only road into the Whispering Kingdom runs along the coast, then hits the three Whispering Gates. The gates are magic too. No way through them unless you're a Whisperer and know how to get the keys.

Not surprisingly, the K&E soldiers failed.

"How can a forest and three *gates* stop a thousand soldiers!" everyone wailed. But that's the sort of thing that magic does. We knew that really.

Next, the K&E Dragon Corp flew over the Whispering Kingdom, but of course, there's a witch-made Mist Shroud pulled right over the place. Very private people, they've always been, the Whisperers. You can't even *see* through this Mist Shroud, apparently, let alone fly through it.

Another fleet of K&E Alliance ships sailed on the Whispering Kingdom in the dark of night, but again, they were roundly defeated.

And so on.

In Spindrift, we all said, "Never mind; they'll get it right in the end," and we waited excitedly for the K&E Alliance to sort things out and bring the children back. Lili-Daisy gazed at the empty beds and up at the top of the wardrobe with a hopeful smile.

Meanwhile, we were busy getting revenge on Brathelthwaite by painting *WE ARE DAFT GITS* on the sails of all their little boats. They take these out each Sunday morning and sail around the harbor.

They retaliated by painting *ORPHANS ARE AWFUL* on the Orphanage wall. We found this to be a very half-hearted, lackluster attempt.

"They're hardly worth our effort," Glim, the twins, and I said to each other.

"If they're not going to fight *properly*, why bother fighting at all?"

But that night I saw the two children again—the boarding school spies—staring up at us from the town square.

I was staring right back at them through the window, dreaming about how we might trick them into taking false information back to Brathelthwaite. Our false information would somehow make the boarding school launch an attack on us, *which would badly backfire* on them, leading to the whole school standing in the town square in their underclothes—

But how? How could we achieve this?

—when I noticed that the dormitory had gone very quiet.

The others were gathered around the wireless. The queen was speaking.

"I have made the official declaration," she said in a grand tone, as if she was pretty proud of herself. She didn't know that the wireless was making her voice come out squeaky. "They *cannot* steal our children. They *cannot* steal our land. The forces of *good* and *right* must, and always *do,* defeat the forces of evil! My people, the K&E Alliance has declared war on the Whispering Kingdom. I have just now sent a telegram stating that the Kingdom of Gusts,

Gales, Squalls, and Violent Storms will stand by the K&E Alliance. My people, we are *at war with the Whispering Kingdom*."

For a moment I thought that a blizzard was blowing through the dormitory, but it was static on the wireless. Also, I guess, the queen's words had cast a chill. The chill mingled with the smell of seaweed. (Daffo's always bringing seaweed back from the beach.)

Lili-Daisy switched off the wireless. Little Ollie had crawled onto her lap and Lili-Daisy was stroking his head in an absentminded way, her fingers getting caught in tangles. Glim was frowning at her own fingers, as if she wasn't sure she recognized her knuckles. The twins had stopped reading their papers and their heads were up like plump meerkats.

Anita, who has a bedroom along the corridor, where she studies her medical textbooks until late each night, appeared in the doorway.

"Are you listening to this—?" she began, but she stopped, taking in the children's faces. Glances darted back and forth between Lili-Daisy and Anita.

"Right," said Lili-Daisy, standing suddenly so that Ollie spilled to the floor. "This is good news! This will put an end to all the nonsense! The Whispering Kingdom will send back the children. Amie and Connor, Bing and Jaskafar..." She pointed to their empty beds in turn. "They'll all be back at last, and we can return to regular life."

"Exactly," Anita agreed at once. "They'll have a bit of schoolwork to catch up on, won't they? But I'll let a few things slide."

"Will there be a war?" little Leesa whispered.

"Of course," Daffo pronounced. "The queen just said so."

"Oh Daffo," Lili-Daisy sighed and she spoke to the room. "*Nobody* wants a war. There will *not* be a war. This will be the end of it—you'll see—and *nothing* is going to change."

✳

"Do you know what I think?" I said to Glim and the twins, much later that night. The other children were sleeping, but us four were lounging on Glim's bed, eating toffees that Glim had saved from her last birthday. She had just told us a story about flying stars, exploding comets, and a giant, fire-breathing roast potato.

"What do you think?" Glim asked obligingly.

"I think we need one, final, major attack on the boarding school. Something that *finishes* this thing between us."

"And shows them who's boss?" Eli inquired, glint in his eye.

"Yes."

Glim nodded slowly. "I agree."

And so we made our plan.

CHAPTER 19
HONEY BEE

Mm.

I seem to remember Finlay calling me a *freight train*, and saying I needed to *pace myself* when I told you about the races at the Spindrift Tournament.

And here Finlay himself has *zoomed* through day after day of attack and counterattack between Brathelthwaite and the Orphanage, not to mention all the news about the Whispering Wars. Like a boy zipping through a fair, whizzing by stalls with scarcely a glance at one.

Fascinating.

He must be quite worn out.

At any rate, yes.

We fought.

They attacked us.

We attacked them.

And so on.

Just as Finlay says.

Meanwhile, my friend Carlos lay half-conscious in the infirmary, tossing and turning and crying out some days, perfectly still, his breath scarcely audible, on others.

We knew the orphans must have spies keeping an eye on us, for they seemed to know our schedule precisely. And one day we spotted the spies.

We had just completed our regular sailing expedition around the harbor. Our sails surprised us that day by announcing to the world that we were Daft Gits in huge, messy painted letters. Very pleasant sailing, then. Guffaws and jeers competed with the sound of seagulls around us. It is marvelous to have pirates shouting and toasting you in their gruff voices: "To the Daft Gits!" swilling their beer on the deck of their ship. We had to rescue one fisherman's lad when he laughed so hard he tumbled from his boat.

We ran into town, painted *Orphans Are Awful* on the back of the Orphanage wall, and sprinted back to the beach just in time for our carriages, breathless and excited. But then we felt a bit flat. *Orphans Are Awful* wasn't up to much.

Riding back to the school — our sails now stowed away, ready to be laundered — Victor tapped my elbow.

"There," he murmured, pointing to the window.

Outside, a boy and a girl, both about twelve, were pressed into the trees that line the road to our school. Both were well-dressed: the boy in a dark gray coat, the girl in sky blue. At first this struck me as odd because the weather was too warm for coats, but then I saw what Victor meant. There was something uncertain about them. Anxious. Agitated.

"They don't belong," I said.

Victor nodded and cast an approving glance at me. "Orphans," he said, low-voiced. "Disguised as proper people. Probably stole those coats. Spying on us."

"Eh?" hissed Hamish, leaning forward excitedly. "Orphans, you say? Spying?"

"Hush," Victor told him. "Usual meeting place tonight."

That was the night that war was declared, so we missed our meeting. Sir Brathelthwaite made us stand and salute the wireless, and then we had to sing the Kingdom anthem, followed by the Brathelthwaite school chant, and we had to pledge to do all we could to rally the spirits of our troops.

"For example," Sir Brathelthwaite announced, "we will send your school blazers away to be starched, and to have their buttons polished."

"In what way—" began Rosalind Whitehall, but Sir Brathelthwaite had moved on to the importance of our having good posture whenever we saw a soldier.

The next few days were thrilling because we scarcely did any lessons. It was all "preparation for the war" this, "hunkering down" that. The school put a rush order on custom-made gas masks—they were striped in the Brathelthwaite colors, with comfortable silk bands—and blacked out all our windows with heavy drapes. The kitchen ordered vast quantities of jams and marmalades, butter and sugar, sherry and chocolate—just in case they ended up in short supply during the war. We would *not* be caught without our marmalade!

Spindrift itself was busy setting up lookouts and watchtowers, along with a system of warning bells around its borders and along its beach and wharves. "Excellent idea!" Sir Brathelthwaite said, and he arranged the same setup for our school. He paid a couple of carpenters extra silver to slip away from their work on the town watchtowers, to build for us instead.

Nevertheless, a number of parents sent servants to collect their children and carry them home. People kept murmuring about how Spindrift would be "strategic" for both sides in this war, since we are on a jutting-out bit of coastline just north of the Whispering Kingdom. We were going to be a "key battleground," apparently. I wasn't quite sure what all that meant, but I found myself feeling rather *proud* of Spindrift for being so *strategic* and *key*.

On the other hand, it meant that our student numbers halved.

"Preposterous," I heard Sir Brathelthwaite mutter to Uncle Dominic. "We are better fortified here than *anywhere*!" He gave a speech that night about how those students had scurried away at the first sign of trouble, cowardly little weaklings!

This was rather harsh, as their parents had not given the children any choice. Still, I found myself feeling proud again, this time for *not* having been scooped up by parents. Here I was! Ready for battle! Or anyway, ready to rally troops with my shiny buttons and excellent posture.

After a few days, life settled down again. All the excitement began to seem foolish. No doubt, nothing would happen, and we'd have to be eating all those extra crates of strawberry jam and chocolate until we turned *into* jammy chocolate.

Victor called a meeting of the Anti-Orphanage League to discuss our next attack.

"Isn't it *their* turn?" I inquired. "Since we were the last to attack. Remember we painted *Orphans Are Awful* on their wall?"

"That was a half-baked assault and you know it, Honey Bee." Victor pursed his lips. "I still think we should use my supreme idea of rendering all the food in their pantry rotten and inedible."

"Well, that would starve them."

"Oh blah," Rosalind put in. "They do that to themselves already. Listen, does one truly *take turns* in a war? Should we not *hammer* them until they beg for mercy?"

"Cripes!" Hamish *tch*ed, frowning deeply. "Do you know, I think you may be right, Rosalind? I have no recollection *whatsoever* about 'taking turns' being one of the rules of engagement!"

"They are clearly making new plans," Victor said, stretching his stockinged feet. It was a surprisingly chilly evening, and we were by the fire. "I keep seeing their spies—the same girl and boy in their stolen coats. The best form of defense is attack."

"Oh yes." Hamish nodded. "Yes, I've read that somewhere. Makes *no* sense to me, I mean, how can you call an *attack* a *defense*? They're entirely different things! Here now, this is attack"—he punched the air—"and this is defense." Now he crouched behind the couch. "See what I mean? Utterly different. But do go on, Victor."

Victor shot Hamish a look. "I have an idea," he said, turning back to Rosalind and me, "for an excellent attack. And this time, Honey Bee, you will not dissuade me. We'll need about twenty silver pieces, Hamish."

"Right-ho," Hamish agreed.

"It will mean getting up before dawn."

"Oh, must we?" Rosalind complained.

"And it will mean taking along our new gas masks."

I straightened up, uneasy. "It will?"

"We are going to spray poisonous gas through the Orphanage windows."

"Brilliant!" Rosalind clapped.

"We'll kill them!" I cried.

"Hold up a moment." Hamish frowned.

"Not enough to kill them." Victor rolled his eyes. "Just enough to give them stomach cramps and a nasty rash. Meet you here. 4:00 a.m. tomorrow."

CHAPTER 20
FINLAY

The grass was frosty under the early-morning moonlight, and the wind kept creeping up on me, sliding its fingers down my neck like some kid playing a super-annoying game that the kid itself finds hilarious. I wanted to take a swipe at it.

"Shift the lantern a tad, would you?" Eli asked. "Can't see here."

Taya repositioned our light. "Better?"

"Thanks."

We were almost done. We were digging trenches across the Brathelthwaite sports field. I got the idea from all the trenches they'd been digging around town for shelters in case the war turned up. Next, we planned to cover up the holes with layers of turf that we'd borrowed from a plant nursery just outside of town. When the morning bell rang, the students would march out here. They'd march into the field. They'd stop. They'd swivel. They'd start their crabapple school chant.

There's a line in that chant that goes like this: "We will never *ever* fall"—at that exact moment, they would fall.

We'd been watching them through a spyglass the last couple of mornings: they always marched in precisely the same formation, same direction, same swivels. Chanted at the same exact time. We'd calculated; measured it out.

It was genius.

When they did fall, we'd be sitting up on the school wall watching them crash into the mud. It would be crackerjack. We'd laugh like sterling silver foxes. Then we'd demand their surrender.

"This one's not deep enough yet," Glim said. Her breath made puffs of steam.

"Here." I grabbed the hoe. "I'll hack away at this and—"

"And what?" demanded a voice.

And there they were.

Four boarding school kids, a row of moonlit silhouettes, staring down at us. Gas masks dangled from their hands.

"Ah well." Eli set down his spade and dusted off his hands. "That's that, then." He's always quick to accept a situation and get philosophical about it, that Eli.

"Why are you all up so early?" Taya demanded. She's not as quick. "Go back to bed and forget you saw anything or I'll break your faces."

I was trying to make out which kids it was in the dark. The one who'd said *and what* was back in the shadows. I recognized a blond one: it was Hamish, the kid who'd beat me in the sprint race. You can't miss him because his hair falls like yellow milk over his face. Honey Bee was there too—tall, gawky, braid. And some fancy girl I didn't recognize who was making sounds like a donkey now: *hee haw!* And *whinny!*

What was she doing? Did she have a problem with her throat?

I figured it out. She was laughing.

"Is that how you always laugh?" I asked. I really wanted to know. It occurred to me that maybe a sterling silver fox had stolen most of her laugh and this was all she had left. That made me feel guilty for asking. On the other hand, as far as I could see, her face was not blue.

Glim sat on the edge of one of the trenches and thudded her heels against its side. "I bet they're on their way to attack the Orphanage," she said.

"I'll do the talking, thank you." The boy in the shadows stepped forward. It was Victor, the kid I'd punched. His voice was like the icy wind only without the playful element.

At this point, a loud jangling started up in the distance. Probably townsfolk trying out their warning bell system again. Nobody paid any attention.

"You are all under arrest," Victor said, rocking on his heels.

"What are you, a constable?" Eli asked. "Small for it."

"Citizens' arrest," Victor said. "You are trespassing. Damaging school property. Looks like..."

I missed the last bit as the distant jangle had stepped up its volume.

"What?" shouted Eli. "Say again?"

Victor kicked at the edge of one of our trenches, loosing a spray of soil. "Looks like you were intending for students to fall into these holes?" he yelled. "Conspiracy to inflict grievous bodily harm? Actually, probably intending to bury us alive. Attempted murder."

"Oh, *crabapple* and *blatherskite*," I scoffed, while at the same time the twins growled: "I'll grievous bodily—"

We couldn't hear the rest—the bells were so loud now my gums were aching. The Hamish kid had hunched down into his jacket and was pressing his hands over his ears. The fancy girl with the whinnying laugh had an expression like she'd just seen someone wearing mismatched clothes.

"YOU WILL SURRENDER," Victor roared. "ALL FURTHER ATTACKS ON BRATHELTHWAITE WILL CEASE. YOU WILL CALL OFF YOUR SPIES. YOU WILL ADMIT—"

The bells seemed determined not to let him speak. Even *louder*. Seemed like they were stabbing my cheekbones.

"SPIES? WHAT SPIES?" Eli shouted back. "YOU CALL OFF *YOUR* SPIES!"

"WE KNOW YOU HAVE SPIES! THE GIRL AND BOY IN THE STOLEN COATS! YOU WILL SIGN A DOCUMENT ADMITTING THAT BRATHELTHWAITE IS *VICTORIOUS* AND—"

That was the point where Honey Bee screamed.

CHAPTER
21
HONEY BEE

I had glanced behind me, you see. Something made me glance. I think I was checking whether any other orphans might have concealed themselves in the grounds and were creeping up on us.

What I saw was a curious, thick gray fog. It was moving towards us at about knee height. I turned in a slow circle and saw that the fog was approaching from every direction. *How strange*, I remember thinking, *I've never seen fog at that height. It's about the height of—*

That's when I screamed.

At the height of radish gnomes, is what I thought, and instantly I knew what it was. I'd never seen a radish gnome onslaught, only heard about them. Thousands of gnomes pitch their razor-sharp claws all at once. Shadow Magic carries the claws vast distances, swarming at dizzying speed.

It is much like thousands of tiny daggers hurtling through the air.

They will slice through your calf muscles.

And here we were, in an open field, the claws tearing towards us. So close now that even with the clanging of the bells, we could already hear the *thwap thwap thwap* of claws, the wind and force of them, spinning through the air towards us.

CHAPTER 22
FINLAY

They spun so fast they were a haze, a blur. Mesmerizing.

Like a git, I stood staring, hypnotized.

Then a *thud* hit my back, and I was toppling into the trench I'd just dug. Glim had shoved me. She's dreamy one minute, mind like lightning the next, that Glim. The lot of us were gawking, thunderstruck, but then Glim shoved me, wrenched Victor's arm, kicked the back of Hamish's knees, *rolled* Honey Bee, and basically *threw* Taya.

"GET DOWN! GET DOWN!" she shrieked.

Even so, the blades slashed through Honey Bee's braid as she fell into the trench, and sliced a layer of skin from Eli's ankle as he kicked out to give himself momentum.

We lay there, perfectly still, for seconds, minutes, hours it seemed like, the bells hammering, the air whipping as the claws flew and flew, a ceaseless rush of sharp silver wind, until I thought this must be my new life now, facedown in the dirt.

CHAPTER
23
HONEY BEE

The Whispering War had officially begun.

At breakfast that day, Sir Brathelthwaite gave a dramatic speech.

"My dear students," he said, low-voiced. "I have news."

Everyone shuffled to look at him, excited.

"An army of radish gnomes attacked at dawn today!"

Gasps. I remembered to gasp myself at the last minute, which meant mine came out like an afterthought. Sir Brathelthwaite frowned at me and cleared his throat. "The dreadful claws flew through Spindrift's streets and fields! Eventually, the Spellbinders repelled them!"

I gasped again, but that was a mistake, as nobody else did.

Earlier, after the attack, the orphans had run back to town, taking their rolls of turf with them, and we had crept back into the building.

Nobody guessed we'd been gone. I myself pretended I'd woken early and decided to cut off my braid. It was lost in the attack, you see. There was a bit of a fuss as it's against the rules to cut your own hair (unless you are Hamish, who is allowed to do as he likes with his hair).

"As the attack took place at dawn," Sir Brathelthwaite continued now, "very few people were out and about."

Very few people did not sound quite right to me. Many Spindrifters arise early—the fishers; the sailmakers; the ship repair crews; Jean-Pierre, the news vendor; Baker Joe.

But it turned out that Sir Brathelthwaite actually meant that very few people who *mattered* had been out and about. In fact, fifteen of the townsfolk had been seriously injured. Three were killed.

"The thing about a radish gnome attack," Sir Brathelthwaite explained, as if giving a fascinating science lesson, "is that your instinct tells you to get down—which means you are at exactly the right height for a claw to cut your throat."

My instinct had made me do exactly that. I had thrown myself flat onto the grass, but Glim had rolled me into the trench. That is how I had escaped serious injury—that's why I was even *alive*. My hand trembled at this realization, so that my spoon jangled against my teacup.

Uncle Dominic flicked his horsewhip, and I flinched and dropped the spoon.

"From now on, dear children," Sir Brathelthwaite said, "you must *never* speak to any child who is not a Brathelthwaite student. Children from the Whispering Kingdom are traveling throughout the Kingdoms and Empires, luring *good* children away."

I noticed Victor nodding solemnly. He looked perfectly serene, as if he had forgotten how close we had come to calamity. Hamish, alongside him, also seemed his usual breezy self, although it's tricky to tell with Hamish, as you only get glimpses of his face behind his hair.

But Rosalind was hissing, giggling, and pinching her friends before leaping away and babbling: "Missed me! Missed me! Now you've got to kiss me!" So she was clearly distressed. Then again, she often gets like this if she is tired, or after too many sugary treats.

"The main thing," Sir Brathelthwaite lectured, "is to get to shelter *the moment* the warning bells ring! I hear that many locals did not *react* to the bells this morning! Can you imagine such foolishness?"

"I *cannot*," Victor chuckled. "What stupid people!"

At this, I dropped my teacup. It crashed to the floor, forming a puddle of splintered porcelain.

Uncle Dominic strode towards me, horsewhip unfurling. Tears sprang to my eyes at his approach.

But Sir Brathelthwaite shook his head. "Honey Bee has always been a nervy thing," he said, "and does not have the strength of character of His Grace here—so talk of war must be difficult for her. Try to model yourself on His Grace, Honey Bee."

"Happy to help in any way," Victor offered.

"Thank you," I managed.

"Meanwhile," Sir Brathelthwaite carried on, "dear students. Take heart from the fact that *our* defenses are an *example* to the town."

After that, he listed the security features already implemented at our school.

"Trenches have been dug on the sports field!" he crowed. "I inspected them this morning!"

I blinked—then realized he meant the trenches dug by the orphans; he assumed his own "security team" had prepared them. Funny.

Bunkers and escape routes would be constructed, he told us next. And on he went, showing off about how our school would be the safest place of all. But I was distracted by the maid crawling around at my feet, mopping up my broken teacup.

"If you are in town," Sir Brathelthwaite continued, "when an attack is launched, take *first* place in a shelter. What the Kingdoms and Empires need is *you*, our brightest and best. We will *not...lose...one...single...Brathelthwaite...student!!!"*

Here, we all cheered, just as he intended.

After breakfast, we did two hours of emergency drills. We practiced sending messages using the semaphore flag system and the dot-dash light system. We also had to learn the alarm codes. Three short rings followed by five long meant *drop and crawl.* Slow, unbroken ringing meant *climb under furniture.*

And so on.

Uncle Dominic ran the drills.

"Again!" he shouted. "Faster!" *Flick* went his whip. "Too slow! Again!" *Flick! Flick!*

"Again!"

"Wrong!"

Flick.

"Faster!"

"Again!"

Until we were gasping for breath and dripping in sweat. Smaller children cried.

Later that day, I went and sat by Carlos's bed in the infirmary. I told him everything that had happened, but his eyes were closed, his eyelids the color of violets, his skin the yellowy-white of old cheese.

Now and then I heard the faint rasp of him breathing, so I knew he was alive.

CHAPTER 24
FINLAY

The day of the radish gnome attack, most of the children were crying.

Three people were dead. Two fisher-folk and a carpenter down at the docks.

Plenty more were injured. Baker Joe's wife, Millie—she'd been crossing the town square with a sack of flour. The news vendor's brother, visiting him from Stantonville, had run outside to help a wounded dog and got his shin sliced open.

Out of respect, all the shops and stalls were closed, and flags were lowered. A bunch of rowdy tourists—big blokes who'd come to town especially to "party"—complained that they were here for the atmosphere and beer and how *dare* we close the brewery!

A couple of local pirates knocked the lot out cold. The constables scolded the pirates, but winked and let it go.

Meanwhile, some of us Orphanage kids went to Oakum Woods to pick wildflowers, and to the beach to collect shells. These we used to make a display in the town square, to say how sorry we were. Ronnie-the-Artist painted a little portrait of each victim and leaned these up against our display, and townsfolk added their own flowers or trinkets or mugs of soup (and other strange things) and stood crying and shaking their heads.

There were no classes that day. We would have been too sad to concentrate anyway, but Anita had to help at the hospital. As well as the people seriously injured, plenty had cuts that needed stitching.

Lili-Daisy let us read books or do crafts, as well as our usual chores. In the afternoon, she gave us cocoa and cinnamon toast. Tough times were coming, she said, and every one of us, even the tiniest, would have to help.

For a start, she said, we should *all* watch out for kids we didn't recognize. These could be Whispering children here to steal more of *our* children. Reporting these children to the authorities would be a big help.

Later, after most of the children had fallen asleep, Lili-Daisy called Glim, the twins, and me out into the corridor. Her face was even more sorrowful.

"I know you four snuck out before dawn this morning," she said, low-voiced.

We were pretty shocked. I swear we'd heard her snoring from her bedroom when we left.

"It was one of the worst times of my life," she continued, "to be listening to a radish gnome attack outside, without a clue where you lot were. Fearing dreadfully that you were out in the open. I *never* want that experience again. Do you understand?"

It's not often that Lili-Daisy gets properly angry, but when she does, the veins around her temples stand up, and her mouth kind of pouts itself out, like a wolf's mouth.

"Do you understand?" she repeated.

We nodded. Too scared to speak.

"This battle you've got going with the boarding school," she said next, still angry—and now we were *properly* shocked. She knew about that *too?* Usually, she hasn't got the faintest idea what we're up to. "I took no notice, thinking it was harmless fun. Oh, don't look at me like that; I may be dim as the deepest ocean most of the time, but you keep turning up covered in flour, or with pink clothes. And you're *always* in the corner having secret meetings. I *can* add two and two, you know. It's—"

"Four," Eli told her.

She thwacked him on the side of the head. "It's got to *stop* is what I was going to say. To be honest, I let it go this long because I *also* wanted to throttle that boarding school. It was *their* cheating at the tournament—yes, I call it cheating; it's the spirit of the thing that makes it cheating—that distracted everyone so that Jaskafar got taken. So I understood. But now you're just caught up in silly vengefulness. *That's* the mentality of war. I am disappointed in you. *Gravely* disappointed. I mean, why not take some action to *help* your town with this war?! Show that you can *work* with your enemy towards a common good! *That's* what I'd expect of you. *Do you understand?"*

Once again, we nodded, staring at her. Eli was twisting his mouth around. Taya's lower lip trembled. Glim blinked fast.

None of us cry much, most definitely not the twins, and here we all were with our toes on the cliff-edge of crying.

"Now," Lili-Daisy said, still angry. "I am going to hug you all, because

I promised myself I'd hug you tighter than a constrictor knot if you made it back—after I'd given you a giant piece of my mind, of course."

"Have you got that much mind to spare?" I checked, but it was not the time for jokes. She grabbed ahold of us in one of those clamping hugs that are part loving and part *I'm-so-angry-I-could-crush-the-air-out-of-your-lungs*. I felt her tears falling past my ears. But then she pulled back, wiped her face, and demanded to know why we weren't in bed.

I'd already felt pretty miserable about the dead and injured people in my town—but now? Knowing we'd disappointed Lili-Daisy? I mean, after we'd *already* let her down by not watching Jaskafar at the tournament—well, now I felt a kingdom's time worse.

CHAPTER 25
HONEY BEE

That night I dreamed about razor blades spinning through the air, muddy trenches, black flags, pools of blood, buckets, sand hills, sea clams, violins, ice-cold wind, and Uncle Dominic shouting:

You
Will
Not
Cut
Your
Hair

Without
PERMISSION!

I dreamed broken teacups, Sir Brathelthwaite flinging knives across the dining hall, children in coats through carriage windows, and Uncle Dominic barking:

Again!
AGAIN!
You
WILL
Not
Cut
Your
Hair
AGAIN!

I woke up tangled in my sheets. Slivers of moonlight found their way between the cracks in the blackout drapes. My neck felt strange and bare without its usual long hair, and I ran my palms down my shoulders feeling where it should be. I missed it. If I am perfectly honest, I had been very fond of my hair! It was just the same color and length as my Aunt Rebecca's, and I liked to think we were linked in this small way. Aunt Rebecca lives in the Kingdom of Vanquishing Cove, one of the few non-wicked kingdoms in this region, and I haven't seen her in almost three years. So I needed that link! I never would have *chosen* to cut my hair!

My heart was beating in a sort of jumble, and images from the day and from my dream were still jumbled in my mind. Everybody seemed to be shouting: Uncle Dominic! Sir Brathelthwaite! The Orphanage children!

Right before the attack, I remembered, we had shouted at each other. How silly that seemed now. How childish! That orphan girl, Glim, had saved our lives! We should try to be friends with them! Maybe even *join up* with them to help with the war effort? I would suggest it to the others. Sir B wouldn't like it, of course, but the mayor might give us medals, which would be very persuasive to Victor.

I lay back in my bed again, sorting through my thoughts. And then I remembered. "SPIES? WHAT SPIES?" one of the orphan boys had shouted. "YOU CALL OFF *YOUR* SPIES!"

Right as I remembered this, an image from my dream leapt to mind: a boy and girl in coats through carriage windows.

They were not just from my dream, they were real children — Orphanage spies, we had thought.

But if they were not Orphanage spies, who were they? They were not Spindrifters!

Another memory came. Sir Brathelthwaite at breakfast: *Children from the Whispering Kingdom are traveling throughout the Kingdoms and Empires, luring good children away.*

The boy and girl in coats.

They were *not* Orphanage spies.

They were Whispering children.

The enemy.

In our midst.

CHAPTER 26
FINLAY

Yes, at the Orphanage, we realized the same thing, only in a less dramatic way.

I mean, without the drama. And romance. And details from dreams that are not actual facts. And without words

running

down

the

page

as

if

they

were

far

too

important

to

share

lines

with

other

words —

far

too

fancy

to

act

like

regular

words.

Rich people's words, taking one line each.

And also without being *terribly upset* about a *lost braid* when other people were *dead* and *severely injured*—but oh no, it's *very* important that *Aunt Rebecca* and *Honey Bee* have the same hair.

Without all that, I mean, we figured it out.

We were sitting up late while the other children slept, listening to Glim tell us a story. The twins and I were crowded onto Glim's bed in our dressing gowns, and Glim was cross-legged on her pillow. As usual, her story was about flying machines and adventures in the stars and, as usual, we were mesmerized. It's one of the only times the twins stop reading newspapers—when Glim tells us a story.

Halfway through an exciting battle scene though, she stopped. "Maybe," she said, "we should offer to help with the war? Like Lili-Daisy suggested?"

"We could ask the Brathelthwaite kids if they want to form a *team* of volunteers with us," I joked—and then realized I was serious. Hadn't Lili-Daisy said we ought to cooperate with our enemies?

Remembering their attacks on us, that seemed a bit too much to ask. Rats they'd sent in, and spies, and the day of the radish gnome attack, they'd shouted at us so nastily—

"Hang about," I said. "Those boarding school kids seemed to think *we* were the ones spying on them."

Eli shifted so the bed creaked. He quoted Victor, remembering exactly what he'd shouted that day: *"We know you have spies! The girl and boy in the stolen coats!"*

(The twins have memories as sharp as fillet knives. I think I've mentioned that already? Have I? Can't remember. *I'm* not a twin. Ha-ha.)

"The girl and the boy in the *stolen* coats," I said. "They think those kids stole their coats?"

"They think they were orphans who stole coats to look posh," Glim said slowly, thinking aloud.

"But *we* thought they were boarding school kids."

"So who are they?" Taya frowned. "They're not from around here."

All four of us realized at once. "Whispering children," we said. All at the same time, we said it. But without any of the drama, as I mentioned, and

without
single
words
or
dreams.

CHAPTER 27
HONEY BEE

Hmph.

Very well, I agree that it was foolish for me to feel sad about having lost my braid.

I apologize.

In my defense, I did *think* a great deal about the lives lost and damaged, *in addition* to missing my braid.

I *disagree* that there was anything wrong with my description. I was trying to capture the way *I* felt that night. Finlay, not being me, has *no idea how I felt.*

I used the words on separate lines for dramatic effect.

If Finlay is not aware of the importance of dramatic effect, then that is a real shame for Finlay.

Poor Finlay.

After breakfast the next day, I asked Victor, Rosalind, and Hamish to meet me in the green common room.

Victor yawned when he arrived and said that all attacks against the Orphanage would stop. They put us in too much danger now that the war was underway.

"So why have you called this meeting, Honey Bee?" he wanted to know. "The Anti-Orphanage League has been disbanded."

"Oh, I *say*," Hamish yelped. "Disbanded, eh? Sounds serious. Here's an idea: What say we *band* it again? Can we do that? I mean, I haven't the faintest idea how to band something. But, tell you what, I bet the school handyman knows! Let's go ask him, shall we? He's a good chap."

We ignored Hamish.

I told Victor I agreed that our attacks on the Orphanage should stop.

Then I said that I thought the two children in coats were Whisperers.

Victor's eyes lit up, very interested. After quick consideration, he agreed that they probably *were* Whispering children.

Hamish was baffled.

Rosalind was thrilled and alarmed by the idea of dangerous creatures like Whispering children. She sidled close to Victor. I believe she might have a crush on — oh, sorry, I cannot finish that sentence, as it would be too *emotional* and *romantic* for Finlay. (By the by, I can't *think* where Finlay got the idea that my chapter was *romantic*. I suppose it's because I mentioned that my heart was in a jumble. Finlay probably thinks the word *heart* is romantic. Poor boy has no clue there is an organ in his chest that pumps the blood around his body. He imagines his own chest is empty. Actually, it probably *is* empty, now that I think about it.)

Where was I?

I was having a meeting in the common room with the others.

I suggested we capture the two Whispering children.

Again, Victor considered.

Quite quickly, he agreed. As I've mentioned, he's terribly bored most of the time, that Victor, and the idea of doing something different excited him.

After more confusion, Hamish agreed to join us. Rosalind was truly frightened now — earlier she'd *enjoyed* being frightened, but the idea of going *near* these children terrified her. She tried to hide this by giggling and flicking Victor's forearm, but she kept making "jokes." For example, at one point she said, "Oh, try this for a tongue twister:

"The Whispering Children use supercharged Whispers,
To steal us away
To the Whisper-filled Whispering Kingdom!"

Two things became clear to me: first, she was not especially good at tongue twisters; and second, she was afraid *we* would be stolen away to the Whispering Kingdom.

I promised her that we were perfectly safe. Those two children obviously did *not* have the "supercharged" Whispers (I reasoned), or they'd have used these against *us* already. We had seen them often enough. In fact (I added), Whisperers probably could not "*whisper*" until they were grown-up. Why else was it only adult Whisperers who had such long hair? As long as we did not allow the two children to lead us to a Whispering adult, we would be perfectly safe (I concluded).

I did not have a clue whether any of this was true, of course. Still, it seemed to make sense.

We decided we would lure the Whispering children to a place where we could lock them up and call the authorities.

"I expect we'll get medals," Victor said, a gleam in his eye. So that was another reason for Victor's participation: he pretends nothing much matters to him, but he likes very much to get medals and pats on the head.

I do *hope* that this chapter has not offended Finlay's sensibilities by being *interesting* or *honest* at all.

CHAPTER
28
FINLAY

All right, Honey Bee. Take it easy.

You can actually *see* her temper catching alight, can't you? Like she's *breathing* dragon fire onto the pages. I was looking around for water to put it out.

I didn't mean she couldn't be *dramatic.* I was just *gently* making fun of her for the dramatic way she acted in her last chapter.

(I *do* know what a heart is, by the way.)

Anyhow, we decided the same thing.

Us four at the Orphanage? We also decided we would capture the Whispering children in their coats. To make Lili-Daisy happy and proud. To show her we were contributing to the war effort. So she'd smile at us again without her mouth looking like a wolf's snarl—she's not very pretty when she does that, no offense, Lili-Daisy, if you ever happen to read this—and without making her cry into our hair.

Only, we decided to chase the kids. Not *lure* them. More straightforward, us lot. More direct.

CHAPTER 29
HONEY BEE

We wrote a note for the Whispering children.

Victor and I composed it between us.

Dear children,

We have seen you about and you seem awfully nice! As we do not recognize you, we think you must be new to Spindrift, and perhaps rather lonely and friendless?

Never fear! Help is near!

As part of our school curriculum, we must undertake one "good deed" each month. We rather thought that YOU could be our good deed for this month!

May we invite you to a tea party? There is a little hut on the Beach with the Yellow Sand that is exclusively for the use of the students of Brathelthwaite Boarding School. It is at the southern end of the beach, and is striped in red and white (our school colors). Perhaps we could meet you there this Saturday? At, say, noon? We will be waiting with tea and treats.

Fond regards,

His Grace, the Duke of Ainsley (also known as Victor) (aged twelve), Master Hamish Winterson (ten), Miss Rosalind Whitehall (eleven), and Miss Honey Bee Rowe (twelve)

Hamish said we had it all wrong, and should say they'd have to sit in broken chairs with sharp bits that poked at their bottoms, while we fed them squashed cockroaches and filled their teacups with sand.

"That way they won't come," he said. "Which is what we want, isn't it?"

The rest of us looked at him.

"Well, old chaps, didn't you say they were *Whispering* children? Ghastly! Little devils trying to steal other children away! I mean to say, we don't want to be having *tea* with them, do we? Or do we? Have I missed something here?"

Once again, we explained the plan to him, and he did seem to understand for a moment. Although a little later he said, "Tallyho, I suppose it's worth it to get those extra points for our good deed this month, no?"

We *invented* the part about having to do good deeds each month, to make our invitation sound credible, but I don't think anybody had the energy to explain that to him.

We copied out the invitation four times, and each took one into our pockets. That way, whoever saw the Whispering children first would be able to invite them.

Rosalind surprised us by being the winner. She has a wealthy aunt who travels throughout the Kingdoms and Empires, and sometimes comes by Spindrift to take her niece to lunch. The day after we had composed the invitation, the aunt telephoned to say she was dropping by to collect Rosalind.

The aunt was trilling as she burst into the entrance hall of our school building: "Rosalind! Rosalind! I'm *here*! This will be our last lunch for some time! It's far too dangerous here in Spindrift with this *war* on! Rosalind? You children there, run and fetch my niece, would you—I don't want to linger a moment longer than I must in Spindrift! *So* dangerous!"

She seemed to guess what we were thinking as we stared at her, for she suddenly rapped on the wall with her knuckles. "Perfectly safe *here* though!" she said. "This boarding school is a fortress!"

Rosalind skipped down the stairs wrapped in her fur stole with pearls around her neck, and she and her aunt set out.

When she returned an hour later, she rushed us three into a corner and breathlessly told us that she'd seen them!

"The Whispering children! I walked *right* by them as we crossed the road to go to the Elegant Swan Bar and Grill with Aunt Clara! We were *this* far apart!" She held up thumb and forefinger. Hamish studied the gap.

"*Awfully* close," he agreed.

"So you passed them the invitation?" Victor asked.

"Of course! I popped it into the girl's coat pocket!"

"Do you think she noticed? Maybe she won't even *find* it there?"

"I tapped her shoulder and pointed it out," Rosalind hastened to explain, "and then I hurried after my aunt."

We all congratulated Rosalind, and Victor shook her hand. She blushed.

I felt a little sorry that it hadn't been me, but I cheered up, thinking of the great deed we were doing for the war effort, and the children we might save.

That Saturday, we gathered in the Brathelthwaite beach hut.

In fact, it is a hut for Brathelthwaite teachers, rather than students, but I've only ever seen Madame Dandelion using it to smoke her cigars after she bathes. However, Victor, being a young duke, has special privileges, including a key to the hut.

It is small but brightly painted with windows on either side, their curtains pushed open. There is a low table, a couple of chairs, a sofa, and a chest filled with beach towels and sporting equipment—racquets, balls, nets, and so on.

We set the table, as if for a tea party. Hamish had bought up half the bakery.

Then the four of us sat down to wait.

Rosalind chewed on her fingernails and giggled. Hamish hummed to himself. Victor sat perfectly still, eyes on the door.

"So," I said. "The plan is, we sit them down, offer them cake, then rush out and lock the door?"

"Yes."

"What about the windows? Couldn't they escape through the windows?"

Rosalind stopped giggling to roll her eyes at me. "You and Hamish will *guard* the hut, Honey Bee, while Victor and I run to get the authorities. Honestly. It's not rocket science."

We carried on waiting.

Twelve o'clock came.

"Perhaps we ought to tie them up?" I suggested. "To be *sure* they don't escape."

"We haven't any rope." Victor shrugged.

Quarter past twelve.

Twelve thirty.

"We can use stockings!" I said. I made the others close their eyes while I unclipped and peeled off my stockings. Rosalind said she would leave hers *on*, thank you, until they got here. This did not seem terribly efficient. Was she planning to request that the Whispering children avert their eyes, please, while she removed her stockings ready to tie them up?

Twelve forty-five.

"Rightio," Rosalind said. "Seems they've chosen not to come. Shall we pack up and go home?"

"Let's wait," Victor said.

"I suppose we ought to eat some of these cakes," Hamish suggested.

That seemed wise. We ate cake.

At one o'clock, I was convinced they were not coming. Moments later, there came a distant shout: *"In here!"* and *"Locked! Try that one!"* Footsteps and panting breath drew ever closer, a violent rattling of the door handle—the door burst open and in crashed the children in coats.

* CHAPTER *
30
HONEY BEE (AGAIN)

"I say," Hamish hissed. "Awfully keen to get their hands on tea and cake, aren't they?"

The two children were hunched over, puffing and panting. At Hamish's voice they sprang up and backed away a little.

Then, unexpectedly, the boy kicked the door closed behind him.

Oh my, I thought. *Now we're for it.*

I looked down at my stockings, rolled ready in my lap. It seemed very unlikely that I would be able to use them to tie up these two. They were brimming with such energy! (The children, I mean, not the stockings.)

Suddenly, I knew I'd been wrong about child Whisperers not being able to Whisper.

They were going to capture us. Not the other way around.

Goodbye, Spindrift, I thought forlornly. *Here we come, Whispering Kingdom.*

The girl straightened her shoulders and tidied her sky-blue coat. There was a jagged tear in its sleeve, which was a shame. "Good afternoon," she said. "I see you are enjoying your tea. We do apologize for the intrusion, but may we...impose upon you for a little and remain in your..." She paused, considering the room. "Is it a sort of beach hut? It's charming."

Oh my, I thought a second time. *She's pretending to be polite. She's awfully good at this.*

I felt around in my mind to see if she or the boy had placed any super-powered Whispers there yet, but it only seemed to be my own thoughts.

Unless perhaps the girl *herself* had made me think that she was awfully good at this?

But she *is* good at this (I argued back inside my mind), she seems so friendly and straightforward! So grown-up for her age! (She only looked about my age.)

Unless her Whispering is making me *think* that?

But no, those are *facts*!

Or are they?

Oh my, I thought yet again. *This is very confusing.*

I tried to brace myself against super Whispers, but I gathered that would be like trying to brace yourself against a stampeding coach and eight. (Difficult, I mean.)

Nobody had spoken yet—Rosalind was as white as fresh cream, Victor was smiling faintly (and a bit ridiculously, I thought)—and Hamish was frowning in confusion.

"I'm not sure—now, listen—I don't quite *see*," he began. "Old chaps, we *invited* you here! Didn't we? Have I got that wrong? I do get things wrong, you know. But I'm pretty certain you two are here for tea and cake. Yes, yes. I'm sure of it. Do sit down and let me take your coats! How do you take your tea? I have it in a thermos flask here. Or hang it, I've got *that* wrong too! We should do introductions first. Hamish Winterson, ever so pleased to meet you. Delighted you could come!"

The girl was staring at Hamish in a baffled way. People always do this when they first meet Hamish: I think it's all the yellow hair falling over his face, not to mention his manner of speaking. The boy, meanwhile, had moved over to the windows and was closing the curtains. He was very striking, this boy, with beautiful skin and flashing black eyes. This was distracting.

Probably part of their wicked Whispering ways, I decided, his being so striking. I mean, I had hardly registered what he was doing—

He was closing the curtains.

Why was he closing the curtains?

Oh my.

Now Victor gave one of his languid sighs. "Marvelous that you could come," he told our visitors. "Rosalind, do you know, I think we're out of milk? Would you mind popping out for more?"

"Old chap!" complained Hamish. "I brought plenty along! In the jug right there! If you'd just—"

"*Rosalind* will fetch it," Victor said firmly, and Rosalind, understanding, leapt to her feet, threw open the door, and fled.

The boy Whisperer was now standing at the window, peering through the crack between the curtains. The girl Whisperer had been straightening her gloves but now she gazed around at each of us in turn.

She was choosing which of us to Whisper first.

At that point, Victor's elbow jutted out, and the milk jug crashed to the floor and sent milk and broken pieces splashing over the girl's shiny shoes. She leapt sideways.

"Well, *now* we *do* need—" Hamish began, but Victor had grabbed his arm and taken my hand, and we were out of the hut, slamming the door and locking it behind us.

We had captured the Whispering children.

CHAPTER
31
FINLAY

No, *we* had captured the Whispering children.

Honey Bee sweeps in to take the credit for that, same way she just swept herself up an extra chapter. Anybody else notice that? It was my turn but she just kept right on talking. Sailing on by. (I know I took an extra chapter once before, but only because Honey Bee suggested it.)

Nice. Very polite.

Rich kids.

That's their way.

What actually happened was pretty simple. We chased the Whispering children down.

Glim, the twins, and I had been keeping an eye out, and first sighting was in the town square. They were reading the signs on the noticeboard. The four of us marched right up to them.

Simple.

See how much simpler we make life at the Orphanage? None of the *invitations* and *tea and cake* and *oh my*.

We just folded our arms and said, "We know what you are, *Whisperers*. Come with us to the authorities right now or we pummel you."

Around they spun and ran.

Which, I suppose, was to be expected.

We tore after them. Ran them all over Spindrift.

They were faster than I'd expected. Ducked down alleys, clambered over fences. The girl tore her nice blue coat on a bit of barbed wire down Yardsley Lane and we almost caught up with her, but she sort of fell over the other side and carried on.

We worked together. Shouted instructions at each other. *You go right.* That sort of thing.

That's us: like a *machine* we are. Or like those dogs they have in the country that round up the sheep or the cows or whatever. Rounding up the Whispering children, basically, is what we did.

Got them trapped on the Beach with the Yellow Sand.

Nowhere to run except into the ocean.

We watched them, the four of us, from the bench up by the lighthouse on the wooden boardwalk. They thought they'd lost us. They were pelting along the sand trying out the doors to beach huts, thinking they could hide from us in one.

We chuckled.

Finally, they found a hut with an unlocked door and threw themselves inside. We decided to wait until they'd relaxed and thought they were safe, before going down to fetch them.

"Give them a false sense of security," Glim said.

So there we sat, watching the door to the hut. Red-and-white-striped it was.

"Those are the Brathelthwaite colors," Eli said after a moment. "That must be their hut."

"Strange that the *Brathelthwaite* hut would be unlocked," Taya mused. "*Common* people could get in and leave their common-people germs."

We all laughed.

Next thing, the door to the hut opened again and we sprang up, ready to charge. A girl came out—but it wasn't the Whispering girl. It was that fancy one from the boarding school, the one with the laugh like a frightened horse. *Rosalind*.

We watched, confused, as Rosalind slunk along the beach huts and cowered down behind the third or fourth hut along. Mysterious.

Now *more* people spilled out and slammed the door, and it was Victor, Hamish, and Honey Bee, locking the Whisperers in and cheering like *they* did all the work.

(Okay, handing over to Honey Bee again. See how I keep things fair and let her have her go? See that?)

(Get ready for a lot of *Oh-my*-ing.)

CHAPTER
32
HONEY BEE

Oh hush up, Finlay.

So, there we were on the Beach with the Yellow Sand, standing outside the hut, **having just captured** the Whispering children. Using our **own wit and ingenuity**. Rosalind joined us suddenly—I'd thought she might have run to fetch the authorities, but no, she'd hidden behind a hut.

But here came the Orphanage children, tearing down the slope from the lighthouse, sprinting along the beach!

"We got them!" they crowed. All four of them. Slapping their hands together. Slapping the side of the hut.

"WE GOT YOU!" they shouted through the closed door, in case the Whispering children had missed this, I suppose. "YOU'RE GOING DOWN!"

"Steady on there, chaps!" Hamish held up his palms. "I think you'll find that *we're* the ones who got them, eh?"

"What are you talking about?" Finlay demanded. He was terribly cross. Really affronted.

Ridiculous boy.

Rosalind stamped her foot. This was in the sand, of course, so there was no pleasing *thwack!* and she only stumbled a bit. This made her angrier.

"Excuse me!" she sang at the orphans. "Just *who* do you *think* you are?!"

"We don't think, we know," Glim said. "We're the children who captured the Whisperers."

"Clearly not." Victor chuckled. "Run along and fetch the authorities for us, would you? We'll keep watch over our prisoners."

"YOU RUN ALONG AND FETCH THE AUTHORITIES," boomed Taya, the girl twin. Those twins, they can boom like pirate cannons!

"WE RAN THEM DOWN," Eli, the boy twin, bellowed (another cannon—*ka-BOOM!*). "YOU JUST *HAPPENED TO BE HERE!*"

"Oh now, for crying out loud," Hamish complained. "It was us! We—what was it we did again? Lu-ellen. No. That can't be right. Lu-ellen is the second maid's name—what is it again, Victor?"

"Lured," Victor said, but he wasn't looking at Hamish, he was glowering at Finlay. "We *lured* them here."

He took a step closer to Finlay.

"If you want to avoid trouble," he said, voice low and menacing, "you will go *right now, fetch the authorities, and tell them that the Brathelthwaites have captured enemy forces.*"

"Yes, tell them we've *lured* a pair of Whispering children into captivity," Hamish agreed. "Perfect. So we are war heroes? Correct?"

"Correct." Victor bit off the word and took *another* step closer to Finlay. The twins and Glim moved in themselves, ready for a fight.

Here, I lost my temper a little. "THIS IS RIDICULOUS!" I shrieked. "WE ARE WASTING TIME ARGUING WHEN *CLEARLY* IT WAS *US* WHO CAPTURED THE WHISPERING CHILDREN! IT IS *JUST NOT SPORTING* OF YOU TO CLAIM THAT IT WAS *YOU!*"

Now *everyone* began shouting. Shoving and kicking. Bellowing and bawling.

"Oi," said a voice.

We carried on shrieking. Sand was kicked. Arms were pinched.

"OI!" came the voice again, much louder.

Silence fell on us, all at once.

The voice had come from somewhere high. The roof of the hut, to be specific.

The Whispering children were sitting up there, swinging their legs and looking down at us. The girl was eating one of the cherry tarts.

"Not much point fighting over which of you captured us," she pointed out, "seeing as we've escaped."

CHAPTER 33
FINLAY

The windows.

They'd climbed out the windows.

Completely the fault of those daft Brathelthwaites.

"What's this about having *lured* us here?" the girl continued from up there on the hut. "I know *these* children chased us"—pointing at us Orphanage kids—"but I don't how *those* children lured us"—pointing at the Brathelthwaites.

"Ha!" I said. Couldn't help it.

"We invited you to a tea party!" Honey Bee cried. "That's why you came!"

"No, we were chased here," the boy said politely—he had an unexpected accent, bit like a pirate's.

"HA!" I repeated, louder. Honey Bee flicked her hand in my direction as if I was an annoying insect. She'd know about those, being one herself.

"But thank you," the boy added, leaning forward to address Honey Bee. "Thank you for inviting us to tea."

"Only we never *got* any invitation," the girl in the blue coat added, looking thoughtful up there. "But yes, thank you."

Honey Bee now became pretty childish. Look up the word *petulant* in the dictionary and it'll say: *Honey Bee, after the Whispering children said they never got invited to tea.*

"Yes, you did!" She stomped and sand sprayed up around her ankles. Her legs were bare, I noticed—no stockings—and striped with puffy crimson welts, as if she had a rash.

"What's up with your legs?" I asked.

But she only wanted to be stomping, not answering my polite questions. "Rosalind *gave* the invitation to you!" she blazed. "She put it in your coat pocket! Didn't you, Rosalind?"

Rosalind's cheeks had turned as pink as all our pink-dyed clothes. "Yes!" she squeaked, and cleared her throat. "Of course I did!"

"Oh *Rosalind*." Victor smirked. "You didn't do it, did you? You *pretended* you'd delivered it because you were *frightened* by our plan."

Rosalind shook her head wildly. "Of course I did it! Of course!"

But Victor was gazing up at the Whispering children. "It is not relevant *how* you were captured," he told them. "The fact is—"

"Oh, so *now* it's not relevant," Glim said, laughing at him. Victor's eyes flashed but he kept on slouching there, as if he'd decided he was too important for posture.

"The fact is," Victor repeated, "you have made the tactical error of climbing onto the roof. We will simply wait. You can't stay up there forever."

"Steady on," Hamish put in. "Let's not antagonize them, old chap? They're Whisperers, yes? They'll use their supercharged Whispers, won't they?" He stage-whispered: *"We pretend they're here for tea! Remember? The plan! And then we grab them! Golly, for once I'm the only one who knows what to do!"*

"There are eight of us here," Honey Bee said firmly. "Four orphans and four Brathelthwaites. They can't possibly take all of us. We'll protect each other."

"The orphans can look after themselves," Victor said carelessly. "Meanwhile, we wait them out."

The girl and boy on the roof did not seem at all troubled. Looking at them, I started to feel sort of funny in my belly.

They must know something we don't know, I thought.

Adult Whisperers were on their way. To take us to the Whispering Kingdom.

We're in a crabapple load of trouble.

But then the boy on the roof spoke again.

CHAPTER
34
HONEY BEE

"If it helps," he called down. "You have it wrong. We are not here to capture any children."

"We are not even *from* the Whispering Kingdom," the girl agreed, taking another bite of the cherry pastry.

"We're from the future," said the boy. "Came here through a gap in a hedge."

The girl brushed the pastry crumbs from her hands and straightened up. "We ought to introduce ourselves. Bronte Mettlestone. And this is my friend Alejandro. Delighted to meet you all."

CHAPTER 35
FINLAY

None of us believed a word of it.

CHAPTER 36
HONEY BEE

When Finlay says that *none* of us believed the Whispering children, he should perhaps have mentioned that Hamish did.

But Hamish believes every word he hears, so he doesn't count.

"Cripes!" he muttered now. "From the future, eh? Welcome to our time! What's it like, then, in the future? Everyone have an automobile? Pastries as good as they are here? I say, they must be better! Evolution and all that. Tell you what, shove some in your pockets next time you visit. By the by, what brings you to our neck of the woods? Or what, neck of the *time*? Ho! Sounds wrong, doesn't it? Quite a phrase, that, isn't it? *Neck of the woods?* I mean, golly, do woods *have* a neck? And do woods have *shins*? And what about—"

"Prove it," Victor interrupted, narrowing his eyes at the children. "Or we fetch the authorities at once."

Finlay was nodding. "Everyone knows that the story about the hedge in the Oakum Woods is just a pile of blatherskite. There is no time-travel hedge. You're not from the future."

"Not a chance," Victor sneered.

Up on the roof, the girl and the boy—Bronte and Alejandro—were beaming down at us. They seemed very sunny.

"Shall we?" Bronte inquired, arching an eyebrow at Alejandro. "Prove it?"

Alejandro grinned in a wicked way. "It is the time to go home now anyway." He shrugged. "Or we will be late for dinner."

Bronte nodded, but then she peered at Finlay. "The hedge is not in the Oakum Woods," she said. "It's in the grounds of my Aunt Isabelle's apartment building. Just beyond the rhododendrons and to the left of the geraniums."

"Forty-five degrees due west of the sugar-coated lily-blossom-daffodils," her friend, Alejandro, put in, straight-faced. Bronte's boot swung sideways, kicking his ankle sharply, so I knew he was teasing her. But he only laughed at the kick.

"The Time Travel Hedge moves all over the Kingdoms and Empires," Bronte continued. "I'm sure it probably *was* in Oakum Woods once, and so people might tell stories about it having been here, but no longer. It's not in your time at all. We're here on a quest. If we had more time, we would explain, but I'm afraid we have to leave in a moment—"

"Over my dead body," Victor murmured.

Bronte cleared her throat. "Oh dear, I hope not. It's been a real pleasure to meet you all. Or anyway, extremely interesting. Are you ready, Alejandro?"

"Yes."

"In the future," the girl announced, "there will be—"

And they vanished.

Not a puff of smoke. Not a *whoosh* or clap of thunder. Quite simply, they were gone.

"Golly," said Hamish.

CHAPTER
37
FINLAY

After that, we all just sort of went home.

I think it was the shock.

I mean, I'd never even *heard* of magic that makes people disappear! None of us had.

We did carry on bickering a bit. The Brathelthwaites thought maybe Whisperers could vanish like that, using their supercharged Whispers, and we said that made about as much sense as their ugly faces would make in a beauty contest.

Then *we* suggested climbing onto the roof to see if there was any leftover magic there that could make *us* disappear? The boarding school kids said that was about as stupid as the idea of us ever learning to tie our own shoelaces.

And so on.

(I *can* tie my own shoelaces, by the way.)

But our hearts weren't in the squabble.

See, we'd been *convinced* those kids were Whisperers with plans to steal us away, and we'd been pumped up on our plan to capture them—but instead they'd told us a cockleberry story about coming from the future, and then they'd up and vanished.

So off we went home, trailing in different directions, thinking our own thoughts.

Probably never see those two kids again, I decided.

*

Three nights later, the strangest thing happened.

It started like this. Around midnight, the warning bells rang and we all ran downstairs in our pajamas, out into the square, and down into the shelter.

By "shelter," I mean the basement of the town hall. It's stacked with rusty old chairs, broken typewriters, and boxes of files. It's papered in cobwebs and noisy with clanking pipes. Locals who live around the town square also use it as a shelter.

Now, the first time we'd come to the shelter had been a right blast. Lili-Daisy had handed around paper cups of cocoa, and Anita had taught us clapping games. That set the grown-ups off, demonstrating the clapping games *they'd* played as children. Right daft their clapping games were, so we fell about laughing, and the grown-ups got defensive, which made us laugh harder. The witches' childhood clapping game had a touch of Shadow Magic about it, which began to weave around our ankles and necks, slowly squeezing and suffocating us, until Mayor Franny noticed this and shouted, "Oi! Cut *that* out!" So then the witches were horrified at their mistake and went around apologizing and offering ginger cake to make up. The whole thing was crackerjack.

But this night was the fifth time we'd come. It was always a false alarm. People were starting to complain, and the little kids were cranky and wanted their own beds. A couple of them burst into tears every time the pipes clanked, which was annoying. Daffo cut his bare foot on a broken plate and walked blood everyplace. Avril knocked over a box of files, sending papers flying, and Millicent Cadger bleated and chased the papers, knocking into people. Baker Joe told Mayor Franny to quit crunching on that carrot, as it was setting his teeth on edge; the cocoa was being rationed and not enough to go around; and a number of grumpy grown-ups told *all* the kids to sit still, shut our traps, and cut out that infernal clapping.

So it was not as good as usual.

Then Lili-Daisy piped up: "Should we listen to the wireless? I've brought the portable one down." People grumbled, then said, "Oh, all right, then. Give it a whirl."

She got a lot of static at first, turned the knobs, and there was the voice of Prince Jakob!

We knew it was him on account of him saying, "Hello, people of Spindrift, this is Prince Jakob."

You could hear he had a cold, his voice had that rusty edge, and he apologized. "If it's too much, switch stations, I won't be offended," he suggested. Everyone in the basement chuckled and said, "No, leave it on. Let's hear what he's got to say."

"I thought the least I could do," the prince said, "is broadcast over the local airwaves here in Spindrift, while everyone is in the shelters. My mother, the queen and I, have been advised to stay put until this cold of mine is better, and I feel I must give something back to this kind town. Give you some updates on the war effort, and maybe — oh, excuse me" — he stopped to cough; you could hear he was trying to muffle it — "and maybe sing some songs for the children?"

His voice caught then, this time on nerves rather than on his cold, I thought.

"Oh, *leave* it out," scoffed the butcher. "He's *not* going to sing. Switch it off, Lili-Daisy."

"No, no," Motoko-the-Chocolatier argued. "Let's listen. I've heard the prince has a very fine voice."

He did too.

He had a grand voice, even broken and husky with his cold. The kind of voice that makes you smile warmly, like cocoa. And he sang those old-fashioned songs that tell tales of battles with dragons, or ancient water sprite romances, so that everyone became still, wanting to hear what happened next. The little children sang along with the choruses, cheering right up, and I noticed Anita smiling in a dreamy sort of way.

Soon, the younger ones snuggled into their blankets, and one by one fell asleep. The adults continued to sway or tap quietly.

Hours went by, waiting for the all clear to sound, and still the prince sang.

"He needs to be sleeping," Anita worried at one point. "He's too ill to be up all night singing for us."

"But it's lovely," Glim pointed out.

"It's *very* lovely," Anita agreed, and gave Glim's shoulder a quick squeeze. "His voice is divine."

Right about then was when the strange thing happened.

The prince cleared his throat and said, "Before the next song, I want to send my congratulations to a particular group of children. Yesterday afternoon, my mother, the queen, received a letter from a *team* of Spindrift children who wish to offer regular volunteer help with the war effort!"

There were murmurs of approval from all around. I felt a bit annoyed with this *team* of children. Showing off by *offering* to help. *We'd* tried to help by capturing Whispering children! Nobody had talked about *us* on the wireless! Not our fault the kids had up and vanished!

"I hope these children will not mind if I read out their names," the prince continued, "for I wish to honor them. There are ten children on the team, and they have come together from quite different backgrounds, which is especially wondrous."

Yes, yes, I thought. *Get on with it.*

Then the prince read the names.

"*Four* of the children are from the Brathelthwaite Boarding School: Victor, Hamish, Honey Bee, and Rosalind. *Four* are from Spindrift Orphanage: Finlay, Glim, Eli, and Taya. And *two* are new to town: Bronte and Alejandro. Children, if you are listening, the queen is so grateful! She will direct you to Mayor Franny, who, she is sure, will be grateful for your help. Children, I salute you. My mother, the queen, salutes you. It is this sort of courage and generosity that will win the war for us."

At that moment, the all-clear bells sounded, which was lucky as it drowned out the sounds of Lili-Daisy, Mayor Franny, and other adults, who were all exclaiming their amazement, hugging us, and congratulating us.

Glim, the twins, and I had no idea how to cope with these congratulations, not having the faintest clue what the prince was on about.

An offer to the queen? A *team of volunteers*?

Look, I know I'd once had a half thought about teaming up with the Brathelthwaites to volunteer, but in all honesty, I never meant it. If you'd told me it would actually happen, well, I'd have told *you* to go jump in a cartload of rotten crabapple.

But that's what we did.

(Not jump in a cartload of rotten crabapple, you daft git.)

Tuesday mornings at 7:00 a.m., we started doing volunteer work.

We had to, didn't we? The prince talked about it on the wireless.

The very first Tuesday, Bronte and Alejandro—the pair who'd been spies and then Whisperers and who were now from the "future"—handed us a letter explaining everything.

I'll get to that letter in a moment. First though, you need to know that the war was heating up, and . . .

A Very Important Thing Happened . . .

CHAPTER
38
HONEY BEE

Oh yes, it did!

The K&E Forces decided to use *Spindrift*, our town, as its *base of operations*! Usually, they're based way across the oceans in Clybourne, but they came swarming into our town! Officers took over the fanciest hotels on the Beach with the Yellow Sand, and regular soldiers moved into the shabbier inns.

Each morning, you'd see soldiers cleaning rifles or shooting at targets on the town green. Or they'd be wriggling along on their stomachs on the beach. Must have got sand in everything. The infantry marching band strode around the town square at noon each day playing their invigorating music.

The people of Spindrift were *very* angry about all this. There was a lot of shouting at Mayor Franny. "Are you *crazy*? How could you *allow* this? You have made us a prime target in this war! We will be *pounded*! *Bombarded!*"

"We would be anyway." Mayor Franny shrugged, chewing on a carrot. "We're in a strategic location for both sides. We've got shipping repair, docks, access to the Whispering Kingdom by sea. This way, at least we get the protection of the army."

In any case, it had not been the mayor's decision to let the forces in. The queen had given permission. She showed no signs of leaving town, by the way. The prince was still sick with his nasty flu.

CHAPTER
39
FINLAY

Yes, that was pretty important. Soldiers everywhere.

But that's not what I meant.

Here, have another go, Honey Bee.

And then...

A Very Important Thing happened...

CHAPTER
40
HONEY BEE

Oh yes, everybody left Spindrift!!

Or maybe not everybody, but *many* people. If soldiers streamed in, locals streamed out! In carriages, in carts, on horseback, on foot! I mean to say, if the threat of attacks wasn't enough, children were still disappearing! So Whisperers must still be around, using their superpowered Whispers!

We were suspicious of anybody with long hair. Or anyone wearing a scarf that might hide long hair. If you got a sudden headache, or an idea popped into your head—*I might go to the cinema!* or *I feel like apple strudel and whipped cream!*—you would pounce on the nearest stranger and tear off his or her hat. Long hair curled into a bun beneath the hat? The person would be dragged to the nearest constable!

The barber's shop was busy day and night, cutting hair so people wouldn't be mistaken for Whisperers. I supposed I was better off without my braid, after all!

Anyway, it was tense. Some people couldn't stand it. Whole families packed up. Parents bundled children onto trains and sent them to relatives in the countryside, or to other, quieter kingdoms. (One family, not being able to afford the train fare, actually took their little girl to the post office and tried to send her package post!)

Other than the Orphanage School, all the local schools closed down! Their buildings were requisitioned by the military.

At Brathelthwaite, more and more parents swooped in—or sent servants swooping—to collect their children. Eventually, only twenty or so of us remained. Our halls echoed hollowly!

CHAPTER 41
FINLAY

Nah, that's not what I meant either.

Not very good at this, are you, Honey Bee?

Take another shot.

And then...

A Very Important Thing happened...

CHAPTER
42
HONEY BEE

Well…

Gosh.

A Top Secret Military Division moved into Brathelthwaite? That happened!

Very exciting! Our halls echoed hollowly, as I said, but only for a bit because this Top Secret Military Division took over the teachers' wing and held secret meetings in the staff rooms! "Codebreakers," people whispered. Sir Brathelthwaite was terribly proud.

CHAPTER
43
FINLAY

Nope.

One last try.

And then…

A Very Important Thing happened…

44
HONEY BEE

Look, I let it go when Finlay did that single-line chapter. Remember that one?

Chapter 35.

None of us believed a word.

At the time, I thought he was showing off about how he's the *opposite* of me because *I* talk for too long and take extra chapters, whereas look at him! Just one line of the story taken! *He* is so generous!

And who cares that it actually means Honey Bee has to do all the work.

Yet still I let it go. *Maybe it's just his hand is too tired to write?* I thought kindly.

However, now he has gone too far.

WHAT IMPORTANT THING, FINLAY?!?!

A *THOUSAND* IMPORTANT THINGS HAPPENED!

A MILLION! A BAJILLION!

Well, perhaps not quite so many, but *a lot*.

And you want me to choose just *one*?!

I think what you're up to is MAKING ME TELL THE WHOLE STORY.

Well, enough! It is JUST NOT SPORTING.

I put my foot down!

WHAT IMPORTANT THING???

CHAPTER 45
FINLAY

The Kingdom of Raffia won the Kingdoms and Empires Rugby Cup.

First time in sixty-five years.

Game almost got canceled, what with war everyplace, dangerous to travel and whatnot. But officials decided to go ahead, to rally everybody's spirits.

And thank the stars they did. Dead heat until the last minute, then Dave Shields scores a killer try as the clock ticks down the game's last seconds. Crowd was on its feet roaring louder than the sea in hurricane season. Lili-Daisy shook the wireless, thinking it had turned to static. Glim and I cried. Lili-Daisy and Anita danced a turkey trot.

Best thing that ever happened to me, that.

CHAPTER 46
HONEY BEE

Now, does anybody recall this?

Finlay savaged me for being sad about my lost braid.

You remember that?

And here he is, jubilant about a rugby game. At a time when people throughout the Kingdoms and Empires were being shot, stabbed, bombed, having their laughter stolen, their memories jangled, their homes burned to the ground or crushed by falling trees.

Very well, Finlay.

Certainly.

That *was* the most important thing. Oh yes, *that* was what counted. That was *everything*.

The rugby game.

Imagine my not guessing that was what you meant.

Just imagine. How foolish of me.

How silly I am.

What was I thinking.

On with the story, then.

You'll never guess what happened next...

CHAPTER 47
FINLAY

Ha!

Nice try, Honey Bee.

See that? She thinks she's got me bamboozled. No more dragon fire, just frost, and she thinks she's got me.

You'll never guess what happened next... she writes, meaning *Finlay* will never guess, so he'll be stuck and crying: *Oh no, what does she mean?!* And sighing: *You got me, Honey Bee. Hats off to you.* And so on.

But I know exactly what she means. I'm keeping my hat on, thanks. If I was wearing one, I mean, which I'm not.

She means the influenza epidemic.

That's what happened next.

Remember the prince was sick? And Honey Bee's friend Carlos?

Now *everybody* started getting sick. I mean, *everyone*. Shops were shutting down on account of nobody left to run them. Half the marching band dropped out; soldiers took to their beds. This was a wicked flu. It would start as a regular cold and then, eventually, feverish fits, hacking cough, hallucinations. We blamed Prince Jakob for bringing his illness into town, even though he actually got sick *after* he arrived. The town council kept sending out urgent requests for Faeries to come and help with their healing magic — we have no Faeries in Spindrift because True Mages don't tend to get on with our Shadow Mages — but the Faeries were too busy helping out wounded soldiers in other Kingdoms and Empires.

A lot of people ended up in the hospital with it, actually, including Lili-Daisy. Meantime, our Anita spent almost every moment at the hospital so she had no time left to teach us. Basically, the only adult in charge was Cook, and he never pays attention to us. He serves up our food, thinking his own thoughts, and scoots off for a game of cards with the sterling silver foxes.

We were left to roam the streets as we liked.

And we did like that. Very much.

So, I know exactly what *Honey Bee* meant with her *guess what happened next*.

She's so *pleased* with herself.

Just like a Brathelthwaite student.

Listen, in case you've missed this, Dominic Rowe, deputy of Brathelthwaite, is her *Uncle Dominic*. He's *family*. She's like the *essence* of Brathelthwaite. (And you wonder why I'm not that fond of her?)

CHAPTER 48
HONEY BEE

Do you know, I am suddenly rather tired?

Weariness pours over me like syrup.

So much bickering with Finlay...

I did used to like Finlay, you know. He is such a wild, funny boy. If there is a brick wall, everyone else will walk alongside it, but Finlay will clamber up the side and run along its top.

He takes no nonsense from Victor either, even if Victor is a duke, and Finlay just a poor orphan. And he can see that Hamish is a dolt but does not mock him for it, or not too often anyway.

In real life, Finlay is friendly and fair, so when he said earlier that he found me "annoying," I honestly thought he was joking!

It has hurt my feelings, rather, as we've gone along and I've realized that he means it.

I do see why he finds me annoying. I chatter a lot, and I suppose my manners are a bit prim. And yes, I *am* related to Uncle Dominic. I hadn't thought of his blaming me for that. But I see it now.

Also, it might seem dreadful that Finlay's important thing was a rugby game, but that is part of the strangeness of war. Ordinary life keeps happening. You learn that the Whispering War is rippling through all the Kingdoms and Empires. You hear that cities have fallen, thousands taken prisoner.

Or you read a story like this one in the paper. Read it. Go on.

Hundreds of men and women from the little Kingdom of Myrtle have marched on the neighboring Kingdom of Rowan and been gunned down. They did not choose to march and, in fact, have always loved their neighbors in Rowan. Unfortunately, they were under the command of Whisperers and could not help it.

"It broke our hearts to attack our friends in Rowan," said one citizen of Myrtle, from his hospital bed. "It's a terrible thing to find yourself raising a weapon against dear neighbors. None of us wanted it. We tried EVERYTHING to resist the Whispers, but nothing worked. Look, I don't blame the Rowans for shooting at us—what else could they do? I know it broke their hearts to have to do it too. I've lost my leg, and my husband has internal bleeding—not sure if he'll make it. But what else could they do when we were shooting at them? They had to shoot back, didn't they?"

A team of Spellbinders rushed to the battle
to release the Myrtles from the Whisperers'
control—but arrived moments too late.

You read that article and you want to sob for days! (That's how I felt, anyhow.)

But you are still happy to learn that there will be peach marmalade for breakfast. Still disappointed to lose a button from your favorite coat. So I suppose you are still excited when your rugby team wins a game.

Actually, in some ways, these small things are *more* important, because they remind you that ordinary life is real, and that hopefully it *will* return one day. You need glimpses of happiness and light.

So I would like to call a truce with Finlay.

I'm tired of fighting him.

Let us simply tell our story: the story of the Whispering War, and how the Kingdoms and Empires have been shredded like coconut.

✳ CHAPTER ✳
49
FINLAY

Well, I have never seen a coconut in my life, so I don't know about this shredding thing.

Also, listen, that news about the Myrtleans marching on Rowan? That made me *hopping mad*. Not sad. I could not *believe* those Myrtle folk would fall under the Whisperers' command and shoot their friends and neighbors!

Couldn't blame the Rowans for fighting back; they had to. But the Myrtles should have resisted!

A Whisperer could *never* make me hurt another person.

I'd just say no. Wouldn't do it. Even if my head felt like it was splitting in two.

But otherwise, okay.

A truce is fine with me. Honey Bee's not *evil*. I mean, she's not even *always* annoying!

When she's fast asleep and can't talk, she's probably perfectly fine.

Ha-ha.

No. She's all right awake sometimes, I guess. In little bits.

So let's get on with the story.

Where are we up to, anyway? It's got muddled.

Life *is* a muddle. I don't understand how people write history books about wartime. Things happen in overlapping ways, and you don't know which bits count.

I think we might be up to that first Tuesday.

CHAPTER
50
HONEY BEE

Yes.

The first Tuesday of volunteer duty we were almost late because there was a fire siren attack at dawn.

A group of sirens is called a blast, and several blasts had joined the Whispering side. Now, a regular siren will attack by howling and shrieking so that your mind gets jumbled and it seems as if someone is plunging a dagger into your ear.

Both ears, I mean. Two daggers.

If you are exposed to a siren attack for more than a few minutes, the jumbling is permanent. From then on, you will always feel as if your mind is a toy box being shaken about by a toddler. In addition, you will go deaf.

Fire sirens, meanwhile, can use their howls and shrieks to ignite flames. What this means is, you *want* to run inside to climb into a wardrobe and press pillows to your ears, but you can't! Because you need to be *outside* with hoses and buckets putting out the fires! Impossible situation!

They are terribly haughty about their superior talents, fire sirens. Regular sirens find them exasperating.

Brathelthwaite Boarding School had been well insulated against siren attacks, but even that only took the edge off the noise. I was dreaming about my Aunt Rebecca that night, I remember. She is a science teacher and I think I already mentioned that she lives in the Kingdom of Vanquishing Cove? Before I came to Brathelthwaite, I used to visit her in the summer every year. Her cottage sits on a hill overlooking the sea.

In this dream, I saw again the golden candle on her sideboard, a pot of tea, and a plate of mango-coconut cakes on the table. My aunt stood in the open doorway, her hands on her hips. She turned to me, smiling her sweet, mischievous smile, and said, "Look, Honey Bee, there's a sun shower outside. Shall we take a walk in the rain?"

But the moment I looked out at the rain, the droplets turned themselves into arrow points. Each point was streaking towards us with a high-pitched whistling sound. *Into* the cottage they spun, through its open windows and door. Aunt Rebecca and I fell backwards, staring wild-eyed at one another.

"Aunt Rebecca!" I shouted. "Aunt Rebecca! Help us! Help us, Aunt Rebecca!"

Hands shook my shoulders.

I opened my eyes to the shadow of Rosalind in her dressing gown.

"Oh, do hush up, Honey Bee," she scolded. "There's enough racket outside without another of your nightmares about *Aunt Rebecca*. It's a fire siren attack."

I fumbled in my bedside drawer for the knitted earmuffs we had all been issued, and joined Rosalind and the other girls at the windows. Our blackout curtains had been pushed aside and we stood in the dim light, listening to the eerie wails and watching flames ripple across the lawn. Bushes erupted suddenly, and sparks rained like autumn leaves from trees. Our security guards scurried about in their soundproof helmets, dousing each fire as it appeared. Once, I saw a security guard stop suddenly and fall to her knees, arms clutched around her helmet.

"Helmets can only do so much against fire sirens," Rosalind muttered beside me. It was strange to hear her sounding so subdued.

There was a shout from another guard, and he ran towards the fallen woman, dragging her into the vestibule. I heard later that she has permanently lost the hearing in her right ear.

At 7:00 a.m., the attack still continued — the guards must have been *exhausted*, but still they sprang from fire to fire, stamping out each in turn — and I thought we would have to miss our first volunteer session.

"Oh dear," Rosalind sighed, "you're right." But her lips twitched into a smile. She didn't *want* to go along at all. "On a *team* with orphans!" she said, over and over. "Why, it's my worst nightmare!"

Neither did Victor but, of course, Sir Brathelthwaite had made such a fuss of how proud he was of his students for catching the queen's attention that there was no way out of it. (Hamish and I admitted to each other that we were curious to see the "future children" again, and just as curious to find out how we had come to volunteer without our own knowledge! Hamish thought he must have accidentally hypnotized himself and done it in a daze.)

Anyhow, just as Rosalind was smiling to herself, there was one of those strange, abrupt silences that feel like noise themselves they are so startling.

Tick, tick, tick said the clock on the wall. Footsteps ran quickly down the corridor outside our room. Voices called to each other.

"Is it done?" I whispered.

On the grounds, the security guards had all stopped still. They were looking up and around, glancing at each other.

A moment later, the all-clear bells rang out.

Beside me, Rosalind gave a little sigh.

Victor asked permission to take a picnic breakfast to our first volunteer session. He is very fond of treats, is Victor. "My friends here," he said — indicating Hamish, Rosalind, and me — "are terribly shook up by the fire siren attack this morning. I think some treats will do them good, don't you, Sir Brathelthwaite?"

"Remarkable," Sir Brathelthwaite murmured. "Always thinking of others. That will be your noble blood. Very well, tell the kitchen to put together a feast. I hope you others realize how fortunate you are to have a friend like Victor here?"

"Oh *yes*," Rosalind agreed, and we sped off.

We were supposed to report to the mayor's office in the town hall. The orphans were already loitering outside her door when we arrived, and all four swung around to glower at us. Before we'd finished glowering back, Bronte and Alejandro strode up, smiling. The tear in Bronte's coat had been neatly sewn, I noticed, and Alejandro's hair was shorter and tidier, but their smiles, I realized—as I studied them—were unsteady. As unsteady as a rowboat that's just been boarded by an elephant.

They were nervous.

"Was it *you* who wrote the—?" Victor began, rounding on them, but the door swung open. Mayor Franny stepped out, exclaiming about what *fantastic* children we were to have joined forces like this! What crackerjack *diamonds*!

Most of us sighed quietly. It was becoming tiresome, you see, playing along with all the congratulations.

Mayor Franny told us that our first assignment would be to take a pony and cart to the Spindrift Junkyard and collect any metal or True Magic trinkets we could find.

"Now, I know most of you," she added, "but I haven't yet met Bronte and Alejandro. You're Bronte? And you must be Alejandro? Greetings! Welcome to Spindrift! Where are you from? Your parents just moved to town, did they?"

"Ever so pleased to meet you, Franny," Bronte said, grinning a little madly. "I hope the others will show us the way to the junkyard? I'm afraid I have no idea where it is. Shall we set off at once?"

"Yes," Alejandro agreed, "before this sun gets any warmer. You say there are gloves with the cart? And sacks?"

Moments later, we were riding through the streets of Spindrift together—Eli driving, the rest of us crowded in the back—and I was thinking how cleverly the pair had avoided Mayor Franny's questions.

"Before anybody says another word," Bronte pronounced, "I have written a letter that explains everything."

"Well," Alejandro put in thoughtfully, "it explains a *teeny* piece of every-thing, Bronte, but *everything* is—how do you say?—big! A very big concept. It is an immense, epistemol—"

"Hush up, Alejandro. He can be very philosophical, you know, but we'd like you to read this letter, so it's not really the time." She drew an envelope from her coat pocket, and Alejandro shrugged (very philosoph-ically).

"And why," Victor sneered, "should we bother reading this?"

"Oh well, I'll throw it away if you prefer." Bronte made to fling the enve-lope over the side of the cart, but Finlay laughed and grabbed it from her hand.

We all gathered around to read over his shoulder, bumped by the cart now and then. From the driver's seat, Eli threatened to break us all into 7,356 pieces if we didn't read it aloud to him. We ignored him and carried on reading in silence.

It was a long letter, which makes sense, as it set out to explain every-thing. Or a *teeny* piece of everything anyway. One curious thing was that the letter seemed to have been got at by the censors—people who black out bits of soldiers' messages home, to make sure they don't give away military secrets. Only, instead of blocks of black, this letter had gaps where sentences simply faded. Pale smudges remained, as if somebody had spilled milk and then brushed it away.

Dear Children of Spindrift,

I expect you are extremely cross with us for sending your names to the queen as a volunteer team. I would be cross too, if I were you.

I do apologize.

To explain why we did this, I need to tell you our story. Please be patient.

As we mentioned, we are from the future. About fifteen years in the future.

My name is Bronte Mettlestone and I live in Gainsleigh in the Kingdom of Rosehip with my parents, my Aunt Isabelle, and the Butler. Two years ago, while on an extensive journey around the Kingdoms and Empires, I met Alejandro. He was a boy with no shoes across a river and, to make a long story short (or to make a 109-chapter story into five words), he and I became friends. He now lives with my family too.

Another important thing also occurred on my extensive journey (well, many important things occurred, but this is the one that counts here): I purchased a genie's bottle from the markets in the village of Lasawftk. (Don't bother visiting, they're pretty standard markets.)

The bottle no longer contained the genie, but it was a bargain at only a few copper coins, and I will tell you why.

It has the power to direct you to the dreams you ought to dream. The genie herself appeared for a moment while I was paying, all got up in lipstick-red shawls—she was terribly mysterious and quiet, left a basket of fruit, and was off again.

The bottle only works the one time per person, and I've already used up my turn, but I still have it. Not long ago, I suggested to Alejandro that he sleep with it by his bed, in order to dream the dream he ought to dream.

He thought that was a fine idea and off he went to sleep.

Well, the next day he came to breakfast looking very pale, and also very interested.

"My dream," he said, "told me I must visit my parents."

We all blinked. Alejandro was raised on a pirate ship and never knew his biological parents.

"My dream," he added, "said I <u>must</u> find my parents, for they are sad."

"Well then," Aunt Isabelle said. "You must. But how do you know who they are?"

"That's what I asked my dream," Alejandro replied.

"Sensible," my father and mother said in unison, nodding.

"The dream said that I should seek out the letters J-A in the town of Spindrift, in the Kingdom of Storms."

"Long journey," my mother pointed out, "from here to Spindrift."

"Spindrift!" I exclaimed. "That's where the Children of Spindrift are from!"

"Stands to reason, Bronte," the Butler put in. "That the Children of Spindrift would be from Spindrift."

(By the way, YOU are the Children of Spindrift. You are very ▓▓▓▓▓ in the ▓▓▓▓▓ and we had just learned ▓▓▓▓ ▓▓▓▓ and I must say, I know that the seven of you ▓▓▓▓▓▓▓ however, I didn't think that ▓▓▓▓▓▓▓▓▓▓)

"The dream," Alejandro continued, "said I must return to the Spindrift of fifteen years ago."

"An even longer journey, then," my mother joked.

"Did you ask how exactly you were supposed to do that?" I checked.

"Of course, Bronte. And the dream told me that it would invite the Time Travel Hedge to our garden, and that the hedge would remain there until I found the truth of who my parents are."

"Good gracious!" the Butler and Aunt Isabelle exclaimed. "The Time Travel Hedge is in our garden?"

We all hurried to the windows to peer down into the grounds. My father spotted it first. A tidy new hedge, the width of your outstretched arms, just beyond the rhododendrons.

Interestingly, back when I used the genie bottle, it gave me a nonsensical dream that I had to puzzle out. Yet Alejandro's dream was so straightforward and polite! I never got to have a question-and-answer session with my dream!

Still, I recovered from this unfairness quite quickly because I was excited at the idea of an adventure. Time travel struck me as adventurous. Also, I saw that it was important for Alejandro to find his parents if they were sad.

The hedge turned out to be marvelous. You just squeeze through a narrow gap in its middle, and it knows where and when to take you. Each time we use it, we find ourselves in the town square in Spindrift. After a few hours here, we fade back to our own time and there we are, standing in the garden again.

So Alejandro and I have been wandering the streets of

Spindrift trying to meet people whose names begin with "J" and "A," as we suppose they are going to be Alejandro's parents. At first, it seemed very easy: we met a Joseph, a Jasmine, a Jacqueline, an Arnold, an Ahmed, and an Abhidi. But we don't know what to do once we meet them. Alejandro won't be born for another few years, and "J" and "A" might not have even met each other yet! And they can't possibly know that they will one day be Alejandro's parents.

Then we thought, "Hang on, J-A doesn't have to be the names of the parents. It could be some other clue. The street name where the parents live! (Juniper Alley? Jeronimo Avenue?) The restaurant where they will have their first date (The Jumping Alligator)?"

So we became frustrated. We wandered the streets of Spindrift each visit, hoping that the answer would spring at us.

Then one day we happened to overhear the matron at the Orphanage calling, "Finlay! Glim!" and we recognized the names.

"The Spindrift Children! It must be!" we cried. Or I did, anyway, and Alejandro agreed.

After that, we got a bit distracted from our search for J-A and began searching out you Spindrift Children instead. We did stare at you rather when we found you. I apologize. I know it was rude. But you can't really blame us! You are and we were keen to tell our classmates and but you.

We never guessed it would lead to you chasing us down! The day when you all tried to capture us in the beach hut,

Alejandro and I were a little frightened but also very excited to be speaking directly to the Children of Spindrift.

However, when we got back to our garden, the genie herself was there, waiting for us by the hedge. All got up in her lipstick-red shawls, just as when I'd seen her the last time, but this time she was not the least bit mysterious or quiet! She was direct, and very chatty (like in Alejandro's dream).

"Whatever have you done?" she said. "What happened back in time just now?"

We told her how you had chased us.

"There," she said. "That's why I've been summonsed by the Board of Time Keepers. You've messed with history."

I became very defensive and said, "We most CERTAINLY have NOT," but Alejandro placed a calming hand on my shoulder and asked the genie, "In what way?"

"Why, the Children of Spindrift have been trying to capture YOU two, thinking you are Whisperers! But history says they SHOULD have been ⸺⸺⸺⸺⸺ and ⸺⸺⸺⸺⸺ in order that they will ⸺⸺⸺⸺⸺ ⸺⸺⸺⸺⸺ which of course will lead to ⸺⸺⸺⸺⸺ and ⸺⸺⸺⸺⸺."

"Oh dear," I said. "If we have messed up history, does that mean time itself will collapse now and Alejandro and I won't even exist?" I'd read about such things in stories.

"Of course you will exist, Bronte!" the genie cried. "Look at you! Existing! Do not be foolish. No, it will be far worse than that. The horizon will tip, becoming awful to see, like a crooked painting. Weather patterns will turn inside out and stars will clatter to the ground like so many marbles. Unless you repair this glitch in history, the Kingdoms and Empires will be flipped like so many pancakes. Many, many lives will be lost before the Kingdoms and Empires settle down and right themselves again."

"So!" said Alejandro, who is an optimist. "We will fix it. How do we do this?"

"You don't have long," the genie retorted, and she turned to frown at the hedge. "You had better forget all about finding your parents, Alejandro, and focus on fixing history. You must make sure that the seven Children of Spindrift ⸻⸻⸻ and that they ⸻⸻⸻ so that they ⸻⸻⸻ All right?"

"Very well," I agreed. "We'll go straight back to old Spindrift now and tell them that they must ⸻⸻⸻ and that they ⸻⸻⸻."

"Yes." Alejandro nodded. "Easy."

"What are you forgetting?" the genie asked, rather drily. "Come on. Don't look at me blankly like that. What have you forgotten?"

Really, she was entirely unlike her mysterious self. I think she must have joined an exercise class in the meantime and it had brisked her up. "Come on!"

We both remembered at the same time.

The Detection Magic.

You see, whenever you go through the gap in the hedge, you get coated in a sort of *froth* of Detection Magic. We found out about this from a book on the Time Travel Hedge that my former governess, Dee, gave me when she heard we had the hedge in our garden. The Detection Magic keeps an eye on you to make sure you don't give away anything about the future. If you even <u>hint</u> that you're about to do so, you get whisked back to your own time. This is how we vanished from the roof of your beach hut that day – we simply said, "In the future..." and the Detection Magic jumped.

This can be handy if you are surrounded by angry, squabbling children, but it can also be a nuisance. The Detection Magic jumps too readily and sends you flying back to your own time even if you were only going to say something like, "In the future, I'll try to eat more apples." It scans the words we say and ALSO the words of the people around us, keeping an eye out for tricks, you see, that we might use to get around the rule. Say if you asked us questions about the future and we gave "yes" or "no" answers. Or if one of you asked for clues or hints about the future? That could be enough to trigger it. It's much too sensitive – too keen to do its job.

Which is why I have written this letter. If we'd tried to tell you all this in person, we'd have been jumped back to the future repeatedly! So tiresome! The Detection Magic will check this letter as we bring it through the hedge with us, and will blank out anything that gives away the future – but hopefully you will still get our key message.

And the key message is this.

We need to fix history.

That is, we need somehow to coax you back onto the right track – the track you WOULD HAVE taken if you hadn't been distracted by trying to capture us. To do this, we need to spend time with you. This is why we signed you up for the volunteer work.

We cannot tell you what to do, and we cannot give you clues, and you cannot ask us for clues. So this is going to be EXTREMELY TRICKY. Probably hopeless actually.

But perhaps somehow you will get the message.

If not?

Absolutely catastrophic.

Yours Truly,

Bronte and Alejandro

CHAPTER
51
FINLAY

All I wanted was to figure out the blank bits. The other kids were flinging questions like arrows at Bronte and Alejandro, but I just sat there, squinting at the blank bits.

No use.

Still blank.

So I looked at the bits I could see instead.

"Hold up," I said. "You seem to think that *we* are these 'Children of Spindrift'? What's that mean exactly?"

"I think your history books must have got us mixed up with somebody else," Glim said apologetically.

"The future is utterly dim-witted," Rosalind said. "There are plenty of children in Spindrift! Why do you have to pick on us? Bullies, you are!"

"I guess it might be explained in the blank bits," I said, and Bronte nodded.

"Well, what's all this about the *seven* children, then?" Rosalind crinkled her nose. "Can't count in the future, hm? There are *eight* of us here! Count!"

"No need," Alejandro said agreeably. He was studying a nail that had been hammered crookedly into the side of the cart. He righted this with his thumb and smiled up at Rosalind. "We know it is eight of you here. One of you is *not* a Child of Spindrift, you see? But do not worry, the rest of you are the Children of Spindrift and we do not think it hurts to have an extra."

There was a pause while everyone considered this. Eli swung around to glare, as he still hadn't seen the letter and didn't have any idea what we were on about. Then he swung back and twitched the reins.

"Still, I like a good mystery," Honey Bee put in eventually. "This *J-A* thing. Let's solve it, shall we? You were raised by pirates, you say, Alejandro? Did *they* tell you anything about your parents?"

"It was different stories at different times," Alejandro replied, shrugging just like a pirate. "They found me on an iceberg with a berg troll. The cook emptied out a sack of flour and here comes little Alejandro, tumbling onto the deck. I was woven from the froth of waves. Such things."

"Which?" Hamish asked, confused. "Which is true?"

"*None* is true, you daft git," I said. "Those are *stories* the pirates told him."

Bronte's voice sang out suddenly, above the clatter of the wheels and clip-clop of the horse's hooves: "You seem," she said, "to have missed the point of the letter."

"Oh yes," Honey Bee said. "The Kingdoms and Empires will go topsy-turvy if *we* don't do what we are *supposed* to do. Oh my!"

"But what?" Taya demanded. "What are we supposed to do?"

We all looked at Bronte and Alejandro, and the pair of them stared steadily back at us.

"One thing the genie asked," Bronte began tentatively, "was that you please write up the story of recent happenings. She wants us to bring this writing back to our time so she can read it and pinpoint where things went wrong. In particular, she wants you to tell the story of how the Orphans and the Brathelthwaites started battling?"

"*I* can tell you *that* story," Eli boomed from the driving seat. "It's the story of the Brathelthwaites being toffy-nosed, cheating, prat-headed—"

"*That's* easy to explain," Victor sneered at the same time. "It's because the *orphans* are the poorest, nastiest, dirtiest—"

"From both perspectives," Alejandro interrupted. "You write *both* sides of the story. On paper, I mean. Taking turns."

Victor and Rosalind said they'd never heard anything more ghastly and that they were too rich to pick up pens. Something like that, anyhow. Hamish said, "What ho, chaps, I suppose I could do this! What a lark! Wait, what am I supposed to be writing? A sort of *play* is it?"

So Honey Bee stepped in and said she'd write the Brathelthwaite chapters.

Glim said she'd like to do the orphan's side but she had a stack of mending to do, and the twins said they prefer to *read*, not write, so that's how I ended up with the job. Wanted to make sure the Orphanage got a good showing, didn't I? Glim said she'd help out when she could.

So if anyone other than the genie is reading this and wondering why we are writing it? Now you know. A genie from the future told us to.

Anyhow, we arrived at the Spindrift Junkyard. This is situated on the hills to the north of Spindrift, and it's like a second home to us orphans. We're always up here looking out for bits of treasure, broken toys that we can repair, chipped old pots that you can have fun smashing against rocks. As usual, there was nobody else around, and I suggested we get on with looking through the junk.

"We can take a break in a bit," I suggested, "and try to sort out this crabapple about how these two want us to fix history without actually telling us—"

"Or in any way hinting," Eli put in—he was finally scanning the letter now.

"Or in any way hinting, what it *is* we're supposed to do to fix it."

We grabbed the burlap sacks and set about looking for metal or magic. Right off I could see a broken umbrella, its spokes like silver spider legs, and an old tin watering can behind it. Bits of metal would be easy. Bits of True Magic were unlikely. Not many True Mages come to Spindrift—sometimes people might import a magic-spelled object, or one might wash up on the beach, but neither thing happens often and the object would be too valuable to end up in the junkyard. You can spot the magic in the silver-blue sheen a magic-spelled object will give off if you squint at it.

Behind us, Bronte had drawn off her fancy gloves and Alejandro had pushed up his shirtsleeves, and those two were getting stuck in. The Brathelthwaites were not so quick. Hamish and Honey Bee mostly looked confused, probably never having seen a piece of junk in their lives. Victor and Rosalind were trying to cover their noses with their coats. It doesn't stink so bad though, really.

"You future children are playing some kind of *dreadful* trick on us," Rosalind fretted, trying to step daintily among the rubbish. "A junkyard! And so horribly, *dangerously* close to the dragon lairs! With *orphans*! Don't you know that it is *physically painful* for people like us to spend time with people like them! Bullying, I say!"

Bronte and Alejandro turned to look at her, their eyes widening slowly. Both at once seemed to decide she wasn't worth it, and they carried on scrounging.

But then Bronte paused again. "Dangerously close to dragon lairs?" she asked. Rosalind pointed to a line of yew trees in the distance. You could just see notices pinned to these, flapping in the breeze. KEEP OUT! DRAGON TERRITORY!

"Beyond the yew trees," I explained, "is dragon territory. Nobody's allowed to go past the yew trees."

Bronte and Alejandro stared at where I was pointing, then frowned at me. Honestly, they must be pretty simple in the future.

"The Dragon Peace Treaty?" I said.

Now they both bit their lips. "I think we learned something about that in history class at school?" Bronte hazarded.

Alejandro shrugged. "Often I am looking through the window at the sea in history class," he admitted. "In every class, I mean. So I do not hear a thing."

Honey Bee stepped in then, and told the future kids about the ancient battles between dragons and people in this and the surrounding kingdoms. How dragons used to breathe fire onto crops so that people starved, and then people began working with witches to slaughter dragons, and a trade grew up in dragon skins. Baby dragons were especially popular, for their gemstones, and adult dragons began setting towns alight, plucking people from streets and tossing them away out at sea.

It all led to the great Battle of the Dragons that lasted over twenty years, and ended with the Dragon Peace Treaty.

Dragons promised to live in their territory and never swoop on or set alight our property or crops, and us people promised to leave them be.

"So nobody around here communicates with dragons?" Bronte asked. "Nobody rides them?"

"To ride a dragon! Ho!" Victor laughed hilariously. "Well, of course, the officers of the Dragon Corp ride *Officer* Dragons—the Dragon Corp is under the command of the K&E Alliance and is based far away, in the Travails of Endiva. You do know what an Officer Dragon is?"

Bronte shook her head.

"Oh my. Well, Officer Dragons were bred centuries ago from a few of the most docile dragon babies—they'd been captured by the army. But Officer Dragons are an *entirely* different beast to wild dragons—think of the difference between a placid old Labrador and the fiercest wolf."

"One day," Glim piped up, "*I'd* like to ride an Officer Dragon."

Now Victor laughed so hard he had to clutch his belly. "A little *slip* of an orphan like you!" he crowed. "No, no, Officer Dragons can *only* be ridden by the biggest, strongest men of noble blood. At Brathelthwaite, we have *two* retired Officer Dragons—they can't fly much above shoulder height now—too old—and only a handful of us are permitted anywhere *near* them.

But *Glim* thinks...well...as if an Officer Dragon would ever respect a mere—a *girl*, a mere *orphan* such as—" He couldn't speak for the guffaws.

The twins closed in on him, fists raised.

"Apologize to Glim," Eli commanded.

"Or we'll break you into three thousand pieces," Taya added.

"And throw all the pieces into dragon territory."

"Oh look!" Bronte exclaimed. "Is this a magic-spelled fry pan? Everybody come and see! Over here! Hamish? Come see! I think you'll like this!"

It wasn't magic-spelled, of course. It was just a rusty old frying pan filled with multicolored rubber bands. She was only trying to distract us. It worked. Hamish did not "come see," but he waved politely at Bronte and said, "Thanks! Ho!" And the twins glowered but carried on foraging.

About an hour later, we decided to take a break. Hamish spread out a picnic blanket on the grass, opened a basket, and started laying out cakes, pastries, cherries, and melon. My eyes blurred up a bit, watching this. All we had was a couple of canisters of water and a half loaf of rye.

"It's ready!" Hamish called. "Sit! Eat!"

"Hamish!" Victor spat. "The food is *not* to share with the orphans."

Bronte stared at Victor. "Whyever not?" she asked.

"Because it's *boarding school* food!"

"Oh, you don't have manners in the past?" Bronte said, smooth as silk. "Or is it that they don't teach manners at this boarding school of yours?"

I have to say I was growing proper fond of this Bronte girl. She's a funny one—you can't figure her out. I mean there's the obviously confusing thing about her being from the future, but I'm talking more about her personality. One minute she'll be speaking in a polite, grown-up voice, tidying her braids and checking her reflection in her shiny, shiny shoes; next she'll be chewing her fingernails in a worried way; and then she'll burst out laughing and give Alejandro a *thwack* across the back of his head. Her face seems to move around all the time, trying out different expressions.

Anyway, in the end, we all settled down on the rug to eat, and it was a bit tense, what with orphans accidentally brushing hands against boarders, and vice versa, as we reached for pastries at the same time. Nobody was speaking and the only sounds were the pages of newspapers turning—the twins had brought theirs along, and were reading as usual.

"You know, we still haven't been introduced properly?" Bronte said suddenly. "Maybe you could tell us a bit about yourselves?"

"Yes," Alejandro agreed, spitting out a cherry seed. "This idea is good, Bronte. This could *coax* them towards the fixing of the history. They must think of the talents that could help in the—that could assist with the—"

"With winning the war?" Honey Bee suggested.

Something plucked at the air. We all felt it, a kind of jarring, or a shudder.

"That's the Detection Magic warning us," Bronte explained. "It thinks we're trying to give you hints. Calm down, Detection Magic, we're just getting to know each other. Perfectly innocent. A picnic in the hills by the junkyard. Somebody start talking."

I started. I told her my name is Finlay and my talents are running fast and getting into trouble.

Glim was ducking her head, too shy to speak—she gets like that sometimes. So I did it for her. "And this is Glim. She's also fast and she's a brilliant storyteller."

"Oh, *most* handy," Victor muttered, his nose doing a sneery thing. "I'm sure that *storytelling* is *just* the talent we need to win the war."

The twins rose up from behind their papers. "Glim's stories," said Taya in a voice like a rumbling volcano, "are *excellent*."

"*Beautiful* stories," Eli agreed, like an approaching hurricane. "Suspenseful and interesting."

Taya nodded. "Victor, tell Glim that her stories *could absolutely* win a war, or I will break you into—"

"And these are the twins," I cut in, thinking it'd be a shame if the feast got trampled while the twins broke Victor into 963 pieces. "Eli and Taya. They're good at remembering things, cursing, beating people up, diagnosing fatal illnesses, and reading newspapers."

This worked like a switch. The twins both twitched their noses, quite pleased to be described in this way, and settled back behind their papers again.

It's Lili-Daisy's fault that the twins read papers all the time, by the way.

The pair turned up at the Orphanage when they were six. (Glim and I have been there since we were two.) They'd been living on the streets when a constable found them stealing clothes pegs from a washing line in town.

"We are water sprites," they told him. "Need the pegs for our noses, 'cause we want to dive back home this afternoon."

None of this was true. They are clearly not water sprites. For one thing, water sprites don't need pegs for their noses when they dive. For another thing, the twins are not dead. (Water sprites can't live for more than twenty minutes outside water.)

The constable disputed their claim.

"But we washed up on the Beach with the Yellow Sand," they complained. "So we *must* be water sprites."

"You washed up on the beach? You're probably a pair of pirate children, then. Seems more likely to me. When was this?"

"Seven hundred thirty-two days ago," Taya replied. "We were four."

"Why, that's two years ago!"

"Two years would be seven hundred *thirty* days ago, you daft git," Eli retorted. "She just said seven hundred thirty-two. That's two days more than two years, isn't?"

Never afraid of a thing, those twins, not even constables, and always quite good at arithmetic.

"Well, where had you come from?" the constable tried.

"The sea."

"But *before* the sea? Which pirate ship?"

The twins shrugged. They held up their nails. "All we know," Eli said, "is that our fingernails were an orangey-gold color."

"More a goldy-orange," Taya corrected him.

The constable hmphed. "Rubbish! Your nails are dirty black!"

"Yes, you daft git," Eli agreed. "They're black *now*. But the day that we washed up on the beach, our fingernails were orangey-gold."

"Goldy-orange," Taya muttered.

They were still arguing about this when the constable brought them to the Orphanage and handed them over to Lili-Daisy.

Glim and I loved them right away. They spent their time smashing things and teaching us curse words. It was the best. One day, Lili-Daisy thrust a newspaper in each of their hands. "Here!" she said. "Read! Maybe there'll be a clue in here that will help you remember your pirate parents!"

Since then, the twins have never stopped reading. Lili-Daisy bites her lip guiltily now and then, as she's the one who started their obsession. "Perhaps you should run outside and get some fresh air?" she suggests.

They frown and keep reading.

"The twins have lost their pirate parents," I said, thinking aloud, "and Alejandro's lost his parents because he was *on* a pirate ship. Maybe there's a connection?"

But Alejandro shook his head. "Thank you, Finlay, that is beautiful. Like a poem. But we are not allowed to look for my parents anymore. First we must save the Kingdoms and Empires." He shrugged.

"What about the Brathelthwaite kids?" Bronte asked politely. "Would you like to introduce yourselves too?"

So Victor announced that he was a *duke*, with "too many talents to list," and chuckled. He pointed to Hamish, who was slicing a plum cake, and said that "Hamish is useful in that he's filthy rich and you don't have to look at his face too often, what with it always being behind his hair." (Another chuckle—I've noticed that Victor sometimes disguises his nastiness as jokes.) Rosalind, he said, was "ace at playing a damsel in distress if you needed one," which made Rosalind blush and giggle.

Finally, he turned to look at Honey Bee. After a long moment, he said: "That's Honey Bee. No discernible skills."

Honey Bee also blushed, but in a whole different way—and then Glim spoke up. "Honey Bee is also a great athlete," she said softly, and you should've seen Honey Bee's face now. Open eyes, open mouth, then a grin like she'd just walked into a surprise party.

Bit of an overreaction, I thought.

"Hamish is fast too," I admitted.

"So many athletes!" Bronte said, setting down her teacup in the grass. Now she did a peculiar thing. She started whispering. Loud enough to hear—like a stage whisper, I mean. Not that long ago we'd thought they *were* Whisperers,

I recalled. But of course, actual Whisperers only Whisper in your head. Not aloud like this. "We should *rescue* you all from here," Bronte was shout-whispering, "and take you to the Kingdom and Empire Games!"

Now that was a daft thing to say. The Kingdom and Empire Games have been canceled on account of the war. Plus you have to be eighteen to compete. *Plus* "rescue" was a strange word to use.

"Yes!" Alejandro put in, and he was *also* whispering. "And somebody must *rescue* that teapot. I think it is tipping over."

Rosalind reached out and straightened the pot.

"We should *rescue* that family of mice I saw earlier, living in the log," Bronte whispered.

"Hold up," Hamish said. "Mice are probably perfectly happy in that log."

"I doubt it," Alejandro whispered solemnly. "We should rescue them. And then we should rescue the clouds from the sky."

"Oh, good idea," Bronte hissed, nodding along. "The clouds seem *so unhappy* up there."

I'd had enough. "What are you two *on* about?" I demanded. I mean, I'd been thinking they were all right, the pair from the future, but now they just struck me as loopy.

Glim breathed in sharply. She scooted away a little and beckoned the rest of us to her side. "I think they might be trying to tell us something," she murmured.

"Like what we're supposed to be doing?" Honey Bee agreed, nodding excitedly. "To fix history."

"*Rescuing* someone?" I tried. "They want us to rescue someone. But why the whispering?"

"Maybe to hide from the Detection Magic?"

"Oh, the Detection Magic has very good hearing," Bronte called sunnily. "We would *never* try to defeat it by whispering. We'd *never* try to get around it at all!"

Glim squinted hard, thinking. "It's part of the message," she said. "Maybe we're meant to go to the *Whispering* Kingdom, and rescue—"

"Jaskafar!" the twins and I hissed at the same time.

"You should try rescuing *all* the clouds from the sky," Alejandro shout-whispered. "Not just the one."

Honey Bee dropped the piece of plum cake she was holding. "They mean us to rescue *all* the children from the Whispering Kingdom!" she cried.

And the children from the future disappeared.

CHAPTER 52
HONEY BEE

On the cart ride home, everybody made fun of me for accidentally sending the future children home. Once they'd tired of that, we discussed the idea of rescuing the stolen children from the Whispering Kingdom. At first, we found it exciting—we would be heroes! How wondrous to bring home the lost little orphan boy Jaskafar and free all the other children!

But then we agreed it was ridiculous. If the K&E Alliance Army, Navy, and Dragon Corp had not been able to rescue the children, how could we?

Glim was frowning to herself. "But I think," she said, "that we *are* going to try to rescue the children—because Bronte and Alejandro want to set history on the correct path, right? And when Honey Bee said about the idea of rescuing aloud, it triggered the Detection Magic. So that must *be* our proper path."

"Could be we're supposed to try it and fail dismally," Eli pointed out.

Taya brightened, and punched her twin brother's arm. "Maybe history says we tried and then we all got *slaughtered*! That's what Bronte and Alejandro are up to — getting us back on track to our destinies — "

" — of being *brutally murdered*!" Eli finished.

He laughed uproariously. They both did. They have rather a dark sense of humor, those twins.

That very night, Finlay wrote the first chapter of this story, and sent it along to me on the following morning's milk cart. I returned the second to him with the baker's wagon. We have been exchanging chapters in this way ever since, although on the weekends we meet up in the town square and sit at the outdoor tables there, passing the story back and forth, knocking over several chapters in one swoop. Finlay is very eager to get it "all squared away," and he sets a cracking pace. We hand over the bundle of chapters to Bronte and Alejandro when we see them — they find us in the town square now and then — and they whisk our words back to their genie friend.

Once we reached the first Tuesday of volunteer work in the story, Finlay made a great show of flinging the pen away and dusting off his hands, terribly pleased to be done. However, Bronte apologized.

"The genie insists you carry on describing what's happening," she explained. "You *seem* to be getting on track, she says, but it's still touch-and-go."

"Right bossy one, she is," Finlay muttered, but he obeyed.

As will I now . . .

The second Tuesday morning of volunteer work, we returned to the junkyard.

I apologized for triggering the Detection Magic, and Bronte and

Alejandro were *much* kinder about it than the others had been. Detection Magic is tiresome, they said; they themselves are always tripping over it.

Rosalind arched her eyebrows and said that Bronte and Alejandro ought to learn from the Time Travel Brothers, our fortune-tellers in the town square. "*They* come from the future," she said, "and *they* know how to tell people what's going to happen without vanishing."

This made Bronte and Alejandro laugh. They'd eavesdropped on those particular fortune-tellers, they said, and they were scam artists from the little village of Wasping, which is two hours east of here. They knew nothing of the future. Rosalind got into a sulk then, and refused to do any more collecting, instead lying moodily in the back of the cart. Victor brought her a bunch of grapes from the picnic basket, which cheered her up, although not sufficiently to get her out of the cart.

As we picked through the junk, slowly filling our sacks, we talked in circles about trying to rescue children from the Whispering Kingdom. You could not reach the place by boat because you would be dashed against the rocks, we all agreed. Nor through the Impenetrable Forest because it would scratch you to pieces and throw you out. Nor from the road, because of the Whispering Gates. And nor, finally, from the sky because—well, for one thing, none of us could *fly*, and for another the whole kingdom is enclosed in a witch-made shroud.

Bronte and Alejandro simply nodded along as we talked, which was rather frustrating.

"By Jove, I've got it!" Hamish said next. "If you want to go to the Whispering Kingdom, you simply ask permission of the king! My father and I vacationed there once, years ago. Father was meeting with diamond mine owners, discussing equipment issues for his own mines. They're such a sweet people, always smiling shyly, never cutting their hair—they can hear the whispers of your emotions, you know! To get in, you ask permission of the Whispering King and he says, 'Righto,' then they unlock the three gates and in you pop! Easy!"

We set our sacks down so we could stare at Hamish properly.

"Hamish," I said carefully. "You do know that we're at war with the Whispering Kingdom?"

He nodded enthusiastically.

"And that battles are going on across the Kingdoms and Empires? Which all started because the *Whispering King* stole children from everywhere and formed a *club* with pirates and Shadow Mages?"

"Yes," Hamish agreed. "Nasty business!"

"But you think we can simply call him up and ask for the children back?"

"Worth a try, isn't it?"

Rosalind and Victor were tittering madly, and Glim cut in.

"Hamish is right in a way," she said. "I mean, not that we can call up the king and ask him to let us in. Sorry, Hamish, things have changed since you visited. But it's true that Whisperers *were* always nice people. Look at Snatty-Ra-Ra. Why *have* they changed so much? Why *is* the king acting like this?"

The twins seem to know about current affairs: all their newspaper reading.

"He was always more ambitious than previous monarchs," Eli said, "then his wife died not long after their daughter, the princess, was born. He turned mean and angry then, shutting the gates to the Royal Gardens and canceling the annual Full Moon pageant."

"How old is the princess now?" Finlay asked.

"A teenager."

Bronte cleared her throat and rubbed her nose. Alejandro glanced at her and placed a hand on her shoulder. Something odd was going on there.

"By Jove, this time I *have* got it!" Hamish said suddenly, hair flying around like the mane of a wild horse. "Bronte and Alejandro are from the future! So they must help us figure it out! Let's make a game of it! I *do* like a good parlor game! Bronte and Alejandro, do give us some *clues* about the fut—"

Once again, the future children disappeared.

CHAPTER 53
HONEY BEE

Me again.

Stealing another chapter. I hope Finlay will forgive me. It's just that I *must* tell you about a very strange incident.

On the cart ride home that Tuesday, nobody bothered to make fun of Hamish for accidentally sending the children home. If you teased Hamish for all the daft things he did, you'd never get any sleep. We didn't talk much at *all* that ride, actually. Nothing to say.

The strange thing happened the following Monday. I haven't told anybody this yet, and I'm trusting Finlay to keep it secret.

That Monday morning, I was in mathematics class, and we were doing a test. I quite like mathematics. It's like a big toy to me, where you snap numbers apart, break them into separate pieces, push them around, and click them together again.

Madame Dandelion, our teacher, was sitting at the front of the classroom. She had pushed off her shoes and her stockinged feet were stretched out on her silk-covered stool. She carries this little stool about wherever she goes.

She was sighing, which she does often, as she is a tragic figure. I know this because she tells us. "I am a *tragic figure,* boys and girls, and this is why I sigh — *sigh.*" It also explains why she has to lean back, put her feet up, and file her nails in class. And why she moves about slowly and asks students to go and fetch berries and cigars for her.

The rain was falling heavily outside, and Rosalind was sneezing.

Achoo, achoo (said Rosalind).

25 apples × 3 gold pieces = 75 gold pieces (I wrote). (*Expensive apples!* I thought.)

Achoo, achoo.

95 slices of cake − 62 slices of cake = 33 slices of cake. (*So much cake!* I thought. *Yum!*)

Achoo, achoo, achoo.

I looked up.

2 sneezes + 2 sneezes + 3 sneezes = 7 sneezes. (*A lot of sneezes!* I thought.)

I turned around. Three rows behind me, Rosalind's head was resting on its side on her desk. Her pen was moving very slowly across her paper. She is never a very enthusiastic student, Rosalind, and mathematics is not her thing, but still. Something was wrong.

I looked at Madame Dandelion. She was admiring her own ankles.

Back to Rosalind I turned. *Achoo, achoo,* said Rosalind. Her pen slipped from her fingers. She reached for it, then appeared to give up, and slumped back down.

"Rosalind?" I hissed.

Madame Dandelion sighed. "No cheating," she said.

As if I would cheat by calling across the room for an answer.

As if I would cheat by asking *Rosalind* for an answer.

"Excuse me, Madame Dandelion?" I said. "I am only wondering if Rosalind Whitehall is quite well?"

The moment I said it, there was a rustle of exclamations through the classroom. Everybody seemed to realize all at once: oh yes, Rosalind *has* been sneezing! The children either side of Rosalind glanced at her, then leapt to their feet and scurried away. Others clutched their knees up to their chests as if a mouse were running across the floor. Even Madame Dandelion pressed a palm to her mouth.

Rosalind remained slumped on her desk.

There was a long moment of suspense.

At last, very slowly, Rosalind lifted her face.

GASP!

(That was the sound of us all gasping. In combination, it was like a wave hitting the sand.)

Rosalind's cheeks burned in bright pink spots. Her eyes were bloodshot and squinting. Snot ran in twin green lines from her nostrils.

More children leapt from nearby desks. Everyone stared, aghast.

"What?" Rosalind murmured, her eyes slowly roaming the room.

Madame Dandelion winced.

"You are ill, Rosalind," she said, sounding bossier and less tragic than I'd ever heard her. "I think you have this terrible flu. You must go to the infirmary at *once*."

Rosalind smiled and wiped the back of her hand across her face. The snot smeared. It was streaked in blood.

"Ew," said Victor.

"EWW!" agreed several other members of the class.

Rosalind blinked. "No, thank you, Madame Dandelion," she muttered. "I'm happy here in bed." Her head clunked back onto the desk.

"Golly," Hamish said. "She thinks she's in bed! Or have I got that wrong?"

Madame Dandelion's eyes rushed around the room. They landed on me.

"You there!" She clicked her fingers at me. Again, she was not at all tragic. "Honey Bee. Take her to the infirmary!"

There was a strange sound from Rosalind's desk. "Oh, and hooray and merry days for me!" It was a song. Rosalind was *singing*.

"Take her at once!" Madame Dandelion urged. "Cut through the teachers' wing!"

I must admit I hesitated. I knew Rosalind needed urgent medical help, but I did *not* want to catch that flu. Now Rosalind coughed. The children closest to her shrieked.

"Go *on*!" Madame Dandelion cried. "Get her out of here! Now!"

I hurried to Rosalind's side, hoisted her out of her desk, propped my arm around her shoulder, and half carried her from the classroom.

Cut through the teachers' wing, Madame Dandelion had instructed.

But I paused at the entrance to the teachers' wing.

For a student to enter that wing is frowned upon at usual times. It is *positively outlawed* nowadays. The wing is being used by the codebreakers from the Top Secret Military Division. "It is an honor to have them here!" Sir Brathelthwaite tells us at breakfast each day. "We are doing our duty in this war!"

Hm, I think. *Pretty easy duty, to have people moving around in the teachers' wing looking after their own food, cleaning, and laundry, and staying well away from us.*

Nevertheless, Sir Brathelthwaite is awfully proud. "They have asked us not to disturb their secret work," he warns each morning. "And we shall *not* disturb their work! It is our great and noble duty not to disturb them!"

This is why I paused.

On the one hand, I wanted to do my great and noble duty and not disturb them.

On the other hand, going through the teachers' wing would take me directly to the infirmary. Going *around* it meant stepping out through the side door into the garden, skirting around the fountain, and climbing the back stairs.

Rosalind snored quietly onto my shoulder.

"Oh dear," I dithered.

"Do you think I'll be a singing star one day?" Rosalind asked suddenly, her voice muffled by my uniform. "Probably I will. They'll throw flowers on the stage! I will swim through the flowers to the grasshopper's waltz and blow bubbles into *all* of the zucchini. Not just some of it, mind. All of it."

Oh my, I thought. *She's completely delusional.*

Rosalind cannot sing a note.

Into the teachers' wing we went.

At first, the corridor was empty, and I clumped along, half dragging

Rosalind past several closed doors. MUSIC TEACHERS' STAFF ROOM, said the sign on one door. CONFERENCE ROOM, said the next.

Then I passed a door that was slightly ajar. I glanced inside. I could not help it. Men and women were gathered around a large table. Mostly strangers, but I spotted our local constable, Rachel Rally—the one I'd seen Spellbinding the queen's guard. *She must be learning codebreaking too*, I thought. I peered at the table and saw the most peculiar thing! It was covered in *looms*. The kind that you use to weave nets! I caught glimpses of hands moving swiftly, pieces of twine crossing back and forth.

Gosh, I thought.

The next door was wide open.

"Slice the dandelions finely," a woman's voice said, loud and clear. "Then add a handful of pink peppercorns and a quart of boiled water."

Oh my, I thought.

The next two doors were closed, but I could hear men's and women's voices in each. They were chanting a verse.

I began to feel extremely uneasy.

Who *were* these people? We had been told that they were codebreakers. But don't codebreakers try to break codes? What were they doing weaving nets, chopping up dandelions, and chanting poetry?

No wonder they insisted on *not being disturbed*!

"Come on," I hissed at Rosalind. She had nestled her head onto my shoulder as if I was a pillow, and her legs were beginning to sink towards the floor. "Rosalind! Please!"

At that moment, a door opened, just down the corridor ahead of me. A woman stepped out, smiling to herself as if something amusing had just happened. She was large, maybe in her twenties, with bright eyes and a great swoop of hair bundled together with a silver clip.

She stopped. Her smile fell. Her eyes flew from my face to Rosalind's drooping form and back again.

"I'm ever so sorry to be in the teachers' wing," I croaked. "It's just—"

"Your friend is ill," the woman declared. Her voice was big and sure. "You are taking her to the infirmary?"

I nodded.

"Here, let me help," she said, and she swept Rosalind into her arms and set off down the hall.

I hurried after her. "I think she has this influenza that's going around," I babbled. "I hope you don't—"

Catch it, I was going to say, but the woman sang over her shoulder, "Don't worry about me! Constitution of a horse! Never catch a thing!"

She swung through the doors at the end of the corridor, kicked open the entry to the infirmary, and deposited Rosalind in the nearest empty bed. Five other beds were already taken by coughing, tossing, turning children. Down at the end of the room, I saw the curtain that hid Carlos from me. He had been "quarantined," the nurse had told me, and I was not allowed to visit anymore.

"Another one for you!" the woman called, and the school nurse straightened, taking a thermometer from a child's mouth.

"*Thank* you," she replied, rather bitterly.

We stepped out of the infirmary.

"Other than a ball," the woman said to me.

I stared up at her. We had paused at the back entrance to the teachers' wing.

Other than a ball.

Was this code? Was she testing me to see if *I* could be a codebreaker?

The woman grinned. "A moment ago, I told you that I never catch a thing," she explained. "Just wanted to clarify that I *can* catch balls. My hand-eye coordination is quite good. Love a good game of catch."

"Oh!" I exclaimed. "Of course! Well, me too! Although track and field is more my thing. But I do like basketball. I'm tall, you see, which helps—I mean, tall for my *age*. Obviously. Not tall compared to *you*. Not that you are *too* tall—"

I was babbling again. Frightened of the Top Secret Military Division and the fact that I was *disturbing* it. The woman, meanwhile, was staring at me fiercely, as if trying to figure out how anyone could be so very foolish.

"May I know your name, child?" she asked.

I blinked. "Honey Bee."

"Honey Bee!" She beamed, and then became serious again. "Honey Bee, if you ever need to speak to me, knock on any of the doors in here and ask for Carabella. In the meantime, will you do something for me?"

I stared.

"Around nine o'clock tonight," she continued, "when the moon is full and high in the sky?"

I nodded, hardly breathing. Was I to run a secret errand? Perhaps become a spy! Help win the war!

The woman's head turned quickly from side to side as she checked nobody was nearby. Then she lowered her voice and hissed, "Look at your toenails!"

And strode back into the teachers' wing.

I decided she was mad.

I knew that codebreakers were intelligent people, and I also knew that intelligent people can be a touch unhinged. I think it's because their brains do so much jumping about solving puzzles. When there's no puzzle to solve, they don't know where to jump.

This woman had jumped onto my toenails. (In a sense.)

Still. I did have a quick look. Honestly, who wouldn't?

At nine o'clock that night, I was in the green common room reading a novel. Ordinarily, I'd have been asleep by nine, but the dormitories were being disinfected and we had all been sent to the common rooms in our dressing gowns. A few other students were also reading, some were chatting, and some, including Victor, were playing board games. Hamish was on the same couch as me, trying to balance a stack of cushions on his palm. That is the kind of game Hamish likes to play. The stack kept toppling and he kept exclaiming and starting again.

Moonlight traced the edges of the blackout curtains.

Well, I thought, *it's nine o'clock, and the moon is full and high in the sky! Let's do this thing!*

I pushed off my slippers. There were my bare feet. I studied my toenails.

Perfectly ordinary toenails.

But then, as I watched, they turned blue.

Every single one. The color of a summer sky.

I caught a faint sound and turned. Hamish, beside me, had stopped juggling cushions and was staring at my feet.

"Do us a favor," said a voice—and both Hamish and I looked up sharply. It was Victor. He had swiveled in his seat at his chess game. "Do us a favor, Hamish, and fetch some cinnamon toast from the kitchen, would you?"

Hamish leapt up from the couch. "Of course!" he said. "Brilliant idea,

Victor! I'll be right on it." As he spoke, he dropped a tumble of cushions to the floor and, with his left foot, kicked them over my toes.

A little later, when I tipped the cushions away, my toenails were their regular color again.

CHAPTER 54
FINLAY

And then what happened?!

You can't end it there, Honey Bee.

DO YOU EVEN KNOW WHAT BLUE TOENAILS MEAN, YOU DAFT GIT??!

WHY HAVE YOU NOT TOLD ME THIS BEFORE??

Did you tell your codebreaker friend?

CHAPTER 55
HONEY BEE

Oh.

Yes, well, early the next morning I did sneak into the teachers' wing and knocked on a door. I thought it might interest the big woman to know that my toenails had turned blue. A friendly man appeared, coffee mug in hand, and I asked if I might speak to Carabella, please.

"I'm awfully sorry," he said, "but she's been called away on an urgent mission."

"Never mind," I replied, turning away and almost colliding with Darby from the kitchen, who was carrying a tray of caramel tarts.

"With the compliments of Sir Brathelthwaite," Darby said. "Treats for the codebreakers' morning tea."

The man looked quite crestfallen and said, "Oh blow, I love caramel tarts, but we're under strict instructions not to accept gifts of any kind. Will you tell Sir Brathelthwaite we appreciate the thought and respectfully decline?"

Darby nodded politely and swung about, while I myself hurried off to our volunteer duty.

On this Tuesday, Mayor Franny sent us to the Beach with the Yellow Sand for our volunteer work, instructing us to half fill burlap bags with sand. Apparently, the soldiers were building sandbag walls around our town.

We did not take the cart but walked, each carrying bags and spades. As soon as we arrived at the boardwalk, Alejandro dropped his spade with a clatter, tore off his shoes and socks, and ran down the sand to the water. The beach was empty—tourists had stopped coming, of course, what with the war and the hotels being full of soldiers—and the others laughed at him, then set to work shoveling sand. But Bronte and I paused to watch Alejandro.

He had rolled up his trousers and was splashing about in ankle-deep water, the sunlight shining on his dark hair.

"He grew up on a pirate ship," Bronte explained, "so he misses the smell of seaweed and salt, the sound of sails in the wind, the shouts of pirates, the swell of the sea."

How poetic she was!

"He's always wanting to talk about wind directions and the mechanics of firing a cannon," she added, "which I find completely insufferable."

Oh, less poetic.

But then Bronte lowered her voice: "He's confused, you see, because the sea runs in his veins and in some ways he loved the pirates who raised him — but when he was a child he didn't know what wicked things pirates *do*, and that shames him, and he's afraid of his memories because they were cruel to him."

Alejandro had crouched down and was trailing his hands through the water.

"To make matters more complicated," Bronte concluded, "he now knows he had parents all along, who have been sad without him."

I nodded, seeing how bewildering all this must be for Alejandro.

"And yet you are supposed to set aside the search for his parents and help us back onto the path to our destinies!" I said. "What a nuisance for you!"

Bronte gave a sudden smile and shrugged.

"Horizon still looks straight enough to me," she said, gazing out to sea. "Maybe the genie was wrong? Or maybe you're on the right track?" She raised her hand and held it level, testing it against the horizon. I did the same beside her. But it's hard to keep your hand perfectly straight.

We giggled at ourselves and looked back at Alejandro, who had stripped down to his underclothes and was diving into the waves!

I blushed, but to my surprise, Bronte went pelting down the sand, stripped down to her shift, and joined him.

So I took a sack and set to work filling it with sand. As I shoveled, I felt a small gust of loneliness blowing through my chest. Bronte and Alejandro seemed such great friends! It made me long for *my* friend Carlos to be well again. Imagine if he were working alongside me now, calling jokes to the others, perhaps running to swim himself! In fact, in some faint way, Alejandro reminded me of Carlos.

But I did not dwell on my loneliness. I shoveled my heart out.

After a while, clouds darkened the sky and it began to rain. Hamish called to everyone, "Hey ho, what say we pop into the Brathelthwaite Beach Hut for our morning tea?"

We all crowded inside and gathered around the little table, shaking rain droplets away. As usual, Hamish began setting out the contents of our picnic basket.

Also as usual, there was squabbling between us boarders and the orphans. At least Rosalind was absent today, so the snide comments were largely from Victor.

Eventually, Bronte asked us all to please shut it as we were giving her a headache. The conversation turned back to how to rescue children from the Whispering Kingdom, which led to the usual sighing about the impossibility of getting in.

Then a voice spoke up.

It was the girl twin, Taya. "*Whisperers* know how to get into the Whispering Kingdom," she said.

The boy twin punched his sister's arm. I've noticed that he doesn't like it when people say obvious things.

"What if we get *a Whisperer* to take us there," Taya explained, rubbing her arm.

Now her brother's eyebrows lifted. "Let them steal us, you mean?"

"We're kids, aren't we?" Taya shrugged. "They take kids."

"Brilliant," Eli declared.

We stared at the twins in wonder, and that's when the warning bells began to ring.

CHAPTER 56
FINLAY

CLANG-CLANG-CLANG.
    CL-CL-CLANKETY-CLANG-CLANG.
CLANG-CLANG-CLANG.

    CL-CL-CLANKETY-CLANG-CLANG.

That's how the warning bells sounded.

More or less.

"Witches," said the twins right away. I was still trying to figure out the warning-bell code, but the twins remember everything.

Gasp! That was Glim. She'd gone to the window and her forehead was pressed to the glass. I joined her there. Everyone did. It was a right crush. I was flattened like a slug beneath a cartwheel.

A coven of witches was marching along the beach through the rain.

Every witch held a broom high in the left hand, while making the *loop, loop, up-and-over* movements of broomstick crochet with the right.

"Empire of Witchcraft," somebody muttered.

"No time to get to a shelter," somebody else put in.

"They're doing broomstick crochet!" a third exclaimed.

I don't know how much experience you've had with witches. They're a wicked lot. Asthma is common, so they're always hacking and coughing. They don't wear black hats, by the way: that's a rumor that started because they sort of *wear* their cats like scarves, slung around their necks. *Black cat* sounds a lot like *black hat* if you say it fast. Try it.

They also usually wear pale brown colors, beads around their necks, socks with sandals. They look pretty harmless. And witches *are* pretty harmless—if they're on their own and you don't catch their eye.

But when they're marching in covens, doing broomstick crochet?

You're in trouble.

Because broomstick crochet is how they cast their Shadow Magic.

"Stay down," someone hissed.

We all crouched low and slunk away from the window. The bells had stopped ringing, and we could hear our own nervous breathing.

Outside, there was the eerie scuffing of hundreds of witches marching. Their hands moved fast and smooth and in perfect synchronicity.

> *Loop, loop, up and over;*
> *loop, loop, up and over;*
> *loop, loop, up and over.*

I had no clue what spell they were casting. Everything outside seemed normal. I mean, the beach was full of marching, crocheting witches. *That* wasn't normal. The rain had stopped. The ocean was placid. Moored boats bobbed around, making quiet *plash* sounds.

Not knowing what the spell *was* made things even scarier.

The coven moved slowly but steadily in the direction of our hut. Now and then, a cat yowled.

"Should we close the curtains?" Hamish shout-whispered.

I'd been thinking the same thing. We didn't want the witches looking in and seeing us, but then again we also didn't want—

"No, you daft git," Victor murmured. "The movement will attract their attention."

Daft gift seemed harsh. "Hang on," I began.

"Everyone stay perfectly quiet," Glim whispered.

"Starting with *you*, Glim," Victor sneered. "You're making more noise telling us to *be quiet* than we already were."

Again, this was harsh. Glim's voice is so soft it's like a breeze.

"Okay, take it easy everyone," I said, trying to take charge.

"*You* take it easy," Victor spat.

There was a deep sigh. I turned around and the future kids were sitting side by side on the couch, watching us.

I felt a bit testy with them, to be honest. It was like they'd decided their job was to be the *grown-ups*. They might have been from the future, but they were still practically the same age as us. No need to act superior.

"What, so nobody ever argues where you're from?" Honey Bee demanded. She must have been feeling the same way.

But we didn't get to hear if people argued in the future, because Bronte and Alejandro had both turned white and they were pointing straight at the window.

A line of witches stared in at us, faces expressionless.

Loop, loop, up and over, went their hands.

CHAPTER
57
HONEY BEE

If you have ever been pushed down the stairs and landed with a *thump* on your stomach so that the air *bursts* out of you, leaving none to breathe, then you will know how I felt as I looked at the witches.

Rows of witches extending back as far as I could see along the beach, the front row *as close to me as the length of my arm*.

Through the glass, I could see the pale gray of one man's eyebrows, the mole on another man's cheek. A woman's chapped lips. Their eyes stared steadily into mine. But their hands carried on, working their broomstick crochet, winding around and around, up and over the handle of the broomstick, around and around, up and over.

What spell are they casting? What spell? I wanted to scream the question. The air in the hut seemed to *froth* with the question.

But we all stayed perfectly silent, staring back out.

And then, as one, the witches turned away. Slowly, they marched again, scuffing sand along. Their faces remained blank, but I caught a slight twitch in one woman's mouth, a tiny smile, a smirk.

Their broomsticks were still held aloft, and their hands still moved in the same quick, smooth motions, but off they went, along the beach, away from us.

We rushed to the opposite window to watch. The coven carried on without pausing, climbed onto the boardwalk, and disappeared around the coastal curve.

"They've gone?" Hamish breathed. "Perhaps they didn't cast a spell at *all*? I mean, nothing is happening, is it? Perhaps it was just a sort of *show*!"

"Perhaps," I agreed, but I was thinking of that witch's smirk.

For a long moment, we were silent, looking back and forth between windows, watching the empty beach.

And then, before our eyes, the spell took effect.

CHAPTER 58
FINLAY

Must have been some wicked Shadow Magic they'd cast, those witches.

I've seen witches' spells before. They favor embarrassment spells, such as making people run into the streets in their pajamas while flapping their arms like frightened geese. Or nasty spells like making trees fall across paths so they snap people's legs. But this was a different level.

The sand was shifting. In every direction along the beach, all the way down to the water, it was collapsing in on itself.

As we watched, giant dips and craters formed, as if dug by huge, invisible spades. Sand was flung up out of these holes and formed hillocks that collapsed into holes themselves. The beach roiled and turned, like the ocean in a storm.

It made me seasick to watch. I reached a hand back to steady myself on the table. Honey Bee was tilting sideways too, and Glim had her hands out to keep herself balanced.

Strange, I thought, *how we're all being so affected just* watching—

My eyes caught Alejandro's. He was frowning to himself, and right at the same time, we understood.

"GET OUT!" we shouted, in unison. "WE HAVE TO GET OUT OF HERE NOW!"

CHAPTER 59
HONEY BEE

The beach hut was sinking.

We flew to the door all at once, everyone yelling, but there were too many of us. The doorway was jammed. I turned back, wrenched open a window, and made to climb out—but where was the beach? A chasm was forming directly beneath the window, and forming so fast that the hut was tilting into it, capsizing. I was flung against the window frame and clung to it, desperate not to fall out.

Glim turned back from the doorway and saw me. She skidded down the slanting floor and helped pry me away. Between us, we managed to clamber up to the open door and throw ourselves outside.

We landed on a firm patch of sand just as the hut slid into the gaping hole.

The others were there too, a tight little crowd, panting and trembling. The twins cursed magnificently. Sand blew on the wind and stung our eyes. The beach had stopped roiling now, but we were surrounded by hundreds of plungingly deep pits.

"It's like honeycomb!" cried Hamish. "The beach is *honeycombed* with holes. Now, I tell you, what I wouldn't give for some honeycomb right now.

Love the stuff. Find it calms me down in a crisis, wouldn't you agree, every-one? Honeycomb?"

"Never tasted it," Eli said, sounding fierce.

"And if you do not shut your mouth about *honeycomb*," Taya put in, "I will—"

"How are we going to get off the beach?" Finlay interrupted. "The board-walk looks all right, but there are too many holes between here and there."

"And the spaces between the holes, they are too narrow," Alejandro agreed.

"It's like the beach is a piece of paper," Glim said, "and somebody has cut out so many sections there are only flimsy bits of paper left between."

"Thank you," Victor said coldly, "for wasting our time with your terribly helpful analogies."

Glim pretended not to hear. "If we tried to walk along the thin bits," she continued, "they might collapse into the pits."

"The pits look *awfully* deep," Hamish said, shuddering. "I wouldn't want to fall into one. Even if I *did* have some honeycomb."

The twins growled at him.

"I think if you fell, the sand would collapse in and suffocate you," Bronte observed. "Look what's happened to the hut."

Carefully, we swiveled to peer down at the beach hut. It had vanished. Buried in sand now, only a corner of the roof visible. Along the beach, most of the other huts had also disappeared. So had our spades and all the sand-bags we'd filled. So much for all that work!

"Should we just wait until the Spellbinders come?" I wondered. "They'll reverse the spell."

"But where *are* the Spellbinders?" Finlay wondered back. "I think the witches might have overcome them."

"Can't stay here," Eli grunted. "This isn't stable either."

"I'm not walking on that sand," Victor announced. "We must simply wait."

Glim's eyes became dreamy. "If we could only fly," she began, but Victor grunted angrily.

"Oh, *Glim* and her *flying* again," he complained. "You really are a tiresome girl. Could you *please* get it *into* your *head* that you will *never, ever* fly?"

There was a silence. The waves crashed onto the shore. Boats creaked out at sea. I took a deep breath.

"I think," I said, "that we must form a human chain."

CHAPTER
60
FINLAY

So that's what we did.

We argued first, of course. Some people, such as Victor, thought we should stay put until Spellbinders came. Some, such as me, thought it was too dangerous to wait because the sand could fall from beneath us any moment. Then Victor refused to hold "an orphan's hand" and kept swatting Honey Bee's and Hamish's hands away from ours, saying, "Germs! Careful! Germs!"

In the end, Bronte and Alejandro formed the link between us.

Fair play to them for hanging around, by the way. They could've vanished themselves into the future at any point during the witch attack, but they stayed it out.

It was a long, long trek along the thin bridges of sand, and even with the future kids between us, we had to trust each other. We skirted holes as their edges slipped and crumbled. More than once, someone skidded downwards, screaming, and the rest of us dragged them out. Honey Bee's shoe slipped off and tumbled into a hole, and we all watched as the sand turned itself over, swallowing the shoe. Our hands were clasped together so tightly that our palms bled from the clutch of fingernails. You could see the muscles in everyone's arms tensing. My muscles were a fair bit more pronounced than Victor's, by the way. I happened to notice that.

We made it.

Obviously we did or we wouldn't be here telling this story. Still. Thinking back now, I can't believe it.

Once we'd collapsed onto the boardwalk, nobody made a sound. We just sort of flopped, and the wood felt good, warm and steady.

"Oh," said a tiny voice, and I looked up. Honey Bee was staring at the beach. The roiling and rolling had started up again with vigor. Sand piles shifting, sinking, and re-forming.

The patch of sand we'd been standing on had *disappeared entirely.*

"Told you so," I *really, really* wanted to say to Victor.

But I showed strength of character and didn't.

CHAPTER 61
HONEY BEE

We stared at the beach as it tossed and billowed like a great beast trying to get comfortable.

"It's like the rules of nature are broken," Eli said. "Like when the currents of the Starling Ocean ran west-east instead of east-west six years ago."

"What makes you think we need a geography lesson?" Victor demanded.

Eli shrugged. "Read about it in a paper once."

"Could we go back to town now?" Glim wondered. "Or would the witches' spell have affected other areas?"

A chill washed over me as I imagined the town square and streets dipping and folding, homes and shops crashing into bottomless pits.

At that moment, several dragons swept over us.

"It's the Dragon Corp!" Hamish cried. "They've come to Spindrift!"

We all looked up, skeptical, but sure enough, there were *people* riding the dragons! Officers! Big, burly men in crash helmets and armor. One hovered low and called out gruffly: "Everyone all right down here?" We gave him thumbs-up signals, and he wheeled around and flew away with the others.

Victor chuckled. "There you go, Glim," he said. "That's the closest you'll ever get to riding a dragon. A glimpse of a *proper* officer."

Both the future children made curious sounds—Bronte's sound was like an angry scowl come to life. But Glim turned to the pair and spoke shyly. "I know you can't tell me about the future," she said, "but is it *possible* that regular people—not just officers—can fly dragons there?"

Bronte bit her lip, frowning.

"Well," Alejandro began.

The air vibrated sternly and the future children vanished.

"Now look what you've done," Victor said, rolling his eyes. "You *are* tiresome, Glim."

"Oi!" the twins said simultaneously, both stepping up to Victor. Finlay also raised his fists, and suddenly everyone was bellowing.

That was when I saw him.

At the far end of the beach, moving along the boardwalk, was a young man. Even from this distance, it was clear he was walking oddly.

A slow dawdle, little skip, slow dawdle, little skip.

"Golly!" Hamish exclaimed. "Whoever is that?"

The others dropped their argument to squint into the distance.

As we watched, the young man stopped. He gazed out to sea.

He coughed. It was one of those dreadful, deep coughs, like the bark of a walrus. It echoed.

The man's body shook and he sneezed. He wiped his hand across his face and his mouth opened: "Hey ho! Hey ho!" A little wiggle.

"Good gracious!" Hamish said. "He's singing! And what is that, a dance of some kind?"

Another chill ran through me. I thought of Rosalind. The sneezing. The singing.

The young man had the influenza.

And then, as we stared, he stepped jauntily off the boardwalk and down onto the rolling, turning beach.

CHAPTER 62
FINLAY

Honey Bee took off first.

She was tearing along the boardwalk while the rest of us gawked in amazement.

Why would he go *down to the sand*?

What, is he *mad*?

That's the sort of thing I was thinking.

Then the rest of us were running too, sprinting and pounding along.

Honey Bee was already skidding onto the sand herself, which was daft-gittish of her, but you could tell she hadn't stopped to think. Just hurtled after the fellow. She grabbed ahold of his hand and started pulling, but he shook her off. I caught sight of his face. He was smiling in a friendly way and trying to head farther down the beach like someone on a picnic. Next I caught sight of Honey Bee's face, and it was not friendly. She was gritting her teeth, wrapping her arms around him, and *dragging*.

The rest of us were on the edge of the boardwalk, screaming: "GET BACK HERE! COME BACK! GET OFF THE BEACH!"

The young man turned and gave us a cheery wave. Barmy.

Right about then, the sand at his feet began to crumble and he swayed in place a moment, looked down, saw himself sinking, and *finally* figured it out.

"I'm *terribly* sorry," he said, stumbling back and turning to Honey Bee. His voice was loud and clear. "I do not mean to offend you, but this seems a trifle *unsafe* as a holiday destination, wouldn't you say? Got any better suggestions?"

Honey Bee, to give her credit, did not sock him in the mouth. She got a firmer grip on his arm, gave a mighty tug, and half dragged him back up the slope and onto the boardwalk.

There he stood, swaying and beaming around. "At any rate," he began—and he collapsed. Head hit the board with a thud.

"He's got the influenza," Honey Bee said, panting. "Somebody fetch him a doctor."

CHAPTER
63
HONEY BEE

He looked *dreadful*.

I mean, you could see he was *handsome* with his black hair and his fine cheekbones, but that was rather in the background. In the foreground was his scrawny neck, the pale purple color that washed over his face, and his glowing white lips. I never knew lips could be white! Blood trickled out of these lips, scarlet by contrast. When I touched his forehead, it was so clammy that I wiped my hand on my skirt.

Finlay and Glim raced off towards town to fetch a doctor—I hoped that was what they were doing, anyway—and the rest of us hovered around the sick man.

"Golly," Hamish said. "Is he dead? I mean to say, he looks *thoroughly* dead to me, and he's *perfectly* still. Wouldn't that suggest that he is dead? What do we—I mean to say, what does one *do* in this situation? When one finds a dead man?"

"Stay away from him, for a start," Victor snapped, sounding a little ill himself. "We're no use to him if we catch it."

Which was nonsense, because you don't catch influenza *instantly*. It would take effect in a day or two, giving us plenty of time to be useful to the young man. However, I let that go.

"Move aside," the twins instructed, and they elbowed their way into place. One held the man's wrist, the other studied his chest. They both patted his cheeks lightly, and each lifted an eyelid.

"He's got a pulse," one twin said. "Faint."

"He's still breathing," said the other. "Just."

Taya's head rested against the man's chest. "Serious rattle, though," she said.

Eli took his turn listening. "Double pneumonia." He nodded. "And he's dehydrated. Anyone got water?"

"We would *scarcely* have water," Victor sneered. "Our picnic is *buried* in the *hut* in the *sand*. Did you *forget* that little *detail*? For goodness' sake, this is—"

Hamish stepped forward, drawing a flask from his pocket. "Here you go! Always carry my water bottle about! Never know *when* I might get thirsty!"

Eli pulled his sleeve over his hand and gently wiped the blood from the man's mouth. Taya opened the bottle and let a few drops fall onto his lips.

We did nothing then. The beach had settled down again, and I began to worry about how many holes might have formed on the road into town. What if Finlay and Glim had fallen into one? Before long, however, the pair appeared in the distance, jogging along the boardwalk with a young woman.

"Oh good," Eli said. "Anita."

"She's our schoolteacher," Taya told me. "Also a doctor-in-training."

"Thank you so much, Taya!" I cried. She frowned. It *was* rather odd for me to thank her, but I was excited that she had spoken an ordinary sentence to me—one without a threat to *break* some part of me.

This Anita was tiny and spry, her black eyes filled with spark. A medical kit swung from her hand, and she pelted the last few steps, fell to her knees, skidded along, and opened the kit, all in one smooth move. It rather took your breath away.

After examining the patient, she unclasped the top button of his shirt and her sparky eyes darted around in thought. She appeared to make a decision, drew a bottle from the kit, pried open the young man's lips, and tipped in a few drops.

"What's in the bottle?" Eli asked.

Anita turned to him. "Store-bought Faery potion. This influenza going around, I think it's *more* than influenza. I think it's witch-made."

Witch-made influenza?

My dearest Carlos had *witch-made influenza*? But in that case, he'd *never* get well! (Nor would Rosalind—oh dear, I reminded myself quickly.)

"Do the doctors at the hospital agree with you?" Finlay asked.

"No, they think it's regular influenza," Anita admitted. "But they humor me and let me give the patients a little Faery potion. It can't hurt them—but it's not fresh-made, so it'll never cure a witch-made flu. You'd need Faeries to administer it. Still, it eases the symptoms."

She straightened and watched the young man's face. "He needs to be in the hospital," she said. "Who'll help me carry him?"

All except Victor agreed. We gathered around the young man, ready to lift.

Before we had done so, however, Anita stopped and stared at the man's face again. Unexpectedly, she grinned. "You know who you've rescued, don't you?" she asked.

We blinked.

"The prince," she said. "This is Prince Jakob. I recognize him from his official royal portrait. All right, on three, we lift. One, two—"

"Here!" Victor leapt forward. "Perhaps I *will* help after all."

CHAPTER 64
FINLAY

Turned out, the prince had climbed out of his fancy hotel bed and wandered onto the boardwalk. His royal entourage had been distracted, watching the witch coven through the windows.

I thought the queen might give us diamond-crusted medals or something for saving her son, but she was busy with the war. She only sent a little note card. *My heartfelt thanks*, it said. Heartfelt is all very well, but it's not diamonds.

Spindrift was wrecked by the witch attack.

Plenty of streets had folded themselves up same way the beach did, scaring the heck out of everyone, even our meanest local pirates.

Our buddy Ronnie lost his art supplies down a pit in the town square. The grocer lost a cartload of cantaloupes. A cantaloupe is not my favorite melon, so I was okay with that, although I heard that the grocer cried. She loved her cantaloupes.

Avril had trouble running to shelter on account of her old ankle injury.

Got hit by a stack of falling shovels from a display outside the hardware store. Cracked three of her ribs.

Also, seven people died falling into the holes, twenty-five were seriously injured, and a lot of families lost their homes.

I said that bit fast, not wanting to think about it.

I didn't know any of the people who died, but I saw plenty of folk crying into their handkerchiefs. It gets you down, that. Men with red eyes, women being hugged and comforted. The sounds of grown-ups sobbing.

Gets *me* down, anyhow.

It turned out that the witch coven *had* taken down our Spellbinders when they arrived in town, using an imprisonment spell on them. By the time the Spellbinders shook off the witch chains and rushed to bind the witch spell, the damage had been done.

The whole town has been angry ever since, arguing about why we don't get *more* Spellbinders, *better*, more powerful Spellbinders.

Fed up, everyone is. Had enough of the Whispering Wars. Novelty completely worn off.

CHAPTER 65
HONEY BEE

One week later, our fourth Tuesday, Mayor Franny sent us to the hospital for our volunteer work.

Finlay is right. *We are* all a bit flat. Not literally flat—we have not been run down by a steamroller. I only mean that nobody is in the mood for much of anything these days. And that fourth Tuesday—which was only a few days ago—was no exception.

Spindrift Hospital is in the north of the town. It is four floors high with a huge basement, concrete stairs, a creaking lift, and slowly turning ceiling fans. The basins have taps that *screech* when you turn them on, and *screech* again when you turn them off. Never happy, those taps.

The matron snapped at us when we arrived. "Can't think what help *you* lot are going to be," she complained, and then she gave us a long list of tasks. We were to roll bandages, mop floors, mix medicines, put wildflowers in vases to "pretty the place up," and carry trestle beds up from the basement.

"Seems to me we can be a *lot* of help." Finlay whistled, reading the list, but the matron only shooed us away, muttering that she was "busy enough as it *was*, thank you very much."

It was rather distressing being in the hospital. Some wards were cheerful: beds up against the windows, patients sitting cross-legged doing crossword puzzles or playing cards with other patients. Other wards, however, were miserable. Patients who had been seriously injured in the war lay staring at the ceiling, moaning softly, chinks of metal melted into their skin. Or they cried out in pain and then quickly apologized for being a nuisance.

One ward was full of people who had lost their laughter in a sterling silver fox attack, and a doctor was doing exercises with them to try to bring it back. Awful gargling sounds they were making, nothing like laughter at all, and their faces were grayish-blue.

The top floor was dedicated to the influenza. I helped Alejandro to carry a trestle bed all the way from the basement to this floor—we used the lift so it was not as bad as that might seem—and it was noisy with coughing, sneezing, and sniffling.

In one bed was Lili-Daisy Casimati, the Orphanage director—the twins had ignored all the matron's instructions and were taking special care of her. She did not look well!

In another bed, the prince lay flat, eyes closed. He looked a little better than he had the day we rescued him but was still gaunt and pale, and we could hear his wheeze even as the lift door opened. As we watched, a little child in a bed near the prince's began to cry for her mother, and at once the prince sat up. "Hush," he said—or croaked, rather. "It'll be all right." And he began to sing—or croak—softly for the child.

Anita, the schoolteacher/trainee doctor, appeared out of nowhere, darting between beds.

"No, no!" she scolded, pressing him back into his bed. "You are ill! You must *rest*. It is very good of you to try to cheer the little ones, but you must *rest*."

The prince smiled faintly, arguing, "I'm fine!" but his head fell back against his pillows. When Anita turned away, I think I saw tears in her eyes.

Behind the hospital there is a courtyard where patients can sit and take the sun. After a couple of hours of work, the matron sent us out there for a break. "Better off without *you* lot underfoot," she complained.

We sat around a table, watching some of the healthier patients digging a vegetable garden. These were being planted everywhere, what with the food shortages. Beyond the vegetable garden was a big sports field, where football games are usually played, but where soldiers were now doing training exercises. This field ran to the hills. The junkyard was up there somewhere, and so was dragon territory. Now and then the silhouette of a dragon rose in the distance, and puffs of smoke faded against the clouds.

We filled in Bronte and Alejandro on all that had happened after they vanished the week before—how we'd rescued Prince Jakob, the destruction in town—and then we tried to make plans to rescue children from the Whispering Kingdom.

But our words kept fading into listlessness. I think we were wondering what we were doing. We were *supposed* to be planning a rescue, and this would "fix history" and stop the Kingdoms and Empires going topsy-turvy.

But who were we fooling? We were mere children ourselves! The Whisperers had become a mighty force, thousands of Dark Mages on their side! Indeed, just *one* witch coven had nearly destroyed our town. And *we* thought we could somehow best them?

Madness!

Also, to be honest, I was beginning to find the Bronte-and-Alejandro situation exasperating. I mean: they *knew* what we were supposed to be doing, but they *could not* tell us anything!

I was in a fierce, glum mood. Do you know that one of the people killed in the witch attack was a girl who had worked in the kitchen at our school? Many a time had I smiled at her as she peeled potatoes in the garden, and she had smiled back, sometimes sighing in a comical way at the enormous pile of potatoes still to peel.

Now she was dead.

No more potatoes would she peel.

A terrible *war* was underway, and a vicious influenza, possibly witch-made, was sweeping our town—my dear friend Carlos and my somewhat less dear friend Rosalind both remained seriously ill. I mean to say, this was—

"This is daft," Finlay said suddenly, as if he'd been reading my mind. "We can't rescue children. We can hardly even rescue ourselves."

"Agreed," said Victor.

"As for you two," Eli added, looking at the future children in his ferocious way, "you're pretty useless. No offense."

So they were *all* thinking along my lines.

This was a relief.

"Yes," I chimed in. "It is terrible that we cannot rescue Jaskafar and the other children, but it was foolish to imagine it. I think it likely that your genie was mistaken about what was meant to happen. I can't imagine *any* history in which we go to the Whispering Kingdom and rescue children."

"And so far," Glim said quietly, "stars haven't fallen from the skies and the horizon is still in its place."

"It's time to disband this group," Taya declared. "Let's volunteer separately from now on."

"Horrible shame," Hamish said. "I will miss you all."

"Let's shake hands?" Finlay suggested. "And then call it a day."

Again, we all nodded, and we reached out our hands and then—

"There!" cried Bronte.

"Look at that," murmured Alejandro.

"*Now* they're ready to rescue the children," Bronte declared. She did not seem the least bothered that Eli had just called her useless.

Alejandro gave a rather lovely shrug. "For the first time, they have all agreed on something. Now they are ready to be a team. To be friends even. And, of course, they have *already* figured out how to *get* to the Whispering Kingdom, have they not?"

We stared. "We have?"

"Last time?" he prodded. "Just before the warning bells rang?"

"But that was when the twins suggested we *allow* ourselves to be captured by Whisperers!" I remembered.

Bronte and Alejandro both opened their hands out, as if concluding a magic trick.

"Are you saying we *should* do that?" I inquired.

They watched us, not blinking.

"Well now, hang about," Hamish argued. "Even if a Whisperer *does* capture us and take us to their Kingdom, how do we *escape*, if you see what I'm saying? There's no way around those supercharged Whispers, is there? Or am I missing something?"

There was another powerful silence from the future children. They simply sat and gazed.

Glim shifted suddenly. She looked hard at Bronte and Alejandro. "They know," she hissed. "They *know* a way around the supercharged Whispers!"

"Oh brilliant!" Hamish said. "They could give us a cl—"

"SHHHHH!" We all turned on him.

There was another long pause. Nobody said a word. We watched the future children and they watched us back.

"Alejandro," Bronte said. "Will you tell us how to fire a cannon?"

I blinked, rather surprised, but Bronte remained still—except for one thing. As she spoke, she touched her own wrist, and then slowly she ran a finger around it.

Beside her, Alejandro also touched his own wrist, and ran a finger around it in the same way as Bronte. Mysterious. "Of course!" he said. "It is like this. First, you must have eight people. It is many, I know. But there it is. One puts the gunpowder down the barrel, and next the cannonball."

He paused. For a moment, he and Bronte sat running their fingers around their own wrists. We all frowned.

Now Bronte stood. She pulled the ties from her hair, tilted her head so that her hair fell over her shoulder, and began to braid it. It made me rather miss my own braid.

Gosh, I thought suddenly. *She's not very good at that!*

She was braiding in such a slow and precise way! I wanted to leap up and do it for her.

"Go on, Alejandro," she said now, rather chattily, as she braided.

"And then this person shouts, *Run out!* And the others drag the cannon to the gunport," Alejandro said.

Bronte completed the braid, ran her fingers through it, releasing the strands, and started over again. "Mm-hm."

Alejandro nodded. "Hold a lit taper over the touch-hole, which makes—"

Now he also stood up. He pointed his boot at a spot on the paving stones. We all looked down. Nothing there. He slid his boot along and stopped. Another jab with his toe. Still nothing there. Just scattered shadows.

"Which makes the cannonball fly out," Bronte finished. As she spoke, her own boot was reaching out to touch the exact spots that Alejandro had just pointed out. *Thud* went her foot. She began to braid again. "And the cannon itself jolts back, a little like those *supercharged Whispers*, which—"

At this point there was a great *surge* in the air. It had a sort of *HEY!!!* quality to it—and once again the future children disappeared.

CHAPTER 66
FINLAY

Ha, that's exactly what it was like. *HEY!!!* You got this sense that the Detection Magic had been leaning against the wall, humming to itself, bored by instructions on how to fire a cannon — *blahdy-blah, ho hum* — and then it *suddenly* cottoned on to what they were doing.

They were giving us clues.

Clues about the supercharged Whispers.

Not especially helpful clues, mind. I mean, winding rings around your wrist and then poking your foot at the ground.

Eh?

We all thought the clues meant different things. Got into a big fight about it right away. Ha-ha. The future children thought we were buddies now and ready to "work together," but there was plenty of fight left between us!

The twins thought the clues meant we should break the Whisperers' wrists and then slam them against the floor, all the while firing cannons at them.

"The cannon instructions were a *cover* for the actual *clues*, you *dolts*," Victor sighed. Between you and me, I agreed with him about the cannon instructions being a cover, but I couldn't have him calling the twins dolts. So I got him in a headlock. He twisted himself out of it.

Hamish thought they'd been teaching us a sort of dance where you spun in place and then pointed your toes. He got himself dizzy trying to demonstrate. When we asked what the dance had to do with supercharged Whispers he said, "Oh golly, is that what this is about?" and sat down.

Honey Bee thought the wrist-winding thing indicated time passing, like a watch going around, maybe meaning that supercharged Whispers wore off after a certain point.

"Time passing, eh?" Victor sneered. "So what, each spin of their wrists was an hour going by? Or a day? A week?"

Honey Bee's face fell. "I'm not sure…"

"And how many spins did they each give?"

"I don't know…"

"*Most* helpful, then, Honey Bee. Brilliant deduction, full of—"

"Nine," said the twins in unison. "Bronte and Alejandro both spun their fingers around their wrists nine times."

That irritated Victor. He crinkled his nose. "Well, *clearly*," he said, "the circling finger is a *universal* symbol for somebody who is cuckoo. And *I* for one—"

"Maybe something is buried underneath this courtyard?" Glim suggested. "They kept pointing out the same spots on the paving stones."

And so on.

Eventually, we gave up trying to figure out the clues, and we all headed off, thinking our own thoughts.

Nobody mentioned the idea of getting a Whisperer to capture us. But we had definitely sparked up. It was the way the future kids tricked the Detection Magic, I think. And the way they stomped all over our decision to call off the rescue.

Anyhow, that's how I'm feeling. A bit more sparked.

And you know what? Secretly, I'm thinking that I'll do it.

Not to fix the future, not to stop the Kingdoms and Empires falling apart. I've started to think, like Honey Bee, that that is a load of crabapple.

No, I'll do it because those children need rescuing.

I'll figure out a way to let the Whisperers take me.

And once I'm in the Whispering Kingdom, no Whisperer will be able to stop me. *I* can stand up to a turbo-boosted, superpowered Whisper!

I'm the boy who rockets down the laundry chute each birthday, and nobody tells *me* what to do.

CHAPTER 61
HONEY BEE

Yes, that's what I'm thinking too, also secretly.

I mean, not *exactly* that. I don't rocket down laundry chutes and people *can* tell me what to do. I'm quite afraid of teachers, actually.

But I'm thinking that I will wander the streets alone until a Whisperer spies me and takes me to the Whispering Kingdom.

And once I get there, I'll *Spellbind* the whole Kingdom and rescue the children.

Because guess what?

I know what my blue toenails meant.

I searched through medical books in our school library right after it happened. They mean I am a Spellbinder.

If your toenails turn blue, especially under the light of the full moon, you are a Spellbinder.

I also know what is happening in the teachers' wing at my school. They're not codebreakers at all. They're Spellbinders. Practicing their art. That explains why Constable Rachel Rally is there.

Net-weaving, potions, and chants are the tools of the Spellbinders, I read in the first book I opened.

And those were the three things I had seen in the teachers' wing. People weaving nets on looms. People making potions of peppercorns. People chanting.

The book I've been reading the most the last week or so is *The Art of Spellbinding: A Beginner's Guide.* I've been studying it. Here's the introduction:

Spellbinders work by TYING UP the Shadow Magic of witches, sirens, radish gnomes, and all the other Shadow Mages. They do this by WEAVING AN IMAGINARY NET around that magic.

When you need to stop a Shadow Mage, begin by closing your eyes and SEEING the Shadow Magic. Visualize it.

Next, move your hands as if you are weaving a net. As you do so, imagine that the Shadow Magic is WITHIN THE NET. Trap it tightly in your net! Do so quick as a flash!

Your Spellbinding will be stronger if you learn some chants and drink some potions. (We recommend reading E. E. Cho, *The Hundred Best Spellbinder Chants* and Litia Ahmed, *Potions That Pack a Punch: Drink Your Way to Superior Spellbinding.*)

But you don't really need the chants or the potions. The key is in your hand movements: try weaving actual nets first, to get it right.

My school library doesn't have copies of *The Hundred Best Spellbinder Chants* or *Potions That Pack a Punch*, and neither does the Spindrift Public Library, but that's all right. The book says the key is in the hand movements!

I plan to find some fisher-folk and ask if they'll teach me net-making. In the meantime, I've been studying manuals on fishing nets and practicing the sheet bend knot, moving my hands about in the darkness of my room each night.

As I fall asleep, a secret thought plays in my mind: *I am a Spellbinder! I am a Spellbinder!*

And each day, a secret song sings in my mind:

> *Of all of us*
> *I am the one*
> *The only one*
> *Who can defeat the Whisperers.*

I know you're supposed to get trained really, and I know this song is a bit conceited of me, and I know it doesn't rhyme or anything.

PART 2

CHAPTER 68
FINLAY

Well.

A lot has happened.

Guess where we are?

I'll give you a clue: it's not Spindrift.

Ah, you'll never guess. I'll tell you.

The Whispering Kingdom.

Honey Bee and I have decided we'll carry on writing the story. Not so much for the genie now, but might be handy for people to know how we ended up here and what's going on.

Our fifth Tuesday of volunteer duty was my birthday. I was pretty chuffed about this. Well, obviously I was. It was my *birthday*.

But what I mean is, I was chuffed that we were doing volunteer duty that day. Not because I wanted to see the Brathelthwaite kids. I'm not saying I'd lost my ruddy marbles.

No, it was because the Brathelthwaite kids brought along their picnic basket each week, and Bronte always made them share it with us.

I tell you, there was enough food in that basket for two hundred kids. Shortages and rationing everywhere else, but the Brathelthwaites could cram a wicker basket with pastries, cakes, apricot conserves, oranges, raspberries, and cream. There was this one particular twisty pastry, and when you unwrapped it from its cloth napkin, it was *warm* and *buttery*, which was something in itself, but listen, inside this pastry?

Melted chocolate.

I am not messing with you.

You'd bite into this thing and there it would be, filling your mouth: warm, oozing chocolate.

A bit dizzy now, actually, writing that down.

Maybe I should end my chapter here—

Nah, I'll be okay.

Thing is, I planned to nab that twisty pastry on my birthday. It was the first thing came to mind when I woke up.

But the picnic never happened.

What *actually* happened that day shocked me more than the time I was six years old and I fell off the wharf into a nest of zapper eels. Now that I look back, I can see that it shouldn't have shocked me at all.

For a start, everywhere you turned around Spindrift, you'd see a sign flapping in the wind:

WATCH OUT, WHISPERERS ABOUT!

There were plenty of strangers in town. People move around a lot in wartime, see, on account of having lost their homes or families.

Or on account of wanting to make some quick cash.

That kind of folk set up stalls in the town square, crowding out our local vendors. They sold Patented Whisper-Proof Helmets, or Anti-Whisper Lime Popsicles, or Crushed Ginger Biscuit Powder with Magical Properties That Will Render You Immune to Whispers If You Take Just a Spoonful Three Times a Day.

Every single one was a con artist.

Charlatans, Glim called them.

The constables kept moving them on, but locals would chase after them anyway, begging for their goods and handing over their silver.

People were pretty scared, see. Every day there were more stories about the Whisperers rampaging across the Kingdoms and Empires, along with their Shadow Mage and pirate allies, stealing children and taking down cities and ports. Not just destroying buildings and killing people, mind. Other stuff too. Newspaper headlines rattled on about how Whisperers were infiltrating everybody's life.

HOW A WHISPERER STOLE MY BOYFRIEND

A WHISPERER GAVE ME A PIMPLE ON MY WEDDING DAY

WHISPERERS MADE ME FAIL MY ALGEBRA EXAM

Some of these headlines were a crate-load of crabapple, I'm sure. But people couldn't get enough of them.

Here comes the point of all this. Those signs and headlines? They never made it clear that the problem Whisperers were not your *regular* Whisperers. Nobody ever said: *Watch out for Whisperers who are using Shadow Magic to give them supercharged Whispers.* It was just plain *Watch out for Whisperers.*

Of course, my version is not exactly pithy. But they still needed to specify! Because pretty soon, everyone forgot that Whisperers had ever been nice, gentle folk.

A handful of Whisperers live in our town, and they've *never caused a single bit of trouble.*

But suddenly, people were gossiping about them. Notices were going up outside restaurants and inns: NO WHISPERERS WELCOME. People were putting rotten fruit in the Whisperers' letter boxes.

Snatty-Ra-Ra is one of our local Whisperers, of course. I'd sort of forgotten that about him because, well, he's *Snatty*. Everyone knows him! Everyone loves him!

But some of the folk with stalls in the town square shifted their tables and blankets way across the square, away from Snatty. Ronnie, our artist friend, moved his things closer, to show support, which led to Ronnie getting hit in the ear by a flying squashed banana meant for Snatty.

One day, a bunch of kids just back from the beach ran circles around Snatty, darting forward now and then to pull on his ponytail. He thought they were just messing about at first and he tried to have fun with them. *"GONG! GONG!"* he said, even though it's his *nose* makes that noise, not his hair. But the kids only pulled his hair even harder, so he winced, then they flicked their damp beach towels at his face. One kicked over his coffee mug and another stamped on his sandwich. *"Whisperer, go home!"* they chanted. *"Whisperer, go home!"*

Their parents stood about pretending not to notice.

We saw all this from the Orphanage window, by the way. The twins and Glim and me pelted down the stairs and across the square and chased them out of there, along with their parents. (Orphans can be pretty scary to the "nicer" sort of folk.) But it was too late: Snatty-Ra-Ra's smile had packed itself away and I never saw him get it out again.

If people were quick to turn on our Whisperers, they were even quicker to pile on the local Shadow Mages and pirates. I mean, *they'd* never had a good reputation. We'd always known they were trouble, we'd just trusted their promise to leave their Shadow Magic or pirating ways behind and start over in Spindrift. Before this war, we'd had plenty of squabbles with *outsider* Shadow Mages—but we'd never blamed our locals for that.

But here we were being *relentlessly* attacked by radish gnomes, fire sirens, sterling silver foxes, ghouls, witches, and pirates—and the people of Spindrift were beginning to look at our *local* radish gnomes, fire sirens, sterling silver foxes, ghouls, witches, and pirates in a whole new light.

"Hang on," people were saying, "why did we let you folk *in* here again?"

Which is why, when I woke up on the morning of my birthday and the things that happened started happening, I should not have been shocked in the least.

CHAPTER 69
HONEY BEE

We were on our way through town to see Mayor Franny for our volunteer duty when it began.

I was carrying the picnic basket. I had asked the kitchen to be sure to include a chocolate twist, as I knew that Finlay loved them and it was his birthday. I also had a candle and a matchbook to light it so we could sing "Happy Birthday."

Rosalind remained ill, so it was just Victor, Hamish, and I.

The downtown area was very crowded. I nearly tripped over a man selling sardines on Rawson Street. He'd sat himself down on the pavement, and his legs were stuck out almost to the gutter.

Just as I had recovered from that, a mangy dog darted across the street and a woman shrieked, "Get him! He's stolen my pork chops!"

We paused to watch her chase the dog, which flew over a brick wall and vanished. A few people applauded the dog's successful escape, and the woman yowled at them, like a ferocious cat. The people cheered at this yowl, and now the woman curtsied as if she'd just put on a show.

Around the next corner, a shiny red automobile stood by the side of Gerbera Lane. We had seen automobiles before—some of the wealthier parents motored to the school to visit their children—but they were rare in town. A crowd had gathered around this one, and both men and women were kicking at its tires or knocking on its paintwork.

We carried on.

"Noisy, isn't it?" Hamish commented.

Victor rolled his eyes. "It's *always* noisy here," he said. "The sooner we get this over and return to the peace of Brathelthwaite, the better."

Funny how people are different, isn't it? I myself had just been thinking how delightfully *lively* it was in town—you never knew what was going to happen next! An escaping dog, a yowling woman, a red automobile! So refreshing after the dull schedules and lessons at Brathelthwaite.

It made me wonder, not for the first time, why Victor was still coming along to volunteer duty.

He is rather self-absorbed, is our Victor, and somewhat... I was going to say *relaxed* or *lethargic*, but the word I'm really looking for is LAZY. Not the sort to leap at an inconvenient task like helping with the war effort, anyway, even if the prince *had* read his name out on the radio. Surely one or two weeks of volunteer duty would have been enough to cover him for that?

At that moment, there was a blast of trumpet fanfare, followed by a rising drumroll. It was coming from the town square.

"Golly," said Hamish. "I think that means the *queen* is here! Is she going to make an announcement, do you think?"

Beside us, Victor had quickened his pace. He was tidying his hair as he walked. *Of course*, I thought. That's *why he's still helping.* He is always so keen to get the attention of important people, and the queen is about as important as it gets. Victor had been sure the queen would invite him to tea to thank him for helping to rescue the prince. He became very cranky as the days went by and it never happened.

When we skidded into the town square, it was bustling with people, all pressing together to see. They were knocking into newspaper stands and stalls, and spilling each other's morning coffees. It felt rather like a party. The queen stood at the top of the town hall stairs, gazing over the towns-folk in a loving way. That's how it seemed to me, anyway.

A Royal Soldier in red stepped forward smartly.

"All rise," he boomed into the megaphone, "for Her Majesty, the Queen of the Kingdom of Gusts, Gales, Squalls, and Violent Storms!"

Everybody was already standing up, so it was tricky to "rise." Still, we straightened our backs, as if he'd ordered us to have better posture.

The queen's turn.

"My people," she said. "My good, fine people of Spindrift! What an honor it is to stand before you today. What courage you have shown in these trying times! I am proud of *every* one of you! Between us, we will *win this war*!"

A great cheer went up. People stamped their feet. A *whooping* sounded from the sky—not the sky, but the Orphanage building. Its second-floor windows had been flung open and the orphans were leaning out, clapping and shouting. The twins were loudest, of course. Glim rested her chin on her folded arms and Finlay had propped himself up on the ledge, one arm curled around the window frame. I worried rather that he might fall.

"Disrespectful," Victor muttered.

"I know that many of you have lost loved ones, and my heart breaks for you," the queen carried on, and now the crowd grew still. Heads bowed. A lady wiped her eyes with her handkerchief. "I also know that a dreadful influenza has been sweeping your town."

Many nodded grimly.

"This morning," the queen said, "I come to you with *news* about the influenza."

Now faces took on interested expressions. Finlay leaned even *farther* out of the window, causing me to bite my lip.

The queen gazed around the murmuring crowd once more, her face sorrowful. "We have received a message," she said at last, "from the Whispering Kingdom. It seems that the influenza is itself a form of invasion. It is a witch-made spell. It has been deliberately introduced into Spindrift and has spread. The Whisperers have offered to send in a witch-made antidote that they say will extinguish the influenza—in exchange for the total surrender of our Kingdom."

It was difficult to hear much of this, for as the queen spoke, the crowd's murmuring became a buzz, and then a drone, and then a roar. Each of her statements was like a lever, propping the volume up, until it *burst forth* into furious shouting and shrieking.

"How *dare* they?"

"My *grandmother* is in hospital with that flu!"

"My little nephew is on a respirator!"

"They think we will *surrender*! After what they have *done* to us!"

"They must be off their rockers!"

"NEVER!"

"NEVER!"

"NEVER!"

The guards blew their horns. The queen held up her palms. Eventually, the crowd settled.

"We will *never* surrender!" the queen declared.

More cheers and stamping. But it was angry cheering and stamping. And a woman near me frowned to herself and muttered, "But my little girl is so sick with it. Could we not surrender just for a *little* while?"

"Hmph," said a man standing next to me. "The queen's own son's got the influenza. Let's see how long she keeps up this *never* of hers."

People nearby *shush*ed him or swatted his shoulder, but he had a point. Would the queen let her own son, the prince, languish rather than give in to the Whisperers' demands? It put her in a rather awkward position.

"Hold up," Hamish shout-whispered to me. His long hair tickled my cheek. "Did the queen just say that this influenza is *witch*-made?"

Hamish is always a few steps behind.

I nodded, straining to hear what the queen said next, but the crowd had gotten itself into a state again and there was a deal more hullabaloo.

"Isn't that what that nice woman said?" Hamish called to me over the noise. "The Orphanage one—a doctor, she was, or a teacher? Helped us rescue the prince? *She* said it was a witch-made influenza, didn't she?"

Oh yes! She *had* said that! I'd forgotten!

"Anita!" I half yelled back to him. "Yes, she used some Faery potion on Prince Jakob, remember?"

Now I found myself, rather surprisingly, shouting at the queen. "WHY CAN'T WE USE FAERY MAGIC TO CURE IT?"

Somehow the queen caught my words! Then she caught my eye and nodded! It really was a treat. I felt my cheeks blush. On the other side of Hamish, I believe Victor scowled.

"THE HOSPITAL IS NOW TREATING PATIENTS WITH FAERY POTION!" the queen bellowed into her megaphone. It hurt my ears, she was so loud. Everyone fell silent. "It seems one student doctor was *already* doing that—"

There were *whoops* from the Orphanage windows. "Hooray for Anita!" various orphans shouted.

The queen blinked. "Yes, Anita has helped a great deal, probably saving the lives of the old people and babies. But a real cure will require actual Faeries. The store-bought potion only takes the edge off the symptoms. Now, we have sent away urgently for Faeries to—"

"BRING IN FAERIES NOW!"

"WHERE ARE THE FAERIES?!"

People were shouting again. They were quite impatient. But I suppose you couldn't blame them. Family members and friends were so ill. And anyone could catch the flu at any time.

"*But*—" The queen held up her hand. "Travel is extremely difficult at this time. Pirates are controlling the seas, and Shadow Mages are blocking the roads. So this may take some—"

"WE DON'T *HAVE* TIME!"

The queen nodded grimly. "We don't," she agreed.

There was a sober quiet.

"How did this witch-made influenza get *into* Spindrift?" somebody demanded.

The queen shook her head. "We do not know. Now—"

But here is where the trouble began.

I believe it was Harriet, the owner of the hardware store, who started it. "Local witches!" she called. "They probably *made* it!"

"*Was* it our witches?"

"It *must* have been!"

"Why do we have witches here anyhow?"

"Why do we have *any* Shadow Mages?"

A sort of rumbling then, as if the crowd had become the engine of an automobile.

"They must be helping with these attacks!"

"Speaking of, why do we have *sirens* here? Who let those fire sirens in that day? Must have been our local sirens!"

That one was just plain silly. Everybody knows that sirens don't associate with fire sirens. They're very tetchy with each other. And nobody had *let* the fire sirens in, they'd just taken down our Spellbinder guard, same way the witch coven did. Our guard wasn't up to much, was the problem.

But this was not a time for reasoning.

Everyone was angry, you see. Angry, frightened, and sad, and nobody knew what to do with those feelings, or how to fight the invading Shadow Mages or the superpowered Whisperers or the influenza. But they needed to fight *something*.

And then I heard a blazing voice: "ENOUGH! THEY'VE BROUGHT IT ON THEMSELVES! IT'S TIME TO KILL THE SHADOW MAGES! IT'S TIME TO KILL THE WHISPERERS! LET'S *END* THIS!"

CHAPTER
10
FINLAY

It was what you'd call a free-for-all then.

Those folks that are mean-spirited or bloodthirsty took up the cry, "KILL THEM! KILL THEM!" fists already out and flying. Those who saw how wrong this was—and who loved our local Whisperers and Shadow Mages—hollered, "NO! NO!" and got their arms in lockholds around the first lot. The first lot didn't like that much and head-butted the second lot.

Meanwhile, people who didn't care either way but like a good dust-up—and we've got plenty of that sort in Spindrift—started laying into whoever was standing beside them.

Frightened local witches and Whisperers tried to duck out of the crowd: "Excuse me! Just let me through please?" and the nasty folk shouted, "There's one! Get him!"

I scrambled out of the Orphanage window. No time for stairs. Scraped up my shins on the brickwork sliding down the drainpipe. Twins and Glim were right behind me.

Couldn't tell you what happened then. Elbow in my eye. My fists pounding someone's gut. We were trying to get to Snatty, to protect him. Pummeled from behind, landed with a crack on my knees. Kept running into sterling silver foxes and sirens who were being hammered, and trying to hammer back. An elbow in my chin. Someone's heavy boot hooked around my ankle, tripping me up. The heel of a hand in my eye.

That sort of thing.

I know the queen was blaring away in her megaphone. "I COMMAND YOU TO CEASE AND DESIST AT ONCE!"

Even if she'd said, *Stop right now!* it wouldn't have worked. *I command you to cease and desist* didn't stand a chance. Most people didn't know what *cease and desist* meant.

I did all right in the fight. Well, not great, actually, but keep in mind these were mostly adults and I'm a kid.

I blacked out for a bit.

Came to when somebody stepped on my face.

CHAPTER 71
HONEY BEE

Oh, that was me.

I stepped on his face.

The brawl went on for *over two hours*! I didn't know that was possible. I mean, if *my* nose were bleeding, I would head straight to the infirmary to get ice. If *my* tooth got knocked out, I'd hurry to the dentist. Broken glass all over the ground around *me*? I'd fetch a broom and sweep it up. And so on.

But these people just carried on wrestling! Getting blood all over their clothes, and spitting out their teeth, and cutting themselves on the glass when they fell on it! Which they did, often—fall, I mean. It turns out that you're always *falling* when you fight. I cannot imagine how they ever laundered the blood out of their clothes.

The local constables tried to break it up, of course—they kept blowing whistles and bellowing, but the whistles were just knocked out of their mouths, and most of them ended up tangled in the fight.

Victor and I took cover in a little alcove under the town hall steps. The picnic basket was knocked out of my hand as we hurried over there. Hamish was separated from us and I couldn't see him anywhere. A chair was flung towards the alcove, and Victor leapt to the side so that the chair hit my shoulder. It hurt, rather. Then Victor must have decided that the alcove was not safe at all, and he scurried away, hands protecting his head.

I tried to find a better hiding place too, but I'll tell you what, you can't estimate people's movements at *all* when they're fighting. You think you can just duck around them, but they pay no attention to other people or objects. They sway this way and that, and they walk *backwards*, glowering at their opponents, stumbling right into tables or children.

Crossing the square was like being thrown about in a runaway wagon. I was buffeted this way and that, knocked down twice, hopped up, stumbled, and stepped onto Finlay's face. Not on purpose, you understand. It woke him up anyway, and he leapt to his feet and back into the fray.

Extraordinary.

All the shops and offices around the square had locked their doors and pulled down their shutters. I tried knocking on JJ Barett Esq., Solicitor and Conveyancer, but JJ shouted, "Get away!" Eventually, Motoko-the-Chocolatier threw open the door to her Candy Shoppe, bundled me inside, and slammed and locked it again. We waited then while shouting and thumping, whistling and swearing carried on outside, the jars of candy rattling on the shelves. Motoko was wearing marvelous earrings, almost the size of teacups, and she seemed pleased when I admired them.

At last, soldiers arrived from the military base to assist the constables. More whistles were blown and rifles were shot into the air, but nothing really happened until they brought in the fire hose. It was quite remarkable to see the power of a gust of water. It can send a grown man flying. Motoko and I giggled.

After that, the constables jangled their handcuffs and threatened to arrest anyone who didn't drop their fists in exactly *five* seconds, *Five! Four! Three!*—that was enough to have everyone shuffling apart, arms hanging by their sides. A number were lying on the ground groaning. They were patched up or carried off to the hospital.

"As if the hospital don't have *enough* to do already," scolded Constable Dabnovic.

Motoko-the-Chocolatier opened the door to her shop and unlatched the shutters. I thanked her for rescuing me, and she gave me a peppermint crisp bar and told me to hurry back to school.

"Things will quiet down now," she said.

I believed her too. And then, just as I stepped out of the Candy Shoppe, I saw the queen's guards unlocking the doors of the town hall—where the queen must have taken cover eventually during the brawl—and she stepped back out with her megaphone and raised it to her mouth.

CHAPTER 12
FINLAY

No, wait, she didn't speak into her megaphone right then, did she?

That happened after the argument with Mayor Franny and the others?

CHAPTER 13
HONEY BEE

Yes, you are right.

I beg your pardon, I'd forgotten. I'm very tired.

The queen stepped out of the town hall, paused at the top of the stairs, and she *reached* for the megaphone, but then a little cluster of important people interrupted. They hurried up the stairs. Mayor Franny was one of them, and other town councillors, and military officers with shiny brass buttons. One of these was a terribly important fellow, I think, perhaps a sergeant? Anyhow, I believe he was in charge of the soldiers in some way.

Some kind of urgent conversation took place. You know, the kind where all the faces are worried and frowny, and people lean in close to each other, hands gesticulating madly. Quickly, it became an argument! Rather than leaning in, people were stepping *back*, voices were growing louder!

I heard several curse words. Mostly from Mayor Franny.

Was the brawl about to happen again only this time on the town hall steps between the queen and the mayor?!

No.

The queen has guards, you see. She is the big boss, able to throw you in the dungeon at the drop of a hat.

Mayor Franny lowered her voice and carried on speaking in rapid, earnest tones.

The queen shook her head. She broke out of the ring of people and raised the megaphone to her mouth.

CHAPTER 74
FINLAY

One of these was a terribly important fellow, I think, perhaps a sergeant? Anyhow, I believe he was in charge of the soldiers in some way.

Ha-ha. I'd like to pass that bit on to General Hegelwink, Commander in Chief of the Kingdom of Storm's Army and Navy, which is the person she means.

That part of Honey Bee's chapter gave me a good laugh.

Still laughing, actually.

But what happened next was not funny at all.

Here is what the queen said into her megaphone:

"By order of the Queen, Her Majesty, Ruler of the Kingdom of Gusts, Gales, Squalls, and Violent Storms, every Whisperer and Shadow Mage, including but not limited to witches, sirens, fire sirens, radish gnomes, ghouls, and sterling silver foxes, whether of full or part blood, and no matter what age, residing or currently present in the city of Spindrift, must immediately surrender themselves to the Kingdom's forces. Any individual who does not so surrender him- or herself will be forcibly arrested. All such individuals will be interred for the duration of the Whispering Wars and for such time thereafter as the queen, Her Majesty, determines. While interred, no such individual will be permitted to speak to or in any way communicate with any other resident of Spindrift,

and neither shall residents of Spindrift be permitted to communicate with the aforementioned."

No, I didn't get it either.

I was still busy thinking, *Jeepers, she's good at queenly gobbledygook, isn't she?* when the person beside me explained it.

They were going to round up all our local Whisperers and Shadow Mages and throw them in a cage.

CHAPTER 75
HONEY BEE

Within hours, the army had set up tents and makeshift bathroom facilities in the fairground. They strung this all around with barbed-wire fencing, rounded up the local Whisperers and Shadow Mages, and locked them inside.

It was remarkable how rapidly they did this. I think they must have been planning it for some time, and the queen just *pretended* it was a last-minute "emergency" thing.

I knew I should be back at school, but I could not bring myself to leave the downtown area. For one thing, I could not stop crying. Embarrassing, I know. But you see, I have been at Brathelthwaite Boarding School for the last three years, and Carlos and I often come into town. So I know most of the local characters. And right before my eyes, they were being arrested.

The radish gnome who works in the bicycle repair shop was stamping his feet and shouting angrily. It took three soldiers to drag him through the streets.

The ghoul who wanders around playing the accordion was very polite: "I do beg your pardon but there's been some kind of mistake," she kept saying. "I *live* here." They took no notice. They pulled the accordion out of her hands, kicked it away along the pavement, and marched her down to the fairground.

The rowdy witches who drink too much beer and dance on the tables in the square made a run for it, their cats prancing along beside them. I heard they were captured hiding under the netting in a fishing boat.

Remember the woman I saw chasing a dog? Two soldiers instructed her to come along with them, please. "No, no," she said. "I'm not a Whisperer *or* a Shadow Mage."

The soldier checked his papers. "You are Wilma Sfanski?"

She nodded.

"You're quarter siren."

"Oh, that's right!" Wilma Sfanski beamed. "My grandmother was a siren. She was *such* a laugh—my mother always said I inherited her shriek. You're out of luck though, she died years ago. Excuse me, I've got to get to the butcher's. That blasted dog stole my—"

But the soldiers had clasped handcuffs onto her wrists and were leading her away. I could not tell you exactly what she said next because it was spoken in a cacophony of shrieks.

She wouldn't have had much luck with the butcher anyway. Turned out he was half radish gnome—used his long claws to cut up meat—and had been carted off himself.

The sterling silver foxes who play cards in the square argued about the technicalities of the queen's orders as they were rounded up.

Snatty-Ra-Ra and most of the other Whisperers just nodded sadly and followed along, which made me cry harder.

Oh, it was awful.

Whole families were rounded up. Very young children grew excited, thinking they were being taken on a holiday or adventure and reaching up their little hands into the soldiers' hands. There are plenty of mixed relationships in Spindrift, and I saw couples clinging together and being pried apart. In fact, the butcher's wife grabbed on to her husband's legs and refused to let go, so she was dragged along the gravel for quite some distance. A great tug from a soldier, and she finally let go and lay weeping and bleeding in the middle of the road.

Around this time, Randalf, the lighthouse keeper, came wandering into the town square—he needed to pick up a flat head screwdriver, he said—and *he* found himself carted away. I'd forgotten he was half witch. Some people laughed about this, at first.

"You can't lock up our *lighthouse* keeper!" they said. "There will be shipwrecks!"

But the soldiers ignored them. The laughter turned into angry yelling. *Every soul lost at sea will come back and haunt you soldiers!* they yelled, only with very strong language.

"Just following orders," one of the soldiers said. But her face was grim. She didn't want to be haunted, I could tell.

When they took Motoko-the-Chocolatier away, *I* shouted. Motoko had just sheltered me from the brawl! Who *cared* that she was a sterling silver fox! Others were bellowing and clutching at Motoko too, but I think they were worried about their chocolate.

Anyway, I won't talk about it anymore. It upsets me too much. I felt so helpless!

Which is why I was pleased when somebody—it was Ronnie-the-Artist, I think—suggested a protest. We would refuse to leave the town square, he said, until the captives were all set free.

And that is how we came to be gathered together, a crowd of us, in the square. Most of the children from the Orphanage were there—including Finlay, Glim, and the twins, and I also recognized Daffo from the relay team—and I was surprised to find Hamish participating. When he swung his head to the side to say, "Ahoy there, Honey Bee! Here you are!" his hair cleared away long enough for me to see a nasty bruise forming beneath his eye.

"However did you get that?" I asked.

"Oh, remember that enormous brawl?" he chatted—as if the brawl were a stage play we had seen weeks before. "Well, it was *that*! I thought to myself, hold up! I don't want anybody harming the locals! I mean to say, people were shouting, *Kill them!* What? I thought. No, I *like* them! Anyhow, I'm not a bad boxer, so I—"

But I did not hear how he had boxed his way to a black eye as, right then, the chanting started up. "SET THEM FREE! SET THEM FREE!"

That was how the protest worked, it seemed. We all linked arms in rows and chanted, "SET THEM FREE!"

Hamish and I joined in.

Now this is where things went wrong. A few of the local buskers stepped up to accompany the chant. I suppose this was thoughtful of them, to add musical flare to a *rather* dull chant, but the fellow who plays the violin stood *right* beside me. I think I have mentioned before that I cannot abide the sound of violin? I truly cannot.

I decided I would just duck around the corner, into an alleyway, until the violin had stopped, and then I would rejoin the protest.

The moment I saw them, I knew what they were. Something ran down my spine like hot tea. A man and a woman, both dressed rather casually in overalls, linen shirts, and high-collared jackets, were standing close together, just along the alleyway.

If you had not looked closely, you might easily have missed the long, tightly wound braids tucked into each of their jacket collars.

But I did look closely, and I saw.

I could have spun around and run straight back to the square.

I could have screamed.

I did neither.

I walked directly to them, smiled, and said, "Hello there, my name's Honey Bee. I'm twelve."

CHAPTER
76
FINLAY

ARE YOU TELLING ME THIS WHOLE THING STARTED BECAUSE *HONEY BEE CANNOT ABIDE THE VIOLIN*??

Again with the violin!!

I never knew that's why she ducked around the corner! I am shaking my head here. That's all I can do: *shake, shake.*

Well, I'll let it go for—no, still can't.

Still shaking my head.

Shake. Shake.

Sigh.

I guess it *was* our plan to get ourselves captured by Whisperers, and that *is* exactly what Honey Bee did.

But I was going to make a few more preparations first!—sigh (again)—

Of course, if I'm honest, I'd have done the same as Honey Bee. Pounced on the opportunity. Because who knew when you might run into a Whisperer again? Plus, after the day we'd just had, I was pretty het up and ready to pounce on anything.

Fair play to her, actually. Marching up to a pair of Whisperers like that takes guts.

Look at that, I've written myself around to Honey Bee's side! What are the chances?

At the time, I myself was in the town square with the protesters, and my main thought was that we ought to sit down. It was my birthday, and my legs were tired.

You should not have tired legs on your birthday.

Everything about me was tired, in point of fact. When you fight and shout for hours, it wears you down, see, the same way sucking on lemon wedges wears out your teeth. (Lili-Daisy told me that—come to think of it, was that true or was that her way of stopping me stealing lemons off local trees?) Anyhow, like a worn-out tooth I was, half leaning against Glim, and she was leaning against Eli, and he was not leaning against anyone. He was standing straight like a proper solid tooth that has never seen a lemon in its life. Taya, beside him, was also a good tooth. Those twins are unstoppable.

Now, protesting was a very good plan. But the queen did not seem the type to hear the news and say, "Hold up! Fifty people in the town square chanting? Well then, I'll revoke the order at once! Set them free! On the double! Quick-sticks! Spit spot! (And so on.)"

I suspected we'd be hanging around here chanting a few weeks. Maybe a year. This was another good reason for us to sit.

It was nearly two o'clock in the afternoon. "Set them free! Set them free!" I said, while watching the clock tower. I'd have to nip away at three, to pull the lever for the laundry chute.

Of course, it wouldn't be the same without Lili-Daisy screaming when I hit the cart—she was still laid up with the influenza in hospital, so Cook stands on the pavement supervising these days. He'd be more likely to scratch his ear and say, "Oi, boy, outta there."

Still, it was tradition for me to slide down the laundry chute, and that was what I intended to do. I'd come straight back to the protest afterwards, of course. They'd be all right without me for a minute.

"What's she up to?" Glim murmured, between chants. I followed her gaze and there was Honey Bee, striding along on those long legs of hers.

She'd broken away from the protesters and dashed around the corner, into Mariah Alley.

Next thing, Hamish was hurrying after her.

I don't know why I followed. I think it was just that I'd got accustomed to keeping an eye on Orphanage kids, making sure nobody went about in groups of less than three. Two kids alone in an alley? Dangerous.

"I'll check," I said to Glim.

They looked like a happy family out for an afternoon stroll. A family that had chosen a really nutty place to go strolling, I mean. Two adults, two kids, arms linked, heading down the alleyway away from me, over broken cobblestones, past spilling garbage cans, sidestepping rats, into the shadows and the dark.

"Oi," I called.

They spun around, the four of them. Shuffled a bit as they turned, and then relinked their arms.

The man and the woman, I didn't recognize. That made me suspicious, but they had that posh sort of face. You know, smooth with very tidy smiles? Teeth like sunlight? And they were dressed pretty smart, so my first thought was that they must be boarding school teachers come to fetch Honey Bee and Hamish back to the school.

Then I looked at Honey Bee's face. Couldn't see Hamish's, what with his hair covering it, but Honey Bee—well, she appeared to be sliding down a laundry chute. Eyes half-closed, mouth half-open: mad, wicked, blissful.

I'd never seen that look on her face before.

Something was wrong.

I jumped my gaze back to the adults—they widened their tidy smiles—and the man ducked his head. That's when I caught it: a glimpse of coiled braid at his neck.

Whisperers.

The Shadow kind.

Honey Bee and Hamish had been taken.

"Here now," said a voice inside my head. *"I'll pop along with them to the Whispering Kingdom too."*

It was a bit like that purple flower, what's it called? Wisteria. Bit like wisteria, the voice was.

HONEY BEE

Right, well, I never would have imagined Finlay using the word *wisteria*.

I don't mean that in a snobby way. He just doesn't seem like a wisteria sort.

But he's right. In the Spindrift Gardens, there is a lane that runs beneath wooden trellises and, in the late spring, it overflows with wisteria. Lacy purple flowers that dangle overhead—delicate, exquisitely pretty—and you walk beneath them in a sort of dream.

That *is* how it felt, that first encounter with the Whisperers.

"Hello there, my name's Honey Bee," I said. "I'm twelve."

I thought I should tell them my age so they knew I was a child. I suppose they would have figured it out from looking at me, but I *am* tall, and for all I knew, Shadow Whisperers might be a little simple.

"Hello yourself, Honey-Bee-who's-twelve," the woman replied with a quick little grin—teasing me but friendly at the same time. "Quite a day Spindrift seems to be having! My husband and I are tourists here, and we're taken aback by all the goings-on. Aren't we, William?"

At this, the man nodded gravely. He pushed at the cuff of his shirt and I saw he was wearing a wristband of woven red-and-black twine. "Indeed we are, Eleanor," he said, before turning to address me. "Are you a local, dear child? Only, we appear to have got ourselves thoroughly lost and would be glad of your help."

This seemed silly. The noise from the town square was a *little* muffled down this narrow alley, but still perfectly clear: the chanting of *Set them free! Set them free!*, the thumping of drums, even the screech of the violin. Behind all that you could hear Jean-Pierre, the newspaper vendor, shouting, "Read all about it! 'How a Whisperer Spoiled My Potato Soup'! Read all about it!"

I arched an eyebrow at the man, William. I'm quite good at raising one eyebrow at a time. My Aunt Rebecca taught me this skill. She has many other talents: cricket, cake-baking, the lark's head knot you use to make string bags for grocery shopping, how to cheep like a bird by curling your tongue.

"The town square," I told him, pointing, "is just down there."

They both chuckled. "Oh yes!" they said. "Hard to miss with all that racket! Only, we are trying to find our motorcar. It's a bright red one, and I believe we parked it on a street called Gerbera Lane? Do you know it?"

Now I felt a little foolish about my arched eyebrow. This was when I noticed the voice within my head. In fact, it had been speaking to me from the moment I approached the pair, only it had been buried. Now I rummaged through my regular thoughts and there it was, glowing softly: a faint, lulling voice. It was rather like tossing aside blankets in a wooden chest to find an emerald necklace beneath.

"I'm going to accompany these people to the Whispering Kingdom," said the voice. *"What a lark!"*

The couple looked down at me with the same friendly smiles.

"Do you know it?" the man repeated.

"*I'm going to accompany these people to the Whispering Kingdom,*" said the voice again. "*What a lark!*"

Oh my, I thought. *They can do their super Whispers at the same time as carrying on a normal conversation!*

"Gerbera Lane? Yes, I do know it," I began—but they had raised their chins, their attention caught by something behind me. I turned around, and here came Hamish, his pale hair swishing as usual.

Oh dear, I thought. *He's going to mess this up.* Still, I was happy to see a familiar figure: I realized my heart had been thumping rather fast.

I don't really remember what happened next. It was so puzzling because we all chatted and introduced ourselves and then we set off, arms linked, to show the strangers the way to Gerbera Lane—and then *Finlay* joined us, which cheered me even more—and we reached the couple's motorcar and us three children admired its bright colors and fancy wheels—and next thing, the doors were opening and we were all hopping in. We *all* found ourselves pretending that the strangers were taking us for a spin around town, for a treat. The automobile slowed down at some point—near the boarding school, I think, and there was Victor strolling along—and the woman called out the window to him in her sunny voice. Victor climbed inside too, and we all said, "Hello, Victor! What about this motorcar, eh?" And carried on exclaiming at the leatherwork but at the same time, over and over, this terribly pleasant, shining golden-emerald voice was chanting softly inside my head: "*I'm going to accompany these people to the Whispering Kingdom. What a lark!*"

CHAPTER
78
FINLAY

Yeah, it was like that, the voice—pleasant, shining, emerald—all those sugary words.

Or like wisteria, as I already said.

But this was before we'd tried to resist it.

We all fell asleep in the motorcar and woke up inside the Whispering Kingdom. Annoyed me, that, as I'd been looking forward to seeing the famous Whispering Gates. I'd planned to keep a sharp eye out and notice where they hid the keys.

But no, we woke on a grassy bluff overlooking the sea.

Actually, when I say we fell asleep, I think they Whispered us to sleep. Thing with these super Whispers is, you can confuse them with your own thoughts. *Might as well have a wee snooze now*, you think, *I'm that tired*, and it will seem like the warmest, sensiblest thought you ever had. You get so snug with the thought that you forget to even check if it's your own.

Also, when I say *we woke up on a grassy bluff overlooking the sea*, that probably puts a picture in your head.

Long yellow grass blowing in the wind and a crumbling cliff edge is what you see? With sounds of waves crashing onto jagged rocks way down below?

The picture is wrong.

Well, I mean, it's *right*—the grass, cliff, waves, and rocks, they were all *there*, right enough.

But add a high chain-link fence, mounted on wooden posts and running along the hilltop into the distance as far as you can see. In the other direction, have the hill tumble down into a wide valley that looks a lot like a junkyard on account of it being a shambles of open mines, shaft mines, wagons, woodpiles, stables, sheds, cottages, and mounds, heaps, and hillocks of rocks and dirt.

And then?

Place fifteen wrecked battleships on the bluff.

I am not messing about with you.

That's what was there, laid out before our eyes: fifteen big, hulking ships, resting on their sides like the larger sorts of tourists on the Beach with the Yellow sand. They'd been salvaged from the sea or rocks, I guess: sails missing, worn and forlorn, iron rusting, wood rotting, hulls breached and torn.

We were all pretty excited by this.

To be fair to us, who doesn't like a shipwreck? You try waking up in a motorcar, hopping out, and seeing *fifteen* wrecks just waiting to be clambered over.

And it turned out we'd be sleeping in these! Crackerjack! There was nobody else about at this point—just the four of us kids and the Whispering couple, William and Eleanor—and all of us *still* acting like this was a holiday. Rubbing our eyes, stretching, smiling at each other, pointing out beetles in the grass.

"Around twenty children sleep and eat in each wreck," Eleanor told us.

"Plenty of hijinks, as you can imagine!" William added, smiling like a good-natured dad.

Eleanor pointed to the second wreck. "Run along and choose yourselves a bed," she advised, "before the other children return."

We pelted up the gangplank, found the way below deck, along a narrow passageway, and there, sure enough, was the berth deck. It was patched-up, weather-proofed, in fairly good nick, and strung all along with hammocks.

Most of these hammocks were sort of sunken and gray, with bundles sat on them, as if already taken. But there were four bright ones near the end, so we ran up to these. Then we just stood by them. Swayed them a bit, I guess.

Not having any sort of bundles ourselves, I wasn't sure how Eleanor meant us to reserve one. Hamish leapt onto his and lay there with his hands propped behind his head. Which was one way, I guess, but not convenient. He'd have to stay there, wouldn't he, from then on?

Honey Bee placed her hat on the hammock next to Hamish's. Much more sensible. Next thing, Victor had taken out a penknife from his pocket and was cutting a little *V* into the canvas.

That seemed a bit destructive, but I was impressed by the penknife. A likely weapon, I thought, if we ever need —

That's when I sort of snapped awake.

Weapons.

Of *course* we'd need a weapon.

This wasn't a picnic or a pajama party. I didn't even *have* my pajamas with me. This was an undercover rescue operation. This was a *military maneuver.*

How had I forgotten?

Back on deck, I noticed the mast still looked good and strong. No sails, a few rotting ropes dangling from it.

I climbed it.

Below, the others called up, asking what I could see.

I could see ocean stretching out, smacking into the horizon. A couple of ships lurking out there, maybe K&E Alliance. Looking back inland, dipping just below us, was the valley with its mess of mines, equipment, tiny cottages with smoke threading out of their chimneys. Beyond that, the hills carried on, little villages, more mines, and then the thick, dark green of forest. That was the Impenetrable Forest, a wide belt of it curving right around the kingdom. I followed the green around, swiveling, until I was looking behind us, and there was the road we had traveled, winding through hills, dipping and turning until it reached the main city of the Whispering Kingdom itself. From this distance, it was just a little play-town: castle turrets, toy houses with brightly painted roofs, ponds, parks, teeny carriages rolling down narrow roads, the houses petering out into a bigger green space, then the road ran on into the Impenetrable Forest, emerging on the coast, where a great sprinkling of blues and blacks suggested a Whispering guard.

"Not much," I replied, and climbed back down.

Back on the grass, William and Eleanor began chatting again right away. They explained our schedules. How we'd rise at dawn and have our oatmeal and then away to the mines for the day—a brisk, pleasant, thirty-minute march to get there—with a bread-and-cheese break at noon, back for dinner and sleep. Some days, as a treat, we'd get to do some weaving! They made it sound like a right lark.

At that time, I thought they must be diamond mines—the Whispering Kingdom has a few of them—and I was quite keen to see a real live diamond in the ground. Maybe I could slip some in my pockets and use it to help with the escape somehow? Bribe a guard, say? Each wreck had a supervisor, Eleanor continued, and we should go to them with any questions.

We nodded along as if all of this made sense.

Eleanor waved her hand at the cliff edge. "Stay well away from the cliffs," she advised. "Anyone who falls over is dashed to pieces by the rocks."

William gestured towards the mines. "Beyond, the hills meet up with the Impenetrable Forest. If you *did* reach that, you'd only get yourself thoroughly scratched and thrown right back!"

This time everyone chuckled as if he'd made a great joke.

Now we all seemed to turn at once to look at the chain-link fence that cut along the hill behind us. *I will not climb this fence*, I thought. *I will not climb this fence.*

I looked up in surprise.

I climb everything, see. I'd just climbed the mast of the shipwreck! I don't reckon I'd *ever*, in all my days, had the thought: *I will not climb.* This looked an easy fence to climb. Flimsy enough that it would shake as you jumped on it, and you'd cling to it with your fingers, find your feet, clamber up, swing your leg over the top, and then — well, I'd just let myself fall to the grass on the other side. Maybe do a bit of a tumble as I landed to stop the landing jarring.

I will not climb this fence, I thought.

But this would be the only way out! If the cliffs and rough seas stopped us *that* way, and the hills were cut off by the Impenetrable Forest *that* way, then *this* was how we got out of here. This was the way we'd escape, rescuing all the other stolen children. Over the fence, carry on along the road, creep through the city, then out the Whispering Gates, somehow get past the Whispering guard there — and we'd be free.

I will not climb this fence.

I nodded to myself. It was a good thought, it made beautiful sense. Sweet as —

It was a Whisper.

Of course it was.

All right, then, I decided. *Time to have a go at resisting.*

Yes, I will, I thought right back at the Whisper. *I AM going to climb this —*

Tell you what, it was nothing like wisteria then. Couldn't even get the sentence finished.

CHAPTER
19
HONEY BEE

No, it's not like wisteria.

I've tried to resist a few times since then, and each time the Whisper stops being a flower and turns into a mighty pair of cymbals. *CLANG!* They come from either side of your head, these cymbals, as if a giant pair of hands is banging them together: *CLANG!* And all your own thoughts—all the *you* of you—are between these cymbals, which then begin squeezing together. It's not just giant hands, actually, it's a sort of device with screws, and the screws are turned and turned, and then you realize that the cymbals are made of fire, they are red-hot, like molten lava, so that the *you* of you is being both crushed and burned alive, and then there are sledgehammers and these are being used to *beat* against the cymbals, from either side, to pound and slam you—the essence of *you*—ever tighter, closer and closer—

I have never felt such pain.

Not even when—

Well, I won't talk about that, but I have never.

But the moment you do as the Whisper asks? It's back to wisteria. The cymbals simply dissolve. Such a beautiful relief.

Anyway, that's how it feels to me.

I know the other children have different ways of describing it. We've *all* tried to resist at least once, but most don't try again.

I remember the exact moment when Finlay tried to resist the Whisper that first day. We were standing about between the motorcar and fence, chatting sunnily, and Finlay's face suddenly turned the most ghastly gray.

Like when you wash a paintbrush in water and the water swirls with darkness. His hands rushed up and clutched around his head, and he staggered back a few steps, making a strange rasping sound.

It was over so quickly that I don't think Hamish or Victor noticed. Abruptly, Finlay had straightened up again. He was blinking quickly, and his mouth was open in shock, but his face resumed its ordinary color. Certainly, the adults pretended nothing was going on. They carried on smiling and pointing out the sheds where we would bathe once a week.

Once a week! I thought.

I was actually quite pleased. Bathing can be dull.

But oh my, what a fool I was to be pleased.

Anyhow, after that the day became sleepy again. I think that these Whispers make you very tired: it's part of how it works. I remember Eleanor and William driving their motorcar away through a gate in the fence. *I will not follow the automobile through that gateway*, I thought. Eleanor hopped out on the other side and shut and padlocked the gate. Then she called, "Toodle-hoo!" and waved and hopped back in. Off they drove, chugging along, puffs of smoke behind them.

Next, I remember the sun setting over the ocean—and here came the children.

Trailing up the hill from the mines they came, each group led by a Whispering adult, and oh my, you should have seen them.

There was a cry of excitement and Finlay went sprinting over the hill to one of these children—and it was Jaskafar. The little boy who had given flowers to the queen and been taken the day of the tournament. The one who started it all.

Finlay lifted Jaskafar clear off the ground, spun him around in a circle, gave him a great hug, and set him back down again. Then he lifted him once more. It was very touching.

Another few children gathered around and were hugged and spun in turn. "Connor! Amie! Bing!" There were other names too, of local children—Motoko-the-Chocolatier's niece, for one—as more children gathered around Finlay.

I was glad to see Finlay happy, but Hamish, Victor, and I were staring wide-eyed from the lines of children to each other and back again. For the children—*all* the children—appeared to have been dunked in blackest mud. They were walking in the slow, hunched way you might walk if you had a terrible tummyache. Their faces as they drew closer were so gaunt you could see the bones; their ankles and wrists were as thin as sticks of hard candy.

"What is *happening* here?" I murmured.

Hamish, beside me, breathed in deeply. "Quite," he agreed.

The next day, we found out.

✶ CHAPTER ✶
80
FINLAY

We went to the mines and picked out these crabapple, blatherskite bits of stupid thread.

Don't believe it? I didn't either.

But that's what happens here in the Whispering Kingdom, where we are now writing this story. (We're hiding the chapters in the bucket of gravel behind the washhouse, by the way.)

Each night, we're locked up with the other stolen children. Kids here are from Spindrift, from other parts of the Kingdom of Storms, and from all over the Kingdoms and Empires. The youngest is a four-year-old from the Sayer Empire who won't quit yapping on about her first wobbly tooth. The oldest is a thirteen-year-old from Carafkwa Island.

Each morning, at dawn, we walk to the mines and work until a gong sounds. And like I said, our work is plucking strands of thread—some black, some red—that are jammed into the rock walls.

Now, I don't know much about yarn, but I *do* know that cotton and hemp grow in fields, silk is made by silkworms, and wool is sheared from the backs of sheep. And so on.

But I've never once heard of a yarn that is *mined* out of the earth.

But here it is.

It's often buried deep inside crevices, and you have to tweeze it with your fingertips, grazing your knuckles as you grasp at the fine end, then tugging with just the right pressure.

We're raised back out of the mine, coated in mud, as the sun sets.

Once a week, we get a break from the mines. On that day, we have to go down to the shipwreck at the end, sit at a table, and twist the threads together. This is supposed to be a "treat," but it gives us terrible blisters.

We've been here five weeks now, and every escape attempt has failed.

Yesterday, we woke to a thunderstorm, a great commotion in the sky, and our supervisor said we should stay in. From the rainy deck, we watched the Whisperers over at the mines, little beetles running about, hands over their heads. Mudslides over there, apparently, and we're all cheering, thinking the mines would be closed for weeks.

But today the sun shone, and it was back to the routine.

At the mine, you step onto a sort of wooden plank and you're lowered down. A long, long, rickety ride, deep into the earth, darker and darker as you drop. I never knew the ground could go so low. It runs about the depth of two football fields straight down.

Clunk! The plank stops. You've reached the bottom. And there you are in a black, muddy, dripping passage, pathways heading off in every direction. Some paths are tall enough so you can stand up in them, but most are so low you've got to get down on your hands and knees and crawl.

One I went in today was so close that I had to scoot along on my stomach. Rocks above me grazing my back.

The mines always drip with water—we're that close to the sea—and sometimes the water splatters you. Today I kept swearing my head off, thinking someone was tipping bucketloads all over me.

It's mud and rock you have to crawl through, and you can't even see your hand if you hold it up in front of you. You have a candle to start the day, but dripping water puts it out or it gets knocked against the wall and snuffed, and then you just have to feel your way.

Most of us pick out the stupid thread, but a few of the bigger kids get harnessed to wagons and drag these along the passageways, collecting the thread from us. The littlest kids sit by trapdoors that are dotted here and there in the passages. They open them up when someone knocks, and close again once they're through. Doors have to stay shut, see, to keep the air flowing. Seems like a simple job, but I tell you, those kids forget how to talk. Sitting in black silence for hours each day, waiting for someone to knock.

Evenings, everyone is tired and tetchy. We eat our bowls of sticky flummery and then we sit on the hills looking at the dark sea—sometimes staring out hopefully at the ships on the horizon—and chatting a bit. And then it's bedtime, and sleep.

There's a supervisor—a grown-up Whisperer—in each of the wrecks with us. They hand out rations or tell us when it's our turn to bathe. Ours is a young guy, Malik, who strums on a guitar each night and gives people thumbs-ups or winks, never talking much.

Doesn't need to talk. Sends out his orders as Whispers in our heads. All the supervisors do.

I will eat now.
I will stop eating now.
I will go to the mines now.
I will work all day in the mines.
I will eat now.
I will stop eating now.
I will go to sleep now.
I will not chat with the other children now.
I will wake up now.
I will line up behind this man and follow him to the mines.

And so on.

Whispers come at you from every direction. And each night, the same one: *I will not climb the fence.*

I try to resist at least one Whisper a day. Each time it's more vicious than the last. I'm always wrecked for the next hour or so. Yesterday I couldn't get up the courage to try even once.

The worst is that Jaskafar and the other kids from the Orphanage were excited to see me. They thought I had it sorted and would get them home.

I thought I had it sorted too.

I'll be straight with you: I am *that* disappointed in myself.

* CHAPTER *
81
HONEY BEE

Yes, me too.

I am also disappointed in myself.

Before I go on, though, I must say, I cannot *believe* that Finlay tries to resist a Whisper each day!

I've only tried a few times and even the *memory* of those times frightens me! This pencil seems to scorch my hand just to write the words! My body is *cringing* away from the paper! Look at me! Look! Oh, you cannot see me.

Well.

But my disappointment in myself is not about resisting Whispers. I always knew that would be impossible—Finlay is being too tough on himself. That's the *point* of the supercharged Whispers: they're supercharged, they're *irr*esistible.

No, with me, it's this: I'm disappointed in my Spellbinding.

Remember how my toenails turned blue under the moonlight? And I decided that meant I was a Spellbinder? So I came here planning to Spellbind the whole blasted kingdom, set the children free, and possibly even win the war?

Ha.

Ha-ha!

I feel so silly.

To be honest, I am no longer sure that I even *am* a Spellbinder.

Maybe I imagined the blue of my nails? Or dreamed it? Rosalind was hallucinating that day, and perhaps I *caught* one of her delusions somehow? Can that happen?

I don't know.

I will now tell you everything I know about the Spellbinding of Whispers. Are you ready? Here it is:

ABSOLUTELY NOTHING.

AND A LITTLE MORE NOTHING.

And so on. I could go on leaving blank spaces and saying *"Nothing"* in different ways for pages! But that would be very wasteful. (And boring.)

Yes, all right, I *had* read *The Art of Spellbinding: A Beginner's Guide*. It told me I needed to weave a net. Fair enough. So I practiced net-weaving, didn't I? With my hands? At night?

But I never got a chance to try with *actual* rope, did I? We got taken by Whisperers too soon!

(Yes, yes, I *know* that was my fault. I chose to be taken. Idiot that I am.)

But before you start weaving the blasted net, you need *something* to weave it *around*! *Visualize the Shadow Magic*, the book said.

But *what does Shadow Magic look like?!*

Every night I lie in my hammock, listening to the children muttering and snoring, the quiet crying, the wind blowing outside, and the waves crashing against the cliffs. I close my eyes and try to *see* Shadow Magic.

All I get is a blank.

Or sometimes a sort of squiggly black cloud.

I've tried to use my imagination! I've visualized as many nasty things as I can. Spiders, snakes, snails, slugs, stubbed toes, torn fingernails, sore throats (I get laryngitis a lot), Uncle Dominic's horsewhip, the curtain that hides Carlos from me in the infirmary. Horrible thoughts like these could be a sort of gateway to the Shadow Magic, I thought. But no. The thoughts just wriggle around in my mind being nasty. And when I try to move my hands about, weaving an imaginary net to capture the nastiness?

The nastiness just wriggles through the holes in the net.

I mean to say, nets have *holes* in them. Didn't anybody notice that? That RIDICULOUS FLAW IN SPELLBINDING!!

I am sorry. It's just that I'm cranky. I thought I was a Spellbinder.

I'm not.

CHAPTER
82
FINLAY

Ha! Cheer up, Honey Bee.

I'm sure you're a Spellbinder. Your toenails turned blue, remember?

You're just a really bad one.

A terrible one.

Like, a bottom-of-the-class sort of Spellbinder. One of those people who only just *scrape* onto the team? The sort of Spellbinder they put on the reserve bench. Or whose only job is handing out wedges of oranges to the rest of the team.

Don't be tough on yourself, though. You can't have known you'd be useless at it. And oranges are good!

Well, that cheered me up for a moment.

Not sure why, though. Ever since Honey Bee mentioned her blue toenails, I've had them in the back of my mind —*she'll* sort things out if I can't resist the Whispers! She's a Spellbinder!

But she can't.

Back into the pit of despair, then. You know what this is?

A complete and total disaster.

CHAPTER 83
HONEY BEE

One day a week, as Finlay mentioned, we go to the ship at the end and braid the thread together.

It's easier in a way—not so stifling and dark, not so hot and close, less dangerous. But over time, the thread begins to burn and blister our hands. The burns shoot up our wrists and circle our forearms, like the tentacles of sea stingers.

Mostly the blisters become calluses and our hands toughen up, but sometimes they get infected. The Whispering guards treat the infections with ointment that they keep in a locked cupboard in the washhouse.

Today, I saw a tiny child with a bright red blister on the palm of her hand. She was picking at it, and a Whispering guard shook his head at her to stop. As he crouched down to apply the ointment, I saw a glimpse of kindness in his eye. He was once kind, I realized—they were probably *all* kind. What has happened to these Whisperers?

Tonight, there are three empty hammocks in our ship. A boy was crushed by falling rocks and debris in another mudslide today. And two children were suffocated after a little one fell asleep, forgetting to close the door that keeps the air flowing.

CHAPTER 84

FINLAY

Can't write much tonight.

My head feels like it's been thwacked by a swinging boom about seventy-five times.

Here's why.

I tried resisting every single Whisper today. After those three kids died the other day, I got a surge of fury. We *have* to do something. We *have* to get out of here. I *have* to learn to resist.

So I went ahead and gave it my best shot.

I will get up now—was the first Whisper of the day, as usual—but I didn't let it in.

No, I said to myself, *I'm staying here in this*—

That's where I had to stop. Couldn't get to the word *hammock* before the Whisper had me. But it was a start. Here's how it went the rest of the day:

I will brush my teeth now—Nope, skipping that tod—
I will line up behind this man and follow him to the mines—Actually, no, I'm heading—
I will eat now—Nah, not hung—
I will stop eating now—No, I will carry on eating as long as I like. I'm actually starving.

See that?!

The first few times, the Whispers shut me down before I'd got too far.

(Shut me down *extra* fast when I tried to resist the *eat now* command. I was hungry.)

But the last one? *I will stop eating now?*

See that?

I resisted long enough to finish TWO WHOLE SENTENCES. Long enough to take an extra mouthful of food. My head was being *crushed* and *seared*, but I kept on thinking my own thoughts and eating that sticky flummery.

Our supervisor, Malik, blinked. I saw him. We were all sitting around the campfire eating, as usual, and he was strumming his guitar—and he stopped half strum. Blinked and looked straight at me. Fiddled with the band he wears around his wrist, then sniffed and carried on playing like nothing had happened. But I'm pretty sure he'd noticed.

I'd surprised him, see.

Forget what I said about being disappointed in myself.

Oh, and they want me to do a different job tomorrow too. Kid from another wreck just gave me the message. Someone's noticed how fast I can run, and they want me to do some deliveries for them.

Which means time outside the mines tomorrow. Time under the sun.

Just exactly what I need to give me even more strength.

I am on my way.

I'm going to bring those Whisperers crashing down. I'm going to get us out of here. I'm winning this battle.

Nobody tells Finlay what to do.

CHAPTER
85
HONEY BEE

Oh, I'm so excited by Finlay's chapter! I feel like I did when they made me carry a sack of rocks on my back to clear a passage one day, at the moment when the sack was lifted clear away!

Hooray for Finlay!!

Just as he said, he went off somewhere different this morning—running deliveries, apparently—and he's still not back. I hope he doesn't miss out on his dinner!

I wonder how quickly he will be able to resist Whispers altogether? And how he will rescue the rest of us? Because, I mean, *we* can't resist the Whispers, so *we* can't climb over the fence.

But I trust he has an idea. Soon we will all be home! Perhaps this will be the last chapter of our story?

By the way, Finlay and I chose to start writing again on our fifth night here. That was the night when things got fiery between Finlay and Victor.

Victor, Victor, Victor.

Sigh.

Now, I wouldn't call myself Victor's number one fan (ha-ha), but things *have* been rather tough for him here. He is a duke after all, and what usually happens is that people fluff up his pillow, and ask if he needs a foot rub, and bring him chocolate-coated cherries. But *here*, when he explains that he requires smoked salmon and poached eggs for breakfast, please, Malik smiles at him and turns back to tuning his guitar. Victor has to eat oatmeal like the rest of us. And when Victor says he will require a lamp affixed to a helmet before he enters any mine—the mine supervisors simply wave him onto the shaft lift, and down he goes. You see his face crumple occasionally, and I think that's him trying to resist.

Each evening, after dinner, Victor strolls about on the bluff. He never joins any games or conversations. Trying to look like a duke, I think, to impress the supervisors. Often I see him striking up conversation with a supervisor. He wants to wheedle his way *in* with them. They smile at him politely and turn away.

Anyhow, this whole thing is a shock to *all* of us, but it's a serious shock to Victor. He tried to explain this to Finlay on the fifth night here.

There was an icy wind blowing off the ocean that night, despite the season, and it found its way into our sleeping quarters through the cracks. We were shivering and trembling in our hammocks, curling ourselves up into tight balls, trying to get warm beneath our one thin blanket.

"Here now," Victor said suddenly. He hopped off his hammock and stood in the darkness by Finlay. "Give me your blanket."

Finlay chuckled.

"It is not a joke, Finlay. I am quite serious."

Nobody was asleep yet and you could feel the place growing still, all the children listening.

"Sure it's a joke." Finlay turned over in his hammock. "Crackerjack joke. Go back to sleep, Victor."

Victor cleared his throat. He was trying to sound calm and dukely. "I am *cold*," he said. "I *require* an extra blanket."

This time Finlay laughed aloud. "You think the rest of us lot *aren't* cold, Victor?"

"You may be cold," Victor retorted, "but you are *accustomed* to being cold. You are an orphan. You are *used* to being hungry and dirty and wearing ragged clothes and just generally *suffering*. This is *easy* for you. It is *far* harder for me. I have never been this dirty in my life. Certainly, I have never been cold. In any case, I am a duke, and you are a mere orphan. It is only right that I take your blanket." He reached out and fumbled around at Finlay's hammock.

"*Get* off," Finlay growled, shoving him away.

Victor stumbled, landed on the floor, and swore to himself. He stood up. "Oh very well, I'll take *this* one, then," he said, and swiped the blanket from a little girl—Sienna, six years old. She immediately began to cry.

"HEY!" came the shouts from many angry children, all beginning to rise in their hammocks. I was rising myself, or trying to—it's tricky to get out of a hammock in a hurry. They do sway so. *Nobody* was going to let Victor get away with this, but Finlay had already tumbled out and was flying towards Victor, fists at the ready.

Next thing, the two of them were going at it hammer and tongs.

That is an expression that means they were fighting.

It was difficult to see what was happening in the dark, but there were many thuds and slaps, and more than once they seemed to be rolling about on the floor.

The door opened.

There was Malik, holding a candle. He sleeps in a little cabin adjoining our quarters. You have to go right through it if you want to get out at night, and he always wakes. Embarrassing if you need to use the washroom.

He did not speak, but simply stood there.

Finlay and Victor untangled themselves and stood up, panting.

So Malik must have Whispered them to stop fighting.

They both approached him—I could see their shadows feeling their way across the room.

So Malik must have Whispered them to come to him.

It was very quiet. I was frightened for the boys.

But Malik simply lowered the candle to study both boys' faces. Then he spoke.

"Go along to the washhouse and clean yourselves up," he said. "And then to sleep. Good night, everyone!"

"Good night, Malik," we all replied.

I might go along and see if they need help, I thought. *There are bandages in the locked closet in the back of the washhouse. Malik will give me the key as I pass him now.*

That thought was like wisteria. He was Whispering it to me.

Honestly, I thought, *would it* hurt *you to suggest things out loud now and again? I do not need a Whisper to tell me to go help!*

When I reached the washhouse, Victor had already cleaned himself up and was striding back to the wreck, scowling fiercely.

"Are you all right, Victor?" I asked. "I have the key to a closet, which —" But he gave me a little shove and carried on.

Finlay was friendlier. He was inside the washhouse, holding a towel to his bleeding nose. You couldn't see much of his face on account of the towel, but his eyes were cheerful. I think he had enjoyed punching Victor very much.

He didn't need any bandages, but we unlocked the closet anyway, just to see what was in there.

It was your regular supply closet: bandages, ointments, swabs, and a pair of blunt scissors on one shelf, cleaning products on another, and curious bits and pieces — buttons, nails, on the rest. A stack of notepads sat on the bottom shelf, along with a handful of pencils.

Finlay took the scissors. He found a bucket of gravel behind the washhouse and hid them there.

"You never know," he said, coming back.

Then I reached for one of the notebooks on the bottom shelf and flicked through its blank pages. The paper was yellowing and old.

"Useful?" Finlay wondered.

We both stared at the notepad. We were thinking the same thing: that we could send a letter, telling somebody we were here—but the Kingdoms and Empires already *knew* that the lost children were here. They had *tried* many rescue missions and failed!

"If we could get a message to someone," I began, "telling them the things that are happening to the children here...?"

"The mines."

"It would be a rather *long* message," I said. "Like a story."

"Like carrying on the story we wrote for the genie? Keep taking turns with chapters? Whose turn was it anyway?"

I reached for another few notepads from the stack. "Yours," I said. "We were up to chapter sixty-eight."

And that is how we agreed to carry on. In the evenings, after dinner, Finlay and I sneak away and write behind the washhouse. If a supervisor strays near, we quickly hide the book in the gravel bucket. Pretend we are playing hide-and-seek.

Of course, I have no clue how we will get our story out of here! Finlay says we'll figure out a way.

But it's not going to fit into a *bottle*, is it? We can hardly toss it out onto the ocean.

Perhaps several bottles? A chapter in each? But where will we *get* the —

Oh, Finlay is back! I see him walking towards me!

He can write the next bit. There's still enough time before bed!

CHAPTER
86
HONEY BEE

Me again.

Sorry.

Finlay did not want to write last night.

Actually, he's done with the whole thing, he says.

"No more chapters," he said, when I offered him the notebook again tonight. And he sort of flung it back at me. It didn't hurt, as he was flinging in a very listless way. *Fling* is probably the wrong word, actually. It was more he *slowly* —

Oh dear, I'm blathering, sorry.

I'm upset.

I'm *frightened* actually. Finlay does not seem like Finlay anymore.

When he got back last night, I said, "Hello, Finlay, how was your day? Deliver anything interesting?" And his face crumpled up like old newspaper.

He refused to talk.

Simply trudged off to bed.

He did not do his push-ups this morning. Each day since we got here, he's done twenty push-ups first thing in the morning. Even though he must be quite worn out by working in the mines, as we all are.

And he has stopped paying attention to the little children. Usually, he tries to jolly them up a bit, putting on funny voices, challenging them to races, pretending they are quicker than him. But today: nothing.

Finlay, listen, I think you must have had a bad day yesterday. Maybe if you talk about it here you will feel better? Always good to talk.

Your turn.

* CHAPTER *
81
HONEY BEE

Hm. That didn't work. Still me.

Hey, Finlay, remember that long-ago first chapter? When you promised readers that they only had to put up with me for one chapter at a time? Well, this has been *three chapters of me*!!

Keep your promise! Come back! Readers will be *desperate* to be rid of me!

Oh my, I am sad today.

Do you know how much I hate the thread we pick out of the mines? Filaments and wisps get under your fingernails. They touch your lips, catch your eyelashes. You brush it away, but you always have this shuddery sensation—as if you've just walked through a spider's web and no matter how much you slap at your face and body, you cannot seem to peel the web away.

It rained last night, and the noise of it reminded me of gravel or pebbles falling, and the wind brought sounds from way across at the mines. The tarpaulins they use to cover equipment rustled like low thunder. You could even hear the voices of the Whisperers who live in the little cottages over there and supervise us during the day, their laughter and calls.

I tried to Spellbind again as I listened to these sounds.

What I did was, I imagined a sort of muddy black blob of Shadow Magic, and my hands moved about pretending to weave a net around it. Nothing happened except that Victor swore at me to stay still.

"We are *trying* to sleep here, Honey Bee," he snapped. "Stop *wriggling* like a *worm*."

What a charming boy he is, a ray of sunlight.

Eventually, I fell asleep and dreamed of mines caving in on me, while Whispering supervisors chatted and laughed.

It's hot these days. Summer is strong in the sun. It's a half-hour trek in the heat to the mines, and then inside the mines is even hotter.

In the evenings, as we sit about on the cliff tops watching the sea, we look out for things on the rocks below. "Oh, it's a seal!" children say sometimes. Or: "It's a water sprite! It's a mermaid!" But it never is: it's just the sun glowing on dark rock, or sparks of light on the water.

When I watch the sea, I see how the waves lift up, hurling themselves backwards to show you all the craggy, sharp rocks beneath, and then they *slam* down on those rocks. It's like a teacher slamming a cane onto a desk to show you what will happen if you carry on the way you are. The ocean is warning us, warning us all the time, watching us, keeping an eye on us: *if you come any closer*, it seems to say, *WHAM!* And it slams onto the rocks.

Tonight, after dinner, I chatted with some of the other children. I asked Hamish to join me, and he agreed.

I've forgotten to mention Hamish lately, but that's because I've almost completely forgotten *him*. Do you know he stopped speaking on our second day here? After one day in the mines? And he has not spoken since? It's so strange, as usually Hamish is a chatterbox, even if his chat is all nonsense. All he does now is borrow Malik's guitar sometimes, and he takes it off to a quiet spot on the bluff and plays it rather badly. That's it.

Anyhow, there's this one group of children who always sit together on the very edge of the cliff watching the dark ocean as they talk. I'd never taken much notice of these children before, as they are quite young, most about seven or eight. But tonight, something about the brightness of their eyes in the moonlight made me ask if Hamish and I could sit with them.

They introduced themselves in a very grown-up way, and I realized the group included Connor, Amie, and Bing from the Spindrift Orphanage, as well as a few children from various other Kingdoms and Empires. Even in the dim light, I could see how thin and bedraggled all these little children were, and the deep shadows under their eyes. *This is ridiculous!* I thought. *We MUST get these children out of here!*

To cheer them up, I pointed out the three ships now lined along the horizon. "Perhaps they are K&E Alliance ships," I said. "And they will soon rescue us?"

"Yes, they are K&E Alliance ships," Connor told me politely. He's the skinniest little thing with ears that stick out and hair that stands straight up on his head. "If you squint, you can see they're flying the K&E flags."

Oh, he was right. I felt a bit silly.

"We're hoping they'll launch another attack on the Whispering Kingdom soon," redheaded Amie put in, "but we saw the last one and it was awful. They tried to attack at night, but pirates and Whisperers were ready for them. They used a classic naval maneuver called 'crossing the T.' Risky move, but they executed their turns perfectly and hammered the K&E

ships—flagship was lit right up, a battleship capsized, another one was spinning around in circles. We sat here watching the ocean on fire; you could hear the sailors screaming as their ships sank."

I stared at her. How did she know all the military terminology?

I looked up and pointed out a particularly bright star, rather to change the subject.

"Yes. And there's another one," said a child lying flat on his back.

We all stared at the black sky awhile. Several dragons soared overhead and disappeared.

I rubbed my eyes.

"Am I just tired," I said, "or are the stars here *blurrier* than they are at home?"

"It's the Mist Shroud," a boy with a scratched-up face said. (He looked as if he'd been playing with many angry kittens.) "It stops anyone above from seeing through. It's transparent from our side, of course, but it still has a slight haze. Like frosted glass."

I'd forgotten about the witch-made Mist Shroud. It made me lonely, thinking that the stars and dragons we were watching up there could not watch us back.

I realize that stars cannot see. And that dragons are dangerous beasts. But still.

The children confided in me that they often sit here after dinner, staring at the ocean and the stars, trying to get ideas how to escape.

"Here are the options," Bing said, and he tapped them off on his fingers: "Cliffs, forest, fence."

"The cliffs are too steep and there's only wild and rocky ocean below," a freckled girl told me.

"The mines carry on until they hit the Impenetrable Forest," the boy with the scratched-up face said, and he pointed to his scratches. "And you can't get through that. Already tried, didn't I? Took me a day to walk by the mines, over the hills, around villages, and then I couldn't even get past the first shrub."

Oh my.

Here were Finlay and I thinking we'd come to rescue these children, but they'd been bravely working on escape all this time.

"So the chain-link fence is the only way out," the boy lying flat on the grass piped up. "We can't climb it because of the Whisper — once a Whisper gets into your head, it lasts about a day. Then it fades. That's why the supervisors reinforce their Whispers each morning. *I will not climb the fence. I will not climb the fence.* We get that message regularly."

"So we tunnel under it," Amie said. "Or cut through it. *Those* things are not forbidden by the Whisper. That's what we've been thinking."

Why had I not thought of that?!

"Clever children!" I told them. They nodded, to show they agreed with me.

But the ground along the fence is rock-hard, the children explained, and there are no spades for digging. Also, no scissors to cut through the wire.

"I know where some scissors are hidden," I said, "but I doubt they'd be sharp or strong enough. You'd need wire-cutters really."

Now Hamish cleared his throat as if to speak. I was happy to hear this.

We all turned to him.

But he said nothing. Simply slumped down behind his curtain of yellow hair. Not yellow anymore, more muddy brown.

By the way, little Jaskafar has taken ill. He is curled up in his hammock and has been sleeping feverishly the last three days. At first, he sucked his thumb, but he no longer even does that—he simply lies there, mouth open, breathing raspily.

Malik feels Jaskafar's forehead and frowns each morning, then he tips a little medicine into the boy's mouth. Otherwise, no notice is taken.

"Is it the flu?" I asked the children by the fire now, but Connor shook his head.

"It's something to do with the mines," he told me. "Other children have got it too. The thread gets into their lungs or something. And they don't—they never—"

He did not finish the sentence. *They don't get better*—I think that's what he was going to say. *They never survive.*

We need to find a way out.

We need to get Jaskafar to safety. To a hospital. *He* is the one we came here to rescue—and instead we are watching him die.

Also, we need Hamish to speak again, even if he drives us mad. His guitar-playing is quite dreadful.

Come on, Finlay! Write your next chapter! It will cheer you up! I promise! And then you can get back to resisting Whispers! Remember? You were on your way!!

YOUR TURN!

CHAPTER 88
HONEY BEE

Oh, sigh.

That didn't work either.

Another two days have passed and no change in Finlay.

Like Hamish, he has stopped speaking.

Worst of all, Finlay has been *walking* everywhere.

This might not seem odd to you, but you don't know Finlay.

In fact, it cannot be imagined! Finlay never walks! He leaps, climbs, runs, sprints, turns somersaults. He grabs an edge of something and swings himself up onto it!

To *walk*!

Unthinkable.

It is clear to me that this is the end of our story.

Finlay refuses to write any more. He has given up. There is no way that we can escape from here. This must be our new life, here in these wrecks and these mines.

The good news is that one of the children has found me a stamped envelope that I can use to send out this story. Redheaded Amie, from the Orphanage, says that mail is collected from a sack by the mining office each day. She has stolen an envelope for me. I will put our tale into it and Amie promises to sneak it into the sack.

I will address it to Waratah Teevsky, Director of the K&E Alliance.

✳

How should I finish?

I know!

The first part of our story began with the Spindrift Tournament. So I will *end* it with some final thoughts on the Spindrift Tournament.

And I shall say, for all the Kingdoms and Empires to hear, that Brathelthwaite Boarding School *won* that tournament. We won it fair and square. The Orphanage School cheated. They changed their team at the last minute, and they did not change it in the proper way.

Also, Finlay is not a very fast runner. I believe that everyone is faster than him.

Especially Victor. His Grace, the Good Duke Victor, is the fastest runner in all the Kingdoms and Empires, certainly faster than Finlay.

Thank you and farewell.

THE END

CHAPTER 89
FINLAY

VICTOR IS FASTER THAN ME, IS HE???

Of all the BLATHERSKITE you have written, Honey Bee, this is the biggest truckload of rotting crabapple blatherskite of all.

I will challenge Victor to a race ANY DAY OR NIGHT OF THE YEAR. I could beat Victor running on my hands! I could beat Victor chained to a tree! I could beat Victor while I was taking a bath!

Victor, fastest boy in the Kingdoms and Empires. Most ridiculous thing I ever heard.

AND WE DID NOT CHEAT AT THE TOURNAMENT!!

IF ANYONE CHEATED, *BRATHELTHWAITE* CHEATED!

WE WON THAT DAY!

WE WERE <u>ALLOWED</u> TO CHANGE OUR RELAY TEAM! IF MILLICENT PUT IT IN THE WRONG COLUMN OR WHATEVER SHE DID, THAT <u>*SHOULD NOT HAVE CHANGED ANYTHING!*</u>

THAT TROPHY BELONGS TO US.

SO, okay, fine, if you want to send our story out now, go ahead, Honey Bee, but only with THIS chapter as the FINAL chapter. You CANNOT end it with those lies, I FORBID IT.

You want to know about my day doing deliveries? I'll tell you. The truth will end our story.

Here's what happened.

They took me out of the Whispering Kingdom in the red motorcar. Through the gate in the chain-link fence, past the castle with waving thistle flags, along the cobblestone streets, by houses with flower boxes in every window. We skirted marketplaces crowded with Whisperers, baskets over their arms, long hair streaming down their backs. A man in a smock painted at an easel on a street corner.

All very pretty, I thought, shaking my head.

All very sunny here, while the Kingdoms and Empires burn thanks to the war you people started.

But then, as we passed, the artist turned to stare at the motorcar, and there was something dark, like bruises, around his eyes. He chewed on the end of his ponytail, blinking slowly.

I looked more closely then, and saw that the paint on the flower boxes was flaking, that a tree on a corner had withered and died. A *Missing Person* poster flapped on a pole, and a woman sat in a gutter scratching violently at her wrist. A long line of people waited, silent, at a bakery, and then, as we drove by, a man leaned out and hung a SOLD OUT sign on its front door.

It reminded me of home. *They're at war too*, I realized. Even if they're safe from direct attacks — on account of their gates, the ocean, the forest, the witch-made shroud — they're still at war.

But they started it! I argued with myself — and then stopped. Their *king* had started the war. What if our queen led *us* into war? Could we stop her? What good had our protests in the town square really done?

Around the next corner I saw tiles missing from a roof, a small crowd squabbling over a stack of firewood — and a man getting arrested, his hands being cuffed behind his back.

Through the three Whispering Gates, we drove.

Out of the Whispering Kingdom.

Along the coastal road.

Now I grew excited. Peering through the windows, looking for details that might help us escape. A man I didn't recognize was driving. A Whispering officer, he was, all got up in a uniform, a rifle lying alongside him. Pale cheeks, friendly smile, hair in a coiled-up braid at the nape of his neck.

Didn't say much—didn't tell me his name—but offered me water from a canister every now and then.

Whispering soldiers lined the roads, defending their kingdom, waving us on as we passed.

We drove about an hour, slowed down eventually.

Pulled over.

Hid the car behind some trees.

The officer led the way through a patch of forest. Gurgling sounds turned out to be a river. I tossed in a pebble or two as we walked by it. Sunlight dappling the water. Wildflowers and reeds. Nobody about.

Came out at a dirt road. Big warehouse in a clearing ahead. *NINA BAY CIDER*, a wooden sign said. Carts standing about. People wheeling barrels, or leaning their heads together to speak. Someone called something and pointed, another person held up a clipboard and shook her head.

The officer smiled at me again. Held a finger to his lips, meaning I should be quiet. Gestured for me to crouch beside him. At this point, we were behind a bunch of shrubs.

"Now we wait," the officer said. He took an apple from his pocket and crunched a few bites. "Want some?" Held it out to me. I didn't want his half-eaten apple.

Soon a whistle blew. More people poured out of the warehouse, chatting to each other. A lot of waving and calling. A few barrels trundled along, people pushing them.

Then they all headed off, most around the side of the warehouse, a couple right by our shrub. Three barrels remained, standing upright in a row.

Things went quiet. I could still hear the river gurgling away.

The officer checked his watch. "You have three minutes," he told me.

"Three minutes for what?"

"To make your delivery."

He reached into his pocket and drew out a tiny glass jar with a screw-top lid. Pale purple liquid swished about inside it. He tilted it back and forth, and it sparked, making me blink.

"Witch-made flu," he told me, winking. "Latest batch. Far stronger. Lethal to all who contract it."

Lethal.

That means it kills you.

Now the officer curled the jar in his big palm and reached out, pointing to the row of barrels.

"Pry open the lid of each," he told me, "and sprinkle in a few drops."

I stared at him. "In the barrels?"

"Apple cider. Nobody will taste the difference. Shipment being collected and sent to Clybourne in—" He checked his watch again. "Two minutes. Heard you're fast. Go on, then. Run."

I stared at him. Actually, I grinned. "No," I said.

I am going to take the jar from this man. I am going to sprinkle it into those barrels.

All I have to do is resist that Whisper. Two minutes. All I have to do is resist for two minutes.

"No way," I began—

I AM GOING TO TAKE THE JAR FROM THIS MAN. I AM GOING TO SPRINKLE IT INTO THOSE BARRELS.

That's how big it was. The Whisper.

Louder, fiercer, sharper than any the supervisors do at the mines.

I AM GOING TO TAKE THE JAR.

No, I am not — I only need to make it —

I AM GOING TO TAKE THE JAR <u>NOW</u>.

And I did.

Took it from his hand.

Sprinted over there, sprinkled it into the barrels, sprinted back.

A horse-drawn wagon rolled in. Couple of guys jumped down and started lugging the barrels away.

Anyone in Clybourne who drinks that apple cider will catch that witch-made flu and die, I thought. *I am a murderer. <u>Two minutes.</u> I only needed to resist for two minutes.*

Now I am going to remain silent. I will follow Officer Clegg back to the motorcar, back to the Whispering Kingdom, back to the shipwrecks on the bluff, and I will never attempt to resist a Whisper again.

So that's his name, I thought: *Officer Clegg.*

And I did exactly as he said.

THE END

CHAPTER
90
HONEY BEE

Oh, Finlay, no!

That Officer Clegg is the *vilest, most* MONSTROUS man in all the Kingdoms and Empires.

He murdered those people in Clybourne! Not you! You must *not* blame yourself! Officer Clegg must be an even more powerful Whisperer than the supervisors here. There is NOTHING anyone can do to resist! It's *not* your fault.

They were afraid of you, I bet! Because you were learning to resist the Whispers! Malik must have told them! So they wanted to crush your spirit!

Oh, but what a horrible way to do it. What an awful thing to happen to you.

I am so sorry.

I know a little of how you feel. Here is why.

I will tell this story quickly as I never like to tell it.

When I was nine years old, I was visiting my Aunt Rebecca in the Kingdom of Vanquishing Cove. This is a teeny kingdom, not far from Spindrift. It is hidden on the coast amongst the various nefarious Kingdoms and Empires. My parents were entomologists, which means they studied insects. Their favorite insect was the honeybee—that is how I got my name. Anyhow, each summer, they attended the Annual K&E Entomologist Conference, and I stayed with Aunt Rebecca in her cottage by the sea.

The summer that I was nine, the conference was taking place in the Dzopfy Empire, which is right next door to the Kingdom of Vanquishing

Cove. So, one weekend, in the middle of the conference, my parents surprised us by dropping in at the cottage!

It was wonderful. I wanted to show them *everything*: all the things that I did with Aunt Rebecca. The local markets where we bought bread and cheese, placing these in the string bags that we ourselves had made, the woods where we picked raspberries, the hills where we rode our bicycles and then picnicked on treacle cake and lemon and poppyseed muffins. Aunt Rebecca borrowed bikes from her friends for my parents to ride, and the four of us rode together!

As the sun was setting that day, I told my parents that the most exciting part of the day was yet to come. On Saturday evenings, the local orchestra plays on the beach and everybody comes out to hunt for pipis along the shore.

My parents were sitting on Aunt Rebecca's couch, their arms stretched along the back, their feet up. Glasses of wine stood on the table before them, red for my mother, white for my father.

"Here!" I said to my parents. "You take the best buckets! Ready to go?"

They glanced at each other. Bit their lips. I knew they were going to say something disappointing.

"Perhaps we could do that next time we visit?" Mother suggested. "It's just I strained a muscle riding the bicycle today, and I rather think I should rest it."

"And darling, I'm so sorry," Father added, "but my eyes just want to *close*. I was up until late last night labeling my ants, and I'm so weary."

They both looked at me ruefully.

But I shook my head.

"No!" I said. "We have to! What if you don't come again on a Saturday? What if the tradition changes? What if the pipis all disappear! This could be our *last chance to hunt for pipis*!"

My father sighed. My mother smiled.

"We're so sorry," my mother began—but I would not let her go on.

I begged.

I pleaded.

I even cried and stamped my foot.

Anyway, I made them come pipi gathering with me.

I *made* them.

Aunt Rebecca stayed behind, as she had planned a splendid roast dinner for my parents' visit, and had to tend to the potatoes and ice the chocolate-cherry mud cake.

We did have a fun time. My parents both splashed their faces with cold water to wake themselves up. Crowds of local folks swarmed along the beach swinging their buckets and doing the "pipi shuffle." Pipis are a kind of clam, in case you don't know, and you catch them by twisting your bare feet into the sand and then scooting back until you hit one. That's the shuffle. Father and I were laughing our heads off at my mother's shuffle. She wiggled her hips and pursed her lips and really carried on!

The orchestra played on the beach, as usual, and the sky turned pink with sunset. Everything was perfect—until the first arrow.

Zip.

A flash of light passing right by my nose.

It wasn't really an arrow—it was a quill from a passing berg troll. When berg trolls get too close to the shore, the water is too warm for them. They become feverish and release their quills like arrows.

"HEY! HEY!" Father shouted, trying to alert the berg troll that people were on the shore. Others joined him in yelling. Nobody was very worried at this point. Berg trolls usually mean no harm: you just have to let them know that you're there. My parents and I waded into the waves, cupping our hands around our mouths to shout more loudly at the troll.

Then came the sky-full of quills.

That is the only way I can describe it. The air was suddenly alive with quills, bristling with them, some arching high, some skimming fast and low over the water.

"It's a *herd* of trolls," my father said, amazed, and then he was hit.

He was beside me and then he was facedown in the water. Mother and I lunged down, wrenching him over. Blood formed a butterfly shape on his shirt. His eyes were closed.

"We need to get him out of here," Mother cried.

We set about dragging him, but there came a second wave of quills. Mother and I plunged down into the water, trying to hold Father aloft, at the same time as protecting ourselves.

When we burst up again, gasping for air, we tried again to pull Father from the water. He was too heavy for us.

"Help!" I shouted, but all around us people were running, or throwing themselves flat on the sand.

Aunt Rebecca's house is up on the hill, overlooking the beach. I could see her shape through the window, moving around in there, setting the table for dinner.

"Help us, Aunt Rebecca!" I screamed. "Aunt Rebecca, help us!"

But she could not hear over the sound of the violins. You see, most of the musicians had realized what was happening and had set down their instruments—but the three violinists, caught up in the music, eyes closed, were still playing madly.

Here came another wave of quills. Back down into the water we splashed.

"Help us, Aunt Rebecca!" I screamed.

A storm of quills again, and this time my mother was hit.

Water sprites rescued us in the end. A division swam up from the deep and worked together, using their magic to form powerful currents. They washed the berg trolls out to sea.

But it was too late. My parents both died in the hospital later that day. Several other locals were also hit by the quills, and injured, but the only people who died were Mother and Father.

CHAPTER 91
HONEY BEE (AGAIN)

Sorry, the page was getting all wet from tears! I had to start a new chapter.

Anyhow, Uncle Dominic came and took me to live at Brathelthwaite with him. He is my father's elder brother, and he paid lawyers to make grand speeches to a judge. "Imagine the *marvelous* life this child will have in an *exclusive* boarding school!" the lawyers said. Then they sneered at Aunt Rebecca: "But *she* wants the little girl to stay here in a *teeny, tiny* cottage with *holes* in its flyscreens?!"

Aunt Rebecca promised to fix her flyscreens, but it wasn't enough. The judge sent me off with Uncle Dominic.

Uncle Dominic must love me very much to go to court for me! I thought, to comfort myself.

However, it turned out that he gets all my parents' money until I'm twenty-one. That's what he was after, you see. My parents wrote a book called *Curious Insects: Magic and Otherwise*, which you might have heard of, as it was a bestseller. So lots of cash royalties come in.

In fact, I don't think Uncle Dominic even *likes* me!

Anyhow, Finlay, there *is* no envelope. Amie has *not* found a mailbag. We don't have a way to send out our story at all.

I was tricking you to get you to write. Sorry about that.

I wish there *was* a way to get our story out there.

I'm just staring at the ships on the horizon right now, imagining that I am the *best* pitcher in the world, with the sharpest aim. I could roll the notebooks into balls and *throw* them onto the deck of a ship!

Or I could turn each page into a paper dart and send it soaring across the sea!

If I had the biggest, loudest voice, I could *shout* the words of the story!

Actually, we did learn how to send messages using semaphore flags and dot-dash lights at school. Ha! I could stand on the cliff edge and send the *entire* tale in dots and dashes of light! Funny. It would take me all the night long and all day tomorrow and the next day. I'm sure the supervisors would give me time off from the mine to do that!! "Go for it, Honey Bee," they'd say. "Enjoy!"

Ha-ha! They are always patrolling, you know—I'd be caught in a flash. I'd send the first few *words* and—

WAIT
RIGHT
HERE…

All right, I'm back.

Just had to pop over the cliff edge.

Ha! Not *over* the cliff edge, I mean *to* the edge of the cliff.

I sent a message in dot-dash lights to the ships.

THREE BARRELS OF NINA BAY CIDER HAVE BEEN
POISONED WITH WITCH-MADE FLU. THEY ARE ON
THEIR WAY TO CLYBOURNE.

Just that.

I was going to add: *Please let them know! Don't let them drink the cider! It is dangerous! It is lethal*, and so on, but one of the supervisors—a woman named Jenna who is friendly to the littler children and lets them braid wildflowers through her hair—anyhow, she came strolling by. She frowned at the lamp in my hand.

I don't *think* she guessed what I was doing.

But a reply flashed from one of the ships just as Jenna passed:

MESSAGE RECEIVED. WILL ALERT CLYBOURNE.

I don't think Jenna noticed it.

But anyhow! Great news. The cider won't have reached Clybourne yet, as it takes about a week to sail that far. And Finlay delivered the poison four days ago. So the ship will radio the message to Clybourne just in time.

All will be well, and that concludes my —

Oh, almost forgot to say: I do NOT believe that Brathelthwaite won the Spindrift Tournament at all! The Orphanage School won! That was just part of my trick to get Finlay angry enough to write.

And of *course* Finlay is faster than Victor!

Finlay is like a spark of light! As quick as a water splash! Actually, he *is* a water splash. Spindrift is our town name, as you know, but did you know it is also the word for the spray that flies about on the crest of waves?

That is Finlay: darting here and there, playful and lively, exactly like sparky waves blown about in the breeze. He belongs in Spindrift more than anybody else, for he himself *is* spindrift in the sunlight.

CHAPTER 92
FINLAY

I said earlier that I never cry, but there are proper tears in my eyes right now.

Confusing tears, mind.

Crackerjack, happy tears where I want to dance a turkey trot (one of Lili-Daisy's favorites), BECAUSE HONEY BEE WARNED THE SHIPS!

CLYBOURNE WILL BE SAFE! I am NOT a murderer! Woo-hoo!

But I've also got this boulder in my stomach. Not an actual boulder, that would kill me. I just mean, I'm sad for Honey Bee. The story about her parents. Poor girl, standing in the ocean with her parents dying.

Not your fault, Honey Bee. It's the fault of those boneheaded berg trolls shooting off their quills.

Those are sorrowful tears.

And the things I've said about Honey Bee! That she's annoying! (Well, to be fair, she is sometimes.) (But not *that* annoying!) Blaming her for her Uncle Dominic! When he's only taking care of her for the money! And it's not your fault who your relatives are, anyhow.

(And did Uncle Dominic *horsewhip* her for cutting off her hair that day in the radish gnome attack? That's been in the back of my mind awhile, but I've trod it down. There *were* welts all over her legs the next time we saw her.

Oh crabapple.)

No wonder she can't abide the sounds of violins.

> Honey Bee: I am very sorry.
> Hang about, here she comes. She looks strange.

Honey Bee just told me that Malik has called her aside. "Exciting news, Honey Bee!" he said.

"Yes, Malik?"

"Tomorrow you get a break from the mines!"

"Oh, well, thank you..." (She was suspicious.)

"You are a fast runner, aren't you? You are going to do a delivery for us!"

"A delivery?"

"Yes. To Spindrift, actually. Isn't that where you come from?"

CHAPTER
93
FINLAY

One hour later.

Me again.

Honey Bee says she's too anxious to hold the pencil.

It has to happen tonight. The escape. It's our only choice.

I'm that jittery, the pencil keeps skidding off the paper.

That supervisor Jenna must have seen Honey Bee sending the message to the ship. Now she's being punished. They're going to make her deliver a fatal witch flu to Spindrift tomorrow.

We already knew we had to escape from here soon, but now we know it has to be tonight.

IT HAS TO BE.

We've just held an urgent meeting with a group of kids who meet on the cliff edge and discuss how to get out. Honey Bee recommended them—I found this unlikely, I mean, they're TINY, but she was right. They're sharp as swords.

We told Hamish to borrow Malik's guitar again, but this time to play it for *us*. Like, as if he was giving a concert. His strumming would drown out the sound of our talk.

"At least he's good for something, that Hamish," one of the kids murmured. Not sure if Hamish heard.

"Right," I began. "We need to go around the circle—"

Tricky to hear yourself think over the sound of a guitar.

"Just a *bit* quieter," I suggested. Hamish softened it a smidge, but went to town again as soon as he reached a chorus. Soon we were cupping our ears and squinting, trying to hear each other.

"We need to go around the circle," I repeated, "and everyone suggest a way out of here."

"There *is* no—" Connor began.

But I held up my palms. "Don't want to hear it. There *must* be a way. We *have* to get out tonight."

I told them why. I said that no idea was stupid. (That's not actually true. Plenty of ideas are dim as a rat after a night in a keg. Just had to get them talking.) And off we went around the circle.

And around the circle.

And around it again.

We could climb down the cliff. (We'd fall and drown. It's not your climbing sort of a cliff.)

Tie our blankets together to make a *rope* to climb down the cliff. (Supervisors would be onto us in a flash. Not to mention, we'd fall and drown.)

Sneak back to the mines, steal shovels, and dig under the fence. (They lock up all the equipment at night. Also there are Whisperers living in cottages at the mines.)

Knock the chain-link fence over! The Whisper tells us we can't climb *over* the fence, but it doesn't say we can't knock it down! (That was a good idea, and got us excited for a while. It's a strong fence, but what if *all* the children went at the fence at once? Wouldn't that be enough to knock it down?

But the supervisors would Whisper us to stop before we got any-where...)

We could do it while the supervisors were sleeping? (Get every child out of the sleeping quarters, through the supervisors' cabins, out of the wrecks, and across to the fence without one supervisor waking? Hmm.)

It kept coming back to the same thing.

Whatever we tried, it would only take one supervisor to wake. The superpowered Whispers were just too powerful.

"I swear," said a little girl with a hoarse voice — she must have been only six years old — "we've tried it all."

Hamish strummed once. "Have you tried cutting off their wristbands?" he asked.

We all jumped. Hamish hadn't spoken for weeks.

"Hamish," Honey Bee said. "That is a brilliant idea! Thank you for offer-ing it. Well done! Now, I don't know that they *have* wristbands, or how cutting them off might — "

She was trying to be nice, like positive reinforcement so he'd keep speak-ing, see? But he interrupted her.

"They do all have wristbands," he said, still playing the guitar. "Red-and-black wristbands. Or have I got that wrong? No. No, I really think it's true. I keep noticing. *Hold up!* I think to myself. *There's another of those little wristband blighters on a supervisor's wrist! Must be quite the fashion around here!* Mostly they wear long sleeves but at some point they always push their sleeves up a little? Perhaps because they're warm, or maybe they don't want to get their sleeves *dirty*, say, you know how when you're eating, say — what would you say? I know. Gravy. Say you have gravy on roast beef and you don't want — "

"Ah, Hamish," I said. Very nice to hear from him again and all, but we were on a deadline. "That's good they have wristbands. But I'm not sure how cutting them off would help."

"Oh, as to that," Hamish said, plucking away at the guitar, "do you remember the future children?"

Of course we remembered. The other kids were clueless, of course. Honey Bee and I filled them in, as fast as we could. The kids seemed confused, but no time to clarify. We turned back to Hamish — Honey Bee and I glancing at each other in panic, like how much time are we going to give Hamish for this rubbish?

"Well," Hamish said, "remember when Bronte and Alejandro were giving us clues about how to defeat the supercharged Whispers?"

We all nodded. The other kids can't have remembered, as they weren't there, but they nodded anyway. Humoring Hamish.

"First they kept circling their own wrists," Hamish said. "Around and around they went. Made me dizzy. Anyhow, they were actually trying to tell us about wristbands!"

"Hm," I said. "I'm not sure — "

"Hush," said Hamish. "And the next thing that happened was that Bronte kept braiding and unbraiding her hair?"

"Oh, I don't think that was part of the clue," Honey Bee said gently, "I think she just wanted to tidy her — "

"Shush! The wristbands are *braided* together—we braid them together when we have the days of twisting threads. That's what Bronte was trying to tell us. And what have they been braided out of?"

"Do you know," Honey Bee said suddenly, "those Whisperers who brought us here from Spindrift in their motorcar—the man *did* have a red-and-black wristband! You are right, Hamish."

"Malik has one too," I remembered, surprised. "I saw it when—"

"Oh, do be quiet, Finlay," Hamish cried, playing his guitar very quickly. "I'm losing my chain of thought! Tell me again what the third clue was?"

"They kept stamping at spots on the ground," I said.

"Shadows!" Hamish beamed. "They were stamping at shadows. I didn't take much notice of that at the time. I thought they were doing dance steps. But yes, it was shadows."

There was a long moment of quiet, as Hamish concentrated on his guitar.

"And?" Honey Bee prompted him.

Hamish looked up, surprised. "*Shadow* Magic. The *wristbands* have been *braided* out of *Shadow* Magic."

We stared at him.

"What do we pick out of the mines each day?" Hamish asked. "Thread. Red and black. Don't you remember the old stories about how ancient Dark Mages used to *get* their shadow thread out of the *ground* long ago? Before they just started imagining it? Well, now I think the stories are true. I think Whisperers have uncovered some ancient shadow thread troves. And we are getting the thread out for them, and braiding them into Shadow Magic wristbands, because it's such fine and delicate work they need the small hands of children, and it's shadow thread, so it blisters us and makes us sick eventually. And *that*—" He played an awful *twang* on the guitar. "*That* is how they supercharge their Whispers."

Everyone was silent.

Gobsmacked.

Staring at each other.

"Or have I got that wrong?" Hamish inquired.

CHAPTER 94
FINLAY

Seemed like a good place to end a chapter.

Still me, though.

"No," I said to Hamish. "I think you might have got it right."

So we made our plan.

Tonight, after everyone has gone to sleep, I will sneak into Malik's cabin and cut off his wristband. One child in each of the other wrecks does the same to their supervisor. I'll use the scissors we took out of the storage cupboard. The others said they have sharp-edged rocks they've collected from the mines, which should work to cut through a wristband—the girl with the hoarse voice said she's going to use her teeth. We considered asking Victor if we could borrow his penknife, as that'd be sharper, but I don't trust Victor with the plan.

Next, we use blankets to tie the supervisors up.

Then we wake *all* the kids and storm outside.

We climb over the chain-link fence, run through the nighttime shadows of the Whispering Kingdom, open the three gates, and get away.

I'm not hiding these notebooks tonight. I'm keeping them with me.

The plan is not perfect.

The plan is terrible, actually. What if Hamish is wrong about the wristbands? What if the supervisors can still super-Whisper without them? What if the supervisors' *earlier* Whispers—especially the Whisper telling us not to climb the fence—what if they keep their power even without the wristband?

But the plan is all we've got.

If it goes wrong, Honey Bee and I have agreed we're going to jump over the cliff.

Crazy, I know. We probably won't make it. But we're jumping with these notebooks. Honey Bee will take half of them and I'll take the rest, wrapped in scraps of sailcloth we've found, to protect them from the water. If we survive the jump, we'll swim out to the ships—I know that's batty. We won't survive and it's too far to swim. But maybe we *will* make it? Maybe there'll be divisions of water sprites down there that'll help us?

If we don't make it, we'll wash up someplace, won't we? These notebooks tucked into our shirts? Which means the message will get out to the Kingdoms and Empires.

I'm writing this message in the back of all the notebooks so both Honey Bee and I have it with us when we jump:

It's the wristbands. The supercharged Whispers are all in the wristbands.

Or anyway, we think it is.

Of course, this comes from Hamish.

And Hamish has never been what you might call—well, a genius.

Got to go.

They're calling us in for bedtime now.

My heart's drumming like a downpour on a tin roof.

This is probably the end, but I won't write *the end*.

Oh, I just did.

Wish us luck.

PART 3

* CHAPTER *
95
FINLAY

It's me!!!!

I'm alive!!!

Impossible, I know.

BUT I AM. Just smacked myself in the face to prove it.

Writing this back in Spindrift 'cause we want to finish up the story. Been back here a week now.

Here's what happened.

That night, after everyone had fallen asleep, I snuck into Malik's cabin and cut off his wristband.

Meanwhile, in the other wrecks, other kids were busy cutting off the wristbands of their supervisors too.

We were a team of stealthy super-spies, is all I can say.

In I crept, one tip-of-the-toe at a time, holding my breath. Moon was full, cabin softly lit, so I could see.

Got my scissors to his wristband and he was *still* asleep!

He woke up right about then.

Me standing by him, scissors at his wristband.

Snip, I went.

Didn't work. Scissors too blunt.

"What the—" Malik muttered, half-awake.

SNIP, I went again, and this time the wristband fell away. I grabbed it.

He pushed himself up in his bed, squinting. Still half-asleep, but he got straight to the Whispering, of course.

I am going to step back from Malik, I thought, *and return to my hammock at once.*

Ha!

Nothing but your regular Whisper! A little tickle! The kind Snatty-Ra-Ra used to try in the town square!

Wriggled my shoulders and it was gone.

"No, I'm not," I said aloud, nice and bold. "I'm going to tie you up here."

He blinked. Three times. Eyes went to his wrist, hand clutched at it. Felt around all over his bed, under his blankets.

That's when I knew for *certain* that Hamish had been right.

It was the wristband.

I held it up now, dangled it before him, to save his pointless searching. He pounced, but I'm quick and jumped out of his way.

Panic on his face then. Now he went for me properly, surging right out of bed, but Hamish and Honey Bee were waiting by the door. Pounded in and, between us, we got him trussed up with his own blankets.

He sighed.

"Well done, children," he said. "But what now? Where can you go from here, Finlay?"

"Easy," I replied. "I'm going to climb the fence." I flinched a bit, ready for the Whisper to kick in, but *nothing*. Beautiful! So it was true! Even earlier Whispers disappeared without the wristband. *"I'm going to climb the fence!"* I crowed.

"You're going to climb the fence, are you?" Malik repeated, like a really annoying teacher.

We paid no attention. Already there was a heap of noise outside, and we went out and joined it.

All the kids were waking, or being woken. Everyone was streaming out of the wrecks. Bigger kids carried the little ones or sick ones. A whole lot of half-asleep, confused kids, wrapped in their blankets, standing on the wind-swept bluff.

"EVERYBODY!" I shouted. "WE ARE GOING TO CLIMB THE—"

"Just so you know?" called a voice.

And it was Malik. For crying out loud, he'd got himself out of the blanket knots. Tricky to tie blankets tight. He was standing on the deck in his pajamas, well-lit by the moonlight, *smiling*.

"Just so you know," he called. "That fence is electrified. *Millions* of currents running through it. *Tremendously* high voltage. We switch it on after bedtime each night."

We all stared up at him.

"The Whisper that stopped you climbing it?" he said. "That was for your own *protection*."

"Oh, I don't believe a word of it," Honey Bee scoffed, but with a little question mark on her face in my direction.

Most kids had backed away from the fence. They were looking from Honey Bee and me to Malik and back again. Somehow we'd become the leaders.

"We'll test it!" I announced. "Everyone back!"

They were already back.

Honey Bee and I marched up to it.

Now, one thing I know is how to test for electric fences. Glim, the twins, and I have done enough exploring for that. I put my head close to it and listened.

Hummmm, said the fence. *Hummmm*.

"Hm," I said.

Next I picked a handful of grass, soaked it in a puddle of water, and tossed the lot against the wire.

SIZZLE, said the fence.

Most kids heard it.

"The fence is electrified," I told them. "It sizzles and it hums."

The kid with the scratched-up face marched up to me. (His name is Oscar Cheo, by the way—can't keep calling him *the kid with the scratched-up face*, 'cause the scratches will eventually heal.)

"So we kick it down!" he shouted. "Everyone wearing rubber boots should kick it down!"

Brilliant!

Plenty enough of us with rubber-soled shoes or boots to take down a chain-link fence if we kicked it hard enough!

Or anyway, that's what we thought.

First, of course, was the problem of explaining to all the kids what we wanted from them. A lot were too scared of the electricity to help.

"The bigger kids will be up front," we told them. "If we get a shock, it'll only be a *little* one!"

Plenty of the kids cried at that. They didn't want *any* kind of shock. They didn't want *us* to get shocked. Next thing, a bunch of smart-aleck kids started shouting questions about what we'd do once we'd knocked the fence down—how'd we get through the Whispering Kingdom without more Whisperers coming for us? How'd we get out through the Whispering Gates? What about the soldiers out front?

All excellent questions.

"We'll figure it out!" Honey Bee shouted. "For now let's *kick down this fence!*"

Enough kids were willing to give it a go.

And we did.

Gave it a real, solid shot.

"One!" bellowed Honey Bee. "Two! *Three!*"

Crowd of children, legs out, feet at the ready, hollering to make ourselves tougher and stronger.

Boing!

Bounced right off, didn't we?

Zing! went the electric charge. It actually hurt a lot.

Kids tumbled backwards, clutching their heads.

More crying started up.

"AGAIN!" boomed Oscar. Bit of a leader, that one.

We attacked the fence maybe thirty times. Wham — *boing!*

Bounce. Tumble. And so on.

Toughest fence you ever met.

That was when things really fell apart.

Kids were everywhere.

Some scrabbled around in the dirt, trying to dig under the fence. A whole crowd were at the gateway, pounding at the padlock with rocks. *Clang!* it went. Didn't budge.

A lot of kids started yelling that we'd better go back to our hammocks and pretend nothing had happened.

Most of the supervisors were milling about. Some had got themselves untangled from the blankets like Malik — and littler kids had untied the others, being little and confused.

The worst thing? The supervisors didn't try to stop us or to get us back to bed. They wandered about, letting us *boing* against the fence, or tear our fingernails trying to dig under it, with amused little smiles on their faces.

I wanted to kick those smiles sky-high.

But of course they weren't worried.

There *was no way out*.

And as soon as the sun began to rise, the Whisperers at the mines would notice we hadn't shown up for work. Over they'd come, striding along, and they'd Whisper us back under control long before we could get close enough to snip off any of *their* wristbands.

"Should we sneak across to their cottages and cut off all their wristbands while they sleep?" Honey Bee asked me, like she was reading my mind. She'd been trying to dig under the fence with the others, and was even dustier than usual.

It was not a bad idea, but there were at least thirty Whisperers in the cottages. One would surely wake.

I found Hamish curled up by the side of a wreck, tears in his eyes. "I've mucked this up, haven't I?" he said to me. "We're in for it now."

"Not your fault," I said.

"Of course it's my fault. I told you about the wristbands! And I got that wrong, didn't I? I always get things wrong."

"No, Hamish. You got it right. You got it exactly right. Don't you worry, we'll figure something out."

But the night carried on, the moon rose higher, and we didn't figure anything out.

Dawn nudged at the sky.

The supervisors had built themselves a fire and were toasting marshmallows. As if this was a party! They kept their eyes on the mining cottages in the distance. They might have tried walking over there for help, I guess, but they knew us kids would tackle them if they did. Easier to wait for reinforcements who could Whisper us back under control.

Victor was sitting with them, I noticed. I shook my head at him.

A lot of kids were still working at the gate or the fence, but some had fallen asleep on the grass.

Any moment, the mining Whisperers would wake up. Any moment they'd be here.

And then what?

What would they do to us? How would they punish us?

Honey Bee and I looked towards the cliff edge.

We knew we had to get out of here. We had to tell everyone the news about the wristbands.

We looked at each other. Back to the cliff edge.

"There's a light," someone called, pointing over to the cottages. "They're up."

It was true. A lamp moved around over there. Then another. You could even make out the sounds of doors slamming.

"This is over, isn't it?" Honey Bee murmured. "We've failed."

And that's when the first dragon landed.

CHAPTER
96
GLIM

This is Glim.

As you should know, 'cause I just wrote my name there: GLIM.

Finlay and Honey Bee have asked me to write what was happening back in Spindrift while they were in the Whispering Kingdom. So that the story will be properly complete. "But no more than two chapters," they said. (Bossy, aren't they?)

Anyhow, the day that Finlay and the others were taken by the Whisperers, I saw it happen.

Ran down the alley myself when Finlay didn't come straight back, and then ran about town searching. Caught a glimpse of them climbing into a red motorcar and there went the car, away.

I was scared for them but also proud. Went straight back to the protest in the town square and told the twins. "He'll be home soon," I said, "with all the stolen children." The twins swore a bit, as they'd looked forward to being taken themselves, but were philosophical about it, and soon we were back to shouting, "SET THEM FREE!"

After a couple of days, the protest in the town square petered out. Everyone was hungry and needed a bath, and the queen had taken no notice at all.

We meant to have more protests and marches, but things got busy. Lili-Daisy was still in the hospital with her influenza, so the bigger kids had to run the Orphanage. Cleaning, laundry, breaking apart fights, and so on. Meanwhile, the hospital got so busy that the twins moved in there full-time to help.

There was some fuss about Finlay and the Brathelthwaites having been taken, but nothing could be done about it—and then a string of ghoul attacks took all our attention. Ghouls spread darkness and you have to run about lighting candles against it.

After *that*, there was terrible weather for a week. Hammering rain and lightning every day. Everyone complained, but that's our kingdom for you. Storms.

One night I woke to the sound of the rain quieting to a pitter-patter, and suddenly I knew something was wrong. Three weeks had passed and they weren't back.

They couldn't escape.

I just knew it.

The twins were busy at the hospital. So it was up to me to go in there and get them.

How? In a boat? Through the Whispering Gates? The Impenetrable Forest? Or from the sky?

I chose the sky.

I like the sky.

Everything about it. Clouds, stars, the moon, butterflies, birds, dragon-flies, dragons, swans, gnats, kites, and balloons.

I think this is because my earliest memory is Lili-Daisy holding me up to the window and pointing out a shooting star. My parents were fisher-folk who drowned in a hurricane when I was two. Finlay's parents were lost in the same storm. I don't remember my parents at all but I do remember Lili-Daisy pointing to that shooting star. "There?" she said. "See? That's your mother and your father, Glim. They're stars now." I remember I reached out with my hands and touched her cheeks—the way you do when you're little and you see something soft and pouchy—and the cheeks were wet. *Oh, she's spilled something,* I thought. Now I think it was tears.

So that's why I like the sky.

Of course, it might be nothing to do with my parents flying around up there as stars, it could just be that it looks quiet. No chores, no squabbles, no slamming doors, nobody kicking a goose so that it honks, nobody telling you to speak.

Or because it's mysterious, the sky, like a story no one has yet read.

So I chose the sky.

I'll drop into the Whispering Kingdom from the sky, I decided.

The issue of how to get *into* the sky, I set aside. I'm like that with schoolwork too. I set aside the important bits, like the list of division problems, and focus on coloring the borders of the page instead.

"Well now, that's all right," Anita says to the class. "Glim comes at things sideways! We need more sideways thinking!" But now and then, in private, she says, "For goodness' sake, will you get on with your schoolwork, Glim?"

Still, I didn't think about how I'd get into the sky, I focused on how I'd drop down from it.

I'd need to break through the witch-made shroud.

How?

Witches, I thought. Witches must know how.

They're the ones who made it in the first place.

Now, it did not seem a good idea to travel to the Empire of Witchcraft. For one thing, they were at war against us. They'd joined the Whispering side. For another thing, they're wicked Shadow Mages. *They'd* never tell me the secret.

But *we* have witches. Perfectly *nice* witches.

Right here in Spindrift.

The next day, after dusk, I set off to visit the fairground where all the Shadow Mages and Whisperers were living. Visiting was strictly forbidden, but so was being outside after dark. I stayed in the shadows and crouched behind barrels or trees if I heard any sounds.

Through the barbed-wire fence, I could see that the place was a swampland of mud now after all the rain. Tents sagged. A sterling silver fox was scolding a toddler witch who'd been rolling about in the mud. A pair of Whisperers was pegging clothes onto a makeshift line. Mostly people sat about campfires talking in low voices and eating their supper.

I saw a surprising thing—the headmaster of Brathelthwaite Boarding School! His bald head caught a glint of moonlight. He wears the most ridiculous flappy collars and sleeves, so I'm sure it was him. He was hurrying between tents. How had he got over the barbed wire? I wondered. And what was he doing in there? Then I heard him speaking—although not what he said—and I also heard the sound of a woman cackling. A witch's cackle, it was.

Anyhow, I pressed my face to the fence and called to a nearby child. The child was drawing in the mud with a stick, but he tucked the stick behind his ear and scampered off to fetch Randalf for me.

Randalf is the lighthouse keeper, and half-witch, and we are friends on account of Finlay and me running up the stairs in his lighthouse when we train. He has a reddish face, lines running down his cheeks, and a whiskery chin.

He didn't know the answer to my question, but he set off to ask his old grandmother. After a few minutes, he came back and said his grandmother didn't know either but she had suggested he try Aunty Rada Vix, so off he went to do that. Next he came back and said that Aunty Rada Vix hadn't known either, but she'd had an idea that Uncle Robert Chin might know, so he was off to ask him.

"You don't need to report to me each step of the way," I suggested, but my voice was too soft.

"Eh?" he said. "Speak up!"

I just shrugged and smiled and off he went. His face had turned a darker red from all the hurrying about, but the lines around his mouth were determined.

I lost track of the witch relatives Randalf asked, but I can tell you this. In the end, his Great-Uncle Arthur Lam limped up to the fence and leaned on his walking stick.

"This is a proper witch secret," he growled. "Who is it wants to know?"

Being too scared to speak, I pointed at myself.

"But you're not even a *little* bit witch, are you?!"

I shook my head.

"Well, I don't know that I can tell you, then."

I didn't know what to say. Or even if I could say it.

I simply stared.

He stared back.

There we were, staring through the fence, for quite a while.

Then he gave a great shrug. "You promise you won't tell a soul this secret?"

I nodded.

"You seem quiet enough to keep that promise. Well, so you want to know how to see through a witch-made shroud?"

Another nod.

"Splash it with vinegar."

I blinked.

"You want to know how to get *through* a witch-made shroud?"

Another blink.

"Mix your vinegar with baking soda."

Then he grumbled in the back of his throat, turned around, and limped away.

So I had the trick. Vinegar and baking soda.

But I still didn't know how to get into the *sky* to use it.

I would have liked to write to the queen or General Hegelwink or even to Waratah Teevksy, Director of the K&E Alliance, telling them about the trick.

But I'd promised to keep it secret.

For a few days, I walked around frowning.

I would just have to learn to fly, I decided. It couldn't be that hard, could it?

And I went to the playing field behind the hospital and ran as fast as I could.

If I run fast enough, I thought, *the wind will pick me up and I will fly.*

I get like this when I can't solve a problem: barmy, I mean.

I fell down on the grass, out of breath.

Next, I tried tying balloons to my wrists and sprinting up and down the field. It really seemed like this might work. Especially when I ran down the slopes behind the playing field—I could *feel* myself lifting for a moment!

But only for a moment. Never longer than a moment.

In the end, I jumped up and down on the spot, shouting at the sky: "LIFT ME UP! LIFT ME UP!"

The twins came out of the hospital then. They'd been watching through a window. Eli took my temperature and Taya checked my pulse. Then they shoved me about a bit. That was their friendly way of telling me to cut it out.

I decided that a magic-spelled object might help me to fly, so I returned to the junkyard and searched once again.

For three days I tramped amongst the broken crockery and worn-out saddles, the cracked pots and threadbare rugs. Now and then I thought I saw a silvery-blue glow! But it always turned out to be sunlight hitting an old teapot.

And then, on the third day, I saw it: a gleam of silver, strong and sure!

It was magic! I knew it! Magic for sure!

I scrambled and tripped through the junk to find it—at last, true, bright magic!

Only, it wasn't magic at all.

It was a dragon.

Not a full-grown dragon, you understand. It was a baby dragon, the size of a large dog. The gleam that had caught my eye was its gemstones—the few that remained fixed. The rest must have come loose and fallen out, as there were only pockmarks there. A deep scratch ran right across the little dragon's pale gray flank, and one of its tiny clawed hooves was grazed and swollen.

The dragon looked up at me with wide, golden eyes.

I touched its back with the palm of my hand: warm and trembling.

I picked it up.

I know that this was dangerous and foolish. Even *touching* a dragon is enough to breach the human-dragon treaty. If you see one on land, no matter what size, you're supposed to turn around and run.

Who knew what would happen if a full-size dragon spied me with a baby in my arms?

But there was no way I was leaving the little creature crying in the junkyard. And it *was* crying. Its whole body shivered and hiccuped in my arms as I lifted it, and its snout was damp against my shoulder.

"Oh, poor little dragon," I said, trying to use the voice Lili-Daisy does when the smaller children are sick, "poor little dragon, you've had an accident, haven't you? Did you try to fly too soon? Did you fall and hurt yourself? It's *all* right, little dragon, I'm going to take you home."

I set off through the junkyard, out onto the clear and scrubby hills, and towards the line of yew trees. Whenever I stopped speaking, the dragon whimpered and shivered again, so I kept on.

KEEP OUT: DRAGON TERRITORY said the huge sign affixed to each of the tall yew trees.

My idea had been to set the baby dragon down right here by the trees, but when I peered through a gap I saw nothing but more bare hills with spindly bushes here and there.

I couldn't leave the baby here! I needed to get it closer to its dragon family.

I know what you are doing right now.

You are taking in a huge breath of air.

You are waving your hands at me, frantic.

NO! NO! DON'T GO THROUGH THE TREES (you are shouting at me).

THINK OF THE DANGER!

HAVE YOU LOST YOUR MIND?!

NO! GLIM! YOU WILL BE TORN TO PIECES BY THEIR CLAWS

AND TEETH! THEY WILL BARBECUE YOU WITH THEIR FIERY
BREATH AND EAT YOU FOR SUPPER! YOU WILL BE—

Hush up.

Too late.

(This already happened anyway; you know.)

I pushed my way through the trees and into dragon territory.

Yew trees look soft and billowy from a distance, but up close they're
made of very sharp needles.

These pricked me as I passed, but I curled my arms around the baby
dragon to protect it.

Now, at this point I was still talking in my low, soothing voice to the
baby, but this was more to distract myself. Because my heart was going

boomboomboomboomboomboomboooomboom

And I was thinking: *PUT THIS DRAGON DOWN AND*

SCRAM!

But I could not stop.

On I went.

I got a bit tired of saying, "It's *all* right, little dragon," and began to tell
the baby a story instead. That usually works with the little kids in the
Orphanage when they wake up with a nightmare.

Instead of bushes, there were trees now, growing ever more closely
together, and I was walking through woods. Usually when you tread on
dried bark, it feels good as it crunches beneath your shoe. But today each
crunch lit a firestorm in my heart.

It was so quiet on these wooded hills that, behind the murmur of my own storytelling, I could hear sounds from town—steam engines clunking in local factories, the low sigh of a ship's horn—and then, from the trees ahead of me, came the strangest noise I'd ever heard.

It was like this: *EEP!* Squeak CRUNCH CRUNCH *EEP!* Eruuu!

Birds? I wondered.

Mice?

But so loud! They must be *enormous* mice! The biggest bird I'd ever—

And then I felt a gust of warmth, smoke stung my eyes, and I stopped.

Dragons.

There were dragons just ahead.

"Right," I whispered to the baby in my arms. "I'll set you down here and—"

I crouched and tried to sort of *pour* the little guy onto the grass, making ready to dart away. But the dragon was having none of that. The more I tried to put it down, the closer it pressed itself to me, its claws scratching my arms. Next, it started up a whimpering and whining.

"SHHH!" I said, in a panic. "SHHH!"

I sat right down and pulled it onto my lap. It snuggled in and closed its eyes.

Oh *crabapple.*

Now what?

Well, I'll just quietly rock it to sleep, and *then* slip away.

But the baby dragon opened its golden eyes and stared right at my face.

Eeeee?

Like that. Like a question.

Then it batted the underside of my chin with its head.

"What?" I whispered. "What is it?"

Eeeeeee. Eee ee!

Oh brother, it wanted me to carry on with the story.

EEE!

"Hush!" I begged. "It's okay, I'll carry on with the story!"

The dragon settled down again.

And so I carried on.

I don't remember what the story was. I always make them up as I go along. The twins can recite every tale I've ever told, as they have excellent memories, so ask them if you want to hear one. I know there were dewdrops clinging to spiderwebs in my story, as well as angry water sprites, a splash in the distance, sails on the horizon, and cannon fire. Also, someone was pegging stars up into the sky—I always take my stories to the sky at some point—and then the stars *got accidentally transformed* into dewdrops clinging to the spiderwebs, which somebody crumpled and swept away, and that was a *disaster* for the sky. And so on. There was a chase scene and a thunderstorm too. I always have both.

Anyhow, I knew the dragons were there.

I didn't *let* myself know at first, as I was too frightened. The baby dragon's eyes were closed, its long lashes fluttering with each of its deep breaths, and it was heavy on my lap—but still I kept on talking, telling my story. And all around me were the cracks of snapping twigs, the rustle of bushes—sudden glows and sparks, tendrils of smoke, the smell of burned wood, the rustle of cinders.

I knew I was surrounded by dragons.

I kept my head down, watching the baby dragon sleep, and I carried on telling. It was all I could think to do.

I reached the sad bit of my story—I always do a very sad bit right near the end—and I heard *whoosh*es of air and felt blasts of heat on my cheek.

Sighs.

The dragons were sighing.

But I also always turn my story sharply around and give it a happy ending, so that is what I did.

"And *that*," I said, "is the end of the story."

There was a pause.

At last I looked up.

And there they were, dappled with light: the dragons. There were grays, blues, deep blacks, crimsons, and emerald greens, some snouts narrow, some wide, nostrils flaring or closed, eyes round or squinting, and every one watching me closely.

"Why, that was splendid!" said a dragon, and the baby tumbled from my lap.

After that, we became friends. I visited regularly for the next few days, and the dragons told me that some of them could speak our language, but chose not to. They taught me some of *their* language. It was all a great laugh, and the baby dragon grew better every day. Then, one day, the dragons asked me for another story, like the one they'd overheard. "I have a *true* story for you," I said, "to do with the Whispering Kingdom and stolen children and my friends who tried to rescue them."

They weren't as keen on that story as they had been on my invented one, but when it was done, Dragon Great Claudius, who is the father of the baby dragon, said, "Hmm. I wonder..."

And now, back to Finlay and Honey Bee.

CHAPTER
98
HONEY BEE

Gliding in at speed, the dragon skidded onto the grass. An immense black shadow: jewel-patterns and sharp black eyes glinting in the moonlight.

Everyone screamed. The supervisors scrambled to their feet, alarmed.

"It's all right," called a little voice from the dragon. A voice *on* the dragon, *astride* the dragon.

It was Glim!

Looking tinier than ever up there. The dragon breathed a gust of warm air, and we all shrieked again.

It's true that dragons often cross the sky around Spindrift, but they never fly low, and *never* land near people. They keep to their caves in the hills! The dragons they use for officer training at school are so old their fire is long extinguished, and their claws are clipped. Mostly they just sleep.

But here was a great, vibrant beast, its talons long and gleaming, in amongst hundreds of children!

"Glim!" shouted Finlay, bouncing up and down on the spot.

"*GLIM!*" came a louder, angry voice. That was Victor. Striding towards the dragon—but stopping a fair distance from its talons. "Of all the *preposterous, foolish* things to do! Somehow you have managed to steal an Officer Dragon. You have put us *all* in danger, you silly girl. Now, I'll thank you to disembark at once, while still alive. I will instruct the dragon to depart. Fortunately for you, I have been trained."

He clapped his hands once smartly and barked: "SIT!"

The dragon stared at him. It sniffed.

Glim looked over Victor's head at Finlay. "How many kids are here?" she called.

"About three hundred!"

"SIT!" shouted Victor. "DRAGON! SIT!"

The dragon sighed and turned away.

Glim slithered from the dragon's back to the grass.

"*Finally,*" Victor said to her. "Now step away from the dragon at once and I will send it off. All right, dragon, if you won't sit, FLY!" He waved his hands frantically and bellowed: "FLY! FLY AWAY! DO AS I COMMAND."

The dragon's tail flicked the air.

"He's not an Officer Dragon," Glim called to Victor. "He's a wild dragon. His name is Dragon Great Claudius. They can understand our language perfectly, by the way, he's just choosing to ignore you. But it's more polite to speak to them in their own language." She raised her voice. "Can you children all go over by the shipwrecks? Then I'll ask Claudius to call down the other dragons."

Everybody, including the supervisors, rushed to obey and crowded together, staring wide-eyed at Glim and the dragon. Only Victor did not move.

"Don't worry everybody!" he called. "There's no way she can *tell* this dragon to call more dragons! Too complicated a command. And it *is* an Officer Dragon, by the way, otherwise how*ever* was she riding it?"

But Glim was busy doing the most extraordinary thing. It was a bit like an awkward dance. She touched her toes and elbows, smacked the grass, spun in a circle, and made sounds like this: EEP! WHOA! *Crunch, crunch, crunch* (as if walking on dried autumn leaves). The dragon studied her as she spoke.

Victor burst out laughing.

"Oh, she's lost her marbles!" he spluttered. (I admit, I rather agreed.) "I believe Glim really thinks she's *talking* to the dragon! She thinks she's—"

"WeeeAAAAAAAAAAAAAH!"

That was the dragon.

He had thrown back his head and was *bawling* at the sky in a burst of smoke and flames.

Victor leapt on the spot and scurried to hide behind a supervisor. The sounds of his frightened panting filled the air.

Within seconds, that sound was lost beneath a *whoosh, whoosh, whoosh* like waves rolling in, rolling in, rolling in, and I was almost too afraid to look up.

But I did.

And the *whoosh, whoosh, whoosh* was the beating wings of dragons, hundreds of dragons, thousands, it seemed—but I suppose it was not that many. A sky alight with bursts of flame and the dazzle of their jewel patterns. You could feel the warmth and breeze of it all on your cheeks, you could see the sparks reflecting in other children's eyes. Small children pressed close to bigger ones, but all of us gazed up in wonder.

They landed in perfect formation, with a *thud, thud, thud* that shook and vibrated. You could feel it in your heels.

A long row of dragons facing the row of shipwrecks.

And everyone turned to face Glim. She climbed back onto Dragon Great Claudius, and stood on his back.

"Right!" she called to us. "Each dragon can take three or four children! Bigger children ride with little ones or sick ones. Don't worry about thanking the dragons, they know we're in a rush! I've told them everything! Just climb aboard!"

THANK the dragons?!

Climb aboard?!

Was she mad?

Nobody moved.

Glim pulled on her own short hair. "HURRY!" she shouted. "The Whisperers are coming!"

Still, we stood.

"I can *see* them!" Glim wailed. "Over there!"

She pointed.

And there they were, a small crowd of mining officers, marching along, lamps swinging. If they got any closer, they'd be in range to Whisper us all back under control.

We needed to move now. And fast.

"COME *ON!*" Glim bellowed. "This is the *only way out*! I'll lead!" She touched her dragon once, and it rose in the air.

"THE WHISPERERS ARE COMING!" Glim shrieked from the air above us. *"THEY'RE RIGHT THERE!!"*

And in a surge, in a scramble, we rushed towards the dragons.

You think riding a laundry chute is fun?

Try a dragon.

Easily the best night of my life.

I mean, not only were we escaping the Whispering Kingdom—away from the mines! Getting all the children out of there!—everyone, even Victor—although he had to shake the supervisors' hands goodbye, for crying out loud—but they *all* ended up on a dragon—

Where was I?

Got that sentence tangled.

Because it was such a tangle of happy riding that dragon! Not only did we escape, is what I'm trying to say: *we rode dragons!*

Only just got out in time. The mining Whisperers figured something was up and they were heading our way at speed. One dragon rose, two, three, four, five. Seeing this, the Whisperers stopped dead in shock. Six, seven, eight dragons up. The Whisperers started running. Sprinting even, or something like that: grown-ups don't really know how to sprint. Nine, ten, eleven in a *whoosh* of hot air and a burst of beating wings. So now the mining Whisperers are shouting, roaring, galumphing along, and our supervisor Whisperers are screaming: "Hurry! Whisper them! Whisper the children back down!"

Dragon after dragon after dragon soaring up, all at once now, all in formation.

The Whisperers closed in right as the last dragon took off. I was on that dragon, bringing up the rear, little Jaskafar curled up in front of me, Amie, Connor, and Bing ahead of him. Our dragon knew exactly what to do: shot up like a rocket, it did.

Then we were soaring!

Through the sky!

You need to ride a dragon, you really do.

Up with the stars, the ocean a sort of rumpled-up darkness way below. Its waves look like some strange little game it's playing. Wind in your face, and sometimes a sort of misty dampness: Guess what that is? It's clouds! We were flying through clouds!

There's the freshness of the sky, and the dragon smells like grass after rain, and when it lights its way with gusts of flame there's a wood-smoke smell, sparks curling into the sky.

You feel its wings pumping. You feel that through your body, vibrating through the dragon and into your belly.

The sky lightened to pale gray as we flew through the night. Stars faded, an orange-red glow swept the horizon, and there we were in the midst of a huge flock of dragons, their wing beats keeping time.

At one point, the dragons all banked left, a mighty turn. Ours tilted sharply, so we had to cling on hard. Amie shrieked then.

"Don't be scared," I called, reaching forward to pat her shoulder, but she shrieked again and it wasn't a shriek, I realized, it was a *whoop* of joy.

I joined in. We all did. Even Jaskafar straightened up enough to blink around and grin up at me.

And we *whoop*ed our way home to Spindrift.

CHAPTER
100
HONEY BEE

Oh, well, yes, it *was* fun, riding the dragon, but:

WHAT IF WE *FALL* OFF THE DRAGONS??! WHAT IF THE DRAGONS REMEMBER THEY ARE ACTUALLY *FEROCIOUS BEASTS* WITH *TEETH* AND *CLAWS* AND *FLAME-THROWING MOUTHS* AND THEY TAKE US ALL TO THEIR CAVES AND TEAR US TO PIECES?! WHAT IF WE *FALL* INTO THE OCEAN?!

Those were the questions storming through my mind, rather, and made the experience a *teensy bit less fun*.

Still, there *were* moments when I found myself smiling, or half smiling anyway, the wind sort of *plastering* my smile to my face so it probably looked more like a grimace. Sometimes I *knew* that it was going to be all right. Then I *loved* my dragon and *all* these dragons. So many dragons were flying hard and fast, and they were doing this for *us*, for us children, to save us.

I loved also that we were flying in formation, dragons and children, glimmers of fire now and then—bursts of flame or distant sparks like fireflies—and the silhouettes of the other children, hair streaming back as they clutched on.

We flew across the sea for most of the way, sometimes so low that waves splashed us, and once I was so drenched that I drew out the notebooks from under my pinafore and held them in the air to dry. Then we curved in towards the coastline, and there was our kingdom, the Kingdom of Storms, its forests and roads, hills and towns, spread out like a children's game: toy houses, barns, haystacks, teeny little wagons wending along the early-morning roads. In the distance, I could see a crowd of people crossing the landscape exactly like slowly sliding sprinkles.

Then we flew low towards Spindrift, and there was its curly beach, the lighthouse, the tallow factory, the warehouses, the shipping yards. We swept right across Spindrift downtown: crooked houses leaning together, broken chimneys, piles of rubble, chasms where houses once stood; the enclosure circling the fairground with its rows of tents; the patchy town green, dotted with soldiers' huts, and Danbury Street and Gerbera Lane, the town square—and here came a bucket of water splashing from the open window of someone's house.

Soon we were across town, and there was Spindrift Lake, the Sterling Silver Depot, the grand grounds of Brathelthwaite, with its sports fields and stone walls, the nearby Spindrift Gardens, and there was the Spindrift Hospital, the junkyard, the shrubby Oakum Woods on their low slopes.

My favorite part was when we landed. Ingeniously, Glim had led us to the playing field just behind the hospital. Space for all the dragons to thud down, snorting and breathing dark smoke. Space for doctors and nurses to come hurrying out of the hospital—to see what all the commotion was about and to be horrified by a field of dragons. But then, quick-thinking, practical things that they are, the doctors and nurses gathered the sick or injured children and brought them back to the hospital.

There was also enough space here for townsfolk, just waking up and hearing the news, to run through the streets of Spindrift, shouting, cheering, and sobbing, for here were the children, *all* the children who'd been stolen from Spindrift, back home.

The dragons soared away, back to dragon territory, in one great swoop—Glim said they were shy and didn't want to stay to be thanked, but we applauded, whistled, and cheered for them anyway. I think they liked that.

Spindrift parents wept and hugged their children. The children had been so brave at the mines, but now, with their mothers and fathers holding them, they were children again and remembered how miserable they'd been and how much they'd missed home. Most burst into tears. They were hugged more tightly.

And here was Lili-Daisy Casimati from the Orphanage! I knew she'd been ill with the witch flu when we left and she did look rather thin and drawn, but she was skipping along at high speed, hooting and hollering—she swept the missing orphans up into her arms. Amie, Connor, Bing, and Finlay, she whirled around, hugging each in turn, over and over. They began to look a little like rag dolls.

"And Jaskafar?" Lili-Daisy panted eventually, her voice suddenly frightened. "Where's Jaskafar?"

Some of the orphans took her hand and hurried her across to the hospital, where Jaskafar had already been taken.

While all this was happening, Glim sidled up to me and smiled. "Welcome back, Honey Bee," she said. "Are you all right?"

And she patted me on the shoulder.

I had to bite my lip *so* hard to stop myself bursting into tears!

Mayor Franny arrived, carrying a megaphone, and she called for all the other children to sit on the grass around her. "You will all be billeted out to local homes," she announced, "where you may have baths and breakfast. But first we must record your names and addresses so that telegrams can be sent to your parents!"

The children all cheered, partly because of the parents, but mainly I think it was the idea of breakfast.

"It may take time to get you home," Mayor Franny cautioned, "what with war on seas and land. But we'll find a way!"

She looked to the sky then, maybe thinking that if dragons had obliged everyone by bringing the children here, perhaps they could be called upon to bring these ones back home?

It really was marvelous! People kept arriving and exclaiming. Everyone wanted to shake hands with Glim and ask her *how* she'd done it all. But Glim was too shy to speak and only smiled.

So the people turned to Finlay, Hamish, and me, wanting to hear our stories. (I had tucked my notebooks safely away again, a little damp and singed.) We explained about the wristbands and they all took great breaths of amazement, and congratulated Hamish on figuring this out, and all of us on leading the escape!

Even Sir Brathelthwaite turned up from the boarding school! He embraced Victor and asked how he had helped with the escape. This really did confuse Victor for a moment. "I was there!" he said eventually. "I was most certainly there!"

Sir Brathelthwaite hugged him again and said that Victor would probably get a medal for that.

Next thing, trumpets blared and the queen arrived in her carriage! So the queen was still in Spindrift, and still happily showing her face despite having locked up our local Shadow Mages and Whisperers. She stepped out, waving and smiling. Reporters from *Spindrift Daily News* took pictures of her treading amongst the children, handing out cups of juice and treats, and offering blankets. It was quite warm, so nobody really needed a blanket, but it was sweet of her to offer.

So exciting.

Until the queen crouched down by Oscar Cheo and asked how he'd gotten those scratches. He told her about his earlier escape attempts through the Impenetrable Forest. "Oh!" the queen said, and "Golly!" and "What a chap you are!"

"Now then," she said at last, straightening up. "Would you like a red or green licorice strap?"

"Neither, thanks," Oscar replied, "I'm not much keen on licorice. More of a toffee boy, I am. Oh, and by the way, Your Majesty, did you know there's a great coven of witches heading this way?"

At this, I swung around to stare at him. Everyone within earshot did.

"The dragon I was riding swooped low over them," Oscar explained, "close enough so I could spot their broomsticks and sandals. Biggest coven *I* ever saw. Marching across the countryside. Heading this way."

Of course! The crowd of people I'd seen crossing the landscape! I'd thought of them as sprinkles!

Not sprinkles!

Witches!

Already, the queen was stalking back through the crowd. "Get the commander in chief *here*!" she barked. "Sound the alarms! Alert the Spellbinders! We want *every* Spellbinder! Go out to Brathelthwaite Boarding School and fetch all the Spellbinders-in-Training! Yes, I *know* that's top secret, and nobody's supposed to know they're there, but I don't give a hoot. This time *we will NOT let the witches in! Every single Spellbinder in this town will get out there NOW and stop those witches!!!*"

She paused, recovering her breath. "Oh," she said, "and somebody get that boy some toffee."

CHAPTER
101
FINLAY

Townsfolk who lived nearby scampered off home, taking bunches of rescued kids along with them.

The rest of us headed to the basement of the hospital—the nearest shelter.

Of course, a shelter's not much use in a witch invasion, because you never know what spell they might crochet. Still, off we ran.

Pretty crowded in there, it was. The queen set up shop in one corner, doing serious consultation with General Hegelwink, Mayor Franny, and a bunch of other advisers and guards.

All the patients were carried downstairs from the wards, for their safety, and tucked up in rows of cots—along with the sick children from the mines. Doctors and nurses scurried around, stethoscopes swinging. In the corner, Lili-Daisy was arguing with a nurse, demanding the nurse cure Jaskafar *immediately.* (Lili-Daisy wasn't thinking straight.) Anita whizzed by, stopped to hug me, held me at arm's length, nodded briskly, and carried on.

The twins were here too. Wearing white coats like proper little doctors.

"Been here every day last few weeks," Eli told me. "So many war-wounded and witch-flu affected. Hospital couldn't cope."

"We're quite good at *health*, it turns out," Taya put in.

"Diseases come at us? We break their face," Eli confirmed.

"Prince Jakob got better," Eli added. "Still visits sometimes though—to help out, he says, but he's actually in love with Anita. Well, she saved his life, so why not? He's all right when he's not trying to have picnics on witch-spelled beaches."

"That was just the fever," Taya said sagely. "Don't touch anything, Finlay."

"You're covered in mud," Eli agreed.

"Have a bath."

"He can't. He's in the basement."

Both nodded, punched me in the shoulder to say *welcome back*, and got back to work.

I looked for somewhere to sit. There were only a few seats and those were taken. Sir Brathelthwaite and Victor had both "come over faint" from the "shock of it all," so *they'd* snaffled the two comfiest ones. I found a crate, sat down, and looked around.

Everything was good.

Queens (well, one of them, but still), rich folk, commanders, soldiers, orphans, sick folk, and the rest, here we were, all mingled together and getting along, chatting and squawking and tripping about. Someone handed me an apple, which was not the feast I'd hoped for as a welcome, but it was green and crunchy. Honey Bee pulled up a crate next to me, eating an apple of her own.

Crunch, she said.

Crunch, I said.

Crunch.

Crunch.

Then came a pounding on the basement door.

Everything went quiet.

"Have the witches got through? Is it the witches?" someone hissed.

"Hush," barked the queen. "Witches wouldn't knock. It's Colonel Spoforth. Somebody open that."

A soldier stepped in. Young guy, bristly sideburns. He bowed at the queen, saluted the general, then spoke fast to the general.

We were close enough to hear.

"Hostile force approaching from the north, sir. Approaching this facility as we speak, sir. The third and fourth regiment are in defensive position, sir. What are our instructions if hostiles open fire, sir?"

The general growled: "*Instructions?* Defend the town, of course, Colonel! Fire back!"

But the queen's face was twisting strangely.

"Why?" she snapped. "Why are you asking?"

"It's civilians," the colonel admitted, his voice dropping. "The hostile forces are actually our *allies*, but they're being controlled by Whisperers. We'd rather not engage, but—" He gave a helpless shrug.

"You mean it's not a real army?" the general roared. "Whisperers are *making* them attack us?"

"Correct, sir. Every adult citizen of the Kingdom of Vanquishing Cove—that's a tiny kingdom so it amounts to no more than two or three hundred people. But all are armed with bolt action rifles."

"We need Spellbinders," the queen said sharply. "Spellbinders must bind the Whisperers and set the citizens free!"

"Correct, Your Majesty. But the Spellbinders are all facing the witches."

"*Every* Spellbinder? Surely we have *a few* left!"

The general's nose twitched. "*Every* Spellbinder is dealing with the witches in the northeast, madam. Those were your orders, if you recall."

"I recall," snapped the queen. "These are innocent people, you say? And they are about to attack us?"

Colonel Spoforth nodded. "They're approaching the Tulevsky farm. The third and fourth regiment are at the ready on the lower slopes of the Oakum Woods."

So close!

The queen turned to the general. "What do you advise?"

"We have no choice here."

The queen pressed her hand to her forehead. "Innocent people," she murmured. "Only engage if absolutely necessary, Colonel. Only if they open fire first."

The general nodded. "Agree, Your Majesty. I've no interest in a massacre of innocents. But neither can we risk the town, Colonel. You understand?"

Spoforth bowed, saluted, marched to the door, and pushed it open.

Stillness crossed the basement.

Then Honey Bee leapt up, kicked aside her crate, ran to the door, and disappeared outside.

Now what in the world, I thought, *is she*—

"What's that girl doing? Come back, child!" the queen quavered. "Why would she—"

Of course.

The Kingdom of Vanquishing Cove.

Where her Aunt Rebecca lives.

CHAPTER
102
HONEY BEE

Quick footsteps crunched behind me.

Crunch-crunch

Crunch-crunch

Crunch-crunch

I was crossing the dragon-scorched grass of the field.

Crunch-crunch, went my running footsteps.

Crunch-crunch, came from right behind, and then *crunch-crunch*, as he caught up with me.

It was Finlay.

"Go back," I said, not turning.

"I'm your friend," he replied.

"Go back," I repeated, panting. "It's dangerous. I insist that you go back to the shelter!"

"Righto," Finlay said.

But *crunch-crunch, crunch-crunch*, went his feet beside me.

Then came another voice.

"Honey Bee! Come back at once! It's dangerous out here!"

It was Sir Brathelthwaite, stumbling along, his bald head sweaty and shiny under the hot sun, sleeves flapping about.

Good gracious, I thought. *He* cares *about me! Perhaps it's just the reputation of his school, but still. Good gracious.*

Of course, later I found out that the queen had barked at him, "Isn't that your student? Go after her!"

Finlay and I quickened our pace, leaving Sir B far behind.

The field behind the hospital hits a small hill, which in turn gives way to more little hills, rising up into the Lower Slopes. The junkyard is over to the left, Dragon Territory is to the right, but we were running through the hills in between. These are mostly bare, shrubs here and there, patches of dirt amongst the dandelions and crabgrass.

We ran up the first hill, into a valley, up the second, into a valley—and there they were: a battalion of K&E Alliance soldiers, covering the slope. Arranged in neat lines like columns of mathematical figures. Uniforms, boots, helmets strapped at their chins, guns held firm and diagonal across their chests.

I zipped through the soldiers so fast that most only had time to swing their heads sideways in surprise. At the crest of the hill, the first row of soldiers was crouched at the ready, each resting on a single knee, guns raised to their shoulders, trained on the valley below.

I pushed through this row and emerged onto the hilltop.

"Eh!" came a voice.

It was Colonel Spoforth, right behind me. He must have only just arrived here himself.

"Child!" he called.

But I was staring down into the valley.

There, arranged in straggly lines, were the people of Vanquishing Cove.

They were so close I could have spoken to them without raising my voice.

Dusty and grass-stained, sweat dampening their torn clothes. Their faces were drawn, worn, and wet with tears, their eyes bloodshot.

"Get back behind the lines, child!" Colonel Spoforth commanded. I ignored him.

Ranged around the outskirts of the group below were ten Whisperers. I counted them up quickly, recognizing them as Whisperers at once. Not only did they have long hair draped over their shoulders, they also seemed to be *taller* than everyone else. *Strange!* I thought. *I never knew Whisperers were tall.*

But it was just that they held their shoulders straight, while the people of Vanquishing Cove slumped and drooped.

I ran my eyes along the rows and—there was Aunt Rebecca! My Aunt Rebecca! Oh, I wanted to sprint to her! Bundle her away from there! She did not see me: her face was bowed, her knuckles pressed to her temples.

She was trying to resist the Whispers.

Others were doing the same, I could see. Most simply stared up towards the hill, desperately miserable. They'd probably already tried resisting the Whispers and given up.

Colonel Spoforth hurried over. He placed himself between me and the Vanquishing Covers. This was brave I suppose, but now I had to tilt my head to see around him.

"Who is the commander of these troops?" he boomed.

One of the Whisperers raised a hand. She appeared to be chewing gum. "I am."

"Tell your force to stand down," Colonel Spoforth ordered. "Let's talk."

The Whisperer giggled. "No," she said. "Thanks all the same."

I was wasting time listening to this.

I needed to Spellbind.

To Spellbind *ten* Whisperers.

I squeezed my eyes tightly and sought out the Shadow Magic.

Nothing.

Still nothing.

Just the usual *black* you see when you close your eyes. I pressed the heels of my palms to my eyes, and now I could see the usual threads and wires of light, the dashes and darts of color. It's just tricks of sunlight.

"Surrender at once," called the gum-chewing Whisperer. "Or we attack."

"You are outnumbered five to one!" Colonel Spoforth spluttered. "You are leading your troops to certain death!"

I bit my lip sharply. I slapped my own cheeks. *Where is the Shadow Magic? How can I bind you if I cannot see you?*

I can't do it.

I am *not* a Spellbinder.

Aunt Rebecca is going to be shot down right before my eyes.

"Honey Bee!" barked a voice.

It was Sir Brathelthwaite, wheezing and panting, crushed in amidst the soldiers. He'd caught up with us at last.

"You are in the line of fire! Child! Get back here at once!"

I closed my eyes. I could not look at Aunt Rebecca down there.

But behind my closed eyes, I saw her anyway. Aunt Rebecca in her kitchen baking cakes. Aunt Rebecca making *cheep*ing noises like a bird. Standing in a courtroom, begging a judge to let me live with her. Riding her bicycle alongside mine. Filling our homemade string bags with peaches, grapes, and plums—

String bags.

Homemade string bags.

A string bag *is a kind of net*!

I *know* how to make a string bag!

Why do I keep trying to make *fishing* nets?!

"Perhaps," agreed the Whispering commander. "But we *will* attack unless you surrender. If you want to save these people, surrender your town within the next ten seconds."

"You know that's not going to happen," Colonel Spoforth said, his voice low with terrible sadness.

"Ten seconds," the Whisperer called, "and then we attack."

What if I forgot the Shadow Magic for a moment, and made the perfect net for it?

I squeezed my eyes more tightly shut and looked for it: the loom on Aunt Rebecca's table. Screws in the corners for tying the first knot.

Where's the string?

Ah, here it is. Green-gold plaited thread, thick and strong.

A lark's head knot.

I tied it good and firm.

My hands shook. They moved slowly. I tied the second knot.

"Come on!" Colonel Spoforth pleaded. "You don't want this! You don't want these good people mown down!"

"Surrender," the Whisperer replied. "Surrender the town of Spindrift. Surrender the Kingdom of Storms. Have your queen sign the Kingdom of Storms over to the Whispering Kingdom."

"Let's talk," said Spoforth. "Let's find a way."

Now my hands were growing stronger, more confident, remembering just what to do. They moved rapidly, reaching, lifting, threading through. Reaching, lifting, threading through. Faster, faster, my fingers pulled, tightened, my hands had never moved so fast!

The string bag was forming! I could *see* it—

"Ready!" barked the Whispering commander.

Inside my mind, there was a rush of darkness, just to the right of my almost-finished string bag.

At the same time, a clatter of rifles being raised, locked, and loaded in the valley below.

A louder clatter directly behind me, as our soldiers did the same.

"Hold your fire," Colonel Spoforth ordered his troops frantically. "Not until they fire the first shot!"

"Honey Bee!" called a voice, and it was Finlay, crouching, shuffling towards me, reaching out his hand. "How can I help?"

I looked from his outstretched hand to his worried face. His eyes held mine steadily. He knew what I wanted to do. He remembered I was a Spellbinder.

He gave a little nod.

As if to say: *Yes. You can do it.*

I'm your friend, he had said when he had chased me here.

"Aim!"

Another bolt of darkness, right by my string bag.

My hands carried on with their frantic weaving, but I looked to the side, and there they *were* in the darkness—

The Whispers!

Ten Whispers, each like a single polished stone, metallic gray and scribbled over with the red and black of shadow thread.

My string bag was ready. I held it up, opened its mouth.

"Fi—"

And I lunged. Right as the Whispers fell I caught them, the ten new Whispers, ten sturdy Whispers, each a single word—*FIRE!*—and I slid them all at once into the bag.

Drew the bag tightly closed.

Held it firm to my chest.

Kept my eyes closed.

Silence.

Silence.

Then the sound, from the valley below, of weapons thudding slowly to the ground.

CHAPTER 103 FINLAY

She did it!

Honey Bee *Spellbound*!

Just in time too! (Might not want to cut it so fine next time, Honey Bee.)

But she didn't just Spellbind!

Wait for it...

(Drumroll...)

She *Spellbound ten Whisperers*!

Never heard of a Spellbinder doing that. Honestly. I once read about a Spellbinder taking on three Whisperers at once—but *ten!!*

Well, I am that proud of her.

Here we were then, on the hillside.

Honey Bee's eyes still tightly closed.

She's got her hands sort of wrapped around herself like she's holding on to something for dear life. Drips of sweat pouring down her forehead.

Must be a pretty tough gig, I realize. *This Spellbinding.*

Around me, our soldiers are holding fire, but they're still in position, weapons at the ready.

Down in the valley, the people of Vanquishing Cove have slumped to the ground.

But the Whisperers? They've come together out the front. All ten of them, lined up down there. Their faces are shocked. They're staring up at Honey Bee, amazed.

But there's also a kind of ferocity to them.

They're fighting her, I realize.

She's holding on; she's got them bound, but they're fighting hard to break her binds.

"Somebody," Honey Bee hisses. *"Somebody go and cut their wristbands!"*

Of course!

Should've thought of that.

"Now?" I check.

"Yes! Now! I'm holding them. But I don't know how long—"

I skip around her and run down the slope, scuffing right up to the Whisperers.

They see me coming but pay no attention. I'm just some kid. Their focus is on the girl on the hill who's got them Spellbound.

Scissors still in my pocket from back in the Whispering Kingdom. I pull them out and sidle up to the first Whisperer.

There it is, peeking out of his shirtsleeves: the red-and-black wristband.

I reach out my hand and—

I will not remove these wristbands.

It's a Whisper.

A big one too. More like:

I will not remove these wristbands.

It's come swooping in like an arrow. I look along the row of Whisperers. It's none of them. They're all bound by Honey Bee; I can see by their faces, they're fighting her hard.

So who Whispered this?

Oh well, I think. I take a deep breath.

I'll resist it.

Yes, I will—I think back. *I WILL remove the wristbands!*

And there it is again. Red-hot iron bars crushing my brain. Where is the Whisper coming from?

Someone else can do this. Can't be me.

But it's got to me. I'll just—

I will not remove these wristbands.

No, no, you're right.

I will not.

Good. Instead, I will go back up and distract Honey Bee. I will prevent her Spellbinding.

Yeah, and maybe one of these Vanquishing Covers can deal with things down here? *They* can cut the wristbands. I'll just tell them—

I will not tell anybody else to cut the wristbands. I will go back up and distract Honey Bee. I will prevent her Spellbinding.

The Vanquishing Covers all have these blank, drained looks. They don't know about the wristbands, plus they're probably still held in place by earlier Whispers. I need to cut the wristbands to kill those earlier Whispers.

But I won't. I won't cut any wristband.

When I turn back, the ten Whisperers have taken a single step forward in the direction of Honey Bee.

They're wearing her down.

She can't hold on much longer.

I have to cut the—

The sledgehammers in my brain!

I push against them. Push against the force. Hold my hands out and *shove*, and *shove*, but it's like trying to shove against a thick stone wall!

Got to keep trying.

Okay, *push*—

Nope.

Try again. Like with the shot put at the tournament, you put it in your shoulders and you—

Hold up.

Hold up here.

I'm not a shot-putter. The twins do that.

I'm a runner. A sprinter.

I'm *spindrift*, Honey Bee wrote.

Sparks of spindrift on the waves!

Quick as a splash of water, I am.

I will not remove the wristb —

Yeah, yeah, whatever.

This time I don't fight it.

I duck around it.

Simple.

It comes at me again.

I jump over it.

And again.

And, as I dash and spin and climb, I'm dodging and weaving my way up that row of Whisperers.

Rip

Rip

Rip

Rip

Rip

Rip

Rip

Rip

Rip

Didn't bother with the blunt scissors, did I? Tore them all off with my bare hands.

RIP!

Last one falls into my palm.

That's the gum-chewing commander. She whips around—they're all whipping around, grabbing at their wrists, confused. They've been so fiercely trying to take down Honey Bee, it took them a moment to know what I was doing, but now they are proper mad.

But I'm already sprinting back up the hill again.

Honey Bee's hands fall to her sides. She opens her eyes and smiles.

✳ CHAPTER ✳
104
HONEY BEE

We did it!

We saved the people of the Kingdom of Vanquishing Cove!

They were awfully grateful. So was Colonel Spoforth. He actually sat down on the grass with relief, breathing out a great gust of air. Hadn't wanted to order his soldiers to shoot innocent people, of course. He hopped up again quickly, of course, and rushed to arrest the ten Whisperers.

We've been back in Spindrift just over a week now, and Finlay and I have been taking turns writing this the last few days.

The Vanquishing Covers have gone home—all but Aunt Rebecca, who stayed on to visit with me. She and Uncle Dominic are being dreadfully polite with each other, but there's some real frost there. Turns out that Uncle Dominic had *forbidden* her to visit me, or even invite me to her cottage for holidays, these last three years. I did rather wonder why she never did. *How could she be so busy all this time?* I used to think. But after the almost-battle, Mayor Franny marched Aunt Rebecca and me up to the boarding school door and said that I was a *hero* and must be allowed a visit with my aunt. "Town council orders," she said. So Uncle Dominic had no choice.

Anyhow, this is the end of our story.

Finlay thinks there is not another word to write, and that this chapter 104 is a waste of time. He thinks the story should end with the last line of *his* previous chapter: "Honey Bee's hands fall to her sides. She opens her eyes and smiles."

"That's all we need to say," he says, terribly proud of himself.

Yes, all right, it is. But *I* like stories that wrap things up. For example, readers want to know that Jaskafar and the other orphans are all healthy and well and back home at the Orphanage! Shadow Magic from the mines had begun to infiltrate the bloodstream of many of the children, just as Hamish thought, and that's why they were so ill. But Spellbinders have cured them by binding the Shadow Magic.

Most people have recovered from the witch-made flu, although some are still very ill. The school nurse says I'm *still* not allowed to visit Carlos behind the curtain!

"Still in quarantine," she said, "but on the mend."

And the readers *must* want to know about the marvelous, deep, warm, bubbly bath I had on the day we got back from the Whispering Kingdom, after we'd rescued the Vanquishing Covers! Ordinarily, we children have showers, but Mayor Franny said I must get bath privileges.

Oh, you should have seen how black the bathwater turned! Instantly! All that caked-on mud washing away! I emptied the tub and started again with fresh water, because you don't feel like you're getting clean, do you, lying in a tub of black water. So I lay there in the bubbles, soaking away the last shreds of shadow thread, scrubbing them from under my fingernails, rinsing them out of my ear — [scribbly mark]

Sorry, that was Finlay trying to wrestle the pen out of my hand.

He was reading over my shoulder. I'm killing a great tale with talk of washing my ears, he says.

So, now I will finish off the story by telling about the awards ceremony.

It was today!

I will try to be quick.

The queen held the ceremony right here in the green common room of Brathelthwaite! At present, you see, she is staying in the Brathelthwaite Master Guest Suite. The Beach with the Yellow Sand is no longer safe — some of the hotels have been struck by cannon fire! As you might have guessed, the Whispering Wars continue. Even as I write, there is a battle at sea just off the coast.

Several pirate ships attacked yesterday. They sailed close, their ships disguised — they were flying the flags of our allies — and then attacked! A nasty trick. *Not sporting at all.*

But the K&E navy is holding them off and we hear that the Anti-Pirate League is speeding across the seas to help! Apparently, the league has thrilling new leaders named Gustav Spectaculo and The Scorpion. They can take down an entire pirate ship with a single sword, people say. They toss the sword between them while doing tumble turns in the air, I think. So *that* battle, at least, will soon be won.

It was a very relaxed awards ceremony. The queen said there was no need for pomp and grandeur: it just makes people nervous, she said. *Hrmph*, said Sir Brathelthwaite. And he begged her to add pomp and grandeur.

"Hold the ceremony in the town hall," he suggested, "with trumpets and fireworks and the entire town as audience."

Why did this matter so much to Sir Brathelthwaite?

The first award was to him!

It was raining softly outside, and the lamps were lit. There were trays of cakes on the sideboard, along with a teapot, a jug of hot chocolate, and elegant cups. We had lined up the armchairs and couches so that we were all the audience. When I say "we," who do I mean?

First, the children: Hamish, Victor, and me from the boarding school. Finlay, Glim, and the twins from the Orphanage.

Next, the adults: Sir Brathelthwaite, Aunt Rebecca, Lili-Daisy and Anita from the Orphanage, and Prince Jakob.

The queen was up front, alongside Mayor Franny. Oh, and a reporter from the *Spindrift Daily News* was in the back, taking pictures. But her clicks were very quiet. *Click. Click.* It was all quite cozy.

"Sir Brathelthwaite!" said the queen.

Sir Brathelthwaite stood up grandly, patted down his suit jacket, and flared out his fancy shirt sleeves.

"You have generously given space in your school for the training of Spellbinders. Thanks to you, we had enough trainee Spellbinders in town to repel the dreadful witch attack last week. Will you accept this medal?"

"I will," said Sir Brathelthwaite humbly.

"Oh, he *will*, will he?" grumbled Eli. "What a *surprise*."

"He hates it when people state the obvious," I explained, as the queen was looking somewhat bewildered.

The queen nodded her thanks and handed the gold medal to Mayor

Franny, who hung it over Sir B's bald head. *Clunk* went the heavy medal, hitting Sir B's nose as it fell down to his shoulders. "Oops," said Mayor Franny. "Can't think how that happened."

I'm pretty sure she did know how it happened.

By the by, it makes you think, doesn't it, how strange life is? Rather nasty people can sometimes get medals! But I suppose Sir B does an excellent job of tricking most adults into thinking he is a lovely man. We just have to sigh and not let the whole thing give us stomach cramps. And feel pleased when Mayor Franny "accidentally" clunks his nose with a medal.

Next, Anita got a medal, for her "tireless work at the hospital, and for her ingenuity in recognizing that the flu was witch-made."

Anita danced her way back to her seat beside Prince Jakob, and the prince sprang up, took her hand, and twirled her around. They twirled together for a bit, then sat back down laughing. The queen gave them a polite little clap.

The twins received medals for "being jolly helpful in the hospital themselves, *and* for being part of the team that planned the rescue of the children from the Whispering Kingdom."

That led rather smoothly to Finlay, Hamish, Victor, Glim, and me all receiving medals for also being on that "team."

No mention was made of how I had Spellbound ten Whisperers to save the people of Vanquishing Cove, nor of how Finlay had resisted a Whisper — that whole thing is top secret, and only to be discussed with the Director of Spellbinders. (She will be coming along later, Mayor Franny has told us.)

Lili-Daisy hooted when the orphans received their medals, and Aunt Rebecca put her fingers in her mouth and whistled piercingly when I received mine. It was embarrassing but funny too.

When Hamish received his medal, the queen told him what a *particular* hero he was, for having figured out about the wristbands. It was huge news to the K&E Alliance, she said, and would most likely change the course of the war.

"Oh no, that was the future children?" Hamish replied. "Thanks ever so. But it was Bronte and Alejandro. I just followed their clues! Easy! Or have I got that wrong?"

"Future children?" said the queen, puzzled. "Who are these *future* children, please?"

"Oh, we've never seen them since we got back from the Whispering Kingdom," Hamish replied. "They've shot off back to the future, I think."

Here, the queen looked thoroughly bewildered. Finlay piped up. "It's a long story," he said. "We'll tell you later."

He was anxious not to waste time explaining, I think, as he wanted to get on to afternoon tea.

There are only two more things to tell.

The first is this.

When Glim accepted her medal, the queen made a fuss about how brave Glim had been, befriending wild dragons. (I saw Victor scowling at this. He's awfully jealous, and it did make him look a right fool, didn't it?) Glim smiled shyly without speaking. "But Glim, you *must* tell us how you got through the witch-made Mist Shroud at the Whispering Kingdom!" the queen continued. "You *must*!"

There was a long pause.

Mayor Franny leaned forward eagerly. Everyone did. So far, Glim had not explained.

Glim was silent. She took a deep breath, as if to speak, and then went quiet again. Her hands, I could see, were trembling.

"Go on, child!" the queen urged. "Speak up!"

Glim seemed to sink into herself. Finlay hopped up now. "She *can't* say!" he called. "She—"

But Glim's whole body shook, she breathed in deeply, and she spoke.

"Your Majesty," she said, her voice loud and clear. "I am very sorry but I cannot tell you the secret. I promised the person who told me it that I never would. But I *do* have something to say to you. In fact, I have a... *demand.*"

The queen blinked.

Sir Brathelthwaite spluttered. "Lili-Daisy!" he said. "Discipline that child! She cannot speak to royalty that way!"

But Lili-Daisy ignored him, and the queen was busy staring at Glim.

"Let the people out of the fairground enclosure!" Glim said boldly. "The local Shadow Mages and the Whisperers! They are good people. They are loyal residents of Spindrift. They have *nothing* to do with the war, and they deserve to be in their own homes."

Now Sir Brathelthwaite clapped his hand over his mouth. "The insolence! Those are *dangerous* people in there! For the security of our *town*, we need—"

"I don't know what *you're* making such a fuss about," Glim said, swinging around to scowl. "I saw *you* in the fairground talking to witches!"

But nobody noticed this, because Mayor Franny was up and babbling to the queen. "Our locals *are* good people!" she said fervently. "I know I've said this repeatedly but I'll say it again, Your Majesty. Your security advisers were wrong."

The queen admired the ceiling for some time. At least that's how it seemed. There are fine chandeliers on this ceiling, and it really appeared as if they fascinated her, and that perhaps she was wondering about getting some for her palace.

"You may be right," she said at last. "I have been receiving constant petitions from people of Spindrift about this issue. Also, a sterling silver fox named Motoko—a chocolatier, I gather—has been sending persuasive letters from the fairground. I believe she's taken on a sort of leadership role there. Could somebody please fetch her here at once so we can discuss the issue?"

An official nodded and stepped out of the room.

"Well, what an intriguing awards ceremony this has been!" the queen said now. "Give yourselves a round of applause and let's have our afternoon tea!"

We obeyed her, clapping very heartily for ourselves, and Glim sank into her seat, appearing both proud and rather shocked that she had spoken up in this way. Finlay shook her hand.

Victor, meanwhile, sprang to the sideboard and began pouring tea! He placed the cups on a tray and moved about the room, chattering away about which of us wanted milk, sugar, honey, who preferred hot chocolate, and so on.

Good gracious, I thought as he offered me the tray. *Victor has changed! He has become kind and thoughtful! He has realized that—*

"Honey Bee!" said Victor. "Did you just take *that* cup?"

I looked down at the cup in my hand. I took a sip. "Which cup?"

"The one in your hands."

"I did," I agreed. "I did take this cup in my hands."

Behind me, Eli muttered furiously to himself at this obviousness.

"I *specifically* said that the cup with the orange-gold rim was for His

Highness, Prince Jakob! It's the second-best cup we have! The best is for Her Majesty, the queen, of course."

"Oh," I said, mortified. "I *am* sorry. I was lost in thought and didn't hear you. Shall I put it back?"

"Too late! You've just sipped from it! We all saw you! Well, you must *focus*, Honey Bee! You will bring shame on our school!"

What was I just thinking about Victor again?

Ha! Of course, he was only helping to show off to the queen about what a polite young man he was.

Anyway, everybody was staring from me to Victor and back, and I felt my cheeks burning.

"It is a pretty cup," the queen said from across the room. "That orange-gold rim reminds me of a kingdom I visited on a tour I once took. This was many years ago, of course."

Everybody turned to her politely. *Oh*, I thought, *she is saving me from embarrassment. That is sweet.*

"Go along, then," Lili-Daisy said, getting comfortable in her chair with her tea and cake. "Tell us the story. Which kingdom was this?"

It was the rain outside, I think, and the soft light inside. We were all getting so cozy and relaxed, we forgot to be respectful to the queen.

"Oh, I can't remember the name of the kingdom," the queen replied. "It was one of the little ones. Anyway, they had a parade for me, and a concert band played—all the usual—and a little girl presented me with a huge bunch of blue elouisas. Very pretty scent they have, blue elouisa flowers, but after holding them for five minutes, my fingernails turned an alarming orange-gold color!"

"The blue elouisas were orange-gold?" Mayor Franny inquired.

"No! They were *blue* elouisas. Therefore, they were blue."

Eli sighed.

"That's what was so amusing," the queen continued, nibbling on a piece of cream-cheese-frosted banana cake. "The fact that *blue* flowers caused my fingernails to turn such a vibrant shade of *orange-gold*! Took weeks for them to return to their regular color! For the rest of my tour, the press kept reporting about my curious choice of nail varnish! It even became a bit of a trend!"

Everybody laughed, but there was a *clatter*, and we turned to see that Taya had spilled her cake plate to the floor. She was standing, her eyes wide. Her brother, Eli, frowned at her, and then his own eyes widened, and he spilled his *own* cake plate.

"My, *my*," said Sir Brathelthwaite.

Eli faced the queen. "These blue elouisas?" he said. "They turned your nails orangey-gold?"

The queen nodded. "That was rather the point of the story," she said. "Aren't you the boy who dislikes the obvious?"

"They turned your nails goldy-orange?" Taya demanded.

"Orangey-gold, goldy-orange, however you like to put it. Wish I could remember the name of that kingdom. I believe it might be the *only* kingdom where blue elouisas grow, but—"

"It is," Eli said.

He looked at his sister.

His sister looked back.

They blinked furiously at each other and then, abruptly, they both burst into laughter.

"Rather a slow reaction to my story," sniffed the queen, reaching for her cake fork again. "But there we have it."

"Not laughing at your story," Eli told her. "It's just, we've realized where we come from. Haven't we, Taya?"

Taya snorted, and the twins erupted into laughter once more. They slapped their thighs and hiccuped.

"Do tell," the queen commanded. "What's so funny?"

But they didn't tell because then the second thing happened.

The door flew open, the queen's guards standing aside, and a large woman burst into the room. How familiar she was! But she was carrying a boy in her arms, and do you know who this boy was?

I am going to need a new chapter.

CHAPTER 105
HONEY BEE

The boy was my friend Carlos.

His eyes were closed. He was thin as thread. His face was gray as chimney smoke.

He was dead.

That's what I thought anyway.

"Carlos!" I half screamed.

But Anita leapt forward even faster, crying out: "Put him down! Put him down!"

The woman laid my friend on the sofa, and Anita knelt by his side, a palm on his forehead, her ear to his chest, fingers to his pulse. He *was* breathing — I could hear it now — but the sound was like a rake being drawn through leaves.

"Such a faint pulse," Anita whispered. She snapped her fingers. "My medical kit! At once!"

Eli grabbed the kit, Taya opened it, Eli pulled out a glass flask, Taya clicked open the lid, and Anita tipped drops into the corner of Carlos's mouth.

What a team they were! All of that happened like the slide of a wave onto the shore.

"Come on," Anita murmured. "Come on, Carlos."

More drops were spilled into his mouth.

"Should we take him to the hospital?" the queen inquired. "Sir Brathelthwaite! Have a carriage brought around!"

Anita shook her head. "He has the witch-made flu. I see all the signs here. Faery potion is all that will help now. But he is so thin! He must have had this flu for some time!"

"Months," I told her. "He got sick before we went to the Whispering Kingdom."

"Months!" Half the room exploded with the word.

"Sir Brathelthwaite!" the queen cried. "This is a student at your school? Why was he not in the hospital?"

"He has been in the infirmary," Sir Brathelthwaite replied, positioning his medal delicately over the center of his tie. "That was perfectly suitable. This boy was abandoned here as a baby. He is a prince of the Kingdom of Joya Amarillo, where the royal family has been overthrown by rebels. Quite frankly, I do not believe that family will *ever* win their throne back."

Mayor Franny flinched.

"What has *that* got to do with anything?" she demanded. "*Why* is this boy not in the hospital?"

"I believe he means that the boy does not pay fees," the queen said, looking coldly at Sir Brathelthwaite, "and that the boy is unlikely to take the throne one day and reward Sir Brathelthwaite. Therefore, apparently, the boy is better off dead. This Kingdom of Joya Amarillo—I do not know it. Where is it?"

"It's in the northern climes, Your Majesty." Sir Brathelthwaite clutched his medal protectively. "And Your Majesty, you misunderstand! I certainly did not—"

"Whereabouts in the northern climes?" the prince asked. "I know that area well, but I can't recall a Joya Amarillo—"

"That's because there's no such place," Anita murmured. She hovered over Carlos, stroking his forehead, then glanced around at everybody. "I made it up," she said. "Joya Amarillo means Yellow Jewel. That was the name of my family's farmhouse. When it burned down and my parents died, I carried my little brother into Spindrift. He was ill—he had a very weak chest and I knew he would need the best medical attention growing up. I thought he'd get that here, at the finest boarding school in the kingdom, so I left a note, pretending he was royalty—and then I walked myself to the Orphanage."

Prince Jakob placed his hand on her shoulder. "Oh, Anita," he said. "This is your baby brother?"

"Carlos," Anita whispered. "What did I do to you?"

CHAPTER
106
HONEY BEE

"Carlos will recover," the queen announced, as if making a royal proclamation. It was very calming. Everyone breathed out. "We shall continue having our afternoon tea while we watch over him and wait for the Faery potion to take effect. We'll discuss *other issues* later." She kept her eyes forward, but Sir Brathelthwaite grimaced. "Carabella! Thank you for bringing the boy to us," the queen continued, addressing the large woman who had carried Carlos into the room. "It is splendid to see you back in town. Would you like to join us, or do you need to return to work?"

Carabella?

Of course! That's why I recognized her! She was the Spellbinder who had helped take Rosalind into the infirmary, the one who had told me to check my toenails!

"I've only just arrived back in town," Carabella said, "and I went into the infirmary to check on a young girl. Weeks ago, Honey Bee and I took her in there, didn't we, Honey Bee?" (She smiled at me directly, so *she* remembered me!) "But I wanted to be sure she was well. Anybody know?"

"Good afternoon, Carabella!" Sir Brathelthwaite beamed. "Always marvelous to see you!" His flappy sleeves flew about. He patted his bald head. He has a mole a bit like a raisin sitting on his head, and he just missed it with the patting. "Now, I believe you mean Rosalind? She is *quite* well! Perfectly recovered! Gone off to stay with her aunt for a bit!"

He was booming now, happy to show everyone that some children *did* get better under his care. Nobody was impressed. I myself had completely forgotten about Rosalind. Sorry, Rosalind.

Carabella nodded at him. "Good to know. Anyhow, I tweaked open a curtain, thinking that she might be there, and I found this boy. I brought him straight up here, as I'd already been told that Anita, the student doctor, was here for the award ceremony. I *will* stay for a cup of tea. I want to have a word with Honey Bee and Finlay if he's here too? And of course, to catch up with my sister Franny, there!"

"Good to see you, Carrie." Mayor Franny nodded.

Mayor Franny and Carabella were sisters!

"I asked Carrie to come to Spindrift," Franny explained quietly to Finlay and me. "To train up our Spellbinders. She's the Director of Spellbinders. Trouble is, *all* the Kingdoms and Empires need her, so she's worn a bit thin and couldn't stay long."

Carabella did seem very young to be the Director of Spellbinders! She must be a *most* powerful Spellbinder! Anyhow, next Carabella took Finlay and me to the far corner of the room, along with a large plate of cakes, and asked us to tell her what had happened with the Vanquishing Covers.

"Keep your voices low," she added. "This must remain secret." She glanced across to the others. The room is spacious enough that they could not hear us, and anyway they seemed quite distracted. They were pretending to have polite chats, but they kept casting worried glances towards Anita and Carlos, and poisonous looks at Sir Brathelthwaite.

Sir Brathelthwaite happened to be sitting on the very couch where *I* had been seated the night my toenails turned blue. Hamish was alongside him, hiding behind his blond hair. On Sir B's other side was Victor.

Suddenly I remembered how Hamish had thrown a cushion across my feet that night, right before Victor turned around. The memory gave me a curious feeling, a bit like dizziness.

And right now, as I looked in their direction, Victor was staring at me ferociously! As if he was a guard dog and I was a robber rattling his household gate! What had I done to Victor now?

But Carabella was waiting.

We told her our story about the people of Vanquishing Cove and the Whisperers. I said about the string bag net and how making that had somehow allowed me to *see* the Shadow Magic of the Whispers at last. Finlay explained how he had ducked and weaved around the Whisper that had tried to stop him cutting off the wristbands: It was not one of the ten invading Whisperers, he said. It was somebody else.

"Yes," I agreed. "I could feel it at the edges of the Whispers I had bound, but I couldn't reach for it without dropping those ten."

Carabella frowned. She took a great gulp of her tea and set it back down.

"You are both remarkable," she said, her voice quiet and matter of fact. "Honey Bee, you are the strongest young Spellbinder I have ever met. To Spellbind, without training, at your age? Astonishing! But to Spellbind *ten* Whisperers! Well!"

"Thank you," I replied. "But you know, I could not Spellbind *anybody* when we were trapped in the Whispering Kingdom."

"And you, Finlay," Carabella continued, turning to him. "To resist a supercharged Whisper! Your character must be *enormously* strong."

"Thanks," Finlay said. "But I couldn't resist in the Whispering Kingdom, not really. Does it mean HB and I can only do it when we're outside that Kingdom?"

HB, he had called me.

Ha.

I like the idea of Finlay giving me a nickname.

Carabella clicked her tongue quickly, thinking hard. "No, it's not to do with being in the Whispering Kingdom," she said eventually. "That shouldn't make a difference. Do you know what I think? To be a great Spellbinder, you need to draw on the love of your friends and family. To resist a super Whisper, you'd need an enormously strong sense of your own self. Now, could it be that you felt alone when you were in the Whispering Kingdom, Honey Bee? And Finlay, was your belief in yourself a little shaky? And then I wonder, did something happen to change these things when you got out?"

Finlay grinned. "Makes sense," he said. "I don't admit this to many people, but secretly I sometimes think I'm not much of anything. Just an orphan, see? I thought the one thing us orphans had was being champions of the Spindrift Tournament, but the Brathelthwaites took that away from us. So it seemed like I'd always get beaten by the rich kids one way or another. But then Honey Bee wrote down that I *was* spindrift, like I *am* my own town. Well, that was crackerjack. Suddenly I wasn't just an orphan in Spindrift, I *was* Spindrift. That's how it felt to me anyway. It must have been that." He flicked the back of my head. (Ouch.) "Thanks, HB."

Now they both turned to me.

I knew exactly what the answer was.

Without my parents or Aunt Rebecca, and with Carlos sick in the infirmary, of *course* I had felt lonely and unloved.

But then Glim had smiled at me and asked if I was all right. And Finlay had followed me to rescue Aunt Rebecca and told me he was my friend. At last, I had felt somewhat loved.

I felt too shy to say all this, so I shrugged and said I would think about it.

And *now* at last, we are all caught up.

I am writing this at the desk in the corner of the green common room.

The others are chatting quietly, but I wanted to distract myself from worry about Carlos, so I decided to finish up the story.

Nobody has left, as we are all waiting for better news of Carlos. He still rests on the couch, but he is breathing more like ocean waves than dried leaves now. Anita, the prince, and the twins are taking care of him together. Motoko-the-Chocolatier has arrived, having been brought here from the fairground, and she is conversing with the queen, Mayor Franny, and Carabella around a card table. The queen is nodding often, and I rather think she is agreeing with Motoko.

Lili-Daisy and Aunt Rebecca are discussing politics while they play a board game with Finlay and Glim. Sir Brathelthwaite just challenged Victor to chess, and Hamish offered to be "referee, or have I got that wrong? *Is* there a referee in chess?"

"Do you even know the *rules* of chess, Hamish?" Victor demanded—but then happened to notice I was watching all this and he shot me another of those guard-dog looks!

It's very—well, I already feel odd, you know.

Too much cake.

Or it's too hot in here, I think. Freezing too! See how shivery this paper is! Feel it. Go on. Touch the paper. It's like an iceberg, isn't it?

I'll just take a bite of this pen, to warm myself up.

Now why did I do that?

Tired, I suppose.

Long day.

But ink is just EVERYWHERE!

Oh my, I do feel strange.

Honestly, everything is odd.

Trying to write the final words here, but I have LOST them. I KNOW there are more words to ice, but—

FINLAY

Honey Bee slithered off her chair, and her head went *thunk!* on the carpet.

"Good gracious!" Sir Brathelthwaite wrinkled his nose. "Honey Bee has fallen asleep! I do apologize, Your Majesty. That is the height of rudeness. Generally, my students do *not*—"

But the queen winced as if he gave her toothache. "The child must be exhausted," she pronounced. "In what way is it *rude* to be exhausted at your school, Sir Brathelthwaite?"

We all looked at Honey Bee, sprawled on the floor, asleep.

"The last weeks will have worn her out," Aunt Rebecca said, standing up. "Perhaps someone could help me carry her to her bed?"

"Or pop a cushion under her head," Lili-Daisy advised. "She looks so comfortable there. Be a shame to wake her."

So that's what they did. Stuck a cushion under Honey Bee's head, covered her with a blanket, smiled at her in that loving way grown-ups smile when children are asleep. As kids are less of a nuisance when they're sleeping.

And got back to our games and chats.

Tick, tock went the clock.

Tick, tock.

Tick, tock.

Then Victor leapt up so fast he knocked the chess pieces flying. "It was *me*!" he bellowed. "It was *me*!"

And burst into tears.

Everyone stared.

"What was you?" Hamish prompted. "You mean the person who moved the *knight* just now? Yes, I'm certain that was you. On the other hand, the person who moved the *pawn* was Sir—"

"It was *me*!" Victor roared, pulling at his own hair. "Honey Bee's not asleep! (sob, sob, wail) I *poisoned* her! (sob, sob) With witch-made flu! The new kind! The *killer* kind! The supervisors gave it to me when we left the Whispering Kingdom! They said that I'd be *told* when to use it—and I was *told*, so I put it in the teacup—but I don't *want* to *kill* anybody! I don't *like* Honey Bee (sob, sob) but I don't want to *kill* her!"

Anita darted over to Honey Bee's side, along with the twins, and they did doctorly things and looked at each other with serious doctorly faces.

"She's just sleeping, isn't she?" Aunt Rebecca asked.

"Victor's right," Anita said. "This *is* witch-made flu. But a far darker kind than we've been seeing here." She tried to get drops of Faery potion into Honey Bee's mouth, but it kept dribbling out.

"In that case, store-bought Faery potion won't work," Carabella said. Her voice was peculiar and *she* looked like she was going to cry, which was a shock. She'd seemed a very cheery type a moment ago. "If it's the lethal kind, nothing will work. Oh, Honey Bee. Oh, *child*."

"Take her to the hospital!" Aunt Rebecca begged, but the others were shaking their heads.

"I've seen this before," Carabella told Aunt Rebecca gently. "There's nothing anybody can do. We'll lose her in the next hour or so. I'm so sorry."

The queen pushed closer and peered down at Honey Bee. She swung back around to Victor.

"This was meant for the prince, wasn't it?"

Victor stuck his lower lip out. "Honey Bee took his cup."

"And you say someone *told* you to use the poison? Who?"

His head tipped forward so he faced the carpet. He put his hands in his pockets. "I can't say," he mumbled. "He also told me to give the other witch-made flu to the prince that day he came to the tournament. I put it on a cream puff. And I got it into Carlos's breakfast here. And then to as many people in town as I could. But that was just a *flu*, not a *lethal* flu. I didn't mind making people sick, but I didn't want to *kill* people."

"Who?" we all shouted. *"Who* told you to do that?"

"I can't say."

"We'll snap you into a thousand pieces if you don't," the twins promised.

"I can't say."

"Well, *I* can say!" Carabella's voice was grim. "It's a Whisperer. I knew there was one in this school the moment I arrived here. I could sense him, but the signals kept going wrong. And now I know why."

We all stared at her.

"I imagine it's been very helpful to the Whispering King, having a Whisperer ally in Spindrift." She swung around. *"Sir Brathelthwaite?"*

Sir Brathelthwaite spluttered and bleated.

Everyone else looked doubtful.

"But, Carabella," the queen hissed. "Whisperers have long hair. And this man is—"

"Bald!" several people put in, the queen being too polite to say it.

Sir Brathelthwaite grinned and patted his own head. "I certainly am!"

"It's true that Whisperers never ordinarily go bald," Carabella agreed.

"But *anyone* can lose their hair if they've been cursed by a witch. I've known two or three Whisperers who've lost their hair that way—it's very distressing to them. They can only Whisper a few times a day when bald, and are much harder for Spellbinders to detect."

"Well, I have nothing to do with witches!" Sir Brathelthwaite chuckled. "I'm a headmaster!"

Motoko-the-Chocolatier spoke up. "You've been coming to the fairground to ask the local witches for help in reversing a witch curse!" she scolded. "You want to grow your hair back! Everyone in the fairground has been laughing—vain old git, we've been saying."

"I *knew* I saw him there that night," Glim put in.

"He went to the Empire of Witchcraft years ago," Motoko explained, nodding at Glim, "and stole some witch-made diamond diviners. As a childish prank when he was drunk, he says. The witches cursed him for this theft by taking his hair."

Carabella shook her head. "Not as a childish prank when drunk," she said. "I know exactly who he is now. There are stories around amongst the Spellbinders that a young Whisperer once stole diamond diviners from the witches on a mission for the Whispering King. This must be the very man. The king was ambitious and greedy for more diamonds, you see—and now that I think about it, I bet it was the diamond diviners that found the shadow thread troves where the poor children have all been working. The diviners, being shadow made themselves, would have been drawn to buried shadow magic even more than to diamonds."

We all stared from Sir Brathelthwaite to Honey Bee, who was writhing about on the floor. Everyone seemed to be crying, except Sir B.

"This is preposterous!" he shouted.

"No," Carabella said sadly. "You're working for the Whispering King.

You're his inside man in Spindrift. Pretending to run a school but actually distributing witch-made illnesses all over Spindrift. I expect *you* were the extra Whisperer at the battle with the Vanquishing Covers."

"He *was* there!" I said. "He chased after HB!"

Sir Brathelthwaite began to bluster. "If I knew how to supercharge my Whispers, I'd be doing it on all of you right now, wouldn't I!"

"No, you wouldn't," Carabella argued. "Because I'd just bind them. I'm a lot stronger than you are. You're not silly enough to try. Or you've already used up your Whispers for today. But I'd bet a thousand silver you have that wristband."

The twins got hold of his fancy, flappy sleeves, pushed them up, and there it was: a red-and-black shadow-thread wristband.

Taya wrenched it off.

"GUARDS!" the queen bellowed.

"Your *Majesty*." Sir Brathelthwaite placed a hand on her shoulder. "That wristband is merely jewelry! A friendship band! You are not going to listen to these madwomen, are you?"

But the queen brushed Sir B's hand away and ordered her guards to take him to the dungeons.

"Friendship band," the queen sneered as they marched him off. "It would be funny if there wasn't a child dying here. Hold up, guards, before you go, toss me that medal he's wearing."

"Oh!" Sir B yelped. "Not my medal!"

The medal flew through the air, the queen caught it neatly, and the door closed behind Sir B.

We swung back around to Honey Bee. Her face had turned the color of a peppermint. White with a faint blue tinge, I mean.

"She's scarcely breathing," Anita told us. Aunt Rebecca was stretched out on the floor beside her niece, holding her hand and sobbing, *"Honey Bee, Honey Bee, Honey Bee."*

"She's not going to die, is she?" Victor begged. "Not really?"

"She is," Anita said. "Very soon."

Victor began to cry again.

"Wait, has Sir B been *Whispering* Victor all this time?" I asked, suddenly feeling sorry for the kid. "Is that why he's been such a prat?"

"Oh, he's *always* been a prat," Hamish replied. "Years, I've known him, and years, he's been just *awful.* Terribly *pleased* with himself. But he's only recently become *evil?* I've been thinking to myself lately: there's something up with Victor. Something not right. Didn't quite trust him, see? That's why I tossed a cushion over—hold up, can't tell that. That'll be a secret. Anyhow, can't we do *something* for Honey Bee? I *do* like her."

Carabella shook her head. "The only thing that might work," she said, "would be Faery elixir."

"Well, let's get some!"

Again with the shaking of the head. "It has to be freshly made by Faeries. It only works for about ten minutes or so after it's made."

"SO LET'S GET A FAERY TO MAKE SOME!" Didn't realize I was shouting, but everyone jumped and looked at me.

"There are no Faeries in town," Mayor Franny told me, in a sad voice. "I've been petitioning constantly for Faeries to help out with all the illness and injuries here. But they're in such high demand all over the Kingdoms and Empires and, of course, it's too dangerous to travel these days. Even if I tried again, we'd never get one in time."

"SO TRY ANYWAY!" Still yelling, I was.

"Finlay," Lili-Daisy murmured. "It's all right."

"IT'S NOT ALL RIGHT! THERE MUST BE *SOMETHING* YOU CAN DO, WHAT IS THE POINT IN HAVING THE *QUEEN* HERE, WHAT IS UP WITH YOU ADULTS, YOU GREAT, BIG BUNCH OF *CRAPUSCULAR, CRABAPPLE—*"

This is where Eli and Taya spoke up. Both at once.

"Do you have to be trained to make this Faery elixir?" they asked.

"No." Anita was cradling Honey Bee's head in her lap now, trying to get her comfortable. Honey Bee was making little noises like a toad. "But you have to *be* Faery. And we haven't—"

"So it's enough just to be Faery?" Eli asked.

"And you just follow instructions on how to make this elixir thing?" Taya added.

Carabella turned to them. "Exactly," she said. "Why?"

"Because," the twins announced, "we think we might be Faery."

CHAPTER 108
FINLAY

"That's why we were laughing before," Taya said.

"The queen said blue elouisas turned her fingernails an orange-gold color?" Eli added. "When *we* got to Spindrift, six years ago, our fingernails were orangey-gold."

"Goldy-orange," Taya corrected.

"Blue elouisas are only grown in the Kingdom of Kate-Bazaar," Eli added.

"Tsunami hit the coast of Kate-Bazaar six years ago," Taya put in.

"A lot of folks and animals got swept away."

"Same year, the east-west currents in the Starling Ocean ran west-east, on account of water sprite battles."

"So anyone washed away from Kate-Bazaar could have been swept towards Spindrift."

"The only people allowed to pick the blue elouisas are Faery children."

"All we can remember is we turned up on the beach here with orangey-gold nails."

"Goldy-orange."

"As if we'd been picking blue elouisas."

"Therefore—" Taya said.

"—we could be Faeries."

They both grinned like they might burst into laughter again, then remembered Honey Bee was dying and grew serious. "Sorry," they said. "We find it funny. The idea we might be Faeries."

"Yes," Lili-Daisy said doubtfully. "You don't think of Faeries cursing and threatening to break people to pieces."

"But Faeries *are* good at healing," Anita said from the floor. "And so are the twins. You know, people only began to recover from the witch-made flu when the twins started helping at the hospital?"

"Faeries are often fat like we are," the twins said, as one.

"True," Carabella agreed. "But all those links you just made—blue elouisas only growing in Kate-Bazaar, tsunami six years ago, currents changing—how do you know all that? Can you be sure?"

"They can be sure," Glim confirmed. "They read newspapers all the time, and remember every single thing they read."

The queen raised her eyebrows. "Faeries have good memories too. Better than me, anyway. I think it *was* Kate-Bazaar where I got those blue elouisas, and now that I think about it, it was very Faery-centric there—Faery fountains, Faery dust, Faery carousels."

"The only thing we didn't know until today—" Taya began.

"—was that blue elouisas turn your fingernails orangey-gold," Eli finished.

"Goldy-orange," Taya muttered.

The adults looked at each other. "It could be so," they mused. "But maybe not…"

"We might not be," the twins agreed. "We could *easily* not be."

"WHO CARES IF THEY *ARE* OR ARE *NOT*! THEY HAVE TO GIVE IT A TRY! HOW CAN IT HURT FOR THEM TO TRY?" There I was, bellowing away again.

Got the room moving, didn't it?

"There's a collection of Faery literature in the library," Hamish said.

"We have an extensive library here," Victor agreed. "Come on, then, Hamish."

The pair of them raced off. "Meet you in the kitchen once we find instructions for the healing elixir!" Hamish shouted behind him.

"Will we have to bake a cake for it?" Taya asked. "'Cause we don't bake."

Once again, doubt rippled right across the room.

"Faeries generally *do* bake," somebody murmured.

The twins shrugged. "Like we said, we might not *be* Faery. We might have been picking blue elouisas *because* we weren't allowed to pick blue elouisas."

"Oh," said Lili-Daisy. "That does sound like the twins."

"We don't like rules," the twins chanted.

A long pause.

"WE STILL HAVE TO TRY." Me again.

"You probably *will* have to bake," Anita put in, reaching up to pat my ankle. "Most Faery elixirs have cake crumbs and flower petals in them. The key thing is sewing the magic around it."

"Don't sew either," the twins said.

Another, more powerful moment of uncertainty.

I took in a deep breath, ready to shout again.

Aunt Rebecca stood up. "I'll teach you to bake," she declared.

Glim said, "I'll show you how to sew."

A sound like a distant foghorn. It was Honey Bee. She had grabbed her knees and was clutching them to her chest, groaning. Her face was mottled and swollen. Her hair was clammy with sweat.

"We haven't got long at all," Carabella whispered.

"Go to the kitchens at once!" the queen commanded. "Rebecca, you take the children. The rest of us will stay here and watch over Honey Bee and Carlos."

Another moan from Honey Bee.

"Go! Your queen commands you!"

CHAPTER 109
FINLAY

Hamish and Victor found the instructions for Faery elixir.

The twins made cupcakes. Those would bake faster than a big cake, Aunt Rebecca said.

"But will it still work?"

Aunt Rebecca's voice trembled. "We have no choice. Measure the flour into this," she told them. "Up to—no, no, up to *this* line. Quickly! Oh no, but don't spill it!"

You could tell she wanted to grab the ingredients out of the twins' hands and do it herself. Her neck muscles were standing straight up. Her fists were clenched.

Eggs cracked, spilled to the floor. Aunt Rebecca tapped her foot at a high speed, *tap-tap-tap*. "Cut that out," Eli said, studying the milk bottle. "You're distracting me."

"You open it from *that* end! The lid!" Aunt Rebecca cried.

"Steady on," Taya told her.

Mixture flew every which way.

Eventually, cakes went in the oven.

"Now you two have to sew the magic," Glim said, reading the instructions. "You have to imagine silvery-blue thread. Got it?"

"Yep," said the twins.

"Seriously? Close your eyes!"

The twins closed their eyes. "Okay. Got it. Silver-blue thread."

"Now open your eyes again and I'll show you how to move your hands, as if you're stitching the spell into the air."

"You just told us to close them."

"Well, now you need to *open*!"

"THIS IS NO TIME FOR ARGUING!" That was me. Very loud that day, I was.

Aunt Rebecca checked the elixir instructions again. "Quick, run outside and start gathering the flowers, Finlay," she told me. "And someone get the honey! We'll need a rose, a daffodil, a daisy, a chrysanthemum, and wisteria."

"The school has a greenhouse with most of those in it," Victor declared. "Come along, Fin and Hamish. Let's fetch them."

By the time we got back from the gardens, our hands filled with flowers, the cupcakes were ready.

"We've got everything," I said.

"Hurry!" Aunt Rebecca grabbed the flowers from us and thrust them at the twins. "Peel off the petals! Into the honey! Then crumble in the cake crumbs!"

"Take it easy," Taya said.

The twins have always done things in a slow and steady way. Every one of us wanted to grab them by the shoulders and shake them.

"There," said Eli. "Wait. Where's the wisteria?"

"The wisteria! How'd we forget that?" I demanded.

"There *wasn't* any," Hamish said.

"There must be wisteria!" Aunt Rebecca wailed.

Wisteria.

Whispers like wisteria.

"In the Spindrift Gardens," I said slowly. "Hanging over trellises."

Aunt Rebecca was blinking madly.

"Those gardens are just down the street from here, aren't they?" she asked.

We nodded.

"Well, what are you waiting for? Hurry! No, you twins, stay here and keep sewing the magic. The rest of you, get going! We'll meet you in the green common room! Bring the wisteria there! Hurry and order the carriage around!"

"Quicker," I said, "if we run."

CHAPTER
110
FINLAY

Still raining outside, but only lightly. Just a mist of rain.

The moon was out.

Trees shook raindrops in the wind.

And we pelted down the rain-dark road.

Faster than we'd ever run before.

Victor, Hamish, Glim, and I, sometimes side by side, sometimes one or the other of us pulled out ahead.

We reached the gardens.

"Which is it? Which is the wisteria?"

"It's over here!"

Panting, we all reached up and pulled handfuls of wisteria, got splattered with raindrops, turned around, and ran back even faster.

A race, but we were all in this one together.

Racing against shadow magic.

It's a killer poison. Works at high speed. We had to be faster.

I never knew I could run that fast. Never knew *they* could run that fast.

The four of us sprinting, but a runner was missing. Honey Bee should've been running with us.

A blank space on the road where she should be.

She's a beautiful runner with those stupid long legs of hers.

So our feet pounded.

Our hearts thundered.

Our breath rasped.

We *burst* through the front doors of the school. *Lunged* up the staircase.

Skidded down the hallway.

Into the green common room.

The twins reached out their hands and we *all* thrust wisteria at them.

They tore off petals, added them to a glass jar filled with a sticky honey mix.

Then the twins were on their knees, sliding across to Honey Bee. She was curled up tight, and her face had turned into these hideous charcoal-colored welts.

The twins' faces were dead serious.

They took a spoonful of the elixir. Touched it to Honey Bee's lips.

Another spoonful. Pushed it into her mouth.

"That's enough," Anita told them. "Now we wait."

"Keep sewing the magic," Aunt Rebecca begged the twins.

They sat on their knees, watching Honey Bee's face and sewing tiny stitches in the air.

"Come on," I said. "Come on, Honey Bee."

She lay still.

"Give her more!" Victor pleaded.

Anita shook her head. "Wait."

We waited.

The clock ticked.

The queen made a little sound like a groan.

Rain picked up again outside.

"Honey Bee?" her Aunt Rebecca whispered. "Honey Bee?"

But it was too late.

We were too late.

Maybe the twins weren't Faeries after all?

Or maybe we'd got the recipe wrong?

Maybe cupcakes were wrong—it had to be a real cake.

All that mattered was—

We'd lost her.

She was gone.

CHAPTER 111
HONEY BEE

Oh, FINLAY!!! Cut it out!

I had not gone!

CHAPTER 112
FINLAY

Ha. Sorry, couldn't resist.

It suddenly seemed funny to me, to say that.

No, we waited, holding our breaths.

The twins sewed their tiny stitches.

Aunt Rebecca held both of Honey Bee's hands—

And she opened her eyes.

She opened her eyes.

There was a bit of dribble on the side of her mouth, but luckily first thing she did was wipe that away.

Blinked around like a frightened rabbit.

"Oh my," she said.

Everybody shouted, "Honey Bee!" and Aunt Rebecca sort of slumped down like she couldn't hold herself up anymore. You could tell by the faces of the adults that it had been a very close thing.

I am certain there was no dribble on my mouth.

And that I did not blink like a frightened rabbit. My blinks are very dignified.

I think what Finlay meant to say was this: *Honey Bee woke like a graceful princess.*

But yes, I did wake up! I am still pretty cross with Victor, of course, for almost killing me—he says it's my fault for taking the wrong cup—but at least he owned up in time. That was rather brave.

And I'm *very* thankful to the twins. Faery twins! It *is* funny that the twins are Faeries.

And I feel so honored that *Faery* twins once threatened to break me into a thousand pieces!

And ended up saving my life. Along with Aunt Rebecca and my speedy friends, of course.

This will be the last chapter. *Honestly.*

It is now one month later. And guess what?

Today we saw the future children again!

This happened on the Beach with the Yellow Sand.

The queen decreed a Party Day today, to celebrate the defeat of those pirate invaders. It took a while, but at last, the ships of the invading fleet have sunk or surrendered.

Of course, there are plenty more pirates battling the K&E Alliance and the Anti-Pirate League on oceans throughout the Kingdoms and Empires. And the war still bristles away in both near and far-flung lands. But, for the moment at least, Spindrift seems to be having a short break.

Today, the twins baked Faery-healing cakes for everyone—many people are still run-down after that witch flu or wrung out by the war and need a little boost, and the twins have been practicing their baking with my Aunt Rebecca. Motoko-the-Chocolatier provided stacks of chocolate, including some Maywish Chocolate of the Riddle Empire that she somehow managed to bring into town. Snatty-Ra-Ra and the other fortune-tellers gave free predictions. The town band played, but (luckily) the siren sisters sang so loudly that the sounds of the violin (and all the other instruments, in fact) were entirely drowned out.

Everybody came! Including all our Shadow Mage and Whisperer friends! The queen *did* release them, and they have forgiven her. Or they pretend they forgive her—I did see a couple of radish gnomes kick sand onto her beach towel.

We were having a picnic together—Finlay, Glim, the twins, Hamish, Victor, and I—when we spotted the future children. They were standing by the door of our beach hut. It was a warm day and they were carrying their coats over their arms.

"Who's that?" Finlay asked, pointing.

"Where?" Victor asked politely. It's very funny to hear Victor being polite. He is generally much quieter, although he can't help reminding people that he is a duke now and then. The queen pardoned him for his wicked-ness, as he was being controlled by Sir Brathelthwaite's Whispers. I think he is so relieved that she didn't notice his *own* nastiness that he is determined to be better from now on.

"Over there," Finlay replied. "I think it's the future children!"

"Bronte and Alejandro!" I cried, and we all hopped up and hurried over to them. We were very keen to tell them the whole story of how we *had* rescued the children from the Whispering Kingdom! And how Glim had flown dragons! We all talked at once.

But they seemed to have no trouble understanding us.

"Congratulations," Alejandro said. "It is true that we already know all this as it is in history books. But this is good. I think you have fixed history. I am proud of you." It is strange to hear another child say that he is proud of you, but Alejandro can carry it off. It's his accent, I think, and the handsomeness.

Bronte said, "The genie asked you to finish the story today and leave it on a table in the town square please. She wants to see it. She'll use the hedge to collect it herself."

Finlay and I shrugged. "All right, then," we said, being in cheerful moods.

"We also have something from the future to give you," Bronte said.

We hoped it would be a magic futuristic machine that would do our homework and make us milkshakes, but it was only a torn piece of paper. We tried to be polite about it anyway.

"It's from a book called *The History of the Whispering Wars*," Bronte explained. "Written by my Uncle Nigel. Some bits have faded because of the Detection Magic, but most of it's all right since it's already happened by now."

Oh, I have an idea! Finlay and I have been writing these last few chapters in the town square as the sun sets on Party Day. Now and then, we stop to squabble about who will get the last word. We both want it. I mean, he wrote the first chapter *and* he's just added some Opening Words. By rights, *I* should get the last word. But Finlay says that the story will sink like an off-balance boat if he doesn't finish it up.

Now I think the solution is for *neither* of us to have the last word! We will finish up with the page Bronte gave us from the history book! Like a message from the future! The page stops halfway through a sentence so readers will have to *imagine* what the missing words say, which seems to me to be perfect. Anyway, on with the story—

Bronte and Alejandro joined us at our picnic blanket and we pressed cake, chocolate, and fruit on them.

"Maywish Chocolate!" Bronte said. "My favorite!"

Finlay was happy to hear this, as it's his favorite also. They argued in a friendly way about the best flavors.

"Have I got this wrong?" Hamish asked suddenly. "I mean to say, we *did* rescue the children from the Whispering Kingdom, didn't we? But you still haven't found out who Alejandro's parents are! I'm awfully sorry about that. Or *have* I got that wrong?"

"That's why we've come back," Bronte said.

"And because we wanted to see you all again," Alejandro put in.

"That too," Bronte agreed. "The moment we find out who Alejandro's parents are, we'll disappear back to the future and the Time Travel Hedge will leave our garden, the genie says. We'll never be able to see you again—except in our own time, I suppose."

"But we'll be *grown-ups* then," I complained, but I was interrupted by a little kerfuffle on the sand.

Ronnie-the-Artist, who generally paints pictures in the town square, had set himself up on the sand and was offering free Party Day portraits.

"Oh my! I *am* sorry!" cried a voice—and it was Carabella. She'd been passing his blanket, carrying a plate of treats from the banquet table, and had tripped on Ronnie's water pot, knocking it over. Water trickled into the sand. Then, as she leaned down to pick up the pot for him, her treats slid from her plate.

"I'll refill your water pot for you," Carabella promised, but Ronnie was on his feet, collecting Carabella's dropped treats.

"Not at all," he said. "Let's get you some new treats instead. These are all sandy. Or do you enjoy crunchy food?"

"I do like a bit of crunch," Carabella agreed, "in life generally. But look at you! What a marvelously big man you are! A bear of a man!"

Ronnie laughed, and they carried on together to the banquet table, chatting.

Bronte, I realized, had crouched low behind me as they passed. "That's my aunt!" she whispered. "She looks so young! And that's *Bear* she's with! In my time, he's her—oh, I can't say Detection Magic."

"Oh my!" I whispered back. "That's your aunt? But she—" I stopped. I'd been going to say that Carabella was Director of Spellbinders, but of course that is top secret. Even if Bronte was her niece, she might not know about it.

"Director of Spellbinding?" Bronte murmured. "I know. She's a very powerful Spellbinder." Then she lowered her voice further and added: "As are you, Honey Bee."

I blinked. "Oh? How did you—know?"

"I'm part Spellbinder myself," Bronte explained quickly. "The astonishing way you saved the people of Vanquishing Cove is *legendary* amongst the Spellbinding community, Honey Bee—it's not in history books, of course, because you are still alive and your Spellbinding is a secret, obviously." Her voice rose a little, as she noticed the others sending quizzical looks our way. "Guess what else? Mayor Franny is also my aunt. It's funny how she doesn't recognize me, but of course she wouldn't. I haven't even been born yet. My mother is still a young teenager here—she's actually the princess of the Whispering Kingdom, but that's another story. Don't look at me like that—I can't talk about it. There's Aunt Franny now, eating a carrot. Who are those people with her?"

Obediently, I peered through the crowds and there, on another blanket, was Mayor Franny. She was laughing with a group of friends. I squinted and recognized Lili-Daisy from the Orphanage, my Aunt Rebecca, the queen, the prince, Anita, and Carlos.

Did you notice I just mentioned Carlos?

For yes, Carlos is quite well again! Fully recovered! Thanks to the twins and their healing cakes! And he is spending a great deal of time catching up with his long-lost sister, Anita.

"Would you like to come and meet the queen?" I asked Bronte now.

"Why not?" Bronte agreed, so we all stood up, brushing crumbs away. Alejandro tidied his hair, pushing it behind his ears. A bit nervous about meeting a queen, I think.

It took a few minutes to weave between picnic blankets, towels, and sandcastles, laughing people, spilling drinks, and children running in and out of the ocean. Eventually, we drew close enough to the gathering that we could hear their conversation.

Anita was speaking to the others.

"The Kingdom of Joya Amarillo!" she laughed. "It doesn't exist, of course. It was a story I invented when I was little, before I even came to Spindrift. I used to tell my baby brother, Carlos, all about it. He was Prince Carlos in the Kingdom, of course, and there was a Queen Maria, named after my mother, and a King Alejandro—my father's name."

"King Alejandro." Mayor Franny smiled. "Sounds a fine king."

"Yes," Anita said shyly. "If I ever have a son, I will name him Alejandro."

Beside her, Prince Jakob spoke warmly. "I think," he said, "that any son you have, Anita, would *indeed* make a very fine king."

I happened, at that moment, to swing sideways to see if Bronte and Alejandro were listening to this. They were talking feverishly.

"In our time, the Kingdom of Storms is ruled by King Jakob," Alejandro said.

"Yes, and his wife is a famous doctor—a Doctor Anita!"

"And I remember reading something that said both of them were—"

"—*sad*."

"Because their son had vanished when he was a baby..."

"And here they are thinking of naming their son *Alejandro*."

"From a story about a Kingdom called *Joya Amarillo*..."

"*Joya Amarillo!*" they both hissed at the same time. "*J-A!*"

Their eyes widened, and they were gone.

Disappeared.

Back to the future.

"Golly!" said Hamish. "Where have they gone, then?"

I stared at the space where they'd been standing.

"I think," I said, "they just got the truth."

"They know who Alejandro's parents are going to be!" Hamish cried.

"Who?" Victor inquired.

"Prince Jakob and Anita." Finlay frowned. "You daft git."

I suppose he has not quite forgiven Victor yet.

Look, as I conclude this tale I must admit, not everything is perfect.

We now know that Alejandro's parents are Anita and Prince Jakob. But we also know that he will somehow be stolen from them as a baby and spend his childhood on a pirate ship. (Finlay and I want to warn Anita about this, but will a warning help to change the future, or only make her worry until it happens? Or turn history topsy-turvy again? Oh dear.)

We have rescued the children from the Whispering Kingdom—most of them have been carried home to their own Kingdoms and Empires by dragon now—but some had died in the Whispering Kingdom and so those parents have broken hearts.

The puzzle of the supercharged Whispers has been solved—wristbands made from ancient shadow threads—and Waratah Teevsky, Director of the K&E Alliance, has sent us telegrams of congratulations saying we've basically won the thing for them. But I rather think the Whispering Wars will continue for some time yet. And that more and more people will forget that Whisperers are truly a good and gentle people.

Also, Great-Uncle Arthur Lam, the witch who told Glim the secret of how to get through a witch-made shroud, agreed to reveal the secret—but of course the Whispering Kingdom had already reinforced its witch-made Mist Shroud with an upgraded version, so that vinegar and baking soda no longer work.

Finally, Rosalind is back. She didn't come to the party today because she "doesn't like to get sandy," and she is very moody about not getting a medal from the queen. "But I was part of the team!" she complains, tying her hair ribbons tightly. "If I don't get a medal, history will *forget* about me! *I* might turn out not to be a Child of Spindrift! Preposterous! It's not my fault I got sick! And look how much prettier my hair is than yours, Honey Bee? No offense."

So, as I said, it's not perfect.

However, there is some marvelous news!

Hamish's wealthy father, Liam Winterson, came into town last week and snapped up the boarding school! (That means he bought it.) Sir Brathelthwaite is in the Dungeons of Cloudburst, of course, so *he* can hardly run it. His stash of diamonds from the Whispering King has been confiscated, as they were "ill-gotten gains," so he had to sell the school for cash to pay his lawyers.

Mr. Winterson is exactly like Hamish.

"What?" he cried when Hamish mentioned that Uncle Dominic some-times horsewhips children. "What? He actually uses a horsewhip? And what, *whips* children! But that's horrid! Or have I got that wrong? No, no, I'm sure it *is* horrid. I had a horse once you know. Funny, isn't it, the way the words *horse* and *hoarse* sound the same, but they're quite different, I mean to say, one is the *animal* and one is when your throat is scratchy, which makes your voice—but anyhow, enough of that. Uncle Dominic is fired!"

He seems a likable chap, Mr. Winterson. He has already made plenty of other changes, in addition to firing Uncle Dominic. For one thing, he has invited the orphans to come and live at the school!

"Rather more luxurious here," he told Lili-Daisy, "and plenty of space! What ho! What do you think? Pop along over to live here instead?" Lili-Daisy thought popping over was a brilliant idea, and Mr. Winterson found her smile so charming he appointed her as head teacher. She's planning to let the students vote on a new school name, and to scrap their school chant. She'll replace it with a song that she makes up as she goes along each day. Mr. Winterson has also hired Aunt Rebecca as our science teacher, and advised Madame Dandelion to quit smoking cigars and cheer up.

And *that* is the end of our story.

I fare you well, dear readers, with tears in my eyes and a heart full of joy. Farewell! Have a most marvelous life!

CHAPTER
114
FINLAY

No, it's not the end of the story, because Honey Bee didn't say the most important changes Hamish's dad is planning for the boarding school.

I sat him down the other day. "If I'm going to live in this boarding school," I said, playing hardball, "I'm going to need a couple of modifications. Otherwise the deal is off." Then I told him my required modifications.

"Cracking ideas!" he said. "Consider them done!"

So the boarding school is now going to serve those twisty pastries with melting chocolate inside for breakfast every single day and, when it's safe to travel, the Raffia rugby team are going to come visit us. Also, there's going to be a specially made wardrobe with pillows on top where Jaskafar can sleep when he likes.

And a laundry chute, four stories high, which children will be welcome to ride.

Closing Words

The Remarkable Children of Spindrift

The course of the Whispering Wars was dramatically changed as the result of the remarkable Children of Spindrift. These seven children — Honey Bee, Victor, and Hamish (boarding school students), and Finlay, Glim, and twins Eli and Taya (residents of the local Orphanage) — joined forces to plan and stage a most daring expedition.

Bravely, some of the friends allowed themselves to be captured by Whisperers so that they could rescue children then held captive in the Whispering Kingdom. They solved the mystery of how the Whisperers had supercharged their Whispers: wristbands woven of shadow thread, and staged a dramatic rescue. Back in Spindrift, Glim took the astonishing step of befriending dragons and learning their language, a decision that would have far-reaching repercussions for dragon-human relations in years to come.

Glim also engineered the release of the local Shadow Mages and Whisperers in Spindrift. The expert knowledge of these locals was of `central` importance in saving Spindrift from multiple attacks during the remaining years of the war.

Indeed, many historians are convinced that it was the exploits of the remarkable Children of Spindrift that (eventually) won the Whispering Wars.

The seven children are today celebrated as heroes all across the Kingdoms and Empires. Young folk like to dress up as the Children of Spindrift. Statues have been erected in their honor, and films made based on their exploits. Meanwhile, ever since that time, the seven children have

Extra Closing Words

FINLAY

Ever since that time, the seven children have—carried on fighting each other.

That's my guess.

HONEY BEE

That was meant to be the end, Finlay! We were leaving it for readers to guess!

Anyhow, *I* think it's this: *Ever since that time, the seven children have—been firm friends.*

FINLAY

No, I've got it.

Ever since that time, the seven children have competed in athletic tournaments all across the Kingdoms and Empires, the twins winning plenty of medals for shot put and discus; now and then Honey Bee wins a race; often Glim does too, as does Hamish, even Victor (just once, in an obscure tournament in a tiny kingdom where most of the competitors forgot to turn up), but MOST OFTEN OF ALL, THE WINNER IS FINLAY!

HONEY BEE

Oh, *Finlay.*

MEMO

To: The K&E Board of Time Keepers
From: Genie #45278
Re: The Children of Spindrift Catastrophe

Dear Members of the Board,

I attach the full manuscript of the tale of the Children of Spindrift, as completed by **FINLAY** and **HONEY BEE.**

Based on an exhaustive study of this manuscript, I can see exactly where history went awry. It was somewhere around chapters twenty-five and twenty-six. Both Finlay and Honey Bee came up with the idea of joining forces with the other children and volunteering to help with the war effort, as per the original history. In this history, however, they were both distracted by the sudden realization that "the spies" (Bronte and Alejandro) might actually be Whispering children. So then: kerpow! Volunteering idea forgotten.

Oops.

The archives show that in the original history Finlay suggested the volunteer idea to Honey Bee the day after he came up with it. Honey Bee exclaimed that she'd had the same thought the night before. Finlay said that was nonsense and she was a copycat.

Honey Bee angrily said she'd had the idea separately. And so on. The key point is this: in the end, Honey Bee agreed, and went off to persuade the other Brathelthwaites to join this volunteer team, promising them likely medals from the queen. Their first volunteer outing was at the junkyard, where they got into a huge brawl during which Hamish tripped over a rusty frying pan filled with rubber bands. He was so taken by the various colors of the rubber bands he took to wearing them around his wrists.

At each of the following volunteer meetings, the children fought violently until one day Mayor Franny caught them at it. She looked around at their black eyes and bloodied noses and threatened to tell both Lili-Daisy and the queen. They begged her for another chance, promising to agree on just one thing.

The one thing they agreed on was that they should try to rescue Jaskafar and the other children from the Whispering Kingdom. Things then unfolded more or less as in this history except that, while he was in the Whispering Kingdom, Hamish spent so much time twanging at the rubber bands around his wrists that Victor became incensed, demanding that he "throw away those ruddy wristbands." This led to Hamish riffing on "wristbands" until he realized that all the Whisperers wore red-and-black wristbands, put two and two together, and figured out the secret to the supercharged Whispers.

Now, it seems to me that Bronte and Alejandro have done a great job nudging history back on course. I had them keep

Honey Bee and Finlay writing their history right up until the day when the time travel quest was done and Bronte and Alejandro couldn't accidentally cause any more time disasters.

Again, I apologize for this catastrophe, and I humbly request that you now lift your restrictions on my genie magic so that I can carry on with a life of granting wishes and making magical, life-sorting-out dreams.

Thank you in advance.

Yours truly,

Genie #45278

Acknowledgments

I cannot begin to express my gratitude to the following people: my publisher, Arthur Levine who (along with Anna McFarlane and Radhiah Chowdhury in Australia) is insightful, incisive, inventive, lovely, lively, passionate, patient, and many other positive adjectives; everyone else at Scholastic, especially Meghan McCullough, Melissa Schirmer, Starr Baer, Jessica White, Baily Crawford, Lizette Serrano, Rachel Feld, and Elisabeth Ferrari; my fantastic agents, Jill Grinberg and Tara Wynne; my extraordinary parents and sisters, Liane, Kati, Fiona and Nicola (with special mention to Kati, who proofreads all our books and who has been remarkably brave and strong this last year); my brother-in-law, tech-support and web designer, Steve Menasse; my lovely friends at Coco Chocolate (Deborah, Maria and Deborah); to Michael M, Rachel, Laura, Corrie, Jo, Elizabeth, Hannah, Jane, Natalie, Sandra, Melita, Jayne, Ildiko, Katherine, Michael K, Sara, Anna O for friendship and listening-to-me babble; and to Dee (and Patrick), Suzy (and Lucie), Lesley (and Ethan), Libby (and Miranda), Alison (and Rose), Gaynor (and Isabella), Kirrily (and Declan and Sophie), Beejal (and Anya), Maria (and Anita and Eli), and all the other mother-child reader combinations amongst my magnificent friends.

I need to start a new paragraph to thank the extraordinary artist, Davide Ortu. Both Davide and Kelly Canby (who illustrated the Australian edition) have created illustrations that are a dream and a delight, and make me shake my head with wonder and admiration.

To Nigel: thank you for your beautiful enthusiasm, story-telling, listening, and for being part of our family. To Charlie: thank you for making me laugh, and for running, jumping and climbing through life, never mind about the furniture; I'm sorry for not calling this book Spindrift.

Finally, to all the children who read Bronte's story and wrote to me about it, or asked their mothers to write to me about it, or drew pictures, or even just quietly liked it, without saying a word—you are all magical to me.

This book was edited by Arthur A. Levine and designed by Baily Crawford. The body type was set in Janson MT Std, a typeface originally designed by Miklós Kis in the late 17th century. The display types were set in KG Sue Ellen Francisco and KG Happy Henneke. The book was printed and bound at LSC Communications in Crawfordsville, Indiana. Production was supervised by Melissa Schirmer, and manufacturing was supervised by Angelique Browne.